D W SMITH
Fathers' Law

M
MACMILLAN
LONDON

For W H and CAROL FERRY

First published in Great Britain 1986 by
MACMILLAN LONDON LIMITED
4 Little Essex Street London WC2R 3LF
and Basingstoke

Associated companies in Auckland, Delhi, Dublin, Gaborone,
Hamburg, Harare, Hong Kong, Johannesburg, Kuala Lumpur, Lagos,
Manzini, Melbourne, Mexico City, Nairobi, New York, Singapore and
Tokyo

Typeset by Text Generation Ltd., London.

Printed and bound in Great Britain
by Anchor Brendon Ltd. Essex

British Library Cataloguing in Publication Data

Smith, D.W.
  Fathers' law
  I. Title
  823'.914[F]   PR 6069.M4/

  ISBN 0-333-42147-7

1

The warehouse near Heathrow Airport was protected by high walls topped by barbed-wire and by the most advanced electronic security available. Three separate lines of monitors and surveillance devices, hidden cameras and electric eyes were linked to two central control systems – one on the warehouse site, one two miles away at the security company's offices. Shifts of six security guards manned the on-site control point and patrolled continuously. Any intruder would be spotted by human or mechanical means, immediately triggering alarms and automatically alerting the local police. At three p.m. on Monday, 8 October, 1984, the kind of property that demands such intensive protection arrived: approximately eight million pounds worth of gold bullion. About ten hours later it was expertly removed.

As the working day began on the following Thursday, Detective Chief Inspector Harry Fathers sat at his desk at Scotland Yard reviewing the case. All six guards had been knocked out, tied up and drugged. None had seen the assailants. The electronic security had been overpowered just as swiftly and tracelessly. The intruders had even been able to send the coded 'all's well' signal every fifty minutes (an unusual interval which was supposed to add to the impregnability of the warehouse security). Patchy evidence plus logical deductions suggested the robbery had been done by six men who then left in two vehicles – a large truck that also carried the gold and a car. One guard reported seeing a large red car he did not recognise, parked in a side road, as he arrived to clock on for the night shift. A stolen red Ford that might have been the right one had been found the next morning abandoned in south London, but had yielded no evidence to the police.

And that, thought Fathers gloomily, scowling through the taste of poor quality black coffee drunk on an empty stomach after too little sleep, was just about that. He looked up from the reports on his desk, took off his glasses, squeezed the bridge of his nose tiredly and ran his hand through his dark hair. The bullion robbery had demanded the involvement of his entire team in the Serious Crimes Squad. Together with the local scene-of-crime officers and numerous technical assistants, they had swarmed over the warehouse and its grounds. They had questioned all the employees and started going through everybody who worked in the vicinity. The security company's personnel files had been inspected, and its employees questioned. They had attempted to work out the route the truck carrying the gold could have taken. They had asked questions in motorway cafés. Officers from Camberwell CID, augmented by a few from Fathers' team, had started house-to-house questioning in the streets near where the car had been found. All this – but no progress had been registered.

Moreover, Fathers' superior, Chief Superintendent Bastin, was not only pushing for results but also beginning to remind Fathers that this was not the only case in London. In addition to a tart little memo to that effect, Fathers also had on his desk a manilla folder containing a request from the New York Police Department for help on one of their cases that involved the disappearance of a British citizen. Why it had ended up on his desk, Fathers did not know, but there it was, with a note stapled to it in which Bastin asked him to put his 'best available man' to work on it. Not a woman? thought Fathers.

There was a knock on Fathers' door, followed by Detective Sergeant Graves putting his head into the office. Graves was a big man, at six foot two the same height as Fathers, but fifteen stone to his superior's thirteen.

'Sorry, guv,' said Graves, 'but you did say nine and it's ten after now.'

'Yes, skip, thanks. Wheel 'em in.'

Graves opened the door fully and came in, followed by seven men and two women. Most carried cups of the same noxious coffee Fathers was trying to drink, some were smoking. Fathers looked resentfully at their intruding numbers and fumes, turning

2

his reasonably sized office into a cramped slum. He drummed his fingers on the folder in front of him and let his gaze settle on a slim young man of average height, the newest member of his team.

'Yarrow,' he said, 'what are you up to?'

'Er, not a lot, guv,' replied the young detective constable with a start, not expecting to be the first person Fathers addressed. He had a thin face, untidy blond hair and constantly moving eyes out of which he had a habit of looking sidelong at people, especially suspects and senior police officers.

Fathers regarded him broodingly. 'What do you mean, not a lot?'

'Er, well, sorry, I mean I'm working with the skipper, I mean DS Graves, on the route the blaggers took and what I've actually been doing is running the line on the motorway stops together with Bill.'

'Spare him, can you, skip?' asked Fathers. Graves replied with an accommodating wave of his cigarette that Fathers took for assent. 'Right then, cast your eye over this file and when the others have left come back for a word about it.' Yarrow took the folder and returned to his place against the wall. 'Go on then, off you go,' said Fathers, and Yarrow left, looking over his shoulder and edging out of the room. He probably needs some encouragement, thought Fathers, and made a mental note to give him some. 'Pardoner.'

'Present,' replied DS Pardoner.

'Of course you are, skip, but not for long, not for long. Absent yourself this minute, and get the Wadkins file out. A wages snatch of a mere thirty thou is not much compared to the disappearance of eight million smackers worth of gold dust, but I don't think we can afford to let it lie fallow much longer. Pick up the threads and get back to me as you need to.'

'Yassuh, boss,' said Pardoner happily and walked out.

'Does this mean ...?' started Graves, but Fathers interrupted him, guessing the question and not allowing it to be put.

'No, skip, it doesn't mean anything. The bullion job is still our first priority. Pardoner and Yarrow have just been given time off

3

for good behaviour, that's all.' This raised a knowing chuckle round the room. The unadvanced state of the investigation was being disguised from reporters and, through them, the public, by artfully written press releases from the Press Room and bland interviews given by Chief Superintendent Bastin. But it could not be hidden from the men and women actually involved in it.

Fathers surveyed his remaining audience of five men and two women. 'James,' he said, addressing a conspicuously neatly dressed man standing by one of the filing cabinets. Detective Inspector Stevens looked up from the French cigarette he was about to light. His light tan suit perfectly fitted his stocky frame and almost outdid Fathers' three-piece pale grey one.

'Pull our people out of Camberwell. I don't hold out much hope for the door-to-door stuff. But keep on the tail of the local manor. Give Jackson a bell and insist as nicely as you can that he put at least a couple more pairs of legs on the job.' DI Jackson had been reluctant to divert men from enquiries into a rash of local burglaries. 'Let them know we expect great things from them, and so on and so forth. Have somebody phone round the ports again and the Regional Crime Squads, who are doubtless panting to get in on the action. Also get on to West Drayton again and make sure they're still looking out for improperly cleared take-offs by unusually large planes from small airfields. They've only heard from Mr Bastin so far, but they need to know we really mean business on this one.' Stevens nodded and tapped some ash into his plastic cup.

'You, skipperene,' Fathers said to DS Gordon who rewarded him with a friendly scowl, 'can now turn your attention to former employees of our super modern security chums. You know the kind of thing: addresses, new work, anything odd or unexplained. OK?' She nodded at him.

'I need hardly tell you,' continued Fathers, 'what kind of position we are in. However, I do need you to tell me. So bring all reports up-to-date by lunch-time, please, and hand them in to Petty.' The detectives groaned dramatically and in unison. 'Petty: summary by tea-time, please, words of one syllable.' DC Petty, a stolid man in his forties and the oldest present, nodded amiably. He was unlikely to be promoted but was a useful synthesiser of others' reports.

'By now,' said Fathers, 'the gold is well out of the country or else extremely well-hidden. The air traffic people at West Drayton can maybe help us on the former if the ports don't come up with anything, but we have to help ourselves on the other. Which is why, James, you are going to pull out a large map of southern England and start playing with computers. One, who has the form for this kind of job? Two, who are their known contacts with any kind of money or country properties? Three, where are those properties? Then, if anything comes up from the motorway cafés or the Regional Crime Squads to give us some kind of info on their route away from the warehouse, perhaps we can pin down a couple of likely looking places, get a lot of rozzers together and have a jolly good search.'

His words were greeted with a knowing silence by the others in the room. Only two full days had passed since the robbery, and already Fathers was reduced to guesswork.

Stevens stubbed out his cigarette. 'Come on then, my lads and lasses,' he said, 'time to get down to serious detection.'

The detectives filed out, leaving Fathers to open windows and empty ashtrays. He took another sip of his now cold coffee and resisted the temptation to throw it out the window. He looked at his watch. A couple of minutes with Yarrow and he would not be more than a few minutes late for his nine-thirty review meeting with Bastin. Breakfast would have to wait again.

'Yarrow,' he called out, 'let's have you.'

Detective Constable Elliot Yarrow sat and thought glumly about the case he had been given. He was twenty-six years old. He had been on the Serious Crimes Squad for three months, coming from two years in an East London CID with glowing annual reports. Now he often felt that counted for nothing. Today Fathers had taken him off the bullion investigation and given him a task that held no real interest and about which he had hardly been briefed. It felt like a demotion. Fathers' mind had obviously been elsewhere when he ran through the case. When he had finished, he got up and walked round his desk to thump Yarrow on the back and murmur something about it being an important job and how well Yarrow would do it. It had been embarrassingly artificial and did nothing to lift Yarrow's gloom.

Yarrow was a serious man, keen to get ahead. He had been genuinely thrilled when news came through of his transfer to the Serious Crimes Squad, even more so when he was assigned to Fathers' team. Fathers was a detective chief inspector at only thirty-seven years of age. His cases regularly got a lot of publicity, were often front-page news. He and his team had a host of judges' commendations. Yarrow had seen his new posting as a challenge, a privilege and a reward. Now he was not so sure. Used to thinking of himself as sharp, he felt slow alongside his new boss, belittled by his irony and his often elliptical way of talking with its combination of carefully formed, well-educated sentences and rapid-fire slang.

He remembered one of his last acts in his previous post – charging two boys of seventeen and one of fifteen for three amateurish burglaries in the Isle of Dogs. Nowadays, he often felt like one of those dumb, sad, spotty adolescents himself.

He was trying to improve himself. He had switched his newspaper to one more 'upmarket' and had started to read up on the law, trying to really understand the abstractions that were supposed to guide his working life. And because of a couple of comments by Fathers two weeks previously, Yarrow's current nightly reading, interrupted by the bullion case, was a popular introduction to criminal psychology. None of this made Yarrow happier, but he hoped it would pay off by helping him fit better into his new situation. Perhaps, he reflected disconsolately, sitting back at his desk after his brief session with Fathers, what I really need is a steady girlfriend. But that was a useless line of thought. Just as useless as wondering if he would have been better off at his old manor, or trying to think what mistake had led to him being so abruptly taken off the bullion investigation.

The file Yarrow had been given concerned Michael Peter Sampson, a British citizen living in New York, holder of a US

6

Resident Alien Visa permitting him to work there. Sampson, it appeared from the background information supplied by the New York Police Department along with their request for assistance, had done his university studies in Britain, getting his first degree in Politics and his second (making him a Doctor of Philosophy) in Strategic Studies. He had worked for two years at a small research unit based at one of the colleges of the University of London, and had then, eighteen months ago, moved to New York to become Vice-President of a small company called Franklin Research Associates. There, Yarrow learned, Sampson specialised in 'research on policy implications of new satellite technologies, recently with emphasis on Command, Control, Communications and Intelligence and on the Strategic Defense Initiative'. He shrugged at that part. Pinned to the file was a brief memo reporting that Sampson had no criminal record and the British police had never had any reason to be interested in him during his twenty-seven years in the country. The reason for the New York police's interest in Sampson was laconically stated: it appeared that he had disappeared.

The request from the New York Police Department was to supplement their background information on Sampson. They had provided a list of seven names with whom Sampson had had 'extended personal and/or professional contact' before going to the US. Yarrow's job, Fathers had explained, was to contact these people, ask questions, and write out a report giving the New York police the extra background they needed. Quite what it was they needed, Fathers had not stated. But he had told Yarrow not to bother with two of the names on the list – Sampson's mother and sister, whom Fathers saw no need to worry at this point. Yarrow took the point behind this uncharacteristically sympathetic decision: since it was not clear any crime had been committed, and since there was probably an entirely innocent explanation for Sampson's 'disappearance', there was no reason to stir up the sensitivities of his close relatives.

This left Yarrow with five names – four men and one woman, a reporter on a Sunday newspaper. Yarrow started with her, but when he got through to her office he was told she was in Pakistan

7

and would not be back for at least a week, possibly a month, since it was a fascinating investigation and potentially a very big story. Yarrow left a message to await her return and, suppressing envy at people who conducted fascinating investigations in faraway places, looked at his list again and started at the top.

The top, he decided, was a professor at the university where Sampson had earned his PhD. He turned out to be on sabbatical leave and would not be back for a year, but Yarrow was willingly provided with the current address and telephone number, which were in Tokyo. Yarrow sighed deeply. These globe-trotting absentees reminded him that he could not even see out of a window from his desk, and that if he could all he would see were grey buildings beneath a grey October sky.

However, the person he was speaking to was ready to be helpful and, when Yarrow explained what he wanted, suggested Yarrow speak with Dr Davis and offered to transfer his call.

There followed a silence, interspersed by a couple of clicks. Yarrow tucked his phone against his neck and began arranging paper clips into a chain. When he had connected twenty together he decided he had been cut off, hung up and re-dialled. He asked for, and was eventually connected with, Dr Davis, who agreed in melodiously cultured tones that he had known Mike Sampson quite well but had lost touch since he had got his doctorate and moved to London. He did, however, read Sampson's articles whenever they were published, in journals Yarrow had never heard of, but which sounded important judging by the tone in which Dr Davis mentioned them. From the most recent of them he had gathered that Sampson had moved to the USA. Once Yarrow had explained that his enquiry was purely routine, whatever that might mean, Dr Davis was very willing to be helpful.

Sampson had been a very bright student who had completed a fascinating thesis to get his PhD, and done it within the three years allotted, which was apparently very unusual these days. Everybody had agreed that he had a bright future ahead of him. A tidy mind with a penchant for detail, his work was painstaking and usually rather technical. A sad loss to British acadaemia, but who could blame him? There were precious few jobs around, even for the brightest, and America was where the money was. When asked, Dr Davis named two other students of the time with whom Sampson had appeared particularly close, but, sorry, he did not have their current addresses. Yarrow dutifully noted it all down.

Yarrow unpicked his chain of paper clips and arranged them into a question mark on his desk, then called a second professor, at a London college, though not the one Sampson had worked at. He got through immediately to a secretary, who told him in a fruity Home Counties voice that Professor Marks was away at a meeting in another part of town and would probably be back by lunchtime. Yarrow left another message. He had two names left, both at the college where Sampson had worked before moving across the Atlantic. Choosing the more senior to start with, he phoned a Reader called Finlay in the Department of Politics. But Finlay was not yet in, he was told predictably, though he was expected in that day. The last name was David Cairns, a Research Officer in charge of the unit where Sampson had worked. Yarrow was surprised to find him in his office. Cairns agreed that he knew Sampson well, had worked with him for more than a year and counted him a friend.

'What do you want to know about him?' he asked.

'It's just that we've been asked,' Yarrow said, 'purely as a matter of routine, to fill in some background on Dr Sampson.' It was all he could think of saying. There was a silence and Yarrow could feel Cairns weighing up what this non-answer meant.

'Is it a security enquiry?'

'I can't really comment on that,' replied Yarrow. 'But it is certainly in Dr Sampson's interests that we complete this enquiry as soon as possible. It won't take much of your time.' He was grasping for straws.

'Well, what kind of questions do you want to ask?'

'Oh, we just need to have a sense of him, your opinion of him, his work and so on.'

'Well that won't take long,' replied Cairns crisply. 'His work is of the highest standard. That's why he landed a plum job in New York. I suppose you know he works there now?'

9

But Yarrow already knew Sampson's work was of high standard and he did not think Fathers would regard it as a proper enquiry if he left it there. 'Actually,' he said, 'what I need most is to be filled in a bit on the kind of work he does, or, really, how he works, and, in very general terms, you know, how he spent his time when he lived and worked in London.'

'Well,' said Cairns, 'really the person you want is Paul Finlay. He's known Mike longer than I have and they work in much the same field.'

'Yes, I want to talk to Dr Finlay, too. Perhaps I could call round to see you later today, and catch him as well?'

'We don't use his title here,' said Cairns, 'because he's a bit fed up with the jokes, but he'll be in this afternoon, I think, and so will I. You're welcome to come round.'

After thanking him and hanging up, it took Yarrow a moment to think what jokes Paul Finlay might be fed up with, and he again felt slow and dim when he remembered the soap opera his parents had spent excruciating hours of his childhood watching on the television. Worse, as he gathered up his paper clips, he found the theme tune of *Dr Finlay's Casebook* sounding out its cocky rhythm in his head. He considered what to do next. He passed the time waiting for Professor Marks to call back by trying to trace recent addresses for Sampson's old university friends, but as he traced them from university down the tracks of their mobile lives he finally ran out of new numbers to try. He pondered the situation, fiddling with the paper clips. In principle, no honest citizen is untraceable, especially to someone who can call on the Police National Computer and, through it as well as other more human interfaces, several other sets of computerised records. Sitting and thinking, he absently twisted a paper clip and managed to stab himself. Sucking his thumb, he decided it was not worth the trouble in this case, if it could be called a case. Looking up, he saw Fathers glance at him on his way through to his own office. A great way to be seen by your boss, he thought dismally, and took his *Daily Telegraph* off to the lavatory for half an hour. When he came back he found a message saying Professor Marks had called, but when he phoned back, the fruity

10

secretary told him the professor had gone off for lunch. Yarrow put down the phone and looked at it with disgust. Sod it, he thought.

When Yarrow arrived at David Cairns' office at three-thirty the door was locked and knocking brought no answer. He found the general office, where he was told simply that Cairns was out, but he was directed to Paul Finlay's office on a different floor. Surprisingly on such a day, Finlay was in, but he was busy with an attractive young woman Yarrow assumed was a student and asked him to wait.

Yarrow was happy to, having decided it was more important to see Finlay than Cairns. Just after two p.m. he had finally managed to talk on the telephone with Professor Marks.

'I don't really know him at all well,' said the professor, starting out badly. His voice sounded confident and affluent. Yarrow's instinct for voices told him Professor Marks was a large, portly man in middle age. In fact, Marks was in his mid-thirties, kept in excellent shape through regular squash and swimming, and was five foot two. But, since Yarrow would never meet the professor, he would never discover his mistake. 'I met him first some years back, can't remember exactly when off-hand, but I suppose it was when he was still a grad student. It was at a Beezer conference.'

'A what?'

'Eh? Oh, sorry, yes, Beezer – acronym for British International Studies Association.' Yarrow had never heard of it, but dutifully wrote it down in his notebook. 'Bee, eye, ess, ai – Beezer. Anyway, I do remember being very impressed by him then, and I must say that good impression was only confirmed when I met him at several other occasions of one kind and another. Including a seminar when he gave a quite fascinating paper. About verification, as I remember.'

'About what?'

'Eh? Ah, yes, verification, as in verification of arms control agreements, crucial subject, you know, make sure the other

11

chap's not cheating. I suppose this was about four, four and a half years ago. Yes, very good impression he made all round.'

'But you didn't get to know him very well?'

'No, not really. Well, one doesn't, you know? But when he started looking for jobs he asked me to write a reference and I was happy to oblige. He eventually got a job at Finlay's research unit here in town. Before he moved on to greater things.'

'What impressed you about him?'

'Oh, I would say both his manner and his work. Very personable chap, quick brain, great attention to detail, not afraid to study up on things he doesn't know much about, very good listener, great ability to become expert on new subjects very quickly. And he writes well. Rather on the technical side of things, of course, but that's the nature of the subject. I suppose he has a bit of a tendency to slip into jargon, but don't we all? However, Finlay is the man you really want to see. Paul Finlay, you know? In the past couple of years he's been rather specialising in pretty much the same field as Michael, See Cubed Eye.'

'Come again?'

'Eh? Oh, sorry, more jargon, I'm afraid. One has to learn an entire new language to study this field. See Cubed Eye: shorthand for Command, Control, Communications, and Intelligence.'

'Ah yes,' said Yarrow. 'That's one of Dr Sampson's interests, isn't it?'

'Indeed. I suppose his main field is satellites, their multiple and complex uses and implications for all sorts of things. Very sexy field these days, you know, science fiction coming true, Star Wars and all that sort of thing. That's where he overlaps with Finlay. Since they worked in the same building for a couple of years, I imagine each knows a lot about the other's work and they keep in pretty good contact I should say. Finlay certainly knows Sampson's work much better than I do. And that young man who works there, now what's his name?'

'David Cairns?'

'Indeed. Another bright young chap. Though rather too much under Finlay's influence for my liking.'

12

'Yes,' said Yarrow, 'I've got an appointment with him this afternoon, and I'm hoping to see Dr Finlay then, too.' Professor Marks chuckled. 'What is it you don't like? I mean, you said Cairns is rather too much under Finlay's influence.'

'Ah, well, delicate ground. Finlay is most able in his field, you understand – in fact, most able in any field he cares to make his own. But, of course, he's very left wing. Calls himself a peace researcher, which I suppose is meant to distinguish himself from tired old warmongers like myself, eh? Member of CND, so I gather, which is all very well, but it tends to get in the way, do you see?'

'And was Dr Sampson, would you say, under the same influence, that is, er, is he a leftist too, influenced by Dr – er – Finlay as well?'

'Oh, heavens no, I don't think one could really say that. No – Michael is much too interested in the technical problems, far too absorbed in getting the details straight and drawing the appropriate conclusions to go and indulge himself in these politics. I doubt he ever pays much attention to politics, in fact. One of the joys of his writing is that it includes no extraneous matter whatsoever. Entirely to the point. A pure researcher. Of course, I say this without really knowing the man terribly well. Finlay's the one you want to talk to, Cairns, too, for that matter.'

So now, waiting outside Finlay's office, Yarrow felt he might finally be getting somewhere. He waited for twenty minutes until the student finally came out. Yarrow turned and appreciatively watched her walk away. When he turned back he saw Finlay watching him with evident if mild amusement. He was invited in cordially enough, though.

'Come in, Brian,' said Finlay, 'come in and tell me what I can do you for. Don't know you do I?'

Finlay's office surprised Yarrow. It was a small, narrow rectangle with white walls almost entirely covered in bookshelves that were filled with books, filing boxes and loose piles of magazines and papers. Along the right-hand wall, away from the window almost back to the door, was a long narrow desk. At the end of it, behind the door, stood two filing cabinets. The desk

13

and the tops of the cabinets were covered in more piles of papers, computer printouts, unopened mail and general chaos. Against the left-hand wall, at the window end, was a shorter, deeper desk at which Finlay sat, wearing checked shirt, jeans and trainers. He sat tipping back in his chair with his feet on the desk. Next to that was a coffee table, and next to that a low, modern easy chair, the kind which has no arms and is impossible to sit in with either comfort or dignity. Pinned to one of Finlay's shelves was a postcard with the comforting motto: 'A tidy desk is a sign of a sick mind'.

'No, we've never met,' said Yarrow, perching his light frame on the very edge of the low chair. 'I'm Detective Constable Yarrow, and I'd like to ask you a few questions in connection with some purely routine enquiries we're making.' Yarrow pulled out his warrant card, flicked it open, shut it and put it away. But Finlay was looking at him levelly and holding out his hand. Yarrow pulled his card back out and gave it to Finlay who looked at it for a full minute with every sign of serious concentration before handing it back.

'Routine enquires, Brian? And you want me to help you with them?'

'That's right,' said Yarrow. 'I want you to fill in a little background on Dr Michael Sampson who used to work here.'

'Why?'

'I'm afraid I can't tell you that. They are purely routine enquiries.'

'I'm sure they are, Brian. Who am I to doubt it? But I'm very busy right now. The new term is upon us.'

'Well, I won't detain you very long, Dr, er, sir, but it would certainly help us a great deal if you could take a few brief moments to answer some questions. I understand you know Dr Sampson well, have worked with him and share the same interests as him in, er, See Cubed Eye.'

'Um. What do you want to know?'

'I'd like to know your general opinion of him and his work. I'd like to know how well you knew him before he left, what kind of work he was doing here and what kind of contact you've had with him since he left.'

'Why?'

'As I've said, sir, I can't answer that. But I can say that it is in Dr Sampson's interests that we complete these enquiries as fast as possible.'

'Well, Brian, I'm not at all sure I want to tell you anything unless I know why you want to know.'

Yarrow sighed and wondered what this was all about. He looked around Finlay's room for a moment but found no answer. 'Perhaps I should remind you, sir, that it is every citizen's duty to assist the police in the course of their duties, such as, for example, routine enquiries like this.' Yarrow knew it sounded pompous but he hoped it would have an effect.

'Balls,' said Finlay.

Some effect, thought Yarrow. But he leaned forward, smiled, and said, 'Balls it may be, but if I was you I'd start taking it a bit seriously.'

Finlay looked at him. 'Just a few questions,' coaxed Yarrow, 'purely routine.'

'Even if I wanted to help you, Brian, I'm not sure I could. I never knew Michael Sampson that well while he was here and I've had bugger all contact with him since he left.'

'Your research is in the same field.'

'Well, it overlaps. Same in some respects, different in others. And we approach the subject in very different ways. Now, what did you want? OK, general opinion of him and his work. Nice enough bloke, very competent, over-technical, good at what he does. How well did I know him? Not very well: chat about work, cups of coffee in the buttery, occasional lunches together, usually with other people from the department, the odd drink or two after work, went to a couple of conferences with him. All in all, don't know him very well. What's next? Yes – what kind of work did he do here? Glorified filing clerk, really, but he used our files to do a lot of his own research and then nipped off to the States on the strength of it. There was one more thing, wasn't there? What kind of contact have I had with him? Well, he wrote a letter asking for a copy of a bibliography he'd heard I was producing, I sent it to him and he sent back a little card saying ta very much. That was August last year. And there, Brian, are the answers to your questions. Don't help much, do they?'

Yarrow looked up from his notebook. 'I have been told, sir, that you know him well and that you keep in regular contact with him.'

'Really? Who told you that? They told you wrong.'

'Does Mr Cairns know him any better than you?'

'Shouldn't think so. Ask him yourself.'

'I intended to, sir. I made an appointment for this afternoon but he wasn't in when I got there.'

'Really?'

'Really.'

'Well, well.'

'You wouldn't happen to know where he is, would you?'

'Quite right, Brian, I wouldn't. An excellent deduction, but now I'm late for a finance meeting that I do not want to miss, so if you're through?'

Yarrow decided there was no profit in prolonging his stay. And anyway, he wanted to beat the rush hour back to the Yard. He stood up. 'Well, Dr Finlay,' he said, deciding not to pander to Finlay's sensitivities any more, 'thank you for your help. Really, a great help. Perhaps you'd tell Mr Cairns when you next see him that I'd still like a word. Here, this is my number at the Yard. I may get back to you. Bye.'

The end of Yarrow's day was not much more gratifying than either its beginning or middle. Arriving back in the general office where the detective constables and sergeants in Fathers' team had their desks, he saw Fathers sitting at DS Pardoner's desk, smoking.

In principle, Fathers was a non-smoker. When he did smoke, it was never in his own office and it was always a bad sign. Yarrow had already learned that it signalled some kind of dissatisfaction

– usually with a case, or with the behaviour of various superiors or subordinates. Like the rest of the team, Yarrow also knew that the bullion enquiry was not proceeding well and he drew the obvious conclusion.

This was bad news for Yarrow. A disgruntled Fathers was even less approachable than usual, and Yarrow had wanted to have a word with him about his almost stalled enquiries. Of the seven names on the original list, only Cairns was still interviewable. The session with Finlay had been entirely unproductive. Professor Marks and Dr Davis had been willing but unable to be of substantial help. The two additional names he had learned from the latter were not easily contactable. It was not certain or even likely that the trouble it would take to find them would be repaid in hard information. The same was true if he tried to contact the reporter in Pakistan or the Professor in Tokyo. There were also Sampson's mother and sister, who could yet be contacted, but before he did that he felt he had to have Fathers' say-so. Initially, Fathers had conveyed the impression that this was an altogether modest affair involving a few phone calls and not lasting much more than a day, if that. But Finlay's attitude and, when he thought about it, the subject matter of Sampson's research nigglingly suggested to Yarrow that perhaps there was something more to it. If there were, perhaps Fathers would know and could advise him. It was by no means unusual, after all, for the foot-slogging DCs to be left in ignorance about the background to their work – the big picture was not always theirs to know.

Even as Yarrow assessed the possibility of asking his boss's advice, Fathers stubbed out one cigarette and lit another. Yarrow decided against disturbing him.

There were, however, other things he could do. For one, since it was still before five o'clock, he could phone the first university Sampson had attended. That he did and received more information about Sampson's early academic career from the registrar's office. Tomorrow he would call Sampson's old comprehensive school to fill in more ancient history. With the report shaping up to be very insubstantial, Yarrow wanted as much dross as he could lay his hands on to fill up space.

Next, he requested a check on Finlay in Criminal Records. He was wondering about the academic, about his attitude to helping routine police enquiries, about his calm rudeness. Finally, he phoned the library at the London School of Economics, learned that it subscribed to the journals Dr Davis had mentioned, and further learned it was open late into the evening. Casting one last glance at Fathers, he took himself off to the staff café for a coffee and sandwich before going to the Aldwych and the LSE Library. There he spent a tedious two and a half hours reading articles which discussed the possible end of the world with icy calm. He noted the titles and dates of seven articles by Sampson, avoided reading three of them and at last gave up on the day.

Fathers had seen Yarrow come in, registered the surreptitious glances cast his way, half-listened to the phone calls and watched him leave. A few minutes later, he yawned and stretched in Pardoner's seat, rose and walked without knocking into the office DI Stevens shared with the absent DI Queen. A group was gathered round an easel holding a large map of southern England. Coloured pins were being stuck in it, marking various towns and villages. Fathers put his glasses on and peered at the map. Then he looked across the room to where Stevens was sitting on a window sill leafing through a fat computer printout. Stevens shrugged.

'We're not very far into it yet, guv,' he said. 'A couple of interestingly isolated old farmhouses and such, but nothing leaps to the eye. Not that it would I suppose.'

Fathers raised his eyebrows expressively.

'Nothing from the motorway cafés, either,' added Stevens.

Fathers nodded, took off his glasses and shoved his hands deep into his pockets. The more time passed, the less likely it was that the route the gang had taken with the bullion would be established, and the less useful it would be in the unlikely event that it was worked out. And without some hint of the getaway route the list of possible safe hiding places was a lot less useful. As it was, another review meeting with Bastin was coming up in ten minutes, with a lot of activity to report, but no results. Not even a sniff of a result.

'All right, you lot,' he said, 'who has the duty tonight?'

'Short straw's mine,' said Graves. 'Mine, George's and the girl's'

'Fair enough. You three go and get a bite. The rest of you, break it off for now, do up your reports if necessary and get an early night. James, a word.' And with that Fathers walked out, followed by Stevens, leaving behind a happier group.

As he left he heard DC Bunn comment, 'One thing about Daddy, he doesn't flog a lotta dead 'orses.'

2

Yarrow arrived at the office shortly after eight-thirty the next morning. The place was buzzing. Three typewriters were going, several phones were being used, the air was thick with smoke, detectives were walking and half-running in and out, cups of tea and coffee were being drunk, spilled or left to get cold.

Yarrow assumed there had been a breakthrough in the bullion case, sniffed resentfully at his exclusion, got himself a cup of instant coffee and sat at his desk. Waiting for him was the answer to the question he had put to Criminal Records. He read through it with mounting interest. Paul Finlay, it emerged, had a record. He had three convictions from the 1960s, all for obstruction at demonstrations, and another for the same offence in 1977. He had also twice been charged with more serious offences – once for threatening behaviour and once for assaulting a police officer. The first charge had been withdrawn before the case came to trial, and the second dismissed at the trial for lack of evidence. Moreover, Finlay's file had been flagged by the Scotland Yard Special Branch: all enquiries about Finlay were to be reported to them. Yarrow called up, found someone with whom he could discuss it immediately, and took his notes and coffee along with him.

He was back at his desk in twenty minutes, not much the wiser. DC Whyte of the Branch had explained that Finlay was a known and active leftist with a criminal record (even if not a terrible one) who closely studied sensitive areas of military and security policy. As such, he was the kind of person on whom the Branch routinely kept an eye – but not in any very active or intrusive way. When Yarrow explained that his interest in Finlay was secondary to his enquiry about Sampson and that only Finlay's behaviour had led him to check Criminal Records, Whyte lost interest.

20

Yarrow returned to the telephone and picked up more information on Sampson's early academic career, including at school. Finally, he called David Cairns at Sampson's old research unit, reproached him gently for being out the previous afternoon and started in with more questions. It was not a productive conversation. Cairns' attitude appeared to have changed, as did his relationship with Sampson. Now it seemed they had been friendly rather than friends. They had occasionally had a drink together after work or at conferences they had both attended. Otherwise, Cairns had not known Sampson well, had never visited his home, did not know if he had had a girlfriend, had not met any of his other friends, had never discussed either his personal affairs or politics with him. Pressed, he added that Sampson's field was not his, that he found his ex-colleague's work interesting and competent but over-technical, and that he had not had any contact with him for over a year. Shortly after getting to New York, Sampson had sent a postcard saying he was settling in well, Cairns had sent one back in an equally banal vein, and that was about it. Having spent a cagey half-hour drawing out this unrevealing information, Yarrow hung up, sat back and pondered.

The more he thought about it, the less worthwhile it seemed either to bother Sampson's family or to put in the effort of chasing up two of his friends from student days. For the most part, all he would get would be further confirmation that Sampson was serious, hard-working and personable. The family might give him the name of an ex-girlfriend, but that seemed unlikely to be much help unless it had been a steady relationship, and even then it might not help a lot. Young men living in London do not always keep their families fully informed about their latest girlfriends, or about very much at all. Fathers was obviously busy at the moment, and Yarrow did not fancy sitting doing nothing waiting for a chance to approach him and ask for advice. Better to go with what he had, thought Yarrow, show it to Fathers and leave it to him to suggest trying to get more information.

Yarrow arranged his notes and started to type.

21

★

As lunch time approached, Harry Fathers was feeling a good deal older than his thirty-seven years. The adrenalin which had kept him going through the night was beginning to run out.

The hyper-activity which had greeted Yarrow that morning had not been to do with the bullion case. That investigation still refused to make progress. But, just after seven the previous evening, Graves had shouted out, 'Here's a big one! Camden! Security van, cash snatch! In progress!'

Stevens, who had been chatting with Fathers, went to the scene, taking George Bunn with him. Graves and the third duty officer, Cathy Gordon, got on the phones to call back in the detectives who had only just left for the night. Fathers himself, via the Yard Situation Room, coordinated the effort to seal off the area around the scene of the crime, geeing up the CIDs and uniformed forces in the surrounding manors to get all their men out and watch for speeding cars.

In classic fashion, the gang had blocked the security van collecting the day's takings from a large supermarket, and then made their getaway in two cars going in opposite directions. They moved fast enough to evade Fathers' initial cordons, but Stevens soon called in with, for once, good identifications of the cars. As Fathers' team began to reassemble, one of the getaway cars was found abandoned in an alleyway near Primrose Hill. Better, a near-by resident had noted the make, colour and number of a car which had almost knocked her down as it sped off with, she thought, three men in it.

With most of London's police now well alerted, the car was spotted heading northwest. A discreet watch was kept as it was driven to a multi-storey car park at Brent Cross shopping centre, where it was abandoned in favour of another that headed south into Acton and then towards central London. The car was lost to sight in Hammersmith for four minutes. When next seen, it held only two men, but there were no more gaps in coverage as it drove sedately and legally across London to Greenwich. In

Greenwich, a scruffy layabout who was actually a detective constable from the local CID cycled past the car soon after it had stopped in the driveway of a modest house. He was in time to see the two men unload several bags from the boot and carry them indoors. One re-emerged, got into the car and drove off, presumably to dump it. Four streets away, his way was blocked by three patrol cars. A sensible fellow, he let himself be arrested on suspicion without argument or resistance.

Fathers was in a strong position, the kind policeman everywhere like. Close observation and a swiftly arranged telephone tap covered anything that the man in the house might try. The occupants of the house backing on to the one the police were watching cooperatively moved out for the night when the need to use their home and garden was explained. Fathers could afford to wait and watch. If more people showed up, so much the better – they would be pulled in, too. If not, the man in the house with the money would be arrested, charged and eventually offered a deal if he cooperated – that is, if he named a few names. Fathers made sure everything was tight, and, together with most of his team, went to Greenwich where he gave more orders, deployed his detectives and made his preparations.

They waited with some of the uniformed and plainclothes officers of Greenwich, through cups of tea and coffee, excited chatter and, for some, endless cigarettes that fugged up cars and turned fingers yet deeper shades of yellow and brown. They waited until shortly before one in the morning, when a car with two men in it cruised slowly along the street where the watched house stood. It disappeared round the corner and criss-crossed the surrounding streets, its occupants cautiously looking out for signs of anything amiss. They saw nothing, drove back to the house, parked in the street, got out of the car and walked up to the front door. One took out a key and let them in.

Fathers ordered two cars to each end of the street as improvised roadblocks. Then he left the police station and drove to the scene of the coming action. He walked to the roadblock, took a walkie-talkie radio from a local constable and quietly ordered his

23

detectives to move up along the street to the driveway, and over the back fence into the garden.

He waited for the whispered reports that all was ready.

'Right,' he said to the slightly shivering local detective inspector standing beside him, 'let's give them a spin, shall we?' The local man nodded.

'Go,' said Fathers into his radio, 'go, go, go.'

Three policemen ran up the front drive, smashed in the front door with a pickaxe, shouted that they were police and charged in. The three men inside were all on the ground floor, two in the back room from which they rushed out at the first sound, straight into the large arms of DS Graves, the first one through the door. Graves hit one in the face with his right fist and grabbed the other by his hair, banging him hard up against the hall wall. The third man was in the kitchen where he had been pouring out three whiskies. At the first sound of the front door being smashed down, he opened the back door, just in time to let in DS Pardoner, who smiled broadly and informed him he was under arrest on suspicion of robbery and committing grievous bodily harm, adding that anything he might say would be taken down and could be used in evidence. The man nodded and stretched out his hand. Pardoner tensed for trouble and bunched his fists. But the man merely took each glass of whisky in turn and drank it.

By lunch time, Fathers had been up right through the night and had come well down from the high of the chase and the arrests. The excitement of the night had been followed by the usual tedious business of taking statements, allowing the men to call lawyers, sorting out who was to be charged with what, counting the money which had been in the still unopened bags, offering lenient treatment in return for spicy information, drafting a statement to tell the assorted news media how clever and quick the police had been, opening up the drink for celebrations all round, reporting to Bastin and receiving his pompously hearty congratulations, and, finally, by harrying weary detectives into doing their reports before sending them off in shifts to get some sleep.

24

The case was neatly sewn up. As it turned out, one of the two late arrivals at the house in Greenwich was one of the five men who had actually made the snatch. That made three out of five, which was not at all bad, with the possibility of getting the others if one of the men in custody decided to talk – or if simply following up on their known associates produced results. The fourth man under arrest was a specialist in laundering stolen money out of the country in return for a hefty percentage. He was charged with conspiracy and being an accessory. When the London press got on to that, he was described as the 'Mr Big' of the operation.

Fathers' elation was fighting it out with two other feelings: his fatigue and his grim awareness that he would have to turn his attention back to the bullion case straight after lunch. He was more than a little pleased that he had still been in the building when the news of the snatch first came in, and for that he was grateful to Bastin for having dragged the review meeting on long after all the ground had been covered. He was also pleased that Bastin had left the building immediately after their meeting, which meant he had been able to run the case without interference. It had been a successful, morale-building diversion from the bullion case. But now he would have to get back to it. And at that point he totted up his hours of sleep and reckoned he had managed nine in the last seventy-eight. An early night tonight, he decided, no later than midnight.

So he was more pleased than he would normally have been when Yarrow poked his head round the door, cleared his throat and vaguely waved a folder at him. One interruption was as good as any other.

'That's the New York thing is it?' asked Fathers. 'Come on in.'

Encouraged by this unexpectedly cheery greeting, Yarrow came fully into the office. 'Yes,' he said. 'I know you probably won't want to look at it right now, but I thought I could leave it on your desk and—'

'Nonsense,' said Fathers, putting his glasses on. 'Hand it over and I'll look through it. Sit down.'

A few minutes reading told Fathers that Yarrow had found out very little that would help the New York police very much. But that, he reflected, was more their fault for not being more precise about what they wanted to know than Yarrow's for not finding out enough. Although his enquiries had not yielded much, he had made a reasonable report out of them. As well as the typed report, there was a hand-written note stating Yarrow's belief that Cairns had turned unhelpful because Finlay had told him to.

'So you don't think much of your Dr Finlay, then?' asked Fathers.

'Not a lot, guv, no. I reckon Cairns told him I was coming round and he probably told Cairns not to show. See, it did feel like he was expecting me. He wasn't surprised or anything, put out, you know, when I introduced myself. He took a moment to adjust by inspecting my warrant card and then just took it in his stride. And he's got form too, like it says in there.'

'Yes, form of the left-wing variety, eh? Well, you've done OK, but there's not much here that will help our American cousins.'

'No, guv, I suppose not. But I don't really know what they want.'

'Me neither. Background was all they said.'

'Well, I give 'em background.'

'Yes,' said Fathers, 'you give 'em background all right. I gather you don't think it's worth chasing up the mother and blister, then?'

'Not really, guv, no. I reckon I'd just get more of the same, you know? There's also a couple of university mates of his I could try to get on to. But their addresses aren't easily available, and, well, I don't know that they'd tell me anything new either.'

'I tend to agree. It might be an idea to insert a sentence at the top here, saying something about not wanting to disturb the mother and sister unduly without firmer informaion that something is seriously wrong. And take out the references to Finlay's form and the Branch's special interest in him. But leave that in your own file on the enquiry, all right? Then get it on the list for telexing back to New York.'

'So don't tell New York about Finlay's form and everything, but leave it in my own report of work done?'

'That's it. Just in case we have to come back to it. You never know. And thanks for your trouble. Get some lunch when you've finished and then report back to Graves, who'll doubtless find you some essential task.'

'Er, just one other thing, guv.'

'Yes?'

'Well, it's not in the report or anything, but I was just wondering. I mean, that Finlay, he kept on calling me Brian. What do you think that's all about? I mean, I never heard something like that before.'

'Well, Yarrow m'boy,' said Fathers wearily, 'I don't know. Maybe he's a Monty Python fan.'

3

As Harry Fathers walked up the front steps of a modest house in a modest street in the neighbourhood of Stamford Hill, he reflected that he was neither quite sure nor very happy about the train of circumstances which brought him there. Yet it had seemed to make sense when he had decided that he, and not DC Yarrow, should handle this interview. On the one hand, Chief Superintendent Bastin had stressed an undefined importance attached to the case by somebody yet more senior; on the other, Yarrow had made it clear that he regarded the task as beyond him. And in the middle, Fathers suspected that his real reason for coming was to get away from the cursed bullion case again.

He had to ring a second time before the door was opened. When it was, Fathers managed to stop himself gasping. One thing Yarrow had not reported about Finlay was his size. Finlay was enormous. Fathers was not used to being physically intimidated by the mere look of another man. But Finlay was something else: Fathers guessed he was at least six inches taller than he, and from the look of his neck and shoulders about ninety pounds heavier. The impression of size was increased by the fact that Finlay was standing on the threshold a couple of steps higher than Fathers, and that he had opened only half of the wide double door, filling that half entirely, from side to side, top to bottom. Nor was he fat. Remembering Finlay's record, Fathers thought he could understand the charge of threatening behaviour: he would only have to look angrily at a policeman and it would be taken as a threat. But how many coppers had it taken to arrest him each time?

'Hullo. What can I do for you?'

'Dr Paul Finlay?' asked Fathers. Finlay nodded. 'I'm Detective Chief Inspector Fathers, Serious Crimes Squad at Scotland Yard. I'd like to ask you a few questions.' He pulled out his warrant card and put it in Finlay's silently extended huge hand.

28

Finlay scrutinised it for a moment, then turned it over and for some reason looked at the back.

'And what serious crime am I supposed to have committed?' he asked, handing the warrant card back.

'I don't know, sir. What serious crime have you committed?'

'None that I can remember since last Thursday.'

'Ah yes, sir, that would be when you failed to help an officer of the law in the pursuit of his duties, would it?'

'Are you here about the same business, then?'

'Yes,' said Fathers. 'We've been asked to look into it some more, with particular regard to certain discrepancies between what you told Detective Constable Yarrow and what we know.'

'Discrepancies, now. That sounds grand. Such as what?'

'Well, if it's not too pushy of me, I wouldn't mind telling you that indoors, and I could quite fancy a cup of tea.'

'Could you now?' Finlay looked appraisingly at Fathers and then up and down the street. 'I suppose you might as well come in. Don't get the doormat dirty.'

Fathers followed Finlay into a neat hallway. Both doors off it were shut, denying Fathers the chance to develop his sense of Finlay by peering quietly around. Up the stairs in front of them was a half-landing, off which was a closed door. Fathers thought he could hear the grating whine of a computer-printer coming from behind the door. From the half-landing, the stairs turned back on themselves up towards the first floor. To the left of the stairs in front of them were six or seven steps going down. Fathers realised that what looked like a two-storey house from the front had two and perhaps three mezzanine floors tacked on at the back, making a much larger house than appeared from the outside. Finlay led Fathers down to the back of the house, into a large, airy kitchen. It had rural-looking wallpaper, cork floor tiles, scrubbed-pine fitments and a large wooden table with several chairs around it. There was a leather jacket on the table, a pile of newspapers and magazines on one of the work surfaces, another pile of letters, bills and torn envelopes on one of the shelves, a black cat on one of the chairs, children's toys on two others and on the floor. Apart from that, there was the usual

29

paraphernalia, large and small, of a reasonably prosperous middle-class home.

Finlay started to make the tea and said, 'Sit down if you like. Shift the cat if you have to. Put your coat on one of the chairs. Excuse me.' He left the room, returning in a moment with a pipe and tobacco pouch.

The two men did not talk until Finlay had set two mugs of tea, sugar and milk on the table and sat down. Fathers helped himself to milk. He had given a lot of thought about how to deal with Finlay (having listened to a second and fuller account of their interview from Yarrow) and he hoped he had worked out the best approach.

'So why did you give my DC a hard time?'

'Did I give him a hard time?'

'He seemed to think so.'

Finaly shrugged and drank from his mug, looking at Fathers over the top of it.

'You see,' said Fathers, 'it emerges that you really know Dr Michael Sampson a great deal better than you were letting on.'

'Do I?

'Yes, indeed, so you can help us much more than you helped Mr Yarrow last week. So please stop messing around and tell me everything you can, including why you didn't help as much as you could the first time round.'

'Well, Mr Chief Inspector, I know this is nineteen eighty-four and all that, but I don't really care much about police fantasies about who and what I know. I expect Special Branch has a reasonable file on me, so why don't you ask them? They probably don't get as irritated as I do by damn fool policemen asking damn fool questions.'

'Pigheaded academics seem to be just as good at wasting time as damn fool policemen,' said Fathers. Finlay smiled, took another sip of his tea, tipped his chair back and leaned what seemed to be halfway down the kitchen to pick up a matchbox, brought his chair thumping forward, unzipped his tobacco pouch and began to fill his pipe.

'Please, Dr Finlay,' said Fathers, 'please don't use the old pipe-filling routine to waste more time. And don't think you can outlast me. I don't like wasting my time, but I will if that's what it takes. Policemen get used to it.'

'I bet they do,' replied Finlay with a wolfish grin. He gestured with his pouch and pipe. 'It's just that you're making me so terribly nervous. But tell me what you want to know.'

'And what will you do?'

'I'll tell you what I want to tell you.'

'Nope, no deal. But if you tell me what I want to know, I'll tell you why I want to know it.'

Finlay studied Fathers and took a while lighting his pipe. Fathers thought he saw a glint of interest.

'OK,' said Finlay. 'Fire away.'

'Scotland Yard has received a request for assistance from the New York Police Department. It has landed on my desk. They have asked us to provide general background information on Dr Michael Sampson, and they gave us a fairly short list of names, on which you figured, of people who knew Sampson well before he moved to the US. That's why I want to ask you some simple questions, beginning with when was the last time you had any kind of contact with Dr Sampson.'

'Hold on, hold on. Don't think you can get away with that. You haven't told me anything yet. Why do the New York fuzz want to know this background about Mike?'

'Would that I knew. But I don't. They didn't say.'

'Well that's no good then. Deal's off.'

'What do you mean, off? A deal's a deal.'

'Only in a case of fair exchange,' said Finlay, 'but you haven't brought any goods to market, have you? So you'd better run away home.'

Fathers reached into his jacket pocket for the packet of cigarettes he knew he shouldn't have with him. He extracted one, took Finlay's matches and lit it. He was beginning to understand why Yarrow had been less than eager to re-interview this man.

'Well,' he said, 'there's a bit more that I can tell you. It doesn't tell you why my DC came to see you last Thursday, because I don't know more than I've said, but it'll tell you why I'm here now. After Mr Yarrow talked to you and certain other people, we telexed a report to New York. And we thought that was an end of it. But on Monday we got phoned by the man in New York who'd sent us the request. Thanks very much, he said, but what's this about Finlay having no contact with Sampson since August last year? Here we have Sampson's notebook with a date in August this year written down and Finlay's name beside it. Here we have a scrap of paper headed 'Report' with Finlay's name underneath it. Here we have somebody who knows Sampson well and says he often mentions Finlay. So Finlay figures large for Sampson. What's going on, he says, and could you please have another word with your Dr Finlay? And here I am having another word with you. And this time you should be a little bit more forthcoming, or else I'll begin to wonder why not, and I expect I'll begin to have my doubts and suspicions about you. And if you think this is a waste of time, just wait and see what I can do for you in that line once I begin to entertain doubts and suspicions.'

'Well, Mr Inspector-in-Chief, you know how it is. If you have doubts and suspicions about me you will only be the latest in a long line. What I don't understand is how and why the New York fuzz have got hold of these various bits of paper, why they're asking questions around the place, why they're setting the wires humming between there and here, and why it is such a big deal that my humble abode is graced by a copper of such eminent rank as yourself. And, come to that, where's Sampson?'

'These days, Dr Finlay,' said Fathers, 'it is no big deal to make wires hum between America and here. Quite routine, in fact. We're very modern, you know.'

'But it is a big deal, Mr Inspector of Chiefs, for you to be handling it personally, is it not? Now, why's that?'

'That, Dr Finlay,' said Fathers, relishing it each time he used Finlay's title, 'is absolutely none of your business. As for the rest of your questions, I don't know the answers. But I think I've told you enough for you to keep our deal. When did you last have contact with Dr Sampson, what form was it, and what was the substance of it?'

'Well,' said Finlay thoughtfully, 'a deal's a deal, I suppose. To answer your question directly—'

32

'At last,' said Fathers.

'... the last time I had contact with Mike Sampson was just before I went on holiday last year, which was in early August. He wrote to ask for a bibliography I was preparing. I suppose he'd heard about it from David Cairns, or just in general on the grapevine, you know? When the bib was ready, a couple of weeks later – so I suppose he actually wrote to me in July – anyway, I sent it to him. When I got back from holiday, there was an acknowledgement slip from him. Or from his office, rather.'

'And what was your bibliography about?'

'The last ten years' worth of open literature about the modernisation of US See Cubed Eye. That's Command, Control, Communications and Intelligence to the uninitiated.'

'So I understand. Why is it called See Cubed Eye, by the way?'

'Eh? Oh, it's letter cee, figure three, letter eye. Like this, gimme your pen.' And on a scrap of paper Finlay wrote, 'C3I'. 'Some people,' he added, 'put the number in superscript.'

'Mm, how interesting,' said Fathers. 'And I understand that this See Cubed Eye covers all these military functions in one bracket, so to speak?'

'That's right. The functions have always existed, of course, but it's very much a product of the electronic age to deal with them all in a single concept. In fact, it's only quite recently that the Eye has been added. In the mid-seventies, I guess. Before that, it was just See Three.'

'Pee Oh,' added Fathers, earning a grin from Finlay. 'You said open literature. What does that cover?'

'Everything that's not secret. Books, articles in the specialist press, important news items, though I left out the dross, hearings in the US Congress, government statements, NATO communiqués and so on.'

'And how about the material that is secret?'

'Well, it's secret, isn't it? Ordinary mortals don't have access to it.'

'I suppose not,' said Fathers, 'I hope not. So the bibliography you put together was a comprehensive listing of all published material relevant to this category of military operations, except for unimportant news items.'

'You could put it that way, if you wanted to. At least, I hope it was comprehensive.'

'Is it common to produce a bibliography like that?'

'I hope not, otherwise there'd've been no bloody point in me doing it. Oh, I see what you mean. Yes, I suppose it is reasonably common for bibliographies to be put together on this or that aspect of, you know, the general armament and disarmament field.'

'Is it hard to do?'

'Not if you know the sources and have been tracking them for ten years or so.'

'And when you've done it I suppose you charge other people to see it?'

'No.'

'Oh. Why do you do it then?'

'To increase the store of human knowledge, Mr Chief of Inspectors, to increase the store of human knowledge. Also for my own convenience. If you can put aside the time to commit to it, you save one hell of a lot of time afterwards. And once it's done, it's no trouble to run off an extra copy now and then for anybody who's interested. Sometimes these bibliographies get published, but I didn't bother. See Cubed Eye is a pretty specialised field. That is, not many people are much interested in it.'

'So you sent Dr Sampson a copy. What would his interest in it be? Surely he's a specialist in this field in his own right?'

'Well, not quite this field. He mainly gets his kicks studying satellites – and they do a lot of other things besides See Cubed Eye. And, of course, See Cubed Eye is not just satellites, though they're very important. But even if it were his main concentration, it'd still be convenient to have it. Save an awful lot of work. Lazy bugger.'

'All right. Then you received a thank-you note. When after that did you next hear from him or write to him, or receive anything from him, or send something, or meet, or talk on the phone, or have any kind of contact?'

'Like I told your young chap, I've had no contact with him for over a year. And I didn't get a thank-you note from him. I got a printed acknowledgement slip from his office without even so much as his signature on it. Pretty cheap, I call it.'

'Which brings us to the nub of the matter. Why was your name on his notepad with a recent date beside it and on a scrap of paper under the word 'Report'? Why did he talk about you all the time? It sounds pretty unlikely that the pair of you have had no contact for a year, doesn't it?'

'Do I know? Do I care? Maybe he was going to send me something and didn't get round to it. How should I know? Like I said, not many people work on See Cubed Eye outside the military, so perhaps if he talks about his work a lot he mentions my name occasionally. So what? Perhaps something I wrote impressed him. Probably did. What's he done anyway?'

'As I said, I don't know why the NYPD is interested in him. I don't know that he's done anything.'

'And I don't believe you.'

'And I'm not entirely sure that I believe you either.'

'Well, there we are then.'

'Indeed, Dr Finlay, there we are. Let me put a different angle on the question. You haven't heard from him. What have you heard about him?'

'A bit. Not a lot. I've seen the couple of things he's had published this year, but they seemed mostly rehashes of conference papers he did while he was still working for us, so I don't know if they were about what he's been working on since he left. I know a bloke in Washington who does a bit of work in this kind of thing and he told me he'd seen Mike a few times. And an Australian who blew through a few months ago by way of New York and called in on Mike there, but he said he wasn't terribly forthcoming. He gathered Mike was working on a Dee Oh Dee contract and couldn't or wouldn't talk about it.'

'I beg your pardon?'

'What?'

'Dee oh Dee?'

'As in Department of Defense.'

'Thank you. That would be classified work would it?'

'Usually, yes. Or it's classified while it's being done and it's up to the Pentagon to decide whether or not it can be made public, published in any other form, whatever. It depends a lot on what kind of information he's been given access to, but it also depends on what kind of material he puts together, even if it all comes from open sources. In any case, if you're working on that kind of contract and think you'd like to get more of the same in the future, it doesn't make a lot of sense to go blabbing the details round everywhere, whatever the conditions are on the contract.'

'Did you know he was going to be working for the Defense Department?'

'Well, strictly speaking, he's not working for them. They contract research out all the time – scientific, technical, policy implications, the lot. The contract goes to a consultancy company and they appoint somebody who works for them to do it. But, yes, Mike did say before he left that he'd probably be doing a lot of Dee Oh Dee work. And Franklin Research gets a lot of its money that way, also from the State Department, as well as industry and the big foundations.'

'Now, your American friend and the Australian – what did they tell you about him?'

'Nothing that I remember. One said he was only interested in the hardware, which rings true, and t'other said he wouldn't say what he was doing, which is understandable.'

'And what did they tell you about Dr Sampson's personal life – how he is, how he lives?'

'Not a lot. Said he looked well, dressed snappily, seemed all right. You know, they didn't see him for very long and we had better things to talk about.'

'Perhaps I can go back a bit, now, and ask you for your own impression of Dr Sampson and his work?'

'Well, he's very pleasant, I suppose. Good bloke to have a drink with. Interested in the usual things. Not very political. Bit shallow, really.'

'And his work, I gather, is very much on the technical side of things?'

'That's putting it mildly. Mike's chiefly interested in hardware, performance, costs and development strategy. He's very good at digging all those things out and arranging them in order. But he really doesn't do a lot with it once he's got the information neatly arranged, you know?'

'Not really.'

'Well, basically he's just a fact cruncher. That's why he was so good at working at our unit. But when you get to somebody's own research and what they write, you expect a bit more than just the facts. They're the basis from which you then go on, the material for analysis. You ask how and why this has come about, what social or political context is it to be understood in? What are the main trends and what will be their consequences? How will they interact with other tendencies in related military areas – or political, economic, or industrial? What are the costs, not just financial? What are the alternatives? It's the kind of thing I'm always telling my students: don't just tell me what happens, tell me how and why. All Mike does is tell you what, and a very little bit of how. Any newspaper reporter could do it. No, take that back. Very few of them could. But Mike's never had a why thought in his life.'

'Would you be meaning rather much the same kind of thing as Professor Marks meant when he told us that Dr Sampson is a pure researcher?'

Finlay chuckled. 'You've been talking to Karl, have you? Exactly the sort of stupid thing he would say. The very idea of pure research in this field is absolute rubbish. Or in any field in social and political science, come to that. The last thing anyone with any sense would call Mike Sampson is a pure researcher. Nothing pure about Pentagon money. But, in the end, yes, I suppose I mean the same thing that Marks meant.'

'You regard government research money as tainted, then, Dr Finlay?'

'Well, chief, I suppose I do regard Pentagon money as tainted, but that's not the point I was making. What I mean is that if you take money from it you accept certain conditions and restrictions. Like, you may not be allowed to publish. You

37

simply are not involved in the search for pure truth for its own sake. You're doing work which somebody in power thinks will help do whatever it is that they want to do. And whether or not you like what they want to do, working on contract like that is in no sense pure. Those consultancy companies don't just look around to find out interesting things for the fun of it, or the love of it, or the politics of it. They do their research as a particular service that they sell.'

'And what do you do your research for, Dr Finlay – fun, love or politics?'

'All three, Inspector, all three.'

Fathers stood and picked up his coat. Then he said, 'Tell me, how many people work on this See Cubed Eye business in the same way you do?'

'How do you mean?'

'Outside the military establishment.'

'Ah. Well, four including me, in Britain, one way or another. Seven or eight that I know of on the continent, not all specializing exactly in See Cubed Eye, you understand, but in aspects of it, or overlapping fields. In the States, I don't know, maybe ten or so outside of companies like Franklin Research and the Beltway Bandits. One in New Zealand and one in Australia.'

'Bandits?'

'Eh? Yes, the Beltway Bandits. Companies based on the Washington Beltway, the ring-road round Washington. They do classified research for the Pentagon. Then there's magazines that specialize in it and their staff, and probably a few staff people in the US Congress, but I wouldn't know how many people that would add up to.'

Fathers put his coat on. 'Well, in the end, you have been a help. I do hope you haven't tried to mislead me about any contact you've had with Dr Sampson in recent months.'

'As if I would.'

'Yes, well. Thanks for the tea.'

'That's all right. It was only PG Tips.'

As Fathers left the house, he found himself playing word-games in his mind: See Cubed Eye; Seek Used Eye; See Cube Die; See Accused Lie.

★

When he had closed the front door behind the detective, Paul Finlay walked back to the kitchen and pensively put the kettle on to make himself another mug of tea. He took it upstairs to his study on the middle mezzanine. He picked the sheets of paper which had been printed out from the computer up off the floor, checked through them quickly and began tearing off the strips on each side. Then he exited from the programme he had been using, switched the machinery off and put the disks in their boxes. He sat down at his desk and began to drink his tea.

In contrast to his college office, his study was in immaculate order. It was a sparse room with white walls and woodwork, a plain blind on the window overlooking the back garden, one wall covered in book shelves, three filing cabinets, and a very large modern desk on which sat his computer, printer, typewriter, three boxes for index cards and seven for computer disks, a black telephone, several computer manuals, a pile of six books, a large pad of paper and a container for pens and pencils.

On the top sheet of the pad he wrote 'Fathers' and then 'Sampson'. After a moment he wrote 'Franklin Research', 'C3I?', 'Satellites', 'Verification', 'Shuttle' and, finally, 'Star Wars?'

It seemed fairly clear that the detective had been lying when he disclaimed any knowledge of why the New York police were interested in Sampson. It was most unlikely that a detective chief inspector would beetle all the way out to Stamford Hill without knowing the reason why. And it was not likely to be something unimportant which had brought him along. Yet, after a little sparring and a little fishing – which as far as Finlay could think had been totally unproductive – the policeman had gone beetling back to Scotland Yard.

Finlay wondered what had happened to Sampson, or what he had done. Was he under arrest? Sampson was not the kind of person to get into trouble of any kind. Was some kind of major security enquiry being made, in which Sampson was either a central figure (unlikely) or peripherally involved? If it was, why had the enquiry been extended all the way across the Atlantic?

That was no way to keep quiet. Finlay opened a drawer and pulled out his address book. He looked up the number of the *New Statesman* and reached for the phone, but then did not dial and put the address book away.

From a different drawer he took out the neatly bound report he had received in the post at the beginning of the week before. Apart from glancing at the section entitled 'Executive Summary', he had not had time to read it. On its cover it showed the title: 'Verification Implications of the Modified Space Shuttle Program'. On the bottom right hand corner were the words 'Franklin Research Associates, Inc.', together with its address. Under the title was the author's name: 'Michael P. Sampson.' Beneath that it said: 'Report Compiled Under Contract DoD (DARPA) FY 1984 #113b FRA'. And on the next line, in bold print: 'Restricted: Not for Release Until Authorized by Contracting Agency'. Attached to the cover with a paper clip was a compliments slip from Franklin Research bearing a hand-written message: 'Paul: I thought you would be interested in this. Please keep it under your hat for the present. Mike'.

Paul Finlay opened the report and began to read it.

4

After returning from Stamford Hill, Fathers wrote up the notes of his interview with Finlay, then arranged a punishing schedule of meetings for the next morning, and finished by reading the papers and reports necessary for each one. The result was that he got home just before ten o'clock, which caused his wife, Sarah, to explode with rage. Going out that morning he had said that, subject to the usual qualification that a big case could erupt at any time, he would be home in time for an early meal and a long evening together. The fact that he had simply forgotten to phone her only made her anger more burning. After the explosion a grim and hostile silence dominated the last hours of his day. In the morning he was thankful to be up and out of the house before Sarah or the children had woken.

The morning was warm and sunny, but he did not enjoy it as he made his way to work to snatch breakfast during his first meeting, a brief session with Yarrow – preparation for their meeting with Bastin and others later in the day. Before eight-thirty Yarrow was out of his office, his place taken by Detective Inspector Stevens for a discussion of the latest state of the now largely stalled bullion case. He had been the officer in effective charge of the case since the weekend, with Fathers reduced to breathing anxiously down his neck.

Like Fathers, Stevens had a university degree; like his, it was not a very good one from not a very good university, but it was enough to establish common ground and even the basis of an alliance between them. In the non-intellectual environment of the police, Fathers had experienced this kind of alliance several times before. In his team at the moment, there was a similar feeling between two of his detective sergeants – Pardoner and Gordon – both university educated, which to some degree divided them from the others who were not. Since their access to higher education also reflected their more middle-class background, there were grounds there for the resentment and cliquishness that could have a corrosive, debilitating effect. So far, Fathers felt that problem was small enough to be manageable – only in the case of Laurence Queen, his other detective inspector, was it either obvious or difficult. But that was largely due to the fact that they were, by the standards of Scotland Yard, a successful group of detectives with a relatively high rate of cleared cases and convictions.

With Stevens, Fathers felt an ease and rapport he had rarely felt with any colleague since he had joined the CID twelve years ago. More than their common background, the two were united by a similar approach to their work and its problems, and, just as importantly, by a taste for elegant clothes and a liking for elaborate, idiosyncratic and self-conscious slang. The two men would have been close friends were it not for an unstated understanding that comradeship and liking made for a better working relationship than real closeness.

After forty minutes, Stevens summed up. 'By now, guv, the gold has either taken a walk across the water, or been smelted down or put in cold storage. Any which way, we're not going to find out much. Word's out that, to put it mildly, we are very interested in any whispers about this particular merchandise, and willing to trade. Frankly, I think that's our best hope. In the meantime, a little over eight million smackers' worth of the yellow has taken a walk and there's bugger all we can do about it.'

'What you mean, James,' said Fathers 'is that you have done your best and can you please now be taken off the case and given summat else to do.'

'That's about it,' agreed Stevens. 'Reluctant though I am to say so, the blaggers have pretty well stuffed us on this one. It's been so effing frustrating. Not a break anywhere. Not one bit of luck. Nobody talking out of turn about it. We've done a lot of bloody good police work for sweet Fanny Adams. I suggest you knock three times on wood, find a lucky rabbit's foot and pray to your fairy godmother.'

'Yes,' said Fathers, 'I'm seeing him later on this morning.'

Fathers was not surprised that Stevens had led the conversation to this point. Much though it hurt to let the bullion robbery join the all too long list of unsolved cases, Fathers was reasonably reconciled to its inevitability. When active responsibility for an investigation is moved down the hierarchy, as it had been in this case, it is usually because it has become less important in the police's ever changing list of priorities.

Fathers shrugged and handed Stevens a folder from his desk. In it was a report of a tip-off from one of DS Graves' contacts about a forthcoming jewellery theft. He told Stevens to pass the bullion file on to DS Gordon, who would doubtless put it in one of her desk drawers there to remain until either a grass appeared to help them or she had a grand clear-out and transferred it to a filing cabinet.

When Stevens left, DI Queen took his place. At forty-three, Queen was older than both Fathers and Stevens and aware of it. It rankled that younger men had been promoted to his level and above it. He was given to referring to the 'university mafia' to explain why the brakes had been put on his own climb through the ranks. Six years ago, Queen had made his first attempt at promotion to Detective Chief Inspector. He had missed out then and twice more, at two-yearly intervals. He was due, reflected Fathers, to make another attempt soon, and he would be just as unsuccessful as before, partly because Fathers did not consider him to be the right material for DCI. Fathers wondered sometimes if Yarrow would turn out like Queen, who was something of an earlier model of the young DC – ambitious, clever, a working-class lad expecting to make good. And in many respects he had, but not good enough, not in his own eyes anyway.

Queen started in briskly. 'Those fucking animals told young Ricky last night how they want the money. Used notes of mixed denominations. Surprise, fucking surprise. No consecutive serial numbers. They been watching too much sodding telly.'

The previous Sunday, a rock star's nine-year-old daughter had been kidnapped and a ransom of £250,000 demanded. Queen

43

had been called in on the Sunday, returning from holiday a day early to handle the case.

'Any problems getting the cash?' asked Fathers.

'No, fucking rolling in it.'

'And have they set up the hand-over?'

'No, too fucking smart for that, aren't they? Instructions to follow. Do exactly what you're told or else. No police and no press, as usual.'

'At least that means they don't know we're on to it.'

'Yeah. Mrs Ricky's pissing herself, though, about us being there. Says just to hand over the money and get little Zoe back.'

'I suppose you've told her about the statistics?'

'Fucking right I did. Didn't do any good, though. Says so what if the odds are usually better if the police are in on it, nobody would dare harm little Zoe. Sodding animals, what does she know?'

'You were a bit more tactful than that, I hope?'

'Thank you very much,' said Queen. 'Course I was tactful. Didn't stop the waterworks being turned on, though. Course, what makes it hard is I got a feeling they won't get Zoe back either way. Just a feeling.'

Queen outlined his plan. Essentially, it consisted of having a detective impersonating the rock star's agent leave the money wherever the kidnappers instructed. He would be wearing a miniature microphone to keep him in constant communication, and once the place to leave the money was announced it would also be watched.

'Why can't Ricky do it himself?' asked Fathers.

'Have you met young Ricky? Or anyone like him?'

'No.'

'Well then,' declared Queen.

'What's that supposed to mean?'

'Do you know how these pop stars live? They live surrounded by people who look after their every sodding need. They live in mink. Ricky can't even handle going to the shops himself, let alone something like this. He probably has someone hold it while he pisses. Fuck knows what'll happen if he has to be the one to hand over the dough. I wouldn't put it past the little bugger to turn funny under the pressure and go and tell them he's wired for sound. And he has to be wired up or anything and bleeding everything could go wrong.'

'What if they insist it has to be Ricky?'

'He'll say he's in shock, under sedation, drugged to the eyeballs. Pop stars are like that so the animals should believe it. If they say Mrs Ricky can do it, Ricky says it's the same problem, bung full of Valium. Not too far off the mark either. If we rolled that place over we'd like as not pick up our weight in fancy drugs of one kind or another.'

'Has Ricky agreed to this?'

'Not yet, but he will,' said Queen confidently.

'What if he doesn't?'

'Then he's fucked and so's little Zoe.'

'And what if they say it's got to be Ricky whatever state he's in?'

'What if, what if, what if?' asked Queen sneeringly. 'Well, if I absolutely have to, I reckon I can persuade Ricky to wear the wire and we'll just have to take the risk.'

'All right,' said Fathers after thinking it over some more. 'You're the man in charge. Work out what you need and get back to me. This afternoon, line up the cooperation on the ground you need from the local forces. Go through the county headquarters for that. And brief them thoroughly. And not just the Surrey police, either. Kent, Sussex and Hampshire as well. Need any help, get back to me.'

When Queen had gone, Fathers looked at his watch and sighed. Of all the men and women who worked under him, Queen was the one he had most trouble with. Most of the time they were barely on speaking terms. Queen did not normally sprinkle his conversation with swear words. He did it with Fathers because he thought Fathers was prim and middle-class and would be shocked. And maybe I am prim, thought Fathers – because although he was not shocked he was offended.

It was after nine-thirty. Time to see Bastin.

★

Chief Superintendent Bastin pressed a button on his desk intercom. 'Has DI Walters arrived yet?' he asked. The intercom replied that he had. 'Good. Send him in then, Celia, would you? Also Messrs Whyte and Yarrow. Oh, and coffee for five, thank you.' The intercom said something back and the door opened. Bastin rose to shake hands with DI Walters of the Special Branch, gesturing him to sit down at the conference table at which Fathers was already seated, stretching and yawning, praying silently for decent coffee and lighting an illicit cigarette. Detective Constables Whyte and Yarrow were left to find their own seats, receiving only a nod from Bastin and nothing from Fathers.

Bastin sat himself down at the head of the table. The men from the Special Branch were to his left, the men from Serious Crimes to his right. 'Now then,' he said, 'the Sampson file, Or is it really the Sampson file? This Finlay seems to have consumed a lot of our interest, is that not so, Harry?'

Fathers looked at his boss, a bulky six-footer in his fifties whose muscle had only recently begun to slacken into fat, nodded and stretched again. Bastin appeared to have chosen the most uncomfortable chairs in the Yard's inventory. There they had sat for sixty-five minutes going over the kidnapping of the rock star's daughter and the bullion robbery. Fathers had finally managed to convince Bastin that the bullion investigation was genuinely stalled and would remain so unless they got a tip-off, that this was not the fault of an unthorough investigation, and that Stevens would be far better employed looking into the forthcoming jewellery theft. Bastin had not seemed very interested in the jewellery tip-off. Fathers suspected this was because the kidnapping was more glamorous. The tip-off had been bought by a Detective Sergeant for a mere fifty pounds.

'Finlay,' said Fathers, 'is an interesting case study in instinctive non-cooperation with the police. Yarrow here had the distinct impression that Finlay was not only holding something back, but also got in the way of his enquiries by encouraging another man, Cairns, the research officer, into taciturnity.'

46

Bastin looked at Fathers with a glow of approval. Words of five syllables mark out the high-flyers.

Fathers continued. 'I'm more than inclined to accept that judgement, having interviewed the man myself. He's a prickly soul who enjoys teasing the police, and I'm certain he was holding something back from me, something of some importance, though what it was I can't say. On the other hand, fascinating though Finlay is, our interest in him is entirely secondary to the enquiry about Sampson, which itself is merely derivative of the New York Police Department's case, whatever it is.'

'Indeed,' said Bastin, 'this is barely our case at all. Yet it is our case, and our major point of entry at the moment appears to be the man Finlay. I think it best to start there. You have, I take it,' he said to Walters, 'had an opportunity to peruse the Sampson file itself?' Walters nodded. 'Good, then let us familiarise ourselves with Finlay. Yarrow, perhaps you'd care to start? Whyte, you can fill us in from the Special Branch angle as appropriate? Good. I should add, Harry, that Mr Walters is here to keep a watching brief on the Branch's behalf. Yarrow?'

Bastin nodded courteously, first to Walters, then to Yarrow. His little peroration had been delivered with both hands flat on the table and the comfortable air which comes from possessing undeniable superiority in a particular gathering. Detective Constable Elliot Yarrow had no such luxuries to sustain him. He gazed at his notes, looked up briefly, and then delivered his report in a monotone.

'Paul Theodore Finlay' he said, 'was forty-one years old in April. He gained a Bachelor's degree at Oxford University in Politics, Philosophy and Economics. Then he went to Manchester and got a Master's degree in Political Science. He returned to Oxford for three years more, studying for his Doctor of Philosophy degree. He actually got that a few years after he'd left Oxford, when he was already a university lecturer. Apparently, that's quite common.'

Yarrow looked up. 'More common than getting the PhD in three years like Sampson did,' he added and looked back down again. 'His doctoral thesis was on Hungarian politics after nineteen fifty-six. During the nineteen sixties, while he was a student, he was an active member of the Socialist societies at both Oxford and Manchester. He took part in several demonstrations, both in those towns and in London, and was three times charged and convicted of obstruction. Fined in each case. He was charged again with obstruction during the riots on the Grunwick picket line in North London in the summer of nineteen seventy-seven. Convicted and fined again. In nineteen sixty-nine, at a demonstration about Vietnam, he was arrested and charged with threatening behaviour, and in nineteen seventy, at a demonstration about South Africa, he was arrested for assaulting a police officer. But he wasn't convicted either time. Case withdrawn the first time, and dismissed in court the second. He was appointed as a lecturer in politics at his present college in nineteen seventy-two. He was made a senior lecturer in nineteen seventy-seven and reader two years ago.'

Yarrow looked up briefly again. 'Reader is just below professor,' he said, and then went back to his notes. 'He's published four books – author of three of them, editor of one – and also numerous articles in various places.' Another look up. 'I've got the list here if you want it, sir. It includes some very academic journals, but also other papers and periodicals like *Marxism Today, New Socialist*, the *Guardian* and *New Statesman*, as well as some other less well-known leftist publications.'

He looked down again. 'Since about nineteen seventy-three, his research has specialised in what's called strategic studies, but with a very left-wing slant, what he and others apparently call peace research. He's been a member of CND since early in nineteen eighty. That's right at the beginning of their revival. And he's spoken several times in public for them, as well as writing articles calling for Britain to disarm itself, cut defence spending and so on. He's also attacked NATO on several occasions, and has written a lot recently about what he calls the USA's plans for nuclear war fighting, and attacking the US President's plans for defence against nuclear attack from the USSR. His current speciality is a very sensitive field known as

See Cubed Eye, which is shorthand for Command, Control, Communications and Intelligence, and he cooperates in that work with like-minded researchers in Britain and abroad. Dr Michael Sampson's own speciality is in satellites, which overlaps with Finlay's field. They worked in the same college for about two years, and Finlay appears to be the person who would have appointed Sampson to that job. Other people say Finlay knows Sampson well and has kept in contact with him over the eighteen months since Sampson moved to New York. But Finlay himself denies it on both counts.'

Yarrow leaned back in his chair and took a deep breath. At that point, a knock on the door announced the arrival of coffee for five. Setting it down, pouring it and sorting out the milks and sugars took some time, during which Fathers took the opportunity to mutter a quick 'Well done' to Yarrow, who smiled wanly but gratefully.

'So,' said Bastin when the coffee was all straight. 'Yarrow, I am most grateful. Whyte, you have something to add?'

'Merely to say, sir,' said DC Whyte, 'that the Branch has an interest in Finlay. So, too, I shouldn't wonder, has Box Five.' This jargon reference to MI5 brought an appreciative nod from Walters, a 'harrumph' from Bastin, a scowl from Fathers and a look of puzzlement from Yarrow who did not understand what it meant.

'As you can probably tell from DC Yarrow's report,' continued Whyte, 'Finlay's militancy has calmed somewhat as he's got older. Still supports the usual causes, but he's not to be seen so often on the violent demos these days. Keeps his head down a bit more.' Fathers smiled.

Whyte carried on. 'He joined the Labour Party in nineteen seventy-three. We do not know of any previous party memberships, though he was close to the old International Socialists for a time in the late nineteen sixties, and he may have been an actual member for a short period. Nothing confirmed though. He was clearly a Marxist during the nineteen sixties, but his colours seem to have faded a bit since then. Our current interest in him is chiefly a product of the combination of his research interest in a highly sensitive area of national security, together with his political views which, as DC Yarrow has said, include opposition to British membership in the Western Alliance, topped off by the fact that he has a criminal record. On his research, one should do him the justice to add that, on technical grounds, it is well respected in his field, even by those who do not hold with his politics. On the other hand, he is one of those who walk the knife-edge between reporting and analysing what is already in the public domain and actually revealing classified information. So far he hasn't tipped over into actually spilling secrets. I would say it's our estimate that one day he probably will.'

'How do you read his motives?' asked Fathers.

'Well, sir,' said Whyte, looking at Walters, 'I'd say we're not much interested in motive, you know?'

'Quite,' said Walters. 'But I think one could say he is something of a classic case, representative in his way of the disaffected intellectual who despises the way things are, the established order, and also, therefore, those people whose duty it is to uphold the established order. Thus, I would imagine, his attitude to the two of you, representatives of what these people like to call the repressive apparatus of the state.'

'What I really mean,' said Fathers, 'is whether or not you have any hint that he is a genuine security threat, in the sense of working for the Russians?'

'Ah,' said Walters. 'No, we do not see him as consciously working for the Soviets. Box Five might see it differently. He can, of course, be a security threat even if he isn't working for the other side.'

'If I could say, sir,' put in Whyte, 'he seems to be one of those socialists who hates the Russians almost as much as he hates the Americans.'

'Your Box Five would probably say that was just cover,' said Fathers.

'Perhaps,' said Walters, 'but only if there was hard evidence.'

'Really?' said Fathers. 'You surprise me.'

'If anything,' said Walters, 'I would say his motive on most occasions seems to be to cause as much mischief as he can.'

'Yes,' said Bastin, 'that's the best they can manage usually, isn't it? However, let us try to advance. Is it your contention, Harry, or yours, Yarrow, that he has deliberately and knowingly witheld information?'

'What's a contention?' asked Fathers. 'If you mean something that would stand up in a court of law, the answer is no. But if you're asking me and Yarrow what our feeling is, having interviewed the man, the answer is yes. I'm sure that not only when Yarrow interviewed him but also when I did he was withholding information, knowingly, as you put it, and deliberately. Or, to put it the other way round, he was telling me as little as he possibly could without obviously obstructing my enquiries. I doubt he told any actual lies, though that's possible. It's just that when he told the truth, he didn't tell the whole truth. Our problem is that if we don't know the questions to ask, and we don't, we can't back him into a position where he has to choose between telling us everything we want to know or blatantly obstructing us. And, of course, if we did know the right questions, we'd probably know the right answers already. So we could have the fun of nailing him but it would no longer be relevant to advancing our enquiries.'

'So what do you conclude, Harry?' asked Bastin.

'That unless we are given the right questions by New York, we have got everything we are likely to get from the good doctor. We should forget about him now and get back to Sampson. Or rather, we should forget about him and let New York get back to Sampson. This isn't our show.'

'Mr Walters?' asked Bastin.

'Broadly speaking, I concur,' said Walters. 'Of course, our interest in Finlay will continue, enriched by this episode. But on present showing, I see no reason why it should be raised to a higher and more active level. We could keep a much closer eye on him, of course. No technical or legal problem. But so far I see no grounds for directing extra resources that way. Subject, of course, sir, to your own judgement and any decisions my commander might take should you raise the matter with him.'

'Of course,' said Bastin, 'and I'm grateful for your summary. I doubt I shall raise the matter with him, except to comment favourably upon your cooperation. But I should tell you, gentlemen, that the Sampson file is the object of great interest from higher quarters. I shall be presenting a report based on a compilation of what you have provided. It may be we shall be called upon to take this further. For the moment, however, I see no reason to ask that you undertake any further actions or enquiries. Dr Sampson has a clean sheet here, and Dr Finlay is a secondary concern. And I imagine the Branch is not out looking for extra work.'

'Quite so,' agreed Walters. 'We're more than stretched as it is, what with the Brighton bomb and the miners' strike.'

'Nineteen eighty-four,' said Fathers, 'what a year. But this one really isn't our show. We've done our bit and that's an end to it.'

'Provisionally,' said Bastin. 'Thank you very much, gentlemen.'

5

At six p.m. that day, Thursday, 18 October, Detective Inspector Laurence Queen arrived at the Surrey home of Ricky Punter, the rock star whose daughter had been kidnapped. He came with his driver and a Drug Squad detective, borrowed for the occasion because of his long hair, wearing a white suit to impersonate Punter's agent. He found a household waiting in distraught tension for the phone call which would tell them how and where to hand over the ransom money. Punter's manager had already arrived with £250,000 in cash.

Queen started straight in to persuade Punter to follow his plan. Punter's wife, Jessie, refused, which Queen had expected. But Punter, with an obstinate grit which surprised Queen as much as it offended him, also refused, rejecting all counter-arguments for over two hours. Finally, Queen changed tack and suggested that Punter wear the miniature microphone and radio which had been brought for the Drug Squad man to wear. The police could track him unobtrusively and listen to anything he had to report, or anything the kidnappers said to him if they were at the hand-over point. Jessie Punter again refused – for her, only complete cooperation with the kidnappers made sense – but her husband seemed more amenable. Yet Queen did not make enough progress. When the phone call came shortly after ten p.m., Punter was still undecided.

Punter was sitting right by the phone and answered it immediately. A voice briskly described a milestone on a road near Burgess Hill in Sussex. He was to be there in forty minutes and leave the money beside it. On the stone he would find instructions for where to go to pick up Zoe. Any funny business, the voice told him, even a sniff of police, anything, and the deal was off. If Ricky Punter wanted to see Zoe again, he would do exactly what he was told and nothing else.

Punter put the phone down, picked up the brown grip holding the money and ran for the door.

'Here, you're not wired,' called Queen.

'No,' said Punter. 'No.'

'You must let us decide,' said Queen. 'We know what's best.'

'What do you fucking know?' shouted Punter, almost at his Mercedes in the driveway. 'She's not your daughter. Keep out of it.' And he got in, started up and drove off. He had decided to obey the kidnappers, not the police.

'Fuck it,' said Queen, and, 'Play it back, Sergeant,' to the man who had been taping the telephone conversation. Despite Jessie Punter's vehement objections and sporadic efforts at sabotage – such as grabbing his arm and trying to pull him away from the telephone – Queen arranged for Punter to be tracked at a distance by the neighbouring police forces. The telephone tape told him where the drop was to be made, and he arranged for a discreet watch there by the Sussex police through their head-quarters in Lewes. When he left the house twenty minutes later to follow in his own car, he thought he was in direct touch with all the people he needed to be to rescue the case from catastrophe.

The milestone where Punter was to leave the money was on a quiet country road south of Burgess Hill. For the most part, the road twisted and turned, but the milestone was on a short straight patch. Queen and the Sussex police did not risk anything obvious. Every few minutes an unmarked police car – a different one each time – drove down the road past the milestone. The third one to make the pass reported that there was a stone on top of it which might be holding something down – a piece of paper, perhaps, with Punter's next set of directions. So the kidnappers – or some of them, or one of them at least – were in the vicinity, hiding. Caution was essential. Around a couple of bends about half a mile westwards of the milestone was a layby. There the police put a quiet watch, in the form of a couple apparently courting enthusiastically. Slightly further eastwards from the milestone was a T-junction with a lonely street light. There another watch was kept, by a young lad working desperately on a wonky motorbike under the inadequate light.

Punter broke the speed limit most of the way as he drove south, then slowed to a more legal pace as he neared the milestone. He got to it within two minutes of the prescribed time, stopped his car, pulling it over onto the verge to let another pass him, got out and put the bag holding the money down behind the milestone. Fifty yards down the road, another car stopped and four young men got out; laughing and talking loudly as they walked over to relieve their evidently bursting bladders against a large tree. Punter picked up the piece of paper on top of the milestone, got back into his car and switched on the internal light. Letters cut out from a newspaper and pasted onto the paper formed the name and address of a pub near Lewes and outlined directions for getting there. He clicked off the light and, as he began to move off, saw the four men up the road. Assuming they were police, he wound down his window as he passed and hissed, 'Fuck off out of it, cunts.'

The four men at the trees looked at each other, shrugged and zipped up. One of them walked to the roadside and looked after the departing Mercedes. The three others joined him. 'Well,' said one, 'shall we investigate?' The four rolled along the fifty yards towards the milestone. Another car passed them. They got to the milestone and one bent down to pick up the bag. He put it on top of the milestone and unzipped it. He turned to the others, and at that moment the car that had just passed them came speeding back followed by another. A third car converged on them from the other direction. The three cars screeched to a halt, doors were thrown open and men charged out, throwing themselves on the four at the milestone. One of the four was punched in the stomach, lay down and began to vomit. One who tried to run had his legs kicked from under him. The other two were grabbed and slammed face first across car bonnets. Then all four were bundled into the cars which raced through the countryside to the police station at Haywards Heath, where they were dragged out of the cars, through doors, down stairs, through more doors and into four separate cells.

'Christ,' said Queen when he got the news on his car radio that four kidnappers had been picked up with the money. He turned to his driver. 'Let's hope that hasn't fucked it for little Zoe.'

'But I thought you thought she was already booked for the cemetery, guv,' said the driver.

'That's what I think,' said Queen, 'but I don't know it. Put your foot down.'

When Queen arrived at the police station, he went straight to an interview room and sat down at the table. The first of the four was brought into him. He looked about twenty years old and smelled of drink, vomit and urine. He had his hands in his pockets to hold up his trousers because his belt had been taken from him, his shoes too. He sat down opposite Queen. A uniformed constable sat in a chair by the door.

'Right then, animal,' said Queen, 'we've no time to mess around. Tell me where Zoe is or it'll go the worse for you.'

'What's going on?' asked the man.

'Don't mess me, animal. Zoe – where is she?'

'What's this all about? What've I done?'

'Look, mate, kidnapping's bad enough, but you're right up the creek if anything happens to her, all right? The game's up so there's no point in you messing about, understand? Just tell me what I want to know and we'll tell the beak you were a good boy. Keep on like you are and it's porridge for life. Zoe Punter – where is she? Now.'

The man finally seemed to register Queen's words. 'What are you talking about?' he asked, panic rising. 'What do you mean, kidnapping? I don't know what you're talking about. I want a lawyer. I want my father.'

'Don't gimme that,' said Queen. 'Just give me Zoe. Where is she?'

'I want a lawyer,' insisted the man. 'You can't do this. I got rights.'

'Rights?' Queen turned to the constable at the door. 'Just pop out and get me a cup of tea, would you, lad? he asked. The constable left, shutting the door behind him. Queen got up, walked round the table and picked the man up by his shirt collar. 'Look here,' he said, 'do you want my knee in your balls? Because that's what you're going to get unless you tell me where Zoe is. And I mean now.'

'Look,' said the man, 'I don't know what you're talking about. My father is a Just—'

Queen kneed the man in the groin as hard as he could. The man screamed and clutched himself, falling to the floor, his trousers sliding down around his knees.

'Zoe Punter,' said Queen kneeling down and grabbing the man's hair. 'Where is she?'

The man did not answer. He groaned and heaved, trying to be sick, but nothing came up. He wept. But he did not answer. Disgustedly, Queen let go of the man's hair so that his head thumped down onto the floor, and walked out and into the next interview room.

For the next fifteen minutes Queen tried his luck with each of the other three arrested men, with mounting frustration. He stamped on the stockinged feet of one and poured scalding tea down another's back. With the third he changed his tactics, offering tea and cigarettes, chummily suggesting that a little cooperation would not go amiss. But neither hard nor soft approach worked. When Queen had them locked back in their cells he was no nearer knowing where Zoe Punter was to be found.

As Ricky Punter drove to the pub in the countryside near Lewes, he felt sick with tension and fear. Visions of his daughter and what might have happened to her jostled in his head with pictures of his reunion with her. Had he been right or wrong to go against the police? Why had they been at the milestone like that?

Twice he missed his way, and the police lost him at his second mistake. But at last, towards eleven-thirty, he turned left in a village and the pub was on the right, a large car park to the side of it. All the lights were off and only one other car was there. He stopped in the car park, leaving his headlights pointing at the other car, and got out.

'Zoe,' he called into the dark, 'where are you, my love? It's all over now, it's all all right. Are you there, little one? I've come to take you back home, come on.'

The dark silence scoffed at him. He went over to the other car and looked in. It was locked and empty.

'Zoe, my lovely,' he shouted, 'come on, where are you? It's all right. Come on, Zoe, it's me, Ricky.'

More silence. He tried the boot of the empty car. It was locked. He put his ear to it: no sound.

He got back in his car and turned the internal light on. He reread the note. He had followed the directions correctly. He got out again and walked over to peer at the pub sign. He was at the right place. At the far end of the car park there was an inky darkness. He guessed it was a field. He walked towards it until he bumped into some kind of fence. 'Zoe!' he shouted. 'Zoe, are you there?' He called again. 'Zoe! Zoe! It's Daddy. Zoe!' Silence. He walked back to his car. Tears ran down his cheeks. 'Oh, those fucking police,' he whispered. 'Oh, those fucking police.'

Lights in the pub and the car park were switched on. The landlord, golf club in hand, ventured out to see who was making the racket. He found a man in his late twenties standing beside a big car, sobbing quietly and saying, over and over again, 'Oh those fucking police.' The landlord could not make him say what the trouble was or even listen to his offer of a drink. So he went inside and telephoned the police.

After his first encounters with each of the four men Queen went through the contents of their wallets. They were local men – not, as Queen said to the desk sergeant, that that proved anything. The father of one of the men – the one Queen had kneed in the groin – was well known to the locals: he was a headmaster and a Justice of the Peace. 'A black sheep in every family,' muttered Queen when he was told.

Four sets of parents were called from their homes at about midnight and brought to the police station. They recognised their sons, and began to fume about the state they were in, inflamed by a deep and righteous anger when they learned that the four were being held on suspicion of having committed an extremely serious crime. The police, they all confidently asserted, had the wrong men. A doctor was allowed to examine the four and a solicitor was brought in.

58

Statements were taken. The four had been drinking at a country pub. They had been driving home. They had stopped for a moment. They had seen a man leave something at a milestone. As he drove off he said something to them. They had gone to look at the bag. They had been attacked. They had been brought to the police station where three of them had been attacked some more. Except in the details of Queen's treatment of them, the four stories were identical. As witnesses to their whereabouts that evening, they variously mentioned the landlord, barman and barmaid and three or four other drinkers.

Amid their complaints and anger the parents also gave statements. All four of the young men lived at home. Three had jobs, one was unemployed. None had been away during the previous week. None had behaved in any way unusually. All were fine, upstanding boys.

Queen was unimpressed. 'Every villain's got a loving mum somewhere,' he said to the local detective inspector.

But he realised three things. First, the explanation of how they came to be on that bit of road at that time was credible and could easily be checked. Second, if it turned out to be true that the behaviour of the four had been entirely routine and unsuspicious during the previous week, and that too could be checked easily enough, then the odds were that they were not kidnappers. Third, if they were not the men he'd been after there could be serious trouble about their treatment at the police station.

Queen also discovered that when a uniformed inspector from the Lewes police turned up at the pub where Punter was, by then sitting in the bar with a sympathetically provided whisky, there had been further trouble. Punter had recovered enough to say who he was and ask for a lift home. The inspector demurred gently. The officer in charge of the case, he explained, was now at Haywards Heath and would want to talk with Mr Punter. He could be taken there, and then given a lift to his home, where his car could also be driven in the meantime. Punter shook his head. There was still a chance of a happy outcome, explained the inspector, so, though Mr Punter was undoubtedly most upset, he could surely see that the best thing would be to call in at

Haywards Heath, just for a moment.

Punter stood up. 'If you haven't got the common decency to help me, just shut up,' he said. 'You've just killed my daughter. I'm not talking to any of you.' And he walked out.

The inspector was apologetic to Queen on the phone. 'I thought it was the right thing,' he said, 'but I didn't realise how wound up he was.'

Accordingly, Queen began to prepare his defences. Firstly, he indicated to the parents, when he managed to get them to give him a hearing, that their sons might have been arrested through a mistake which was no fault of their own or of the police. On the other hand, he pointed out secondly, they were technically at fault for having opened the bag. Accordingly, he said thirdly, although he was willing for the four men to be released on bail, they must stay in the locality and the appropriate enquiries would be put in hand. The parents heard him out in grim silence and he made a quick exit before another eruption of outrage overwhelmed him.

Next, he asked who had given the order to go in and pick the four men up instead of having them followed. When he was told it was a detective sergeant, he cursed and muttered something about people with not enough experience being given too much responsibility. When this remark was reported to the detective chief inspector by the detective inspector to whom he had made it, more preparations of lines of defence began.

Finally, Queen called Scotland Yard and left a message for Fathers. It was brief but carefully thought out: 'Sussex police may have arrested wrong men in Punter case. Zoe not found. Ricky furious'. And then he left for London.

When Fathers saw Queen's message on his arrival at the Yard next morning, he shivered. He passed it on to Bastin's office, and then called the Press Room, alerting them to the possibility that Ricky Punter would want to pillory the police in public and suggesting that any press enquiries that could not be fobbed off should be referred directly to himself for comment.

Next he phoned Detective Chief Inspector Barnsley, the senior CID officer at Haywards Heath. The man was not in a good mood. He gave Fathers a crisp summary of the night's events and then delivered his views about thugs who came down from London, beat up people in police cells and departed leaving the people on the spot to pick up the pieces. An angry retort rose to Fathers' tongue but he suppressed it, knowing he would regret it later if it came out uncontrolled. Later in the day Barnsley phoned back to apologise for shouting. As Fathers then gathered, he had had every excuse. To take Fathers' call he had had to leave a session with the four fathers and two of the mothers of the arrested men, now released.

'My boy is innocent,' one mother had said.

'If you will forgive me,' said Barnsley stiffly, 'it is our job to investigate the situation and to determine—'

'And you had no right to treat him like that,' she added.

'Madam, it is not pleasant to be arrested, but our officers had every reason to suspect all four of the boys and—'

'They didn't have any bloody right to beat them up,' said a father.

'I think I have made it clear that all the injuries were actually sustained at the moment of arrest when, sad to say, there was a fight.'

'What about the tea down my boy's back?' shouted another father.

'I have tried to explain,' said Barnsley, 'that that was a genuine accident – a friendly offer of tea, but your son was naturally in an upset state and, let's be honest, he'd had a bit to drink and it was actually his sudden action that caused the officer to spill the tea. The other one, now, your son I believe, sir – he was offered tea as well, was he not, without accident?'

'That's bloody irrelevant,' said the father whose son had not been maltreated in the police station. 'He was still in a shocking state. Cuts and blood all over the place.'

'Yes, well, if somebody, however much in the right they feel, resists arrest by police officers who have good reason—'

'A knee in the crutch is standard procedure, is it?' snapped the Justice of the Peace.

'Well, no, but in a fight such things happen, and I'm afraid I can't tell my men to pull their punches when, as far as they know, their lives might be on the line. It's an unpleasant consequence of resisting arrest.'

'It did not happen,' said the JP, 'at the arrest; it happened in the police station.'

'No,' said Barnsley, 'it happened at the arrest.'

'And they didn't even resist the arrest,' said one of the mothers. 'They didn't have time. They were attacked.'

'No,' said Barnsley, 'I'm afraid that's not right. They attempted to get away after the officers had identified themselves, which is, of course, one way of resisting arrest, and there was a brief scuffle as a result.'

'My boy doesn't lie,' said the JP.

'Nor do police officers,' said Barnsley.

Therefore, he had shouted at Fathers.

When Queen arrived to report, he wasted no time in coming to the point. 'Right balls up, I'm afraid, guv.'

Fathers listened carefully to Queen's account. When it was finished, Fathers reflected that police officers made mistakes just like ordinary people, that they liked them as little as anybody else did and that they had the human habit of denying they had made any. Without having heard a detailed report on the previous night's events from anybody else, he could already see where and how Queen was tailoring his story to put himself in the least bad light. For all Fathers could tell, this version was what Queen really believed. The more he repeated it, the more he would believe it. If it came to an enquiry, he would repeat it again and, as he would see it, he would be telling the truth.

According to Queen, three serious mistakes – none of them his – had been compounded by bad luck. The first and most serious one was Punter's in refusing to cooperate with the police at the last moment. 'We were fucked from then on, guv,' he said. 'I could smell trouble coming.'

The second mistake was to put a detective sergeant in immediate charge of activities at and near the milestone. It was too much responsibility, Queen declared, for a lad of such low rank and little experience. The third mistake was the detective sergeant's for assuming the four men examining the bag were the kidnappers. 'Even if they were the animals we was after,' said Queen, 'we wanted to follow them, not nab 'em then and there.'

The bad luck was that four drunks should roll up at that exact moment and not a few minutes later. With what Fathers considered to be a masterly touch, Queen then conceded that he had, perhaps, made one mistake himself: 'It could be said that I was at fault in not saying, in so many words, that if anybody was spotted taking a dekko at Master Ricky's bag, then they should be left well alone. But then again, I couldn't know they'd be so fucking green, could I?'

Fathers moved on to the events in the police station. 'As I understand it,' he said holding up four fingers of his right hand, 'you encouraged one of the suspects to talk by means of a knee.' He folded his little finger down. 'With the second one you stepped on his little piggies.' He folded down his ring finger. 'The third one you talked things over with, with the help of a pint of tea down his shirt.' He folded down his index finger and squinted at Queen past his middle finger. 'And with the fourth one you finally got round to asking questions.' He folded down the middle finger, keeping his now clenched fist in the air. 'That right?' He let his fist drop to his lap.

'Look', said Queen, 'the message I got was that four of the gang had been picked up and were held at the Haywards Heath nick. Obviously, I had to get them to say where Zoe was. Right? If they had been the animals we were after, one of 'em would've pissed in my lap, no trouble. Trouble was, they weren't the men we wanted.'

'You do realise,' said Fathers, 'that we – and that especially means you – are in serious trouble on two fronts. Screwing up the

63

actual case is bad enough. A man like Punter is no stranger to the world of the media and the Sunday papers. He knows how to use them and you can bet he will.'

'Master Ricky's only got his fucking self to blame for the screw-up,' interrupted Queen, 'and that'll come out clear as you like in any stories that get done about this.'

'His name's Punter,' said Fathers, 'and you'd better start using it.'

Queen opened his mouth, then closed it.

'And our second front,' said Fathers, 'is comprised of a Justice of the Peace and several other respectable citizens. Roughing up four innocent boys is not going to look good in the local press. And don't doubt the Sundays will be on to that, too.'

'If they'd been the ones we were after,' said Queen, 'you'd be congratulating me on a bit of—'

'But the point is,' said Fathers, 'that they were not the ones you were after. Handling them like that simply compounds the first mistake.'

'All right,' said Queen, 'it was a bit naughty, I grant you. But it happens. It has to happen. Everybody knows that. And when it comes down to it, that JP won't cause too much fuss. People like that know which side they're on. He's angry now, but he'll calm down. You know he will.'

'When it comes down to it,' said Fathers, 'it's down to you. You were the officer in charge of the case and it went wrong. And I said, *were* the officer in charge. You're not now. I want your report immediately, I want it straight and I want it complete.'

When Queen had gone, Fathers leaned back in his chair, blew his breath out and ran his hands through his hair. DI Stevens walked in.

'Right mess, I'm afraid,' he said.

'Yes, isn't it, James?' agreed Fathers. 'But I 'spect we shall survive it.'

'Er, no, actually,' said Stevens, 'I didn't mean the Punter mess. I meant a different mess. The one I've come to tell you about.'

'Oh no,' said Fathers, 'not two before lunch. All right, God save us, tell me all.'

'Terence Brown,' said Stevens. 'Known to Graves as Terry the Talker.'

'Yes,' said Fathers. 'Your man who knows everything about the jewellery.'

'Right,' said Stevens. 'Or did.'

'Eh?'

'He's croaked.'

'He's what?'

'Croaked. A goner. Passed on. He is an ex-grass. Gone to be a sneak in the sky. Dead.'

'James,' said Fathers, 'I think by now I'm reasonably familar with the appalling slang in which otherwise able police officers are wont to express themselves.'

'It happened last night,' said Stevens.

'How and where?'

'Well, as we professionals would say, he had the shit beaten out of him. He was found lying in a gutter, unconscious and very bloody, around closing time last night, just off Gray's Inn Road.'

'Who found him?'

'A member of the public, who called an ambulance. Brown was taken to Bart's hospital and died in Casualty without regaining consciousness. The list of injuries is really wicked. Badly cracked skull, broken cheekbone, one arm broken in two places, broken ribs, cracked pelvis, one knee and one ankle broken, more I've probably forgotten, internal bleeding, cuts and lumps all over the place. He was given a total working over, but total. Probably died of an internal hæmorrhage, though one of the medics said the poor bugger might well have been a virtual vegetable if he'd lived.'

'As you say,' said Fathers, 'wicked. What are you doing about it?'

'Brown died a little after midnight. A man from the local nick who went to the place where Brown was found got the feeling the dirty was not done right there. So he had the bright idea of phoning round to see if there'd been any incidents reported. None have, as far as we can tell, but one of the places he phoned was here. Yarrow was Duty and he recognised the name, pulled me and Graves out of bed and we've been going on it since. I'd've told you sooner but I only got back from the hospital when you had Queen in effing and blinding with you, so I thought I'd wait. I've put Yarrow and Gravesy on to tracing Brown's movements last evening. Shouldn't be too hard. They'll find out where he was drinking and who with, if anybody, and they'll track them down, too. So we shouldn't be too badly placed. But it's a bad business.'

'Who knew Brown was giving you the word about the jewellery blag?'

'You, me, Graves and Yarrow.'

'So perhaps Terry the Talker talked too much?' suggested Fathers.

'Perhaps.'

'What exactly had he told you?'

'OK – the word was that Carteret's is going to be rolled over, a snatch during working hours with a fast getaway car and everything. That's the first thing he told Graves. At their second meet, he said it wouldn't be for some days yet because there's a new line in diamond jewellery that Carteret's is bringing out, and that's the target. That checks out; we've talked with Carteret's and their new autumn line is late this year for some reason. It's not going on display until a week today, and the centre-piece is indeed some extremely exclusive and expensive ice, worth about sixty grand in all, most of which they would have actually in the shop. Anyway, yesterday afternoon Terry left word for Graves setting up another meet for tonight. Last time they talked, Graves promised him a monkey for either the day of the snatch, or some names, or both.'

'Five hundred quid?' asked Fathers. 'That's going it.'

'Worth it, I reckon. It wouldn't be small fry who'd go in for something on that scale. They've got to have the experience and the contacts to get the ice out of the country. We could have landed some pretty big fish.'

'What were you going to do?'

'Keep our beady eyes on the place,' said Stevens, 'inside and out. Carteret's agreed yesterday to take on a new trainee

66

manager – one of ours, of course, fully wired for sound at all times to give us the word and otherwise stay low when the snatch was made. Meanwhile, we'd be ready outside to seal the street at both ends and get the blaggers as they came out. If it hadn't been for last night, I'd've been asking you today for extra personnel to set the watch going and for somebody to work on the inside.'

'Very sweet,' said Fathers. 'You've moved quickly on this, James. But let's think about the beating your talkative friend got. He could've got a bit stewed and blabbed where he shouldn't last night or some other time. Or our villains could have somebody themselves at Carteret's who got wind of our interest in the case. Either way, they worked out Brown was giving us the word, and decided to do for him. Or maybe Brown's death has got nothing at all to do with the Carteret's business.'

'That's about where I am,' said Stevens.

'And where do you go from there?'

'Well, Graves and Yarrow can handle the murder enquiry. They'll sort out where Brown was last night and who with, who he owed money to, what bets he'd welched on, who he's done down recently and all the other grimy details. That may give us a motive that's got bugger all to do with the blag.'

'Right,' said Fathers.

'If that's how it turns out, we assume the job is still on. We know where it will be. We know it won't be before next Friday – at least we hope we know that. We've got Carteret's agreement to let one of our lads or lasses in. We set up the watch outside and stay on our toes.'

'Right.'

'However, if Brown blabbed where he shouldn't've, or if the villains have their own insider at Carteret's, we assume the job's off.'

'I see your reasoning, James, but I think you're wrong. Or you might be wrong. And if you were, you would feel very foolish.'

'If the villains have got an insider, our man could be in real trouble.'

'Let's take it a bit more slowly,' said Fathers, 'and see where we get. Begin by assuming that Terry the Talker talked too much. He tells somebody he knows the job's coming down. We don't know that he says anything more. Even so, the villains may think they can still get away with it. Sixty thou is a big temptation. On that assumption, it's worth putting somebody into Carteret's and keeping a watch on the place. What would it take? Two car loads, and a couple of vans with two bobbies each? Ten men the lot, plus our insider. Eleven in all. Worth it for a week, at least. All right, now assume they do have inside information. Who have you talked with at Carteret's and who have they talked to?'

'Just the managing director and the company secretary. And we've impressed upon them the need for secrecy. They say they've told nobody else. Even the manager of the store doesn't know, and doesn't need to.'

'Fine. Unless it's either of them, you're in clover.'

'OK,' said Stevens, 'but at the least, the villains will be extra double careful. Even a new staff member might warn them something's up.'

'True. Then there'll be no crime. Don't look so disappointed.'

Stevens thought a bit, and then said, 'I'm short-handed now.'

'I was coming to that. First, though, how do you read Brown's beating? Deliberate murder, or a severe warning that went over the top?'

'Probably the latter. There's easier ways of killing somebody than breaking every bone in his body.'

'And who do we know who has a certain amount of form in the line of jewellery and an over-enthusiastic way with his fists? And who just got out of clink?'

'Pigface Pelham,' said Stevens. 'I should've thought of that.'

'I'll put Hands on to sorting out his whereabouts. You can have Pardoner and Waddell to replace Graves and Yarrow. We'll leave them on the Brown business. And Gordon can liaise with Carteret's for you.'

'Yes, they'll like her, won't they?' said Stevens. 'She's got class, she has, real class.'

'That's the first nice thing anybody's said about anybody in my hearing all morning.'

'Harry, this is terrible,' said Chief Superintendent Bastin.

'Terrible,' agreed Fathers. 'Maybe worse.' He had just finished recounting the story of the previous night's work. He had also mentioned the murder of Terence Brown, but refrained from giving a full account and, as before, Bastin had seemed less interested in it than in the Punter case.

'You think we can expect a roasting about this, do you?'

'I think we can expect Punter to try.'

'And how about the, er, incidents down at Haywards Heath?'

'A lot depends on whether the locals feel in the mood to let it all out, cover themselves by coming clean and blaming it all on us, or whether they'll stay mum in the name of police solidarity. Queen reckons the outraged JP will calm down and not make a fuss in the end. Could be, I suppose. Not that I'm too inclined to trust his judgement right now.'

'Yes. Queen. What about him now?'

'Well, he has a story and he has a point. Those four lads turning up like that was the most atrocious luck. Why did they have to pick that precise tree at that precise minute? And it was a crass mistake to haul them in then and there. Even if they'd been the villains, it was still a stupid thing to do. Then again, whoever put that skipper in charge obviously picked the wrong man. And Punter didn't help by refusing to cooperate. It probably would have helped if Punter could have spoken straight to Queen when he saw the four lads.'

'So Queen's account does stand up then?' asked Bastin with relief.

'No, not for one second. All I said was that he has a point. There was bad luck, and God knows how we depend on luck in this business, and other people made mistakes. But that's not the whole story.'

'All right, Harry,' said Bastin, 'lay it out for me then.'

'Queen was the officer in charge of the case, and he didn't keep the reins tight enough. That's number one. He let everything important get out of his hands. He didn't have direct contact with the men at the drop. He didn't know who was going to be in

69

charge. He never talked to them – not by phone beforehand, not directly from his car once he'd left Punter's place. He didn't know they'd be dumb enough to do what they did. Number two: he entirely misread Punter. He believed the man was spineless and that he could get him to do what he wanted. He didn't like him and he didn't trust him. When Punter rejected Queen's plan and wanted to go his own way, Queen was just shocked. It was the last thing he expected. And he didn't have a back-up plan. Probably, the dislike was mutual. He didn't get any kind of rapport established where it really mattered. And number three, which I suppose is down to the Sussex men too, because they ought to know the area, he hadn't even got the drop properly covered. It would have been all right if the money had been picked up by somebody in a car. But I had a look at the Ordnance Survey just now. Suppose someone came through the woods, picked up the bag and nipped off the same way? It's only about three hundred yards to another main road on one side, about half a mile on the other. Say one minute to get to a fast car if they were parked on the short side, three or four minutes on the long side, and then they'd be away. No watch kept on those roads. None. Even if those four lads hadn't happened along just when they did, we'd probably still be discussing disaster today.'

Fathers stopped and looked at Bastin, who was making notes.

'Queen's account,' said Fathers, 'and his whole basis for declaring himself pretty much blameless is about what happened on the night. He's concentrating on the execution. Where he went wrong was in the preparation.'

'I take the point, Harry,' said Bastin. 'Yet I've always thought of Queen as a pretty solid fellow.'

'Then,' said Fathers, 'there's the matter of roughing up three of the four lads they pulled in.'

'Yes,' said Bastin. 'Well, as you say, much depends there on how the Sussex police themselves react. I can have a word about that, of course, in the right ear.'

'It happens,' said Fathers. 'We all know that. And, as Queen says, if they had been our villains one of them might well have coughed up. Then Queen might have been in time to get to wherever they were holding Zoe, if she was still alive by then, pick them up and deliver her back home. The means might have been justified if the end had turned out all right. But the point is, it didn't. They weren't our villains. So Queen's in deep trouble over it. And that's the thing about means which aren't justified in themselves. Once the fuss has died down, I want Queen off my strength.'

'You're sure you're not being vindictive, Harry? I wouldn't like to think a personal element was getting into this.'

'It's not a question of vindictive,' said Fathers tightly. 'It's a question of what's right and what's wrong.'

'I've always thought of Queen as a very solid policeman,' said Bastin.

'Solid,' said Fathers. 'He tried to rescue a lost cause with a kick in the crutch. That's not solid. That's panic with a vicious edge.'

'Has he done it before?'

'Yes.'

'You've not brought it to my attention.'

'It's on the record in a discreet kind of way. Look, one of our problems is that it happens all the time, which everybody knows but denies because nobody takes it very seriously. And if we got to wherever they were holding Zoe and found her dead, and if some copper put a boot in here or there, it would go down as the result of resisting arrest and nobody would worry. But this is different. And I do worry if I've got a man on my strength who tries to get out of problems of his own making in that kind of way. I don't like it. I don't need it.'

'Yes, yes, you've made your point,' said Bastin. 'What now?'

'We sit back and wait for the flak. I very much doubt if the kidnappers will make another effort to get the money from Punter. They might do, not that Punter will let us know. It wouldn't harm to bug his phone and watch his mail for a while. But I doubt it. They've been too clever this far. I'd expect them to cut their losses and get out.'

'I don't know about that. It doesn't seem as if the drop or the time was well chosen, in view of what happened.'

'I disagree, sir. The time was right: some cars still on the road, even in country areas, but not enough to slow them down. As for the place, well, it was their bad luck as well as ours that those four turned up when they did. Zoe's bad luck, too.'

'Yes. Zoe.'

'Anyway, I've taken Queen off the case. If anything breaks, I'll handle it. But I doubt it will. Not till some kid finds her body in some ditch.'

'Well, Harry, it's terrible. But you're right to take Queen off the case. No other thing for it, I'm afraid. Well now. Then there's Carteret's and this man being found dead. Not having much luck, your boys, are they?'

'Oh, I don't doubt we'll get the man who did for Brown. And we've got a plan for Carteret's, just in case the job comes down after all.'

'Good,' said Bastin, 'glad to hear it. Stay in touch with the Press Room, will you, over the Punter case? And let me know immediately if anything happens on that front? Now, how are you fixed this afternoon?'

'Badly as usual.'

'Yes, well, try to keep a slot free in the region of four o'clock or thereabouts. There may be a meeting at the Home Office which you'll be required to attend. If it happens, it'll be about the Sampson file.'

'I've told you everything we've got about that.'

'Yes, even so. You will be required if the meeting takes place.'

'When will I know?'

'If you haven't heard from my secretary by, say, two-thirty, it won't happen. All right?'

'I suppose so.'

6

It was a formidably high-ceilinged room overlooking Whitehall.
It had a dark patterned carpet on a dark polished wood floor. The
walls of corporation green were hung with portraits of stern men
in Victorian clothes. In the middle was a large conference table,
and at one end of it were five notepads and pencils, as if they were
placings laid for dinner. Three men were already sitting there,
two talking, one gazing out of the large window at the far end of
the room. Set off in one corner were two smaller tables at which
sat a man and a woman. In another corner was a trolley with all
that was needed for tea and biscuits for seven.

One of the men at the main table rose as the door closed
behind Bastin and Fathers. 'Ah, George, good to see you,' he
said, walking forward and extending a hand to Bastin. 'And this
must be Mr Fathers. A pleasure to meet you at last.' They shook
hands. He spoke with a mild Scottish accent – Edinburgh rather
than Glasgow, Fathers guessed. He was a balding, stocky man of
about average height, wearing a dark grey suit and a striped tie
which had a quiet air of prestige. He looked to be in his early
fifties.

'Let me introduce you,' he said. 'My name is Hanson; I'm
based here at the Home Office. This is Douglas Foster, from the
Defence desk in the Foreign Office. Chief Superintendent
Bastin. Detective Chief Inspector Fathers.' They shook hands
with Foster, a thinner man with fair hair, a few years younger
than Hanson. He, too, wore a dark grey suit with a striped tie.
His hand was slender, his face aristocratic, his back straight.

'And Frank Witherspoon of DS9 at the Ministry of Defence
across the way here.' Hanson gestured vaguely at the window
and beyond it as Witherspoon stepped forward to shake hands.
He was younger again, about Fathers' age, dark-haired, brown-
suited, a little below six foot tall, slightly overweight.

'The tea has been delivered,' continued Hanson, 'so I suggest we equip ourselves and then settle down.'

Fathers looked towards the other man and the woman in the corner, but no attempt was made to include them in the introductions, and he joined the other four principals at the tea trolley. Only when they had their tea and biscuits did the other two get up and serve themselves.

Hanson sat at the head of the table. To his right sat the two other Whitehall civil servants, to his left the two policemen. He cleared his throat and, in a calm, precise voice, opened the business.

'As you know,' he said, 'what brings us here today is the case of Michael Peter Sampson and his disappearance in New York. It is a case of potentially far-reaching and certainly subtle ramifications. It both involves the plight of a UK citizen abroad and has security implications. It is a police matter since the New York Police Department elected to seek assistance from the Metropolitan force here, and, therefore, it is also a Home Office matter. Those dimensions of the case suffice to explain, I think, the nature of the representation here.'

He paused and looked up, as if seeking either dissent or agreement. Foster of the Foreign Office and Bastin nodded, Fathers looked down at his notepad and Witherspoon had gone back to looking out of the window.

'There has been some discussion about the ground rules,' said Hanson, 'so let me start by laying out what has been agreed. The police dimension is central in this case, which makes it appropriate for the Home Office to host this meeting and, in the person of myself, also to chair it. The Foreign Office, however, will open with the information available as a basis for our discussion.' He paused to glance round again. Foster nodded cheerfully. None of the others responded.

'There has also been some discussion about the reporting of the meeting,' Hanson continued. Witherspoon left what Fathers felt to be his rather wistful gazing out of the window to pay attention.

Hanson nodded and went on. 'Formally speaking, the discussion will be off the record. That is, no minutes circulated. However, the Foreign Office and ourselves both feel the need to take, for purely internal purposes, an unofficial and private record of the discussion to serve as an *aide memoire*, and we do, therefore, have note-takers present.' He glanced at the anonymous pair in the corner. 'Defence has decided not to follow suit. Thus our discussion will, so to speak, be recorded, but off the record. Is that agreeable?'

'*Verbatim ad hominem*?' asked Witherspoon.

'No, no,' said Hanson. 'Purely a summary of points made and conclusions reached, without attribution.' Foster nodded.

'Then I have no objections,' said Witherspoon.

'Very well, then,' said Hanson, 'I think that should suffice by way of preliminaries. Unless there are any other points? No? Good. So perhaps I can ask the Foreign Office to kick us off.'

Foster bent down to pull a thick folder out of his briefcase. He put it on the table in front of him and opened it. He took a moment to glance up and down the top sheet.

'A British citizen abroad,' he said, 'who has apparently disappeared. A citizen engaged in research on sensitive security issues under contract to the US Department of Defense. A delicate and troubling situation.'

He paused and looked irritably at Fathers, who had risen to walk over to the tea-trolley and serve himself with another cup of tea and four more biscuits. He waited for Fathers to sit down before continuing. He spoke without hurry, checking the papers in front of him from time to time, enunciating clearly and elaborating each point to is full extent but no more. He took several minutes going through who Michael Sampson was, his background and what he worked at, before repeating himself on the delicacy and troubling nature of the situation. He paused again as Witherspoon followed Fathers' example by getting more tea for himself, throwing a dirty look at the detective as he put the last broken biscuit in his saucer. Fathers shrugged and put another biscuit in his mouth.

Foster continued by describing how Scotland Yard came to be involved in the affair and outlined the two reports that had been sent to New York, before he came to matters Fathers decided to pay attention to.

'It is now almost three weeks,' said Foster, 'since the weekend Dr Sampson disappeared, and we now come to those events. Let me just sketch in the immediate background. Dr Sampson lives – or perhaps, I fear, I should say lived – in an apartment in Manhattan with a woman, Rosemary Willis. They are not married. She went away for a weekend on Friday, the Twenty-Eighth of September. She went to visit her family who live in upstate New York. She went, it seems, directly from work. She returned on Monday directly to her office. That is, she was out of the apartment from early on the Friday morning until the evening of Monday the First of October. When she returned, the apartment showed signs of having been burgled. In particular, the bedroom that she shared with Dr Sampson had been ransacked, while the room that he used as a study had been entirely emptied. Furniture, books, papers, everything. Apart from that there was some other damage – broken ornaments, lamps, that sort of thing. She immediately called the police. It would appear that they initially took the view that either Dr Sampson may have surprised some intruders, in which case they feared the worst for him, or, less dramatically, he might also have gone away for the weekend without informing Miss Willis, the burglary having occurred while both were absent. On the following day they visited Dr Sampson's place of work, Franklin Research Associates, with the intention of interviewing him. He was not there and they left. The next day – we are at Wednesday the Third now – they were called back to Franklin Research. It emerges that when Dr Sampson was absent for a third day running, and in view of the police having called on the Tuesday, it had been decided at the company to force open the locked door of Dr Sampson's office.'

Foster paused to turn a page, and looked round the table. 'I understand, by the way, that security at Franklin Research is reasonably strict and extends, at least, to all offices being routinely locked at the end of each working day. The point being that classified and confidential material of various kinds is commonly kept in the offices. In any case, on examination, it was discovered that Dr Sampson's office had, like his study at the apartment, been emptied. Everything had been taken out except the wallshelves and the carpet. It seems the police now inclined to the view that Dr Sampson had decided to move both to a new job and to a new apartment over the weekend, taking his possessions with him. Apparently, they hypothesised that either there had been a break-in at the apartment after he had gone, or that he himself disarranged and broke things as he left, in something of a fit of rage. They informed the British Consulate in New York of the facts of the matter and instituted enquiries of, I gather, a somewhat routine nature in the attempt to ascertain his new home and place of work. If I may inject a surmise at this point, it appears that the police would have been happy to leave matters to stand there.'

Foster paused again, turning a page and glancing at its contents before he continued.

'However, Miss Willis seems to be a woman of some resource. She is acquainted with a Congressional Representative for one of the New York districts, and turned to him for assistance. He responded by exerting the kind of pressure over the weekend of the Sixth and Seventh that resulted in a definite intensification of the policy enquiry on the following Monday. I should add that the Consulate also applied what pressure it could, and this, too, had a definite effect. Naturally, moreover, the more days that passed without news of Dr Sampson's current whereabouts and employment, the more it appeared that foul play was indeed involved, and thus the more receptive the New York police were to arguments that their efforts should be enhanced. At that point the police also decided to seek assistance from their London colleagues, who supplied the two reports I earlier mentioned, the second one, of course, concentrating heavily on the connection with Dr Paul Finlay, the leftist researcher here who addresses similar matters to those in which Dr Sampson specialises. Or specialised.'

The silence after Foster finished was broken by Witherspoon. 'Finlay,' he said.

'Indeed,' said Hanson. 'I rather think we shall be coming to him in due course. However, to begin with, are there comments or questions on what we have just heard?' Witherspoon shook his head. 'Mr Bastin?' asked Hanson.

'Of course,' said Bastin, 'much of this is new to us, especially the details of what happened in Dr Sampson's flat and office. I need a moment to absorb the implications. Harry?'

'Yes, Mr Fathers?' invited Hanson.

'Do you know why the New York police opted for the least likely explanations of what happened?' Fathers asked Foster.

'I'm not sure I follow,' said Foster.

'First they thought he'd surprised intruders and, presumably, been killed for his pains or beaten up. But if that happened, they would hardly take his body off with them – simpler to leave it there and get out as fast as they could. And you'd expect to see signs of violence in that kind of case – blood, maybe a bullet hole in the wall, ejected cartridge case, something – not just broken objects. They could've ruled that explanation out in two minutes. Also, it obviously wasn't any ordinary break-in – not with the contents of his study entirely removed. Especially since it wasn't a total removal job. I mean, the bedroom was ransacked, you say, but it's only the study that was emptied. And it was even less ordinary once they found the same thing done at his office.'

'I see,' said Hanson. 'And the later hypothesis that he had left in a hurry and perhaps a rage?'

'From everything we know of Sampson, that's so unlikely it's laughable,' said Fathers. 'And they'd only have to talk with this Rosemary Willis or some of his work colleagues to come to the same conclusion. It's wildly out of character.'

'People do act out of character from time to time, do they not?' suggested Foster.

'Yes,' said Fathers, 'but it's always more likely that they'll act in character. And if you're constructing a working theory to help guide your enquiries, the first thing you do is assume the more likely possibilities, not the most outlandish you can lay your hands on. In any case, if you follow the theory that he left like that, there's an obvious discrepancy.'

'Which is?' said Hanson.

'That you don't just walk out with the complete contents of a study or an office in your pocket on the spur of the moment. You think about it, organise it, wait for the right time to do it, get a van or something. But the idea was he also left in a fit of rage.'

'The two are not entirely incompatible,' said Hanson.

'And there was also the possibility that after he'd left, only then did the break-in occur,' said Foster.

'But that was ruled out as soon as they entered his office and found it in the same state as his study at home.'

'Yes,' said Foster, 'quite so.'

'Do you know,' asked Fathers, 'whether anything was in fact stolen from the Sampson apartment outside of the contents of his study?'

'We've received no information on that score,' said Foster. 'I take your point to be that such information would be decisive in laying the break-in theory to rest?'

'Well, the common or garden break-in theory,' said Fathers.

'Although,' said Hanson, 'even if some objects were removed, would it be too fanciful to regard that as a mere distraction, deliberately effected? It would be demanding rather too much of coincidence to expect that two separate burglaries of precisely the same nature against the same man were unconnected, would it not?'

'Did they question Rosemary Willis about the state of her relationship with Sampson?' asked Fathers. 'Or Franklin Research about the state of his work relationship with them, how they felt about his work, whether he was happy in his job, frustrated, or anything?'

'Again,' said Foster, 'we lack that information. I presume you mean that knowing the state of his home life and work life would provide some basis for assessing his state of mind, and therefore gauging the likelihood of him leaving both home and work without forewarning?'

'Mm.'

'In the absence of actual information about what questions the police asked on those points, you will have noted my surmise that, once they instituted enquiries to ascertain his current whereabouts, they seemed reasonably content to let matters rest there. The surmise is based on a report from the Consulate which noted a relative lack of activity after that point.'

Fathers pulled a cigarette out of the packet in his pocket. Before he lit it he asked, 'You still haven't answered my first question: do you know why they opted for the least likely explanation of Sampson's absence and so on?'

'I'm afraid I don't,' said Foster. 'Perhaps they are merely less competent than yourself.'

'Where have their enquiries got to now?' asked Fathers.

'I don't have clear information on that matter,' replied Foster.

'What information do you have?' Fathers persisted.

'Merely that enquiries are continuing, several leads are being followed up and some possibilities have been excluded,' said Foster.

'So they're getting nowhere,' said Fathers. 'In fact, they've probably half given up already.'

'I'm not at all sure that would be a reasonable inference,' said Foster. 'They assure the Consulate that they're giving the investigation the most active attention.'

'That means they've lost the file,' said Fathers.

'But they're looking for it,' added Witherspoon.

'I had gathered,' said Bastin, 'that Dr Sampson's office and study weren't entirely emptied.'

'Oh?' said Foster.

'Yes,' said Bastin. 'Wasn't it because some pieces of paper were found with Dr Paul Finlay's name on them that they made a second request for assistance from us?'

'Ah, yes,' said Foster, 'I must apologise.' He flicked through the folder on the table in front of him, selected a page and moved it to the top. 'Now – yes, there were several scraps of paper in his study and his office that weren't removed. And two chairs in his

80

office and one in his study, though their upholstery had been ripped apart. Also, it seems, a few odds and ends – pens, a map of New York, some cookery books, a magnetic desk toy.'

'But everything heavy – filing cabinets, desks, books, papers, files – that was all taken?' asked Fathers. Foster nodded. 'Was any of the removal work seen? I thought you said security at Franklin Research was reasonably strict.'

'Yes. Or one might say it is not unreasonably strict,' Foster said with a smile. Fathers looked at him through his cigarette smoke. 'I mean that there are several security men in the building, and there are certain routine procedures at Franklin Research itself to ensure that the offices are locked whenever empty. But I wouldn't regard that as being the kind of security we have in government buildings, for example.'

'Are people's identity and bags checked when they arrive or leave?' Fathers persisted.

'Ah. I'm afraid that information is not to hand,' said Foster.

'Share a building, do they,' asked Bastin, 'or have they got one to themselves?'

'I don't have that information either, I'm afraid, but from the address I would imagine they rent one small part of a very large building.'

'There you are, then,' said Bastin.

'Mm,' said Fathers, stubbing out his cigarette.

'I beg your pardon,' said Hanson. 'Would you perhaps reveal to us the meaning of that exchange?'

Fathers shrugged. 'The less you occupy of any building, the harder it is to have really effective security. Probably be relatively easy to break into the offices, take what you want, however much it was, down the back stairs and away without anybody being any the wiser.'

'I must say,' said Foster, 'that having a policeman's mind trained upon this problem merely reveals the tremendous gaps in our own knowledge about the case. Partly, I would think that's because we haven't actually known what questions to ask, whereas to Messrs Bastin and Fathers here it is clearly a matter of virtual instinct. I think, Chair, you'll agree that it's worth bearing that point in mind. It will be increasingly germane to our discussion.'

At that point the discussion was interrupted by a high-pitched, repetitive bleeping sound. Fathers sighed, pulled his telephone bleeper out of his jacket pocket and switched it off. The others all looked at him.

'I do apologise,' said Fathers. 'I left instructions that I wasn't to be disturbed except on an absolutely critical matter. I'm afraid I have enough trust in my team, and serious enough cases on my plate, to believe I have to respond to this call. Is there a telephone I could use?'

'Well, if needs must,' said Hanson. He looked at the woman sitting in the corner. 'Mrs Redmond, would you be so kind as to find Mr Fathers an office and help guide him through the wonders of the switchboard?'

'Certainly, sir,' she replied. 'Please come with me, Mr Fathers.'

'I am afraid,' said Hanson, 'that without the two of you – one to participate and one to record – we shall have to leave our discussion on hold. Perhaps, Mrs Redmond, you'd be so kind also as to rustle up some more tea?'

Fathers followed the woman out of the door. As he closed it behind him he heard Hanson say, 'I quite take your point, Fossie, but perhaps we can let it stand for a moment and retrieve it at the appropriate time.'

Mrs Redmond showed Fathers into an unoccupied office. It was sparse and small, containing only a desk, one chair behind it and one in front, and a line of three filing cabinets. On the desk was a phone which she picked up, dialling nine. After a moment she handed it to Fathers.

'You've got a line now,' she said with a smile. 'I'll leave you in peace and get the mandarin tea. You can find your own way back, I suppose.'

It was Stevens who had called Fathers.

'Hello, guv,' he said, 'I hope I haven't interrupted anything serious. It's about Brown. Or, more accurately, it's about Pelham. He is in London. As far as Graves and Yarrow can find, he wasn't with Brown last night, but guess who they've come up with?'

'Fellowes,' said Fathers.

'Ah, you're no fun. Fat Freddy as ever was. Seen together in three pubs last night, getting drunker and drunker. At least Brown was.'

'So?'

'Oh dear, I have interrupted something serious. Well, my question is, should we pull either of them in for questioning?'

'What do you think?'

'I'm not sure, else I wouldn't ask you. The link's not certain. Already today, just in casual conversation as they've been around and about, the skipper and callow Yarrow have unearthed three other people with reasonable motives for wanting to duff Brown up badly. Unpopular cove. And Fellowes doesn't only work with Pigface. In fact, Fellowes might have been the one whose loose tongue put Terry on to the blag in the first place. But that doesn't mean he's the key man in Brown's killing.'

'So if you pull Freddy in, you might be wrong,' said Fathers.

'That's right, in which case we'd be no further forward on Brown, and probably several steps back on Carteret's.'

'I've told you already, think of it as crime prevention,' said Fathers.

'Shit,' said Stevens.

'What do you lose if you don't bring him in?'

'Hard to say. Maybe material evidence. But if there's any cloth and stuff under Brown's fingernails, it's more likely to belong to Pigface, if he did it, or to whoever did do it, than Fatso who hasn't got the bottle to have done it. And I can't see that we've got anything to trouble Pelham yet.'

'You could talk to Fellowes on the basis that he was seen with Brown last night.'

'And warn him?'

'Come on,' said Fathers, 'if he did set Brown up for Pelham, he's already warned. He'll have a story. He'll probably be expecting you.'

'I suppose we could talk to him without pulling him in.'

'And without mentioning Pelham. Routine enquiry. You know the drill. It'll be a chance to sniff him out a bit. What do the other two think?'

'Graves says pull the pair of them in. But I think he's taking the death of his own private sneak a bit personal. Yarrow says leave them both alone.'

'Well, well,' said Fathers, 'the lad shows promise. And what do you think now?'

'I think we'll have a cold but polite chat with Fat Freddy, trying to remember to call him Mr Fellowes at all times. Is that what you think?'

'Yes. If you don't he'll probably think something's up. He must have an alibi if he did set Brown up. But that in itself could be interesting.'

'OK, and thanks for your time. Sorry to break in like that.'

'That's all right,' said Fathers. 'As far as I can tell this meeting is serious, but it's also deadly boring.' He put the phone down, looked at his watch, and went back to the meeting.

As Fathers opened the door to the conference room, the conversation inside stopped. Mrs Redmond had returned to her station, and the tea trolley had been removed but not yet replaced.

'What was that about, Harry?' asked Bastin.

'Development in the Brown case.'

'Tell me later,' said Bastin. Fathers nodded and sat down.

'Now we are together again,' said Hanson, 'I wonder if there are any more questions to the Foreign Office about the available information from New York, or any further comment upon it.'

'Lots,' said Fathers, 'but there's probably not much point adding to our present list of unanswered questions.'

'I'm most grateful for your restraint,' said Hanson, 'but the Foreign Office nonetheless deserves our thanks for the work it's done compiling the information we have. I think it will serve as an entirely adequate basis for our further discussion. However, I think it right now to move to the issue of Dr Paul Finlay.'

'Finlay,' said Witherspoon again.

'We would value your opinion,' said Hanson.

'One of the new breed of so-called peace researchers,' said Witherspoon. 'In fact, one of the first of the line. Highly political. Labour left-winger. CND. Anti-NATO. Enjoys making trouble and causing embarrassment. One really does have to regard him as essentially irresponsible. Not sound at all, though it has to be said that he knows his stuff.'

'Yes,' said Fathers, 'I was going to say that we had gathered that he's well respected within his field.'

'In a technical sense, certainly yes,' replied Witherspoon. 'A highly accomplished researcher, no doubting it. Not only thorough and efficient but with a nose for his subject. As far as publicly available sources go, I don't recall any serious blunders he's made. And while his general perspective is certainly not ours, you would find plenty of takers inside the Ministry for many of the more technical criticisms and recommendations he's made over the years.'

'How does he do his research?' asked Bastin. 'I would have thought that he'd lack access to much of the basic raw material. What with secrecy, I mean.'

'Yes,' said Witherspoon. 'That's what most people think. But there's a lot more material available in the open literature than is commonly recognised. Sadly. As far as one who has no need of these techniques can gather, the basic method of research comprises a number of rather simple elements. Firstly, the open literature. Finlay and his like get hold of every specialised journal they can lay their hands on, scour the newspapers and not only the British ones, and official statements by government, by ministers and by NATO. The problem, in fact, is to digest the literature because there's so much of it. I gather Finlay is not only diligent but also computerised. Indeed, I am told he was one of the first individual researchers in this field to develop a really thorough data base. Of course, he has help from his own research unit, which he set up, at least partly, for the express purpose of running a data base.'

'How is it run?' asked Fathers. 'Through the university?'

'In principle, yes,' said Foster, 'but in practice directly by Dr Finlay. Its funding comes entirely from outside sources – trusts and so on. It, too, is well respected, if I may say.'

'Certainly,' said Witherspoon. 'To continue, if I may, there are also other research centres, not just in this country, with which Finlay is in constant contact. They would constitute a second element of the research method you asked about. Thirdly, he occasionally discusses matters with over-communicative civil servants who ought to know better. Fourthly, if necessary, he and his kind will actually go and look at military installations – and even over-fly them for reconnaissance purposes. If you know what you are looking for, or if you have a hypothesis for which you merely need confirmation before bursting into print, it is not too difficult to find it. The mere shape of buildings and even their position can be an immediate giveaway. Fifthly, Finlay in particular has made something of a speciality of visiting the USA every year, where they are, regrettably, far more lax than we about these matters. He simply picks up information, brings it back and uses it.'

'You mean,' asked Fathers, 'that material that is secret here is freely available in the USA?'

'Oh yes,' said Witherspoon. 'Part of the problem, of course, is the idiocy of their Freedom of Information Act. Finlay simply gets somebody to use it to dig out particularly juicy items. In addition, it is far easier to talk with defence officials there than it is in London. He can also talk with members of the very large community of consultant researchers, of whom Dr Sampson is, or was, one such. Apart from that, the United States publishes more information than we or any other government – let alone the veritable Niagara of leaks that swamps Washington every week. In all, there is available a considerable amount of information that is not released here, but that pertains directly to our own security situation, or that of other US allies. One of the tricks, of course, is then to get the government of the day here to tell you what you already learned in the US. Then you can

86

always say that we said it first, which makes it no longer secret. But often somebody like Finlay won't even bother with that. He knows it would be enormously embarrassing if he were to be brought to book for saying in London something he probably read first in the *Washington Post*. It's a damnable business.'

'But is it illegal?' asked Bastin.

'Unfortunately not,' said Witherspoon. 'At least, not most of the time. And even when technically it is illegal – the statute is there, after all, and casts a very wide net – the advice we have received when we have sought it is that prosecution would not be tenable.'

'Indeed not,' said Hanson. 'We have no desire to repeat the farce of nineteen seventy-eight, I can tell you. That trial was, in its outcome, a most regrettable occurrence.' Witherspoon grunted assent, but Bastin and Fathers both looked at Hanson uncomprehendingly. 'The Official Secrets trial of the two journalists and the ex-soldier,' he explained. 'However, I feel we may be losing our track somewhat, and I am eager to get us back on course. Our specific interest here is only in the Finlay-Sampson connection, if one there is.'

'Oh, there's a connection, all right,' said Witherspoon. 'After all, Finlay hired him for his research unit. But I'm not sure how relevant it is. Sampson's not at all of the same character. Cut from a very different cloth. Different attitudes; different perspectives. Technically, just as good as Finlay – though less experienced, of course, because he's younger, which makes a difference in terms of what one could call a feel for the subject and the sources. Politically, though, from another planet altogether.'

'You knew Dr Sampson well, did you?' asked Fathers.

'Not personally. Met him once. Read his stuff. Know of him.'

'When Dr Sampson went to work in the USA,' said Fathers, 'and given the nature of the work he was going to do, were you asked for your opinion about him? I mean the Ministry – not necessarily you personally.'

Witherspoon examined his fingernails for a moment and then glanced briefly at Hanson and Foster before answering. 'An enquiry was made, informally I gather, to which we replied.'

87

'Saying?' prompted Fathers.

'That he is a skilled researcher.'

'You didn't comment on his politics?'

Witherspoon looked at his fingernails again.

Foster intervened. 'I think, Mr Fathers, that the lack of a comment on his politics would be taken, in the context of an informal enquiry, as being itself a comment, if you catch my drift.'

'I think so,' said Fathers. 'He was well enough known, was he, for you to be confident in endorsing him?'

'Endorsement,' said Witherspoon. 'Yes, I suppose that's the proper word. I did, of course, check our files when this matter first came to our attention. There are two memoranda: one is a brief compendium of quick reactions from within the Ministry and the other a report on a few queries made of people who knew him a little, people whom we ourselves know and whose judgement would, generally speaking, be trusted. Both the internal and the external queries received the response that I have just outlined to you. Specifically, the comment is to be found that he was not to be regarded as being like Finlay, in the political sense.'

'Finlay himself is rather scathing about Sampson's politics,' said Fathers.

'Confirmation, if such were needed,' said Witherspoon.

'I take it, then, that you conclude the connection with Finlay is of no interest to us,' said Hanson.

Witherspoon again examined his fingernails before replying. 'Two points, if I may, Chair. Firstly, I would be unwilling to say categorically that it is of no interest. Information that it is relevant is not to hand, that is all. Of course, such information may never emerge, but it may do. Secondly, as distinct from Dr Finlay, Dr Sampson is the kind of researcher whose presence and participation in policy debate is, from the Ministry's perspective, entirely welcome. In that sense, the connection is a limited one. We might be best served by leaving it in the pending tray, concentrating our immediate attention on Dr Sampson himself.'

'I would certainly concur,' put in Foster.

'I'm most grateful,' said Hanson. 'Especially because I understand that is also the Yard's view.'

'With the proviso,' said Bastin, 'that it is also our view that Dr Finlay was uncooperative, probably obstructive, and possibly in possession of relevant information, which he held back.'

'The last is very much an impression,' said Fathers. 'A feeling. I wouldn't go to court over it.'

'Well,' said Hanson, 'let us put it all in Mr Witherspoon's pending tray and follow his advice. With thanks to Defence for their assistance.' Witherspoon nodded.

'The question then arises,' continued Hanson, 'of what can or should be done about this matter.'

There was a respectful knock on the door. Hanson looked up eagerly and said, 'Come.'

It was the new tea-trolley, brought by a woman who pushed it into its corner.

As she was leaving, Hanson said, 'I think we might recharge our batteries, gentlemen, and then consider that question.'

The five men rose, served themselves and returned to their seats. Then Mrs Redmond and her corner companion rose and got theirs.

'Well then,' said Hanson.

'Chair,' said Foster, 'if I might bat first on this: it is very firmly the Foreign Office view that we currently lack adequate information. This is a matter not only of the plight of a British citizen abroad, which is of great concern in itself, but also of the added dimension of security – UK security, Alliance security, international security. In such a context, the paucity of information, so swiftly shown up by some of Mr Fathers' questions a little earlier, is a severe handicap.'

'The Ministry, if I may add,' said Witherspoon, 'is of one mind with our Foreign colleagues on this.'

'Thank you,' said Foster. 'Accordingly, it is our strongest recommendation that we must have somebody in New York to fill in as many gaps in our knowledge as possible.'

'But you already have somebody there,' said Fathers before Hanson could respond. 'He's called the British Consul.'

'Certainly,' said Foster. 'In whom and in whose staff we have the greatest confidence. However, in a matter such as this they have little or no experience. Apart from tourism, its promotion in this direction and its problems in that direction, their main expertise is trade. This problem outreaches their knowledge, their skills and their brief.'

'So send somebody up from the Washington embassy,' suggested Fathers.

'Again, the problem of expertise intrudes,' said Foster.

'What?' said Fathers. 'Don't you keep spies in Washington any more?'

'There are, of course, intelligence officials based in the US capital,' said Foster stiffly. 'Their main task is liaison with the US security and intelligence community. They tend not to be field agents. However, I think your suggestion – helpfully though it was made, no doubt – rather misses our point. Our essential need is to gain greater access to the New York Police Department's own enquiry, perhaps to spur them to greater effort, and, potentially, to conduct a few discreet but independent enquiries. We want somebody there, and we want somebody to be seen to be there. I do not think that assigning an intelligence officer from Washington would be welcomed, either by the NYPD or by the US State Department.'

'In any case,' added Witherspoon, 'the information we need demands an experienced investigating officer. It is police work we're talking about, not intelligence work.'

'Well, there's nobody on my strength who's free to go,' said Fathers. 'You're certainly not turning my DC Yarrow loose in New York. He's too busy and he's too green. And he's the only one who's been involved in this case.'

'Not quite,' said Witherspoon.

'Special Branch?' asked Fathers. 'I doubt it – not after the Brighton bomb.'

'I think you've missed the point,' said Foster. 'Again.'

'The proposal, Mr Fathers,' said Hanson, 'is not to send Detective Constable Yarrow, for the reason of his inexperience as you point out. Nor is it to provide a previously uninvolved officer with the details of the case and send him across the sea.'

Fathers looked at Bastin who was busy doodling on his notepad.

'Out with it, then,' said Fathers with a sense of foreboding.

'The proposal is to send yourself,' said Hanson.

'Impossible,' said Fathers. 'Out of the question.'

'Not at all,' said Foster. 'You have all the qualities we need – an experienced investigating officer. Better yet, one with an enviable record and a reputation for a certain flair in his work. You are familiar with all the details of the case. You have been involved in it directly from the outset. The perfect choice, if I may say so.'

'Thank you,' said Fathers ungratefully. 'But no. Proposal declined. Think of something else.'

'Come now, Mr Fathers,' cajoled Foster, 'if you look head-on at the problems we face you have to admit that you are the obvious, and perhaps the only, choice – as well as the perfect one.'

'I am the least obvious choice,' said Fathers. 'I am required in court next week to give evidence in two major cases. My team is currently involved in several investigations, including one, perhaps two murders, a kidnapping, several major robberies including a hitherto unsolved series of country-house burglaries, apart from anything else that may have come up since I left the office today, or which will come up before I leave the country, let alone what will happen after I leave, if I do, which I won't.'

By the standards of the Civil Service, what followed was pandemonium. Foster's attempt to flatter Fathers by explaining the need for somebody of the highest calibre to represent the interests of Her Majesty's Government was interrupted and swept aside by Father's declaration – delivered leaning across the table and wagging his finger – that the proposal was reprehensible, irresponsible, inconceivable and idiotic. This provoked Foster into shifting ground and pointing out at some length Fathers' inability to see the larger picture. Bastin muttered something about delaying the court cases until Fathers' return or having Stevens substitute for him. Fathers interrupted his flow to snap that Stevens knew nothing about either case, and then went on to question Foster's appreciation of the crime rate and the problems of the Metropolitan CID, upon which he began to

91

elaborate in detail. Having unavailingly suggested to his junior colleague that he was out of line and out of his depth, Bastin muttered an apology on Fathers' behalf to Hanson, which the Scot did not hear as he attempted to restore order, thumping his fist several times on the table and repeating with rising volume his plea of 'Gentlemen, please'. Witherspoon shifted his chair away from the table and leaned back with his hands behind his head, smiling comfortably and apparently enjoying the disarray. Foster, meanwhile, had gone on to the defensive, conceding that the Metropolitan Police were fully occupied, but insisting on the importance of the proposed mission, which Fathers had now denounced as unthinking and unnecessary.

Foster and Fathers finally subsided, glaring at each other across the table.

'Gentlemen, please,' Hanson said again, 'I must insist on some semblance of decorum.' He pulled his notepad and pencil back into their positions, from which they had been shifted by his thumps on the table. Bastin put out a hand to pat Fathers' arm. Fathers shook it off, pulled out a cigarette and lit it.

'Now,' said Hanson. 'Please believe me when I say that this proposal has not been made unthinkingly, far less irresponsibly.'

'Certainly not,' said Foster.

'If you please,' said Hanson. 'We have to balance out the considerations that, on the one hand, Mr Fathers, you have enunciated, with those that, on the other, the Foreign Office has represented.'

He held out his hands in front of him, palms upward, then closed his left into a fist.

'On the one hand, Mr Fathers, I do assure you that the pressure on the London police is very well understood, in this building at least, and has been included in the assessment of this matter. I do assure you of that. For myself, speaking for the interests of my own department, I agree with you: you cannot be spared. Now or at any time. You and your colleagues cannot be spared to take your holidays, nor to go home at night and sleep.'

He closed his other hand into a fist. 'On the other hand, this case is particular. Dr Sampson worked not only in a highly specialised field on secret work, but also in one in which the deepest dimensions of our security are profoundly involved. Given his work, the nature of his disappearance and the surrounding circumstances, let me say to you quite bluntly that the list of possible perpetrators of what must clearly appear to be a crime begins with the KGB and gets more outlandish from there.'

'A security job, then,' said Fathers. 'I've no wish to tangle with the KGB.'

'Indeed not,' said Hanson, 'and nor would we wish you to. But even were it to end as you suggest, it begins as a police job – a task of detection. You're to go to New York and find out what happened, not do anything about it. Having found out what you can, you report back o us, and we'll decide what is to be done.'

'What makes you think I can find out what the New York police can't?' asked Fathers. 'Why can't you simply ask for copies of their reports?'

'Ah,' said Hanson. 'I am tempted to refer to your record of cleared cases compared to theirs. Or merely to comment that you will give it your total attention, while they must necessarily be concerned with many other cases at the same time – as you are here in your normal work. However, a third and more delicate element is also involved. Mr Foster?'

'Ah, yes indeed,' said Foster, not looking at Fathers, 'a matter of some delicacy. To put it no more strongly than this, we are less than totally convinced that the New York Police Department is playing with all its cards on the table. This, at least, is the strong impression of the Consulate in New York. I find it plausible. By comparison with other cases where the Consulate has had an interest because of robbery, murder or other mishaps involving UK citizens, the NYPD, now appears both uninformative and rather slow. Secondly, they no doubt have appreciated the security implications and would therefore have grounds in their own eyes, for not revealing all, while continuing to maintain, as far as possible, the appearance of routine cooperation. Accordingly, because it appears to us that they may be withholding information, we haven't felt it politic to request copies of their written reports. That might have the effect of slamming the door on us.'

'You think they'd say no?' asked Fathers. 'So why would they let me have a look?'

Foster raised his eyebrows and blinked a couple of times.

'No,' said Witherspoon. 'We think they might say yes, modify their reports to hold back anything they wanted to and only tell us what we already know. Then, when we asked for more, they'd say there was no more and we'd be left to choose between staying quiet or accusing them of bad faith, which we don't want to do.'

'So why do you think they'll let me have a look, then? I can see myself going there and just sitting on their doorstep kicking my heels.'

'Ah, we think not,' said Foster. 'In fact, we know not. We've already asked if you could have access to their reports, transcripts of interviews, files, material evidence and so forth. The request was made via the State Department, through the New York Mayor's Office, to the Police Commissioner. And, via the same route in reverse, the answer has returned in the positive.' He paused. Fathers looked at him sceptically.

'Let me explain what we take to be their thinking. Not difficult, because it is something of a mirror image of our own. For them to refuse your presence would be a firm refusal of cooperation. In the present state of Atlantic relations, they do not wish to annoy the British government. They can no more say no to us than we can explicitly accuse them of bad faith. That is, of course, why we put the request through the State Department, where such considerations carry some weight. We assume State would have exerted such pressure as necessary to gain consent from New York. It is these diplomatic considerations that make it possible for you to be in New York and have access to everything and everyone you need, whereas we cannot have a similar confidence if we merely ask for their reports. Do you follow?'

'I follow,' said Fathers, 'to the point where they simply remove from the files anything they don't want me to see.'

'Point taken,' said Foster. 'In such a case, we have every confidence in your ability to sniff out covert non-cooperation.

You would tell us, we would make the right representations to the State Department, and they would press the New York police into full cooperation. I assure you we've covered all eventualities in our thinking on this.'

'Except,' said Fathers, 'for the eventuality you now face, which is that I'm not going to go.'

'Oh yes you are,' said Foster.

Fathers thought of responding 'Won't', but felt a bit silly.

Hanson stepped in. 'Mr Fathers, you put us, I fear, in the disagreeable position of turning our proposal and our request into a straightforward instruction. This has already been agreed at the very highest level. Ministerial.'

Fathers looked bitterly at Bastin. 'I'm afraid so, Harry,' said Bastin. 'You're assigned to this case. Your flight's already booked.'

'I'll want it in writing from the Assistant Commissioner.'

'It'll be on your desk by the time we get back to the Yard.'

'And you can expect to receive my written protest,' said Fathers.

'I assure you, Mr Fathers,' said Hanson, 'that we would have preferred to persuade you of the merits of the proposal. They are strong enough to override my own feeling, and Mr Bastin's, I may say, that you should ideally not be removed from your duties here.'

'We had hoped,' said Foster, 'for your full cooperation.'

'Oh, you'll get it. I sometimes do things under protest, but I do do them. If I know what it is I'm supposed to do. Which I don't.'

'Information,' said Witherspoon. 'What do the police there know? What do you conclude from what they know? If necessary, go back over their tracks – what can you find out on your own account? What are the facts and what are the probabilities?'

Fathers turned to Bastin. 'It had better all be in the AC's letter.'

'It will,' said Bastin.

'Who will I be working with?'

Foster checked through his folder. 'Grolsch. Lieutenant Ulysses Grolsch. We'll provide you with a full briefing on

Monday morning. You fly on Tuesday.'

After some placatory niceties, Bastin and Fathers left. They returned to the Yard, with Bastin maintaining a cold and disapproving silence. When they had gone, the three civil servants rose and attempted to smooth their feathers.

'You'll keep that fracas out of the report, Mrs Redmond?' asked Hanson.

'Of course,' she replied.

'Do you think he'll do, though?' asked Foster.

'Having met him,' said Witherspoon, 'I have no doubt of it, But I do wonder exactly what he will do.'

7

Fathers' morning flight from Heathrow left thirty minutes late and lost a further hour circling Kennedy airport. The captain apologised to the passengers, but explained it was not his or the airline's fault.

'Rotten airport, Kennedy,' he said after they had landed, 'dreadfully inefficient, but welcome to America and I hope we have the pleasure of your company again.'

In the immigration hall, Fathers was approached by a man in uniform. 'Mr Fathers?' he asked. 'This way please, sir.'

He took Fathers into a side room where he was greeted by a woman in her mid-thirties. 'I'm Mary Wardingley of the Consulate,' she said. 'If you'll just give me your passport and forms, we'll get all that seen to. And your baggage checks, please. Thank you.' She gave them all to the man in uniform, who left through a second door. 'This way then,' she said, and led Fathers out through a third door, along a short corridor and into another room where there were armchairs, low tables and coffee.

'We find it more pleasant to do it this way,' she said, pouring the coffee. 'Well, Mr Fathers, you are now in the United States, and in a moment, when you get your passport back with your visa approved, you'll be here legally.' She chuckled and led Fathers into conversation about the flight, the fact that it was his first trip to the USA, jet-lag and the unusually warm weather. After a while the man in uniform returned to give Fathers back his passport and tell them his luggage was at their car. On the way into Manhattan, Mary Wardingley explained that Fathers was booked into a hotel on the West Side.

'We thought you'd feel freer than if we put you up ourselves,' she explained. 'Also, it's very convenient for you in terms of the police station, Dr Sampson's office and even his apartment. I'm sure you'll be comfortable there. Do let me know if there are any problems.'

At the hotel she checked Fathers in and accompanied him to his room. 'I expect,' she said, 'that you'll feel the need for a shower and suchlike. I hope you don't mind, but I've arranged dinner for you this evening. With Geoffrey Spray from the Consulate. He's been handling liaison with the police department on this. So it'll be something of a working dinner. I'll be there, too. Let's see, we're running a bit late. I'll have to re-book the table. Should be all right. Would you be happy if I picked you up in, say, an hour and a half?'

Left to himself, Fathers took her advice and, after unpacking, showered, shaved and dressed in clean clothes – a dark tan suit over a cream shirt and yellow tie. He still had almost an hour to wait for her return when he sat down and began leafing idly through the hotel literature. A picture of a happy family eating in the restaurant reminded him of the Punter kidnapping case. Across the weekend, as he had shifted caseloads and responsibilities around in his team to accommodate his absence, he had scratched at the case is if it were a sore. A phone tap on Ricky Punter's house had been approved at the Home Office, but had revealed nothing, except that Punter had called some journalists on the Friday. However, the Scotland Yard Press Room had dealt with the resulting questions successfully.

'We're taking the line that the case is open, enquiries proceeding and the situation very sensitive,' the Press Officer had told Fathers on Saturday afternoon. 'We're appealing to them to be responsible, not to endanger the girl's life by bursting into print, even if the father is very upset and perhaps not seeing quite clearly enough. So far, they've all gone along with it. Luckily, they're in a pretty cooperative mood – one of the spin-offs from the miners' strike, I'd say. Nobody's out to knock the police right now, except the usual ones, of course. It's an ill wind, as they say. Mind you, I don't know how long we can keep it under wraps like that. If it all ends badly, they'll be back in no time, but if it turns out for the best the media probably won't mind too much about the odd snarl-up, you know?'

From everybody's point of view, 'turning out for the best' meant finding Zoe Punter alive and well. Before the Thursday night fiasco there had been no chance of tracing any of the kidnappers' calls to the Punter house, no whispers from the underworld about them, and no random clues or lucky breaks to suggest where they might be holding Zoe. They had not contacted Punter again, and Fathers did not expect them to. The choice of places for the ransom money to be left and for Punter to collect Zoe suggested detailed local knowledge of Sussex, but no police officer in Sussex could help with a hint or a hunch about who or where the kidnappers could be. He supposed Zoe was dead by now, her body dumped somewhere, possibly at the other end of the country. Even when – if – it was discovered, they might be no closer to identifying the kidnappers and making a case against them. In the end, Fathers had left the case with no progress registered, passed the file to Chief Superintendent Bastin and turned his back on it.

Mary Wardingley phoned up from the lobby. They went by car to the restaurant, several blocks away. They were shown to a table at the back where a portly man in his forties sat reading a menu and sipping a cocktail. He stood up, introduced himself as Geoffrey Spray and suggested a drink. Fathers ordered a dry Martini by which he meant the aperitif he occasionally bought from his local supermarket at home, but when it came and he took a sip it turned out to be the vilest drink he had ever tasted.

Spray saw his grimace and chuckled. 'Common enough mistake, old man. Brits tend to have forgotten what a real Martini is. Something of an acquired taste, especially when they make it as dry as they do here. Why not try a gin and tonic? That's international enough. I'll take that one myself – it's my own poison.' He ordered another drink for Fathers, setting the rejected Martini down beside the one he had been drinking when they came in and the one he had ordered after they sat down.

The meal was good, the surroundings sumptuous, the waiters efficient and quiet. Fathers drank cautiously, Spray copiously, shifting from Martinis, once he had drunk them all, to red wine. Mary Wardingley led the conversation through small talk to a discussion of the Presidential elections. As far as Fathers could gather, the only point of interest left was whether the President would win the vote in all the States.

'It's fascinating,' said Spray. 'What they call the sleaze factor doesn't harm him. Even his joke about launching World War Three didn't hurt him. Probably helped if anything, to judge from the opinion polls. No wonder they call him the Teflon President: no dirt sticks, do you see?'

Only when coffee had been ordered and served, together with Armagnac for Spray, did the man from the Consulate direct the conversation to business.

'Can't say I envy you your task, old man,' said Spray, lighting a cigar. 'You'll be batting on a pretty sticky strip, if I can put it that way. I suppose you've been fully briefed at the FO?'

'Yes. And the Defence Ministry. At least, I think it was full.'

'Wisely cautious, if I may say so. Nobody seems to be telling everything on this one, eh? Grolsch, who you'll meet tomorrow, is a fine chap, but he's under pressure from many sides on this one, and it's not all pressure in the same direction, if you follow. I may say, he as good as told me he couldn't tell me everything. I doubt he likes it one bit.'

'I'm surprised,' said Fathers, 'that he agreed I could turn up and rummage through their files and so on. When American citizens get beaten up, robbed, killed, kidnapped, whatever, in London, we don't expect and wouldn't accept the American police descending on us.'

'I'm sure you wouldn't,' said Spray. 'But this is different. Are you sure you won't join me in a brandy? Not just for company's sake? No? Mary, surely? Ah well, I shan't let that put me off a second one. Waiter. This is rather a special case. I'm sure you don't need me to explain that, all the considerations of grand strategy and high diplomacy and so forth, eh?' The waiter approached. 'Another Armagnac, please. Thank you. But you see, there's the added consideration of the different nature of the American police, especially here in New York. I mean, you take that woman, Dr Sampson's girlfriend ...'

'Rosemary Willis,' said Fathers.

100

'Yes. Fine woman, lots of resource, spunky, you know? How does she react when she thinks the police aren't pulling their fingers out? Gets on the blower to a Congress chap, that's how. And pretty soon the police are giving every indication of having pulled their fingers out sharpish.'

The waiter approached again. 'Ah,' said Spray, 'thank you. Oh, and bring the check when you have a chance, would you? Thank you so much.' He finished his first Armagnac and fingered his new glass as he spoke. 'Check – as they say over here, where many things are different. For example, the police here cannot entirely afford to ignore the political winds, you follow? So – friend Grolsch may not like it too much that you've come along to say hallo, but until he's told different he'll put up with it because he wants to make Captain. Poor bugger. Sorry, Mary.'

'So, in the end, do you think he'll be cooperative?'

'In the end? Who can say? But tomorrow, yes, he will.'

'Thanks very much.'

'As they say over here, endlessly, you're welcome.'

'Can I ask you what you make of the case?' asked Fathers.

'Certainly, old chap, but I don't have an answer. That's what you're here for, isn't it? I doubt there is an innocent explanation for your man Sampson disappearing, but what the guilty explanation is, and just exactly how guilty it will turn out to be, heaven knows.' Spray paused and finished his brandy. 'And it is to be hoped that you will, too, in the end. Shall we go?'

Twenty minutes after Fathers had got into bed he turned the light back on and sat up. He felt alert and dissatisfied. He got out of bed and took his briefcase to the table, sat down, pulled out the notes he had made from his briefings at the Foreign Office and Ministry of Defence the day before and began to read through them.

After five minutes he stopped. His alertness was electric and artificial, no basis for concentrating on paperwork. He turned on the television. The late night news was on. After a few minutes he realised he wasn't following it and changed the channel, then changed it again, flicking from one to another through what seemed an endless variety. Several were showing the news, some were running old films, there were a couple of chat shows, a preacher, what appeared to be a soft porn film, some basketball. He watched that for a few minutes but decided he couldn't follow it when one commentator remarked that, at only six foot nine, one of the players was physically quite outmatched by his opponent. 'Sure,' said the other commentator, 'they need to get somebody with a bit of height in there.' Fathers laughed, thought of Finlay and turned it off. He decided to phone his wife. It would be just about supper time at home and he could have a word with the children as well.

Sarah had been less than pleased when he had phoned her from the office on Friday after his meeting at the Home Office to tell her that he would be home late that night, busy for most of the weekend and flying to America on the Tuesday.

'Bang goes our bloody weekend,' was her first reaction.

'Aren't there any other bloody policemen?' was her second.

'Do they know you have a family?' was her third. 'Do you?'

'So you'll be swanning around in bloody New York leaving me to cope,' was her fourth.

'As usual,' she added.

Fathers could not blame her. The more accustomed Sarah had become to the demands his job made on him, the more resentful and unhappy she was about them. And that particular weekend they had promised themselves and the children a shopping spree on the Saturday and a walk in Epping Forest on the Sunday.

Fathers had become increasingly unhappy with the way his marriage was going. Or, rather, the way it was not going. He realised, and not only because Sarah frequently commented on it, that she had become an addendum to his professional life, an unpaid servant, ironing his shirts, making sure his suits were clean and pressed, providing the comforts of home and the pleasures of family for him, making them permanently available for those occasions when he could enjoy them. He relied on her utterly to make his working life practicably possible. Apart from his income, he was not at all sure what he gave her in return. Time after time, plans to go to a film or a play, to have friends for dinner or spend a quiet evening together had to be scrapped because of his work.

They had been married nearly ten years. Their daughter was eight years old, their son six. They had married when Fathers was a detective sergeant, in his early days at the Yard, and clearly destined to make detective inspector soon. In the first years of their marriage, Sarah had put up with his absences, with his cancellations of plans for evenings or weekends on short notice. She had put up with them throughout the hard-working years of babies and toddlers. She had put up with them partly because she was thrilled by his work and his success – a detective inspector before he was thirty, a detective chief inspector by thirty-four – and partly because they both believed that as he was promoted, so the demands on his time would be reduced. But Fathers was too conscientious, too much the grammar school boy, to ride his rank into complacency and comfort. Now, when their life was easier materially than it had ever been, and when the exhausting labour of parenting little children was beginning to diminish, and when by going back to work as a librarian she had established a life that was less completely dependent on him, Sarah was refusing to put up with it. She lost her temper at him more often, both when he forgot to warn her of some new cancellation of a cherished plan for their pleasure and when he remembered. When she kept her temper, it was usually to be coldly sarcastic with a weary, pessimistic edge to her complaints.

At one time she had complained only about the dangers of his job. Perhaps the danger had even added a certain spice to their relationship, making the times they spent together more intense and passionate, even the times spent doing mundane things about the house, walking in the park or country, going to a pub or the supermarket. But the dangers of his job, though they were real, were about what might happen to him, and therefore to her. Like him, like every police officer, like every police officer's spouse, she had learned to live with them. Moreover, she knew realistically that the more senior a police officer is, the less exposed he is to danger. It was not Fathers any longer who bashed down doors and charged into a houseful of villains. What worried her now was not what might happen to him, but what actually did happen – his absences.

When Sarah lost her temper at him, he rarely shouted back. Only extreme tiredness or frustration with a case would bring him to snap at her, usually with a graphic description of one of the more frightful aspects of his work. Normally he met her rage with silence, her sarcasm, too. For he knew she was right – and he knew he was not going to change. And he also knew that if she did not love him, she would not get angry or sarcastic. When he could not sleep, he would lie and worry that one day his devotion to his work would destroy her devotion to him. He lived in dread of the day when she would cease to complain because she had ceased to care.

The hotel literature explained how to dial direct to England. He did so, and immediately heard the ringing sound. Sarah sounded confused and sleepy, and when he asked to talk to the children she sounded cross too.

'Harry,' she said, 'it's the middle of the night. It's nearly five in the morning, damn it.' He had calculated the time change the wrong way round – England was five hours ahead of New York, not five behind. But she brushed his contriteness aside to ask about the flight, how his hotel room was and when he was going to start the job he was there to do.

The unsatisfactorily brief conversation over, he sighed and wondered if he was ready to sleep yet. The answer, he decided immediately, was no. He pulled the Duty Free whisky he had bought at Heathrow out of the plastic bag and poured himself a generous measure in one of the tumblers from the bathroom. After a sip, he pulled out the carton of cigarettes he had also bought, opened it and lit one. It would make the room smell ghastly in the morning but right now he needed one.

'When do you start working, then?' Sarah had asked. He knew the answer to that: he was to meet Detective Lieutenant Grolsch at nine a.m. the following morning. What worried him still was the other question that he had asked himself countless times, that he had asked Foster and Witherspoon when he met them separately the previous day for his briefing and that Sarah had just asked: 'But what precisely are you supposed to do there?'

Witherspoon of the Ministry of Defence had attempted to explain this over a cup of tea the day before.

'When I said on Friday that we are talking about police work and not intelligence work,' Witherspoon had said, tilting back in his comfortable chair behind an imposing desk in an airy office in the Ministry of Defence building on Whitehall, 'I may have given a slightly misleading impression.'

'Oh?' said Fathers, putting down his bone-china teacup and saucer.

'Yes. You see, one of the differences between the two kinds of work is that in the police you demand and need proof, do you not? You need to construct a case that can be proven beyond reasonable doubt in a court of law. You make inferences and deductions, I suppose, but unless you can back them up with hard facts to prove your case every inch of the way they amount to nought.'

'Usually,' said Fathers, 'though I think you're romanticising a bit.'

'Heaven forfend,' replied Witherspoon, grinning. 'Overstating the case in order to make a point, perhaps – romanticising, never. As distinct from police work, intelligence work is very much a matter of inference and deduction. Let me give you an example. We say, for instance, that the Warsaw Pact disposes of such and such a number of tanks and artillery in combat ready forces. We say that, and we believe it. We're not lying. But do we know it? Not in the sense that I know you are sitting there. Can we prove it? Not beyond reasonable doubt according to the rules of evidence in a court of law. One good defence counsel would drive a coach and horses through our statement in five minutes. Now, that is a very mundane and low-level example. There are others far more exotic and esoteric.'

'I can believe it,' said Fathers. 'I've had some dealings with MI5.'

'Ah, well, yes, I don't wish to make my point by going to the logical extreme and beyond it. We'll forget Box Five for a moment. The point I do wish to make is that, when you make your report, do not feel you must restrict yourself to what you can prove. We are not sending a senior detective to New York in order to have you report facts to us and facts alone. We want to know your feeling about the case, about the police investigation. We want to know the connections you think exist, which you would follow up if you could. We realise you will be limited out there, in terms of resources and time. We realise you may return without proof that this or that happened – unless, of course, such proof exists. We shall be happy with your assessment of probabilities. Do you take my point?'

'Maybe,' said Fathers.

'Only maybe?' said Witherspoon. 'Perhaps I need to reiterate it for the sake of clarity.'

'No,' said Fathers. 'I understand what you've said. And it's in my written instructions from the Assistant Commissioner. But I don't understand what lies behind it.'

'No more do we. That's why you are going there.'

'I have the feeling, since you think my feeling will count for so much, that you know more than you say. Or perhaps that you deduce more than you know. Or even that you guess more than you deduce.'

'From the minute that this case came before us,' said Witherspoon, 'I knew you were absolutely the right person to send to New York.'

'Thank you kindly,' said Fathers.

'No, I'm not just soft-soaping you. If you look behind what we know to what we deduce, and behind that to what we guess, you'll begin to have a fair idea of the probabilities we think you might come up with.'

'Of course, you could just tell me what you guess.'

'No, I think not. I don't want to set preconceptions in your way. Guesses are like the best laid plans of mice and men.'

'Yes,' said Fathers, 'but in my current state of total ignorance I have a feeling I'll be ganging agley in any case.'

'A hint, then. I refer you to a remark made by Mr Hanson across the road on Friday. He said that the possibilities begin with the KGB and get stranger after that.'

' "More outlandish" were his exact words, I think.'

'Possibly.'

'And that's my hint, is it?'

'Yes. Emphasis on the second part of his comment.'

'Thank you.'

'Don't mention it.'

Thank you for nothing, thought Fathers pouring himself another glass of Duty Free Scotch. He had noted Hanson's comment without Witherspoon's prompting, but the only thing more outlandish than the KGB was the CIA, and that seemed childish.

I am, thought Fathers, draining his second glass of whisky, unhappy about this case. I am unhappy because I am out of my depth and out of my town. He poured a third glass and sat on the bed.

Fathers knew he was a good detective. Sometimes, he was not sure about how good a policeman he was. He had learned recently about somebody who made commander – three ranks above him – before he was forty, and like everybody else he had wondered what made that man so special. The answer, Fathers was sure, like many others, was not just a matter of his good policing work. And like many of his colleagues, his first guess at the answer was the Freemasons. Fathers had never belonged to that society, though he knew Bastin did, along with numerous other policemen of all ranks. He was never sure how much effect membership of the Freemasons, or non-membership, had in the promotion process, although, like every London police officer, he knew of several cases he thought were nothing less than scandalous. But even leaving that brotherhood aside, there were skills required to gain advancement that fast that Fathers was sure he did not have. He tended to deal with office politics by charging into battle with his head down. He knew it was a weakness, and a total contrast to his approach to the rest of his work, but he could not rid himself of it. He failed to make judicious alliances, and too often he failed to hold his tongue. As a detective sergeant, and ever since, he had had constant clashes with his superiors – none of them serious enough to hold his career back, but clashes nonetheless. He would argue with his DI about the details of cases when he was a skipper, with his DCI about which cases he should take when he was a DI, and now that he was a DCI he still argued with his boss about anything and everything – about the men and women under his command, about who got the blame and who got the credit, about his priorities, about when investigations should be terminated and when they should be kept going. It did him no good, he knew, but he only argued because he believed he was right and whoever he was arguing against was wrong.

He had never believed that because somebody had more rank he had more knowledge or understanding. Yet respect for the rule of law, on which he based his professional life and personal credo, surely meant respect for authority, which ought to mean respect for the authorised hierarchy. And he knew he was not always as understanding of the people under his command as he expected his superiors to be of him. If need be, he would pull his rank in an argument with a junior officer, and expect that his word would be taken as law because it had been decided that he merited the position of seniority and the other did not. It was the only way that a police force could run: if the police bucked proper authority and hierarchy, nothing was left short of either anarchy or tyranny. It was a rule he regarded as paramount, and one continually broken. He was better at giving orders than receiving them, at respecting his own authority than that of others.

Fathers yearned for things to be simple, black and white, good and bad. He was a pragmatic policeman, prepared to bend the rules of procedure when necessary, but always unhappy about breaking them. He did not believe any tactic was justified to get a villain behind bars, and he was equally unhappy with those who did it and those who turned a blind eye. He thought of Queen and the kidnap case. By any standards, what Queen had done at Haywards Heath was a crime – one for which a civilian would have been charged and convicted. The chances of that happening were negligible. It was a crime most officers committed at some time, including Fathers himself on more than one occasion. Yet at least Queen, as far as he knew, was honest. There were worse depredations than over-eagerness. Unlike most London detectives, Fathers looked back with nostalgia to the days in the nineteen seventies when the CID had been cleaned out by A10, the internal enquiry department of the Metropolitan Police, relentlessly tracking down corrupt officers. He had lacked that form of professional solidarity which led most of his colleagues to regard A10 as traitors. He could not abide the rationalisation that said the lesser evil was necessary in the name of the greater good, when quite clearly the greater good was best served by eradicating what some of his colleagues seemed to think was a lesser evil, but which he regarded as itself the greater evil.

He was happiest when he and his team were left alone to investigate a crime, discover who did it and bring them to trial. But tomorrow he was to meet and presumably work with a man he had been told he could not necessarily trust, another policeman in a very different country. He was working on a case where the crime, if crime there were, was embroiled in undercurrents of unstated supposition, of strategy, of politics.

Fathers slumped into sleep where he was sitting on his bed.

8

'Detective Chief Inspector Fathers? I'm Sergeant Miller. Lieutenant Grolsch asks you to come on up with me.'

Miller did not look the way Fathers thought a detective sergeant in New York should. He did not look worn, cynical and scruffy like the detectives in the most modern and realistic of American TV police dramas. He looked young – under thirty, Fathers guessed – open-faced and athletic; a few inches shorter than Fathers, strongly built, no sign of turning to fat, tanned. His hair was blonde, short and neatly combed. He wore a check jacket, white shirt, patterned tie and dark brown trousers with brown lace-up shoes. He looked the way American policemen used to look in television shows in the years before the demands of realism intruded. Fathers followed him anyway.

Fathers was wearing the same tan suit he had worn the night before and carrying a raincoat. He was hot after his walk from the hotel – as Mary Wardingley had told him, the weather really was warm for the time of year, and very humid. He had woken at six-thirty feeling dreadful. It was too early; he didn't need to have breakfast until eight a.m. in order to make his nine o'clock appointment with Detective Lieutenant Grolsch. But he could not get back to sleep. So he showered and dressed slowly, put his papers in his briefcase and went down for breakfast, where he had ignored the astonishing breadth of choice in favour of toast and coffee. He tried to read a newspaper; it was extremely fat and consisted of several sections. Whether it was because of his lack of sleep, or because of the strange lay-out of the newspaper, with a profusion of stories starting on the front page and continuing on inside pages or even in other sections, or because of the stories' contents, he was unable to concentrate. He tried reading an analysis of the final stages of the Presidential elections, but the writer seemed as bored by it as Fathers felt reading it, so he left it and daydreamed. He had hoped the walk to his appointment would clear his head. It had not.

Miller took him into a lift.

'Elevator,' thought Fathers, and pondered whether he should address Lieutenant Grolsch as Leftenant, which would probably sound pompously English, or as Lootenant, which would probably sound ridiculous.

From the lift, Miller led Fathers along a corridor and into a large general office. Fathers recognised the noise, clatter and bustle as home from home. The decor, though, was dingier, and even spruced up it would have been yet less imaginative and cheery than Scotland Yard. Hitherto, Fathers had not thought that was possible except in schools and prisons. Miller led him through the office to a door at its far end, where he knocked and entered without waiting for an answer. Four men were already in the room, one sitting behind the desk, the others on three of five wooden chairs arranged in a semicircle facing it.

The man behind the desk got up and leaned over to shake hands with Fathers. He was short and stocky, with greying hair and a deeply lined, handsome face.

'Detective Chief Inspector Fathers,' he said. 'It's my pleasure. I'm Detective Lieutenant Grolsch.' He was wearing a dark blue, three-piece suit without the jacket. His waistcoat was buttoned up, but the tie was discreetly loosened and the top button on his shirt undone.

'How do you do,' said Fathers.

'Let me introduce you,' said Grolsch. 'The athlete who brought you in is Sergeant Mike Miller. He's in operational charge of the Sampson case. You'll be seeing quite a bit of each other. This is Agent Weiser.'

Agent Weiser was in his forties, dark-haired, tall and slim, and wearing a dark brown suit with a faint stripe. He got to his feet to shake hands with Fathers. 'I'm with the Bureau,' he said.

'That's the Federal Bureau of Investigation,' said Grolsch.

'I've heard of it,' said Fathers.

'I'll bet you have,' said Grolsch. 'This is Frank Labbat, he's from the District Attorney's Office. And last, but never least, this is Captain Amstel.'

111

Fathers shook hands with both men as they stood up. Labbat was short and slight and looked about the same age as Fathers. Amstel was about six foot tall and strong looking. He looked several years younger than his lieutenant. They all sat down, Fathers next to the captain. The chair was not comfortable.

'In this matter,' said Captain Amstel, 'you will be dealing largely with Lieutenant Grolsch and Sergeant Miller, Mr Fathers. However, I wanted to take this opportunity to welcome you to New York and to the Mid-Manhattan Homicide Department, and to assure you of our fullest co-operation. Anything you need, if Ulysses can't provide, please just ask me.'

'Thank you,' said Fathers, 'I will. I'm most grateful.'

'And,' said Labbat of the District Attorney's office, 'I would like to echo Captain Amstel's remarks. We are fully apprised of the entire situation and, though I doubt it will arise, I want you to know you have but to get in touch with me any time you need to, any time. Here, please take my card.'

'Thank you, too,' said Fathers, pocketing Labbat's card. He looked at Weiser from the FBI, expecting a similar little greeting, but the agent was looking in his briefcase.

'How about some coffee, Mike?' asked Grolsch.

Miller opened the door and shouted, 'Schlitz! Six hot ones.' He turned to Fathers: 'You ever drink horse's urine, Mr Fathers?' Fathers shook his head. 'You're about to. That's not a friendly thing the lieutenant just did.' Fathers grinned.

'Do you object to smoking?' asked Amstel. Fathers shook his head. There was a collective sigh of relief as the others, except for Weiser, pulled out packets of cigarettes, matches and lighters.

'Do you smoke?' asked Grolsch, offering his packet.

'Not just now,' said Fathers, waving away a puff of smoke from Captain Amstel's direction.

There was a knock and the door opened. A youngish man came in carrying a tray bearing six plastic cups of coffee, containers of milk, packets of sugar and spoons.

'Thanks, Greg, put 'em down where you can,' said Grolsch.

'Gregory Schlitz,' said Miller when the man had left. 'What a name.'

'Mr Fathers,' said Captain Amstel, 'let me repeat our readiness to help as you find it necessary. But let me also add that we'd be most grateful of any light you can cast on this affair. I hope Ulysses won't think I'm out of court if I say that our investigation is presently pretty much stalled.'

Grolsch grunted. Fathers decided the captain was speaking out of court.

'I doubt if there's much light I can cast,' replied Fathers, 'but, obviously, if anything comes to mind I won't keep it to myself. I do appreciate your willingness for me to come here and look around.'

'Perhaps,' said Weiser, 'you could begin by saying what your plans are.'

'Very unformed,' said Fathers. 'I'd like to see the various reports of the enquiries so far. Look over the material evidence. Talk with the officers involved in the investigation. I think it would make sense to visit Sampson's office and talk with his colleagues, and probably also interview Rosemary Willis. Beyond that, I don't really have plans.'

Weiser nodded.

'That all seems pretty reasonable,' said Amstel. 'Ulysses, how's the best way for Mr Fathers to go about his business?'

Grolsch looked up from a pad on which he was doodling. 'I guess he should read the last status report I sent to Frank's office, then go through our reports and the transcriptions of witness interviews. I guess by then he'll have enough questions to make it worth his while to talk it over with me and Mike.'

'That sounds reasonable,' said Amstel. 'Go through chronologically, you mean?'

'Makes as much sense as any other order,' said Grolsch with a shrug.

'Well,' said Labbat standing up, 'that all sounds not just reasonable but fine. If you'll excuse me, gentlemen, Mr Fathers.'

He stood up, but Weiser held up a hand.

'If you don't mind, Frank,' he said, looking first at Labbat, then at the floor, 'I want to ask Mr Fathers another question. Maybe you gentlemen already have the answer, but I'd like to know from Mr Fathers exactly why he is here, what his intentions are, what his purpose is.'

As he finished, Weiser looked at Fathers, who smiled at him, shrugged and spread his hands in a gesture of openness.

'To be honest, Mr Weiser,' he said, 'these are questions I am constantly asking myself, questions I asked when I was assigned to come here.'

'And what's the answer been?'

'Very vague and general,' said Fathers. 'I think you'll appreciate that there is a certain special interest in London about the disappearance of Dr Sampson, given the nature of his work, I mean. I've simply been asked to look over your shoulders and report back. That's all.'

Weiser looked at Fathers for several seconds. Finally he shook his head with an impatient, single jerk. 'You play your cards pretty close to your chest, Mr Fathers,' he said.

'I'm not sure,' said Fathers, 'that I have any cards to play. The people who requested me to come here simply thought they would be better informed if I came and reported directly, than otherwise.'

'We appreciate that,' said Weiser, 'though let me say I don't follow the reasoning all the way. Wouldn't it be cheaper to ask for a full report from NYPD than to send a senior police officer across the Atlantic? Easier to ask questions by telephone and telex?'

'I think,' said Fathers, 'that we tend to put some store by the personal touch. You know?'

'But what is it,' persisted Weiser, 'that you expect to find out by being here in person? What wouldn't you find out if you simply requested reports from NYPD?'

Fathers pulled out his packet of cigarettes and toyed with it.

'He won't know that till he finds it, will he?' asked Miller. Grolsch and Amstel both frowned at the sergeant.

114

'But there is something you expect to find out?' persisted Weiser.

'Not necessarily,' said Fathers. 'Probably not, in fact.'

'So why are you here?'

'Why are you here, come to that, Mr Weiser?' returned Fathers. 'I'd been meaning to ask that, just out of interest. We hadn't heard that the FBI was involved in the investigation. That's one new thing I've learned.' He put his cigarettes away.

'Involved,' said Weiser, 'is probably the wrong word. I'm just keeping what you in Britain would call a watching brief. A Federal offence is, or may be, involved. If a crime was committed, it may not have been committed in, or solely in, New York State, and that is an aspect which would, or could, bring on Federal involvement. And there is, as you have mentioned, Mr Fathers, and as we all well know, a particular dimension to this case because of the nature of Dr Sampson's work. With this combination of circumstances, a certain degree of Federal involvement – or, at least, interest – is not unusual.'

'Is it involvement or interest?' asked Fathers, looking at Miller.

'I haven't done any legwork,' said Weiser, 'but I have been kept fully informed of the investigation as it has developed.'

As Weiser was speaking, Fathers saw Grolsch and Amstel exchange a look.

'Another thing,' said Fathers, 'arising from what you said just now. Is there still any doubt that a crime is involved?'

'Not by this stage, not really,' said Grolsch. 'We'd have expected him to have surfaced by now if he was going to. There are still other possibilities, of course, but I guess we'd say homicide is the most likely.'

'Deep six,' said Miller. 'Cement shoes and fish.'

'Knock it off, Mike,' said Grolsch.

'Is that the supposition?' asked Fathers.

'Something of that kind,' said Grolsch. 'By now.'

'But you haven't formally informed the UK Consulate that you've come to that conclusion?'

'No,' said Amstel. 'We've put Dr Sampson on the Missing Persons list and informed your Consulate of that, but we haven't gone any further. With your imminent arrival, I decided to hold off passing on that conclusion which is, as you put it, supposition.'

'I see,' said Fathers. 'Does that mean you are now officially informing me of your conclusion?'

'I guess we are,' said Amstel, looking at Weiser, who nodded. 'Why do you ask?'

'Oh, it's a matter of keeping his family informed. I understand the Consulate has seen to telling them of his disappearance, but I don't think it's gone further.'

'We haven't contacted them,' said Amstel.

'Has Miss Willis?' asked Fathers.

'How would we know?' asked Weiser.

'How indeed?' echoed Miller, getting another frown from his superiors.

'Do you think,' continued Fathers, 'just to be very correct about this, that you could let me have a little note saying you're working on the assumption that he has been murdered?'

Amstel looked at Weiser, who shrugged and nodded. 'Sure thing,' said the captain.

'There was one other thing I wanted to ask,' said Fathers. 'Please correct me if I'm wrong, but I heard that initially the police here were inclined to treat this whole business not as murder, but as what you might call a voluntary disappearance merely coinciding with a burglary at his flat, so I just wondered when the Homicide Department got involved.'

Grolsch, Amstel and Labbat looked at each other with raised eyebrows. Weiser checked through his briefcase. Labbat replied.

'On Monday, October the Eighth, when Dr Sampson had been absent from both home and work for a week, the local precinct requested assistance from the Midtown police, which assigned the case to Homicide. It might have been given to a section specialising in kidnap, but since no ransom demand was received the judgement was that Homicide was more appropriate. My office assented to the transfer of responsibility. Since then, Homicide has handled the case, but when you go through the interview transcriptions you'll be reading some from the precinct as well.'

'Thank you,' said Fathers. 'It was only a small point.'

'The report you have received, if I may say so, Mr Fathers,' said Labbat, 'seems to have been very complete.'

'Really,' said Weiser, closing his briefcase.

'Oh, I don't know about that,' said the English policeman.

'Is he a jerk,' said Miller with Manhattan emphasis as he showed Fathers into a small room which looked as if it was normally used for interviewing witnesses and suspects. There was marked and peeling yellow paint on the walls. The bare floor needed polishing. The table had a wooden chair behind it and one in front of it. The light was inadequate.

'Weiser?'

'His first name's Broderick,' said Miller, 'but we like to call him Bud.'

Fathers sat down. Miller put a folder in front of him, and Schlitz, the man who had brought the coffee, came in carrying a large pile of more folders and dumped them on the table.

'This is the lieutenant's latest report,' said Miller, 'and the big pile is everything else – transcripts, earlier reports, the lot. Anything else we can get you?'

'Yes please,' said Fathers, putting on his glasses. 'Another cup of equine urine, a reading lamp, another table and something that can serve as a vase for the flowers I'm going to buy.'

'Certainly, sir,' said Miller with a half-bow. 'Schlitzy-babe, see to it, will you?'

Schlitz shrugged and left the room. Fathers pulled a pad of paper from his briefcase, set it on the table and laid a pen down alongside it. He looked up to see Miller still standing there. Fathers looked at him interrogatively.

117

'You handled him real nice,' said Miller.

'Did I?'

'Yup. After talking to you he was none the wiser, you know?'

Fathers chuckled. 'He seemed to have a lot of questions. I wish I knew the answers.'

'It's really like that, then?'

'Pretty much.'

'Well, I'll leave you to it,' said Miller. 'The Ritz it ain't, but a few flowers will go a long way. I like your style. The material evidence is in another room along this hallway. When you're all through here, if you want to see it, come and find me in the general office back there.'

'Thanks.'

At the door, Miller turned back to Fathers. 'If you'd care for a hamburger at lunch time, maybe?'

'That would be very nice. Thanks.'

'I'll be back about twelve then. See you.' And he left.

Fathers settled down to read Grolsch's report. It was only three pages long, though its stilted prose meant Fathers read it slowly. It told him nothing he did not already know, and when he had finished it he had made only one line of notes on his fresh pad of paper: 'Weiser: when? why?'

He put the report on top of his pad when Schlitz returned with another man in uniform, carrying between them a table on which were a reading lamp, an empty square porcelain vase, which was only slightly chipped, and a cup of coffee together with milk and sugar.

'That's very nice,' said Fathers.

'Don't say where you got it,' said the man in uniform as he plugged the lamp in and set it on Fathers' table.

'I won't,' said Fathers. 'Thanks. Let's just move the other table into a corner here, shall we? Thanks.'

After the two men had left, Fathers glanced through the pile of folders. He went through them all, looking at the titles on the outside and the headings of each of the reports and transcripts inside. Then he did it again. When he had finished, he uncovered

118

his pad and wrote down a second question: 'Precinct request for assistance?'

'I guess I don't really know,' said Miller between mouthfuls of hamburger. 'I could find out. It oughta be there. Is it important?'

'I doubt it,' said Fathers, feeling full already despite being only half-way through the enormous plate of food he had got when he ordered a hamburger, and realising that when the menu said chips, it meant crisps. 'I just wondered, that's all.'

'You wonder about a lot of things, don't you, Mr Fathers?' said Miller.

'Please call me Harry,' said Fathers. 'It's what I'm paid for.' He started to eat again.

'Being called Harry? That's a nice number you got worked out, then. How's it going?'

'It's a bit big.'

'I meant the work, not the hamburger.'

'So did I.'

'Hey,' said Miller, 'if there's more like you, all I can say is I think you English policemen are wonderful. Tell me what you make of Weiser.'

'I didn't really make anything of him. Tell me about him.'

'Well, the Feds – you know?'

'No.'

'No, I guess not. Well – hey, look, if you're not eating your potato chips, do you mind if I dip in?'

'No, help yourself. What about the Feds? That's what you call the FBI, is it?'

'Anything to do with the Federal government – I guess. It's all the Feds, you know? I don't know this Weiser guy, never met him before this case. He just blew in.'

'Blew into town or blew into the case?'

'Kinda both. At least, I asked a couple of the guys, like in Kidnapping and Narcotics, and they didn't know him either.'

'So you think he was sent here specially for this case?'

'Could be, Mr Fathers, er, Harry, could be. You all done with your plate? Mind if I have the bun?'

'No, help yourself. When did he turn up?'

'Well, as long as I been on the case, he's been on my case.'

'I gather you don't like him that much?'

'You must be the pride of London's police, Harry. Don't put it in your report, OK?'

'I am the soul of discretion.'

'I reckon you are.'

'What's the problem with him?'

'Like I say, it's the Feds. I never like working with them. They're smart and snotty and you can never be sure they're really team players, you know?'

'I think so,' said Fathers.

'Or, you know, he may be a team player, but it might not be the same team.'

Fathers sipped his coffee as Miller took a long drink from a tall glass of Coca-Cola. 'Is it even the same game, though?' he asked.

Miller looked at him. 'Never can tell,' he said finally.

'Of course,' said Fathers, 'I suppose you and your friends might not know him just because he's relatively new and this is the first case he's been on with the Manhattan force, or one of the first.'

'Could be. Look, just pass the plate over and I'll have the rest of your salad, too. But I kinda think he's just up from DC. You know, he doesn't seem to know his way around town.'

'Why do you say that?'

'Oh, just a coupla things he's said – you know, like when we've been going somewhere together he's sorta looked around like it was all new to him.'

'Where were you going?'

'Like to see Rosemary Willis, and to call on that place where Sampson worked.'

'Franklin Research,' said Fathers.

'Yeah. You know, no place special, not like the World Trade Center or the United Nations, but Manhattan is a bit special if you never been here before, and it kind of has an effect. You can always tell who's new in town, you know?'

'I think so. I thought Mr Weiser said he hadn't been doing any legwork on this investigation – just reading reports and keeping informed.'

'Yeah, I guess he did say that, didn't he?'

'Yes.'

'Well,' said Miller, 'it wasn't legwork. We went by car.'

'What did he do?'

'Oh, just sat in on a couple of interviews, you know.'

'One with Miss Willis and one at Franklin Research?'

'Yeah, with Mr Franklin himself, the boss man. Didn't ask any questions. Just sat in. I dunno if he's done anything else.'

'What's Miss Willis like?'

'Oh now, she is some special lady, that one. Some special lady. You plan on meeting her?'

'I think so. It seems to make sense.'

'Well, if you're going to meet her, all I can say is, enjoy. Let's pay the check and go, OK? This is on me. Well, it's on Homicide.'

'The food wasn't that bad.'

'No, but watch out for the coffee. It's worse than the Department's.'

'You didn't have any.'

'I been here before. In any case, hot days need cold drinks. Let's go.'

9

'Harry, be honest with me. Do you understand any more about this case than I do?'

Fathers watched Lieutenant Ulysses Grolsch take a last large bite of pizza. They were sitting at a booth table in a bar two blocks from police headquarters. During the afternoon, as Fathers was working his way through the pile of folders in his small room, Grolsch had looked in to suggest a drink at six o'clock 'to get on first name terms and maybe chew the case over.' Later, he had sent Schlitz along to say more work had come up for him, and how about a drink at eight? Shortly before eight he had sent Schlitz along again to say he would be free at nine. So Fathers had gone out for a meal. Not knowing his way around, he had ended up in a Howard Johnson's. When he returned, Grolsch was still not ready for him. He had finally got free from his work just before ten and taken Fathers to a bar where he could eat as well as drink.

Until Grolsch had nearly finished his food, they had searched and tested each other out. It was a routine Fathers knew well, though he could not be confident here that he knew all the codes as well as he would have at home. They established they could call each other Harry and Ulysses, agreed that it would be good to have a long talk sometime about the different problems and methods of police work in their two cities and talked a little about how they each got into police work.

'After Korea,' said Grolsch, 'I guess I wasn't sure what to do, and this kind of came along and I said I'd give it a try. Thirty years on and some, and here I am, still trying. You go into the military?'

'No,' said Fathers. 'Straight from university into the force.'

'I guess,' said Grolsch a while later, 'I believed in all the crap about serving the public, justice and so on.'

'Is it crap?' asked Fathers.

'I guess not. Just seems that way after a long and mucky day.'

But now, his pizza nearly finished, the New York detective was getting down to business.

'I don't know,' said Fathers. 'How much do you understand?'

'Not a whole lot, let me tell you, not a whole lot. I'm hoping you can fill me in some.'

'What don't you understand?'

'One thing I've noticed about you, Harry, you ask a lot of questions and you don't give a whole lot of answers. No offence, you seem like a nice guy, and it's a good habit for a man in our line of work, but Weiser was sure right about you. Those cards are mighty close to your chest. How do you like your beer? Want another?'

'The coffee at your office is better than we serve at the Yard,' said Fathers, 'but this beer is pretty awful.'

'Do you want another?'

'Yes, please.'

'A straight answer. You're slipping.' Grolsch waved the waiter over and ordered two more beers.

'But what is it you don't understand?' Fathers repeated.

'You for one.'

'I'm an open book,' said Fathers. 'I'm just an ordinary copper doing what he's told.'

'But why are you here?'

'Because I'm doing what I'm told.'

'I thought maybe you don't have enough crime to deal with back home.'

'No, I don't think you could say that,' said Fathers. 'All I know about why I'm here is what I said this morning. Mr Weiser seems to have got the idea that I've come with something more than meets the eye. I got the feeling he thought I had some lead or angle or something that I want to check out. But I really haven't. I've just been told to look over the investigation and report back.'

'Let me be honest with you Harry. You're a nice guy, but if it was up to me you wouldn't be here.'

'I do understand that. In your shoes, I wouldn't be too happy.

In any case, if it were up to me, I wouldn't be here either.'

'I can understand that, so why are you here? Why did London decide to send a senior officer like yourself all the way across the Atlantic? That's one thing I don't understand.'

'What else?'

'Well, I guess I'm never happy with a case with no leads, especially when I have to keep going on it, especially when I'm told to keep going on it, especially when it's taking effort away from other cases. Look, Mike Miller's still working pretty much full-time on this Sampson thing, when I'd much rather take him off it. I'll be honest with you – pretty much all he's done for the past few days is fill in time. And we've got enough on our hands. You know what kept me tonight? I'll tell you: some woman was raped and killed in the street this afternoon. With witnesses. If we can chase them down and put the pressure on, we can get an ID and bring home the bastard who did it. This is the kind of homicide we can get a line on, get an arrest, make a case and put the killer away. But it's the kind of thing that's got to be done fast, when you need all the bodies you can get. But, instead, one of my sergeants has to be spending his time on this Sampson case. Yesterday, we got what looks like a serial killing over on the East Side. Happened Monday night. But Sergeant fucking Miller can't work on it, even though he's been working on others over the past year, because of this Sampson. You see what I mean?'

'Yes,' said Fathers. 'What's a serial killing?'

'Random killing. We got a plague of them in the whole country. Guys who travel around acing folks for the fun of it. No identifiable motive, apart from the pleasure of killing. No connection with the victim. If the victim came back from the dead, we'd be no better placed, 'cause he wouldn't know who offed him, or why. We can't always even identify the body. A lot of times, all we get is a John or Jane Doe in the morgue, somebody who's effectively dropped out from society – not in the hippy sense, I mean, but like they're so low they're not even on welfare. They live on the fringes – homeless, jobless, no family, no friends. Or if they have friends, they're not the kind of people who'll come forward to identify a body and help the police. It's a

124

real nightmare. And we reckon some of these guys just roam all over the country finding victims.'

'You mean there are several of these, what is it, serial killers?'

'Yeah, maybe thirty-five according to best estimates. Some of them have probably killed more than a hundred times.' Grolsch took another swig of his beer and looked at Fathers over his glass.

Fathers shivered. 'It makes the Sampson business seem a pretty small affair,' he said.

'That's my point,' said Grolsch. 'This killing yesterday, for example. We recognise the method. We've seen it seven times already this year. Same method, same kind of victim – always a teenage black boy, always the clothes are torn in a particular way. We're building a profile of the killer. We've got a chance with this one. In time. Mike's been doing a lot of work on it, good work. But he can't work on it right now. But what's he doing that's so important? Getting nowhere on this Sampson case.'

'Why can't he work on the investigation of this killing?'

'Orders. I asked, the captain asked. But the answer is no. The answer from the Commissioner, no less.'

'Somebody seems to think the Sampson case is very important then.'

'Sure thing. But who? And why?'

'I think I can tell you who,' said Fathers.

'Yeah?'

'The State Department.'

'The what?'

'Anyway, that's where the request for me to be present over here was sent in the first place. So I've been told. It went from there to the Mayor's Office, and from there to the police.'

'The State Department,' said Grolsch. 'Well, I'll be.'

'But it's probably not only the State Department. What's Mr Weiser doing here?'

'Yeah, Mike told me you were asking about him at lunch. By the way, Mike also told me you were asking about the copy of the precinct's request for assistance. I got somebody looking for it. It should be in the pile you were given.'

'Thanks,' said Fathers. 'Did you say what Weiser's doing here?'

'I guess I didn't. He turned up pretty much when the case did. It's strange, though. I don't know where he got to hear about it. We didn't ask for the Feds to come in on this one. Might've got round to it, let me say, but he blew in before we did. I suppose the DA's Office might've asked them in, but we didn't.'

'You got given the case because a congressman got interested, is that right?'

'I guess so.'

'And it was then that Mr Weiser turned up?'

'I guess so.'

'So it's not just the State Department that thinks this is important?'

'I guess not. You want another beer?'

'No thanks.'

'Well I will.' Grolsch waved the waiter over again.

'And while he's been here, what has he been doing?' asked Fathers when Grolsch had given his order.

'Looking over our shoulders, reading files – just like you.'

Fathers decided not to press Grolsch. Perhaps Miller had been indiscreet to tell him at lunch that Weiser had gone along with him to a couple of interviews.

'Anyway,' Grolsch went on, 'what do you make of the investigation?'

'It seems pretty thorough. And even if Sergeant Miller's just been filling in time, as you say, he's actually done a lot of pressing to find out where Sampson could be. Doesn't it seem strange that there's no hint about where Sampson is, or his body?'

'Yeah, well, frankly there's several thousand John Does in morgues around the country, and communication between different police forces ain't always everything you'd want it to be. And, of course, if he's been kidnapped instead of killed, then they could be holding him anywhere.'

'But it's not an ordinary kidnap, if it is a kidnap at all. No ransom demand, I mean.'

126

'No, call it abduction rather than kidnap,' said Grolsch. 'If he's not dead, he's being held somewhere for some reason that you have to guess has something to do with his work. Or, to get really weird about it, maybe he went voluntarily into hiding for some reason – again probably connected with his work, though I guess he could just've flipped his lid.'

'And it seems he hasn't left the country. Not under his own name, anyway.'

'No, and that's something we are pretty reliable on. If a foreign citizen leaves the country under his own name and in the ordinary way, we can find out easily enough.'

'But he could have left under a false name.'

'Yeah, or been taken out in the trunk of a car, or hidden in a truck, or in a private plane making a quick hop into Canada, or Mexico, or the Caribbean. Fuck it, he could've got out or been gotten out in a million ways to a million places. And if he has, then we don't know and my bet is that we won't know. Ever.'

'You don't seem very optimistic about this case, Ulysses.'

'No, Harry, let me be honest with you: I am not very optimistic about it at all.'

'Is that why you told the man from the Consulate that you couldn't tell him everything about it?'

'Did he tell you that?'

'Yes. Or rather he said you as good as told him so.'

'Me and my big mouth,' said Grolsch, wiping it with the back of his hand. 'Let's get the check. It's on me.'

'No, let's not. Let's talk about what you couldn't tell the man from the Consulate.'

'Harry, if there was something I couldn't tell him, I sure as fuck can't tell you.'

'I don't see why not,' said Fathers, 'as one policeman to another.'

Grolsch waved the waiter over, asked for the bill, paid it, told him to keep the change and stood up. 'You coming?' he asked.

'One of the key things that I'm supposed to keep my eyes open for,' said Fathers, 'is any sign of anything that falls short of full cooperation from you people.'

Grolsch sat back down. He rubbed his hands together as if he were washing his knuckles.

'The cooperation, Harry, is all there, believe me. You can have access to all of our reports, you can talk to everybody who's been involved in the case, everybody we've talked to, you can have an office, use our phones, even drink our coffee.'

'But when I talk to everybody who's been involved in the case,' said Fathers, 'will you talk to me?'

Grolsch pulled out a cigarette and lit it. 'What can I say, Harry? Do you need me to tell you this is no ordinary case? It's murkier than hell.'

'You're making it murkier than that. What's going on?'

'Harry, what you're suspecting, believe me, is not down to me.'

Fathers lit one of his own cigarettes. 'Shall we have another beer?' he asked, waving to the waiter.

'No,' said Grolsch, 'this won't take long, not if you believe me.'

'One beer,' said Fathers to the waiter. And then, to Grolsch, 'Go on, then.'

'You're reading the wrong thing into it. That guy Spray is pretty smart, and he was pressing me, you know? Finally, I kind of told him I couldn't tell him everything – because I have the feeling that what I know is less than everything. You get me? I've already told you. Somewhere, somebody, or -bodies, place real importance on this case, enough to divert a very good detective from a case he should be working on.'

'Enough to bring in the Feds,' said Fathers.

'But it's not me,' said Grolsch. He paused as the waiter set the beer down in front of Fathers. 'I don't know who or why.'

'Who does?' asked Fathers, taking a sip of beer.

'You told me: the State Department, the Mayor's Office.'

'And the FBI.'

'Maybe. I guess so.'

'Who should I talk to, Ulysses, to find out?'

Grolsch shrugged. 'I guess you should certainly visit with Frank Labbat – the guy from the DA's Office.'

128

'And Weiser.'

'I guess so.'

'Is it all right if I talk to him?'

'Sure it is. Why wouldn't it be?'

'I don't know,' said Fathers. 'I just wondered, that's all.'

Fathers met Agent Weiser of the Federal Bureau of Investigation for lunch on Thursday, in the same restaurant where he had eaten with Miller the day before. Fathers didn't take to the FBI man, and the small talk as they waited for the meal to be served was more strained than it had been with either Miller or Grolsch. Once they were eating, Fathers switched the conversation to business matters.

'What do you make of the case?' he asked bluntly.

Weiser pointed to his mouth to indicate it was full, and carried on chewing. Fathers waited patiently.

'Well, Mr Fathers,' Weiser said eventually, 'I see more questions than answers. Put differently, a lot of possibilities and not one among them standing out as a probability.'

'The man at the UK Consulate here said he thought there couldn't be an innocent explanation, but didn't know which explanation would turn out to be the guilty one,' said Fathers.

'That's neatly put,' said Weiser after another mouthful had been efficiently chewed. 'It looks by now like something pretty final has happened to Dr Sampson, but I don't see my way beyond that.'

'What do you make of these clear-outs of Sampson's office and study? Or, let me put it like this, in the light of them, do you think there can be an explanation for his disappearance that isn't somehow related to his work?' asked Fathers. The length of the question let Weiser fill his mouth again and chew his answer over along with his food.

'I would say the likelihood is that it has to do with his work.'

'And would you say that there could be another explanation, apart from that whoever's responsible for Sampson's disappearance is also responsible for clearing out his office and his study?'

Weiser took even longer this time to finish his chewing, and followed it with a swig of water. 'I would think not,' he said, 'bearing in mind that it could be Sampson is responsible for his own disappearance.'

'And therefore also for clearing out his office?'

'I guess so,' said Weiser.

'Motive?' asked Fathers.

Weiser chewed, drank and shrugged.

'You must have been looking into it,' said Fathers.

Another long pause followed as Weiser continued to chew without speaking. When he'd finished, he said, 'As I think I told you, sir, we're not actively involved in this investigation, merely keeping a watching brief.'

'You did tell me that,' said Fathers, 'and I don't find it plausible. It seems axiomatic that if there is a possibility that a researcher working on contract to the military has cleared off, taking all his work materials with him – probably including some classified material, and especially when he was working on such sensitive issues – the FBI would be bound to do some background checking to see if a motive came to light.' Weiser didn't respond even after he had finished more chewing. 'Particularly when you think of the places he might have gone,' Fathers added.

When Weiser at last replied he spoke very calmly, as if Fathers had not just accused him of lying. 'I don't deny the presence of that aspect in our consideration. And I can't refute your reasoning. But if such background enquiries have been made, I can only tell you I am not aware of them.'

'You've got to admit that it would be a little strange if you hadn't been running some checks on him.'

'A little,' assented Weiser.

'If Sampson didn't go voluntarily, who are the likely candidates for abducting him?'

'Well, Mr Fathers, let's not get over-dramatic about this, but I think you know as well as I do who would top the list.'

'And yet,' said Fathers musingly, 'why would they pick on Sampson? As I understand it, he was doing policy research.

130

He's not a scientist and has no technical training, though I grant he has a reputation for picking up new subjects quickly.'

'True,' said Weiser, 'but he did have classified material in his office.'

'Is that a fact?'

Weiser looked at Fathers for a while before replying, 'Yes, it is a fact.'

'And yet again,' said Fathers in the same musing tone, 'as I understand the way in which your Department of Defense administers these outside research projects, there must be many others with as much classified material, and with more technical knowledge, researchers who are, in fact, working on the technology rather than on its policy implications.'

'You've been well briefed.'

'Do you think there's anything wrong with my reasoning?'

'Well, no, not at first hearing, except that you're pretty much working in the dark, aren't you?'

'I was hoping you could shed some light,' said Fathers, 'by letting me in on your background checks on Sampson.'

'I wish I could, but as I said, I cannot oblige.'

'Was that why you got on to us in the first place, to see if Sampson's British past would reveal possible motives for his disappearance?'

'It wasn't I who got on to you,' said Weiser, 'but that may have been the local police's thinking. I don't know.'

'Of course,' said Fathers with a smile, 'it could be different. If Sampson was, say, the victim of a random killing, or of intruders he disturbed in his apartment, then his research material might have been removed by the very people he was doing it for. Hmm? Or at least by agents acting on their behalf.'

Weiser remained silent, chewing his last mouthful.

'But then,' added Fathers, 'why hasn't his body turned up?'

Weiser shrugged. 'It's not a profitable line to pursue,' he said, 'because the supposition is false.'

'I suppose,' said Fathers, as if he hadn't heard, 'it could have been disfigured beyond recognition and be in some morgue, unidentified and unidentifiable. So the killers, if he's dead, and the removal merchants might not be the same people.'

Weiser shook his head. 'You're wasting your time on that one,' he said.

'You're sure of that, are you?' asked Fathers.

'I would certainly doubt most strongly that his office and apartment would be cleaned out in that way by an official agency,' said Weiser.

'Hmm. That does make it look, then, as if he went voluntarily, or was abducted or killed by – well, whomever.'

'I think that's the way it looks,' Weiser agreed.

'Well,' said Fathers cheerfully, 'that's not that many possibilities after all, is it?'

'I guess not.'

Fathers pointed his knife at the FBI man and grinned. 'If you didn't do it, it must have been them, and if it wasn't them, it must have been you, eh?'

Weiser looked uncomfortable but managed to smile back. 'If you put it like that,' he said, 'it must have been them.'

10

In his hotel room, Fathers looked at his watch, checked his tie and hair in the mirror, and then went down to the lobby. He took a cab to a restaurant on 44th Street which Miller had recommended, arriving a few minutes before seven-thirty p.m. When he had been shown to his table, he remembered the lesson of his first night in New York and ordered a gin and tonic. It was delivered with impressive speed.

A few minutes later a tall woman with short, dark hair approached his table. She was wearing black trousers, a white shirt and a small red scarf at her neck. She had rings on two fingers of her right hand and pendant ear-rings. A canvas bag was slung over her left shoulder. She was slim and attractive. He recognised her from the picture in the file at police headquarters. He did, in fact, know a great deal about her including her age – thirty. He stood up.

'Mr Fathers?' she asked. 'I'm Rosemary Willis.'

Fathers shook hands with her. 'We can have a drink while we decide what to order,' he said as they sat down. 'What would you like?'

'Dry white wine, please,' she said to the waiter. 'Chilled.'

'I'm glad you could come to see me here,' said Fathers. 'So much more pleasant than at the police station, or even your office.'

'Yes,' she smiled. 'It's a good restaurant. I've been here a few times. But I don't know what I can tell you that I haven't told countless policemen and FBI agents already.'

'You've seen a lot of them, have you? Police and – what do they call them – the Feds?'

She smiled. 'Especially the Feds. I'm beginning to wish I hadn't stirred this whole thing up. It hasn't produced the result I wanted – which is to find out what's happened to Mike.'

They looked through the menus and ordered, both opting for veal, neither choosing a starter. On Rosemary Willis' suggestion, Fathers also ordered a carafe of the house white wine.

'I think I should tell you Miss Willis – or do you prefer Ms?'

'Rosemary.'

'Yes, well, I wouldn't want you to entertain false hopes. I don't really have any great hopes myself that I'll find out anything the New York Police Department hasn't. My job is really just to look over their investigation and report back to various people in London.'

'Well, Mr Fathers – or do you prefer Master?'

Father smiled. 'Harry.'

'That's a nice name,' she said. 'Thanks for being straight enough to say that, but I don't think I have many hopes any more that any of this police work will lead anywhere. I guess Mike is gone, one way or another. And all I have left are fears and suspicions.' She drank some wine. 'It's nice to be asked out, though. I haven't been out with a man since that weekend.'

'I'm not really sure you're out with a man right now.'

'Uh huh. What am I out with, then?'

'To the extent that you're out,' said Fathers, 'it's with a police officer.'

'Ah,' she said. 'Do you mind if I smoke?'

'No. Do you mind if I do?'

She pulled out a tin of small cigars, he a packet of cigarettes.

'So you're not a man, you're a police officer,' Rosemary said. 'But you're not one of ours.'

'No.'

'So are you one of theirs?'

'Whose?'

'Whoever,' she said after a pause.

'I'm not sure I follow,' said Fathers, 'but I hope I'm on your side in all of this.'

'Oh yes?'

'Like you, I'd ideally like to find out what happened to Michael Sampson.'

'You'd like to.'

'Failing that, I'd like to find out why it hasn't been found out what has happened to him.'

Rosemary Willis looked at Fathers for a long time, inspecting him. She saw a handsome enough man with short, well-cut dark hair, wearing a pale grey three-piece suit with a pink shirt and darker grey, patterned tie. She saw a small scar by the left corner of his mouth, hazel eyes, slightly bloodshot, and the twin marks left by his reading glasses on the bridge of his nose. He shifted uncomfortably under her gaze, stubbed out his cigarette and finished his drink.

The food arrived. The business of setting down the plates, serving the vegetables and pouring the wine took some minutes and broke the tension. They began to eat. Fathers remained silent. He wanted Rosemary Willis to be the first to speak.

'I guess I'm really not sure,' she said finally. He looked at her with raised eyebrows, fork poised half-way to his mouth. 'I'm not sure what I'll get if I'm open with you. Will you be open with me, or will I get more crap? I don't know.'

Fathers considered this gambit as he chewed. Momentarily, he felt like Agent Weiser.

'Police officers,' he said at last, 'are very rarely completely open about anything with anybody. It doesn't usually pay in our job. And I don't know what you want me to be open about. But if I think I can safely answer whatever it is you want to ask, I will. On the other hand, in what you've already said, and apart from the things I came here wanting to know from you, there's two points that I want to ask you about.'

'You know I don't have to answer your questions.'

'Yes, I do know. I have no real status here at all. And that's why I'm prepared to break my habits, to some extent at least. I will tell you what I can of what you want to know, if I feel that you're being open in return, because I really do want to get to the bottom of this and, frankly, I want to encourage you to talk to me.'

Fathers paused to put another forkful in his mouth and then carried on talking.

'It's funny, you know. When I first heard about this case I wasn't very interested in it. I didn't want come to New York. I put up such a fight I had to be ordered to do it under protest. But I have this problem of industriousness and seriousness. When I'm set a task, and when there's no way of avoiding it, I try my best to complete it. And in this case, that means getting to the bottom of it.'

Fathers paused to sip his wine. Rosemary Willis was looking at him with interest, her knife and fork lying on her plate, but she gave no indication she was about to say anything, so he continued.

'But getting to the bottom of what? I don't really know. That's why a couple of things that you've said arouse my interest. There're too many unanswered questions about this whole thing. Something funny's going on, and I don't like it one bit.'

'No,' said Rosemary, 'I guess not.' She put some more food on her fork, and before putting it in her mouth said, 'Why did you put up a fight about coming here?'

'Too many things to do, too much crime unsolved, that sort of thing.'

'Oh. What have I said that so interests you?'

'One, the FBI. I may be a bit off beam on this, but I get the feeling it might be useful to know what they're up to. You said you'd been interviewed quite a bit by FBI agents, yes? I'd like to know a bit more. Two, you mentioned your fears and suspicions. I'd like to know what they are.'

'I'd've thought my fears and suspicions wouldn't add up to a row of beans for the police.'

'Not normally, I suppose. But in this case, maybe. Have you shared them with either the FBI or the police?'

'I tried to one time, but the man – it was a sergeant, with a Fed in tow – he wasn't interested. I got the impression they might easily mark me down as an hysterical female, which would've made them less serious about the investigation, so I shut up.'

'So share them with me,' said Fathers.

'What's your take on this? Why do you want to hear about my private fantasies and nightmares?'

136

Fathers took a sip of wine to gain time to formulate his reply. 'Before I left London,' he said slowly, 'I was explicitly told that my report needn't confine itself to proven or provable facts. I gather that my suppositions, surmises and, bluntly, guesses can all be included as well. The people who sent me here are apparently interested in probabilities as well as certainties, which is unusual for my line of work.'

'That's not what that sergeant told me. He said, and I quote, "the police are interested only in facts".'

'So we are, most of the time,' said Fathers. 'But what did you tell him or try to tell him? And what are you about to tell me?'

'OK,' said Rosemary. She looked down at her plate, set her knife and fork together and pushed the uneaten half of her meal to one side. She poured them each another glass of wine. And then she began to tell Fathers about Dr Michael Sampson.

What she said at first was not new to Fathers. Yarrow's original report in London had contained it all: Sampson was likeable, hard-working, and keen to get ahead; he was exceptionally good at his job and experiencing a lot of success. But she told it with fondness. And she added a new dimension: Sampson's enthusiasm. She described how they had first met in the early summer of 1983, at a party thrown by the congressman she knew. The young English researcher had mistaken her polite questions for deep interest in his work, and proceeded to bore her for an hour and keep her from her friends with a detailed description of the role of different satellites in verifying treaties between the superpowers.

'Christ,' she said, 'I was making conversation and he came up with a lecture. He was fascinated by his work and he thought everybody else would be. And he seemed so young – he always did. I always expect the English to be a lot more sophisticated and ironical than we are. I guess there are exceptions. My, but he did run his mouth.' She paused and waved to the waiter, pointing at the wine carafe. She looked at the table, then at Fathers out of the corner of her eyes. 'I only went to bed with him that night to shut him up,' she said.

Fathers smiled, repressing the urge to look at a painting on the wall behind her head. 'And that was the start of your relationship?'

'Yeah, sort of. We took a few months to hit our stride. He was very diffident, you know, about it all, especially about talking. That sounds odd after what I just said – but I mean talking about personal things, about himself and how he felt. For a time I thought he wasn't really interested in me – other than, you know, bed. But I guess I was wrong. Men are hard to fathom. Especially English men, begging your pardon.' She took the new carafe from the waiter's hand and poured some for herself. Fathers' glass was still nearly full.

She told Fathers more about Sampson's enthusiasm for his work, about his delight as outer space moved into the centre of the American strategic debate in 1983, about the hours he worked, not only in the office but in their apartment as well after he moved in with her at the end of the summer, and about how he continued to talk and talk about it all.

'I guess I got quite familiar with a lot of what he was working on,' she said. 'And sometimes I worried.'

She stopped and looked to her right, out of the window. Fathers waited for her to start again, but she remained silent. She picked up her glass and took a long swallow of wine.

'Why?' asked Fathers.

'Oh shit,' she said, banging down her glass, spilling wine on her hand, her wrist and on the table. 'Mike is just so fucking naive. He worked full-time on all that stuff and he never once understood what he was really working on. Never once. Fool.'

She looked out of the window again and wiped at the corner of her eye with her right hand, already wet with the spilled wine. Fathers had not seen the tear. When she looked back at him her cheek was wet. She used her napkin to dry her hand and cheek.

'I'm sorry,' she said. She took another sip of wine, then picked up her napkin again to wipe the table. 'You should have interviewed me in the office or down at police headquarters. I probably wouldn't have acted up if you had.' She sniffed, dabbing again at the table.

138

'I suppose,' said Fathers, 'this brings us to your fears and suspicions.'

'I've taken my time to get here, haven't I? I'm sorry to tell you all this other useless stuff.'

'Don't be,' said Fathers. 'It's not useless. Not at all.'

'If this sounds crazy, you say so, OK? Mike thought it was crazy.'

'Go on.'

'Mike went into work each day like any normal person, but the work he did was dangerous. Mike had access to classified material. I don't know what level of secrecy – they have different degrees of secrecy, don't they? So, part of what Franklin Research does, though he'd never see it this way, is examine military projects to see what market opportunities there are for business. And some of those fat corporate cats are among the most ruthless people in the world. I mean, Mike never shows any sign of realising that he's working in a world where bribery and corruption are so standard that people don't know what honest behaviour is any more. It all came out in Congressional hearings ten years ago, but Mike behaves as if he's studying – I don't know, voting behaviour in off-year elections, any bland subject, you know? I mean, it's like a little boy excited by science fiction had grown up – or almost grown up – and been allowed to carry on playing the same games for a living. All he's interested in, all he thinks about is the hardware and the technology and its implications. And industrial espionage is all around, and it mingles in with spying on state secrets. And Mike's in the middle of all this, digging out all the facts he can with about as much concern as if he's out boating on a summer's day. Jesus.'

'Was there any particular thing,' asked Fathers, 'that he was working on in the recent period that made you especially concerned?'

'In spring and summer he was working on the Space Shuttle,' said Rosemary. 'You know what that is?'

'Oh yes.'

'And he was starting in September on a new project that was something to with what the papers call Star Wars – what he insisted on calling the SDI.'

'The Strategic Defense initiative,' said Fathers. 'And his work on one of those particularly worried you?'

'There were a lot of problems about his work on the Space Shuttle. I didn't really get a handle on it, but there was some angle he wanted to follow that John Franklin – that's his boss – didn't want him to. He kept on coming home all upset after endless arguments about it. I kind of got the impression he went ahead and did the work anyway, whatever it was.'

'And you think,' said Fathers carefully, controlling his tone so that no scepticism sounded through to her, 'or suspect, or fear, that maybe he found out something he shouldn't have and that's why whatever it is that has happened to him has happened to him?'

'I guess it does sound a bit stupid, huh? I guess you think that sergeant was right and I am just an hysterical female.' She lit a small cigar and puffed for a moment before speaking again.

'The thing is that Mike never saw that there was anything – I don't know – anything *different* about what he did. I mean, he sent a copy of his report that was causing all this trouble to a guy in England. What a dumb thing to do. I told him it was dumb. He just muttered about it being normal. But, you know, it may be OK in the academic world but he wasn't working there any more. Franklin's not in business to spread enlightenment, you know? Nor's the Pentagon or the arms companies.'

'Who did he send it to?' asked Fathers.

'Oh, that guy he used to work for that he was always talking about. I think he saw him as some kind of father figure, you know? He said a few times that he'd've known what to do with Franklin. A couple of times he said he was going to call him for advice.'

'You mean Dr Finlay, do you?' asked Fathers. She nodded. 'Did he phone him?' She shrugged. 'And are you sure he sent the report? He didn't just say he was going to, maybe when he was particularly upset?'

'Oh no, I saw him put it in the mail. He took an extra copy and did it himself at the weekend. At least he was smart enough not to use the company's system. But it was so goddamn dumb. And typical.'

Fathers leaned back in his chair and clasped both hands behind his head. He looked at the ceiling for a minute, then leaned forward with his elbows on the table.

'Tell me about the FBI,' he said and waved to the waiter.

'There has to be a reason, doesn't there?' she asked. 'I mean, weird things happen, but only when there are reasons for them, right? Something happened, and if he's been killed or he's a prisoner somewhere, God knows, there's got to be a reason, hasn't there? However weird it is. And doesn't it stack up so the reason has to do with his work? I mean, what else could there be? Oh God, I'm sorry.' She brushed again at the corner of her eye and looked down at the floor beside her chair.

The waiter approached the table and Fathers ordered coffee.

'What do you want?' he asked. 'Do you want me to say you're right? I don't know if you are. Nor, I should think, do the New York police. That's why I want you to tell me about the FBI.'

'I want you to tell me that you don't think I'm crazy.'

'Why should you think you're crazy?'

'I don't think I'm crazy, not most of the time anyway, but you do.'

'You think I think you're crazy?' asked Fathers. 'That's crazy.'

Rosemary Willis burst out laughing. She stopped as suddenly as she had begun, leaned forward and put her hand on his wrist. 'Harry, just please reassure me.'

Fathers looked at her hand on his wrist, acutely aware of the light touch. He covered it with his other hand. 'You don't want me to reassure you about yourself, do you?' he asked gently. 'Not really. You want reassurance about me.'

She took her hand back and fingered her glass of wine. The waiter brought the coffee and served it. Both took it without milk or sugar. Fathers lit a cigarette and sipped his coffee thoughtfully before speaking.

141

'Before I left,' he said, 'there was a discussion at the Home Office. I suppose that's the equivalent of your Department of Justice. In some respects, anyway. Well, that was when I was told I had to come here. Something was said then which, the day before I flew, was deliberately underlined by a man from the Defence Ministry. I was told that the possible explanations for Michael Sampson's disappearance begin with the KGB and get more outlandish from there. The Defence man told me to think especially about the second half of that sentence.'

Rosemary Willis took a deep breath, blew it out and relaxed. She rummaged in her bag, picked out a tissue and blew her nose.

'Tell me about these FBI agents of yours,' said Fathers.

'You ever been questioned by the police, Harry?'

He paused before saying, 'Not in the sense I think you mean.'

'Uh huh. It's like being hollowed out. Let's talk about something else for a while.'

'Fair enough, I suppose.' He wondered what they'd talk about.

'Let's talk about you, for example,' said Rosemary as if she were telepathic.

Fathers drew on his cigarette. He had never before known a witness suggest an interview became a general conversation, far less follow up by wanting to talk about him. He decided not to object. She was tough enough to close down the interview entirely if he did, spiky enough to refuse to talk more unless she could turn the tables on him. He had no authority to force her to answer his questions, and no good would be served if he tried to. Even if she had not yet started to tell him about the FBI, which was what he was most interested in at the moment, she had begun to give him his first real feel for the case with what she said about Sampson and his work. This, Fathers reminded himself, was a cooperative witness in what was, for him, a fragile situation. Besides, he was beginning to like her.

'Go ahead,' he said.

'Do you enjoy your work?'

Fathers was surprised. He started to answer, then stopped and poured himself some wine. 'What does "enjoy" mean?' he asked.

'OK, that'll do for an answer.'

142

'No, I'm serious. What do you mean by "enjoy"?'

'What do you mean by it?'

'Most of my job is a boring repetitive grind,' said Fathers after a while. 'Much of it is distasteful, some of it entirely repugnant. It brings me into contact with a lot of tragedy, a lot of grief, a lot of ugliness.' He paused. 'I get a lot of satisfaction out of it when it goes well.'

'And when it doesn't?'

'Then I don't.'

'What do you call "when it goes well"? When the crime figures go down?'

'No, it's politicians and pundits who worry about that. What I mean is when we solve a crime and get some villain convicted.'

'I don't want to sound like a liberal cliché, but aren't a lot of villains really victims themselves?'

'Some,' said Fathers. 'Maybe a lot. But there are also a lot of victims who don't become villains. Nobody's forced into crime. They often slide there through their own weakness, I suppose, and plenty get a push along the way from what gets done to them, or where they're brought up, or whatever. I suppose that's all true. But in the end there's always an element of them choosing it, and plenty actively turn down other ways of making a living. It's true that a lot of them are pretty sad bastards, but most of them are bastards as well.'

'Have you ever arrested somebody you felt real sympathy for?'

'When I was younger, yes. But now, I don't think so. Maybe it's been ground out of me, but also I'm in the Serious Crimes Squad and we don't really deal with much small fry, the little people who commit little crimes. But even a lot of them I feel, and felt, no pity or sympathy for. You'll never make me believe that some kid who beats up an old lady was forced to do it or deserves my sympathy when he's given porridge, or even some sly bugger who cons his way into her house and nicks the silver.'

She argued with him about that for a while, but when she made no headway changed tack. 'How does it feel?' she asked.

'How does what feel?'

'You deal with all that stuff – not just the crime, but the rest: the grief, and the ugliness and the tragedy. Like you said. You people must have a pretty grim view of the world. How does it feel?'

'I suppose it's like psychiatrists,' said Fathers.

'What?'

'They only come into contact with the mentally sick and they construct theories of human behaviour around that. We only come into contact with the socially sick, so that tends to be how we view society. It's an occupational hazard. I suppose we just pray and hope that there are decent people out there somewhere. We don't often meet them, but they're the ones we're supposed to be working for.'

'And are you?'

'In principle.'

'Is that good enough?'

Fathers shrugged. She pressed him some more on it, but he kept his replies to the verbal equivalent of a shrug. 'It's a living,' he said at one point. She looked at him sceptically, but if he was prepared to answer some of her questions, he drew the line at revealing how he truly felt to somebody he did not know, and a witness at that.

A waiter approached the table. 'Was everything satisfactory, sir and madam?'

'Perfect,' said Fathers.

'Can we offer you anything else? A *digestif* perhaps?'

Fathers looked at Rosemary. 'Not for me,' she said, and poured the last of the wine into their two glasses. The waiter nodded and drifted off.

'The thing is,' said Fathers, 'that I'm old fashioned. I believe in justice, right and wrong, good and bad, and I believe in the rule of law. I'm afraid there are enough bad people around that the good need laws to protect them. And if you have laws, you have to have people to enforce them. Which is where I come in.'

'A believer in law and order, already,' said Rosemary. 'I guess most policemen are. It must come with the job.'

'I didn't say that,' said Fathers evenly. 'Law and order is a political issue, and you're right, most policemen do believe in it. In the political sense. But the rule of law isn't political. It's

144

something everybody can believe in whatever their politics – except for anarchists I suppose.'

'Who makes the laws?' asked Rosemary. 'That's political.'

'I don't know how it is here,' said Fathers, 'but in my country even feminists want some laws strengthened – against pornography, for instance – and they want the penalties for rape and violence to women made more severe.'

'I can handle that, and nobody wants to be murdered or robbed. But in your country laws are a political issue right now. What's going on with the miners' strike, for Christ's sake? Or at Greenham Common? Or with the persecution of gays? Or police harassment of young blacks? Or are you going to say that those things don't happen?'

Fathers was no happier with the discussion at this level than when it was about his feelings. He shrugged again. He seemed to be doing a lot of it.

'That's no good,' said Rosemary with a sharpness that might or might not have been genuine – Fathers could not decide. 'Do they happen, or don't they?'

'Yes,' said Fathers. 'They happen.'

'And?'

'And I don't like them. Or do them.'

'Well then.'

'I don't see any "well then" about it. The police do some things they shouldn't, and probably don't do some things they should. That doesn't mean you shouldn't have laws against murder, robbery, violent crimes, rape, whatever.'

'You are a tricky bastard,' said Rosemary, 'throwing in rape like that all the time. Especially when you know that the police are goddamn awful with women who've been raped.'

'So you want a better police force. And maybe you want better laws. But do you want no police and no laws? Do you think vigilantes are the answer?'

'Oh, we have them already,' said Rosemary Willis. 'But come on, now. Come clean. What do you think about those things?'

'I don't know. I suppose I don't think about them. You should talk to my colleagues in Special Branch, really. I'm just a plain copper, catching people what commit plain crimes.'

'And here you are in New York, dealing with a plain crime.'

'*Touché*,' said Fathers.

'Is that all?'

'Don't think I'm comfortable with it.'

'And I thought we were getting along so well.'

The waiter approached their table again. 'Would you care for some more coffee?'

Rosemary waved her hand at him and he drifted off. 'You keep on talking about you, and I'm talking about things in general,' she said, finishing her wine.

'I'm not very good at talking about things in general,' Fathers acknowledged. 'Policemen are usually asked to enforce the law, not philosophise about it. Talking of which, what about the FBI?'

'Oh no,' she said with a smile, 'not yet you don't. I'm just beginning to enjoy.'

'There's more?'

The waiter approached their table again holding a saucer with their bill on it, folded in half. He put it down in front of Fathers. 'Thank you very much, sir and madam,' he said and drifted off again.

Rosemary reached across, picked up the bill and scrutinised it. 'How good are you at doing sums in your head?' she asked. 'It's worth going through the check here, sometimes.'

Fathers took the slip of paper from her and began adding.

'The police,' said Rosemary, 'often act like they're inhuman. But I guess the real trouble is they *are* human, with all the usual fears and hates, and then they deal with all that shit, and I guess they get infected by it.'

Fathers frowned, looked up and then back at the piece of paper and began adding it up again, his lips moving slightly.

'Maybe infected is the wrong word,' said Rosemary. 'Maybe it's more they get tempted. Yeah. But you shouldn't expect anything different, I guess. A sick society gets a sick police force is how it works out.'

Fathers looked at her. 'Infected is the right word,' he said. 'Some get tempted, but everybody gets infected.'

146

'Is it OK?'

'No, it's not, but it's a job that's got to be done.'

'I mean the check. Does it add up OK?'

'I think so,' said Fathers, and put it down on the saucer. He pulled out his wallet, took out the cash to pay for it and put it down on top.

'Hey, that's real money,' said Rosemary. 'You don't often see that these days.'

The waiter reappeared and picked up the saucer.

'Do you get infected, too, Harry?'

Fathers looked assessingly at Rosemary Willis for the umpteenth time. As Miller had told him, she was some special lady. She looked steadily back at him, letting their eyes engage.

'Well,' said Fathers finally, looking away, 'one thing is the way you have to harden up when you deal with a lot of violent crime and general nastiness. Just before I left London, a case we were dealing with involved a man being beaten to death. My DI and I discussed it quite – I don't know – quite lightly.'

'DI?'

'Detective Inspector. My immediate junior. We were mostly worried about how it affected the larger case we were working on. Yesterday, a detective here told me about a couple of quite horrifying cases. Basically, he was concerned about how he would handle them rather than about what had actually happened. It's the same thing. You see it everywhere.'

'But you have to have that sense of distance. Like doctors can't have feelings for the patients they operate on.'

'Yes and no. It's necessary, but different. We don't bring people back to life. It gets hold of you somehow and chews away at what makes you a person.'

'You seem pretty much of a person,' she said, looking at him very directly again.

He ducked his head. 'Thank you,' he said. 'You do, too.'

As they thought about this exchange, the waiter returned with the saucer, bill and change. 'Is there anything else?'

Fathers, in thought, said nothing. Rosemary told him the meal had been excellent. The waiter smiled and drifted away again.

147

'I think he's trying to tell us something,' Rosemary smiled.

'Do you get that impression?' asked Fathers. 'Is there somewhere we can go? I still want to know about the FBI.'

They never got to talk about the FBI, not that evening at least.

As they left the cool restaurant for the warm evening air, Rosemary hooked an arm through Fathers'. 'Are all London's policemen like you?'

Fathers was attacked by a coughing fit. 'More than you'd think,' he said when he'd recovered. 'One thing about us is that we're hard to put off. Let me say it again: the FBI. We can go to a bar and talk some more.'

'Your hotel bar?' Rosemary asked with an archness that surprised him, pulling her arm back. 'Next you'll be telling me your wife doesn't understand you.'

'Any bar,' said Fathers with a prim touch of impatience.

'Not quite any bar I hope, buster, not in this city.'

He looked at her, trying to assess her mood. She had drunk a lot of wine, she was in the midst of coming to terms with having lost her lover, and she was spending an evening in a way that must surely have been unique for her – for him too, the way she had directed it. The quick changes were understandable but off-putting, and he tried to sort out how much was deliberate, either teasing or testing him, and how much was not. He was playing this interview by rules that were very different from the ones he was used to, rules he was making up as he went along. He was surprised to realise he was feeling protective towards her.

'It's a lovely warm evening,' she said. 'Let's walk. See me back to my apartment.' And she set off along the street.

But it was too warm to walk far with comfort. After a few blocks they hailed a cab. When they got to Rosemary's apartment building Fathers paid the driver, telling her he would walk the few blocks to his hotel.

'No. See me to my door. That's only good manners, New York style.'

'Afraid you might get mugged on the stairs?'

'It happens.'

They went inside and took the lift to her floor. Fathers was about to say goodbye and arrange another time to talk about the FBI, but she said, 'Come in and have a drink.' He shrugged and walked in after her, his mind playing over the possibilities now. The front door opened straight into a living room with a small kitchen off it. Opposite there was a hallway leading to the rest of the rooms. Fathers looked around him curiously. The room was neat and uncluttered, but well-decorated. There were three pictures on the walls. He went up to look at them: they were all Matisse reproductions.

The apartment was warm. Rosemary kicked off her shoes. 'Make yourself comfortable,' she said, and went into the kitchen. Fathers heard the refrigerator door open and shut, he heard the clink of glasses and the popping of a cork.

'More wine,' she said, returning with the bottle and two glasses. 'This weather is just beyond it.'

She sat on the sofa, poured the wine, set his glass on a low table and leaned back, putting her feet up on the table and taking a long drink. Fathers was still standing.

'Surveying the scene of the crime?' she asked.

He smiled uncomfortably, took off his jacket, loosened his tie, sat down on the edge of the sofa and picked up his glass.

'It's very weird to think,' she said, 'that something awful happened here. The bedroom, the bathroom and Mike's study are along the passage there. Go look at them if you like.'

He put his glass on the table and looked at her.

'Go on,' she said, 'if you want to. You're a policeman.'

'Never off duty,' said Fathers and went.

The bathroom was on the left of the hallway. It was small, neat and unremarkable. He used the lavatory. At the end of the hall was a small area obviously used for dumping whatever there was no other place for. There were two doors off it, one open, one shut. The open door gave onto the bedroom. He looked in. Behind the other door when he opened it was a smaller, entirely empty room. Bare floor, bare walls, no curtains. He looked at it with a feeling as empty as the room, and wondered for a moment

149

about Rosemary Willis. Then he closed the door and went back to the living room. She was sitting as she had been when he had left, but her glass was full again and he could see tears on her cheeks.

'I'm sorry,' he said, 'that was very unfeeling of me. I should know better. I'm just too much of a policeman sometimes. Really, I'm very sorry.' He sat down on the sofa.

'No,' she said, 'don't be. You can't let my sensitivities stop you from seeing something that might help.' She sniffed. 'I mean it. Anyway, I'm not crying just because you went to look at Mike's study. I do an awful lot of crying in this apartment these days. I guess I'm going to have to get rid of it if it goes on. There are too many memories here, and too many doubts.' She made a noise in her throat which sounded like a growl and shook her head impatiently as she wiped away the tears.

'The hell of it is, if I'm honest with myself, Mike and I weren't doing terribly well. I don't know, I was still awfully fond of him but I found him so young, you know? And he always seemed much more interested in his work than in me. I guess he wasn't really. He just didn't have a language for telling me how much he cared, or a way of showing it. Except in bed. But even that wasn't going so well. I couldn't take it somehow, the way he would come back, not give me a second look, go into his study with his books and his files, and come out three hours later all heated up.'

Fathers lit a cigarette.

'Yeah. Well it led to problems and fights, and I think he just didn't have a handle on it. Anyway, I think we were maybe heading for a break-up. I'm not sure, but maybe. I just felt we were going nowhere. And then this. And all I have is an ache and a loneliness where he used to be. It wasn't perfect, but it was something. Why is it no comfort that I was ready to live without him anyway?'

'Whatever you might have wanted,' said Fathers, 'once you'd decided, it wasn't this.'

Rosemary sat upright on the sofa, shifted closer and looked at him intently. 'You know, Harry, I haven't talked with anybody about Mike in the last couple of weeks as much as I've talked tonight with you. Why's that?' She drank more wine and set her glass on the table.

Fathers shrugged. 'I'm good at listening,' he said. 'It goes with the job.'

Rosemary gently put her hand on his cheek. 'Yes,' she said softly, 'maybe it's because you're just a good policeman.'

He leaned forward and kissed her quickly, gently and ambiguously. What am I doing? he thought.

'And maybe it's something else,' she said. She leaned forward and kissed him, longer. He put his hand on her shoulder. He was very aware of her.

She pulled away to pick up the bottle and pour some more wine for him. As she sat back he put his arm round her and she leant her cheek on his shoulder. Then, in a changed tone, she went back to a comment she had made earlier. 'I guess your wife doesn't understand you, huh?'

He looked at her with surprise. 'No,' he said, after a pause, 'I think she probably knows me inside out and understands me very well. It's me who doesn't understand her.'

'So what don't you understand?' she asked, sitting up and away from him.

He shrugged and blew out a breath. 'The life of a policeman's wife is difficult,' he said. 'I don't really know why she puts up with it. And I make it worse by liking my job too much and doing it too well.'

She nodded. 'Long hours.'

'And unpredictable,' he added. 'Unexplained absences, a permanently disorganised social life, fears.'

Rosemary picked up her glass but did not drink. She looked straight at him. Her expression was a little sad, a little hopeful and a little wary. 'So what now?'

'I'm not in the habit of kissing witnesses,' he said.

'You should try it more often. It could have an effect.'

'That's what I'm worried about.'

She laughed, then put down her glass, picked up his hand and held it between both of hers on her lap. He looked at their hands and he looked at her face. She leaned forward to kiss him again,

151

with a hard intensity that startled him, then softening. She let him go and he took his hand back.

'If you don't want to,' she said, 'say now and go. But I want to sleep with you. Now.'

'No, I want to, too,' he said. 'Would that be good for you?'

She snorted. 'Good for me. That's the craziest reason I ever heard for doing it. Who needs a reason? I want to, that's all. Maybe I need to.'

She stood up. 'I guess I should just say this and get it over: it doesn't mean anything, OK? Except that you're nice, and you're attractive, and I'm lonely. In a way I never have been before. I didn't start this evening thinking I'd bring you back here. Even when I asked you in for a drink, that was all I was asking you in for. But now we've begun it would be a shame not to go on. Well?'

He stood up. They walked together to her bedroom and made love.

11

Fathers woke before seven to find he was alone in Rosemary's bed. He got up, put on his pants and trousers and walked down the hallway to the kitchen. He heard the lavatory flush. With the smoking and drinking of the evening before, his mouth was parchment-dry. He filled a glass with cold water and gulped it down. He turned at a soft sound.

Rosemary stood naked in the doorway from the living room. 'Dry mouth, huh?' she smiled. 'I'll have a glass too, please.'

He took another glass, filled it and passed it to her. Like him, she drained it.

'How do you feel?' he asked.

She did not reply for a moment, and they stood looking at each other, wonderingly. 'Rotten and just fine at the same time,' she said.

He moved towards her and put out his hand to touch her. She put the glass down and moved in to the crook of his arm, resting her head on his shoulder. He put his arm round her and ran his hand down her back.

'That was very good,' he said quietly.

'Well I think you English policemen are just marvellous,' she replied. 'Are they all like you?'

'Am I supposed to know the answer to that?'

She chuckled and kissed his neck. 'You were right. It was good for me.'

'Pleased to be of service.'

'Oh, that's what you call it in England. I was wondering.' She stepped away and refilled her glass.

'Boy,' she said when she had drunk half of it, 'I sure as hell drank too much last night.'

'I noticed.'

'Yeah. But you can console yourself that you didn't have to get me drunk.'

153

'You slept restlessly,' he said.

'But at least I slept, and without pills, too.'

'I wonder why.'

'Booze and sex,' said Rosemary. 'Sure beats any other known sedative. Oh, but it puts the years on you.' She flicked at her hair and ran her hand over her face. 'Part of me feels great – that's your part of me. The rest feels awful. How do I look?'

He took a step away and looked her slowly up and down. She struck a pose, one foot forward and her hands held out from her sides, palms facing him, arms bent. He stepped forward and took her face in his two hands. 'You look fabulous,' he said and kissed her for a long time.

At the end she stepped away and he let his hands drop. She stood facing him with both arms by her sides.

'Yes, well,' he said, 'maybe you'd better put something on.'

'Oh no,' she said, 'not if that's what I get for having nothing on.'

'I'm hungry,' he said.

'Mmm, me too.' She kissed his shoulder and ran her hands up and down his sides.

'Really,' he said, 'I'm hungry.'

'Aw, come on. You've started so well. Why stop now?'

'I'm starving. You wouldn't want to hear me rumbling at the critical moment.'

'OK, let's deal: first we look after your hunger, then we look after mine. What do you want for breakfast?'

'Let me get it,' he said, 'if you'll tell me where things are. What will you have? Do you mind if I have eggs?'

'As long as you don't fry them. They're in the fridge. Muffins're there too, English muffins, how's that? I'll look after the coffee. You're not going to fry them, are you?'

'No. Do you want some?'

'Yeah, I guess so.'

For the next few minutes she interspersed preparing the coffee and squeezing the oranges in an electric juicer with telling him where things that he wanted were and with various comments. In response to his repeated suggestion she went and got a bathrobe to wear.

'Hey,' she said at one point, 'cracking the eggs one-handed. I can see you're a man to cherish.'

'Sex with somebody for the first time,' she said a few minutes later, 'is something special. You feel all soft and warm and soppy.'

'Do I?' he asked. 'Where's the whisk?' She passed it to him.

'You've got a great bod,' she said hugging him from behind, 'and you can make scrambled eggs yet.' She ran her nails down his back.

'It's not scrambled eggs,' he said.

'No?' She reached round to run her nails down his chest.

'No,' he said, catching her hands in his and kissing one. 'It's *oeufs japonnais*. Where's a good saucepan?'

'Oh, I beg your pardon, *Chef* Inspector,' she said. 'In the cupboard there. What are *oeufs japonnais*?'

'A traditional dish,' he said, adding milk and salt to the eggs.

'It was invented by the Samurai,' he said, switching on the electric whisk, 'to give them courage to go out and face evil-doers.'

'They did a lot of that,' said Rosemary.

'Oh yes,' he said, 'in between other things. How do you light the cooker?'

When Rosemary had showed him, he put butter in the sauce-pan and put it over the flame, poured in the eggs and started to stir the mixture. Meanwhile, she split muffins and began to toast them.

'It made them very big and strong and brave,' he said. 'In fact, it made them virtually invincible. A Samurai with a good break-fast of *oeufs japonnais* inside him never got killed in battle.'

He concentrated on the eggs. 'Of course,' he added after a time, 'they died like flies from cholesterol poisoning.'

Rosemary laughed.

'And that's the origin of the old saying,' he added.

'What old saying?'

'You can't make an omelette without breaking a Samurai,' Fathers said, looking over his shoulder at her.

Rosemary moved between him and the stove. She put her arms round him and slipped one hand inside the waistband of his trousers at the back. 'You English policemen are just weird,' she said, trying to pinch him.

Fathers gave an exaggerated sigh and reached over her to turn the gas off. 'The eggs are cooked,' he said, kissing her forehead.

He picked up the saucepan and put it down again quickly. The metal handle was hot. 'Yow,' he said, 'where's the oven mitt?'

'The what?'

'You know,' he said waving his hand vaguely, 'the thingy.'

'Oh,' she said, 'you mean the pot-holder. Here.'

'No,' he said, taking it, 'I mean the oven mitt.'

'But it's not a mitten.'

'No, but it would be if it was sensibly designed. With this, you'd burn the back of your hand in the oven. Sensible oven mitts avoid that.'

'You English,' said Rosemary.

They carried the food, juice, coffee and plates over to the table by the window and sat down. Fathers served the eggs out. Rosemary cocked an eyebrow at them.

'You tell a strange story, fellow, but these look like scrambled eggs to me.'

'Well,' said Fathers defensively, 'they're as Japanese as these muffins are English.'

Rosemary chuckled and began to eat. They ate in silence. When they'd both finished she stood up and put out her hand.

'Right,' she said, 'now for the other half of the bargain.'

After they had made love, they made the bed, put on bathrobes and returned to the kitchen. While Rosemary warmed up the coffee left over from breakfast, Fathers started on the washing up.

Fathers sighed. 'Well,' he said, 'I'm in a great condition to work today.'

'Of course, you could always work by asking me about the FBI, and I could call in sick to my job, and perhaps you could continue with your unusual interrogation methods.'

'Fraid not. I have an appointment at nine-thirty, which I'm going to miss if I'm not careful. And a couple more later on.'

'Who are you seeing? If I'm allowed to know.'

'Oh, yes, I think so. A Captain Molson at the precinct that first dealt with the case, then a man from the District Attorney's Office, and then John Franklin. I fixed it all up on the phone yesterday, about the time I called you. I'm afraid you'll just have to wait for your third degree.'

'My, but you call it funny things in England. Coffee?'

'Please. I do want to see you again, both ways. I mean, both professionally and personally.'

'Oh, for a second there I thought you meant ...'

'No, I didn't. Not that I'm averse.'

'No, that's my role.'

Fathers finished the washing up and dried his hands.

'I want to see you again, too,' said Rosemary. 'In fact, I'm more than half inclined not to let you out of my sight. But needs must, I guess. I have to say, though, that you handle yourself like you know your way around the kitchen. Do you do much cooking at home?'

'Not a lot. Less than I'd like. I used to cook quite a lot before I got married, but you know how it is.'

'I guess so.'

'Mike do much cooking?'

'Not a thing. He couldn't toast a muffin without burning it, even in the toaster. He could just about handle instant coffee on a good day. Total disaster in the kitchen. Wasn't interested in learning, either.'

Fathers looked at her for a while without saying anything.

157

'What's wrong?' she asked.

'Nothing,' he replied. 'It's just reminded me of something. Sod it, is that the time? I must fly. First, I must dress.'

She went with him to the bedroom and watched as he put on his clothes.

'Call me,' she said.

'This afternoon.'

They kissed quickly and he left. She put her arms round her waist, hugging herself, and sighed. Then she went for a shower.

The morning was too warm and humid for an October Friday, especially for hurrying to a hotel, shaving, changing and hurrying on to an appointment with a police captain at a busy Precinct station.

Captain Molson begrudged Fathers the twenty uninformative minutes he spent with him, and made it obvious by looking constantly at his watch and his wall clock. Fathers heard the edge of resentment in Molson's voice. He had evidently not enjoyed coming under pressure from a congressman for not doing his job well enough. Fathers gathered that though Molson had formally requested the assistance of the Homicide Department and effectively handed the case over to them, he had acted under strong advice.

'From the DA's Office?' said Fathers.

'You got it,' said Molson. 'Listen, Mr Fathers, I don't wanna be rude, but we got an important case coming up for pre-trial hearing, and I gotta get to the prosecutor's office.'

'Of course,' said Fathers. 'I do understand, and I'm very grateful for your time.' The two men stood and shook hands. As he was half-way out the door, Fathers turned back and said, 'Oh, by the by, the Homicide people seem to have mislaid your actual request for assistance. They have everything else from your part of the investigation and I've looked for it all over, but the request seems to have taken a walk. You don't have a copy I could see, do you? Just for the sake of completeness.'

158

Molson was shrugging his jacket on as he came round his desk to the door. 'Sounds like them. I guess I do.' He pushed past Fathers and walked down a corridor. Fathers fell in behind him.

Molson led him to a large room lined with filing cabinets and shelves full of box files. There were three tables with folders piled on them, and an even more cluttered desk, behind which sat a large black policeman in uniform with sergeant's stripes on his arm. He looked to be in his late fifties.

'Here, Coors,' Molson said to him, 'this is Detective Chief Inspector Fathers from London. He's interested in Sampson, Michael – disappearance, case transferred, file closed – couple weeks back.'

'Sure,' said Coors. 'I know it.'

'Let him look the file over, will you?'

'Paperwork, Captain?'

'When I get back.'

'Just so long as I get the authorisation.'

'Sure thing. In the meantime, he can see the lot. Nice meeting you, Mr Fathers. Have a nice day.' And Molson left.

'OK, then, Mr Fathers, is it?' asked Coors. 'Lemme see what I can do for you.' He rose from his seat and walked slowly round to one of the shelves of box files that covered the walls of his office. He flicked along till he came to the one he wanted. 'OK, Mr Fathers,' he said, opening it. 'Yeah, here you are. Maybe you'd like to sit at the table there and look it through. Just move the pile to one side, OK?'

Fathers sat down at a spare table and began to look through the box. Coors sat back at his desk. After a while, Fathers coughed. Coors looked up and saw a puzzled frown on his visitor's face.

'Got a problem?'

'Well,' said Fathers, 'I've seen all this at the Homicide Department, but what they don't have is the precinct's formal request for assistance on the case.'

'Yeah?'

'Well, it's not here either.'

'Lemme see.' Coors walked round to lean over Fathers' shoulder.

'You see,' said Fathers, 'it's listed on this index form, but it's not actually in there where it should be.'

'Lemme see.'

Together the two went through each folder in the box, checking each document against the index list.

'Nope,' said Coors at last, 'it's not there. It should be. I wonder how come it's not?'

'It's probably not very important,' said Fathers. 'I wouldn't want to take up your time finding it.'

'No,' said Coors. 'This is what I'm here for. Let's see what we can do for you. OK, I'll check the use ledger.'

He tracked back to his desk and picked up a large, loose-leaf book. He went through several pages, then shut it and put it down. 'Nope, not there. Now lemme think.'

He sat down heavily, and thought. Fathers waited. 'OK, now, maybe Carl's still got his copy. He shouldn't, but maybe. Let's check.'

Coors opened up a folder and ran his finger down a piece of foolscap paper. He grunted contentedly, picked up his telephone and tapped out two digits on it, looking at Fathers while he waited for an answer. 'Detective Zberg?' he said finally. 'Coors here, Records. Come along here, will ya? No, I mean now, and that means now.' He put down the phone. 'He'll be along,' he said to Fathers.

They waited for a few minutes, until a tall, dark-haired man half entered the room. 'What've I done now?' he asked.

'What've you usually done to get me on your ass, Detective?' snapped Coors.

'OK, OK, just tell me.'

'The Sampson case. You was on it?'

'Sampson. What was that?'

'English guy who disappeared.'

'Oh yeah, the limey professor with the angry girlfriend. I got ya.'

'You got me, and you still got the work file. So the book says. We're looking for it, me and this very senior English

160

detective here who doesn't like his countrymen being called limeys.'

'Er, OK, Sergeant,' said Zberg. 'I guess you know we've been pretty busy round here these past couple of weeks. I think that's one I haven't done my own final report on yet.'

'One of many,' said Coors.

'Yeah, yeah, I was just going to put the finishing touches on it. You wanna see it?'

'No, but this man here does. He's Chief Inspector Fathers, but you can call him sir.' Coors dismissively opened a file on his desk. 'And you can get your final work report done and get it to me five minutes ago.'

As Fathers followed Zberg back down the corridor, the American said to him, 'Jesus, paperwork, that guy lives and breathes it.'

'Every man to his own,' said Fathers.

'Er, sure,' said Zberg. They arrived at an untidy desk. A heavily made-up woman in an evening gown was sitting beside it. 'Sorry, darling,' he said to her, 'this won't take a moment.' He pulled open an over-full drawer and took out a pile of folders. He flicked through them, muttering 'shit' as he look at the label on each one. 'OK, er, sir,' said Zberg, 'this is the one you want. Anything particular you're looking for?'

'Yes,' said Fathers taking the folder from him. Standing beside Zberg's desk he leafed through it. 'This is it,' said Fathers, pulling out a two-page document. 'Have you got a xerox machine here?'

'Sure. You wanna make a copy?'

'It'll save bothering you any further,' said Fathers.

'Sure. Scuse me, darling, I'll just be a moment, OK?'

Zberg took Fathers to a photocopier in the corner of the room, talked the man who was using it into letting him butt in, and handed the finished result to Fathers with a smile. 'OK? All done.'

'Thank you,' said Fathers. He slipped the original back into the file and handed it back, closed, to Zberg, folded the copy and put it in the inside pocket of his jacket. He watched Zberg return

161

to his desk and toss the folder into his chaotic drawer. He found his way back to Coors' room, poked his head round the door, said, 'Well, never mind, I won't trouble you further, many thanks,' and left.

As he trotted up the steps of the building that housed the Homicide Department he patted his breast pocket and smiled.

Fathers walked into the room that held the material evidence on the Sampson case. It amounted to those contents of his study at home and office that hadn't been removed. They had been collected by the police, the scraps of paper put in plastic folders and, like everything else, labelled. Two chairs, ripped so badly that they were unusable, stood on the floor. The rest of the items were on a shelf. There was not much. Fathers had looked it over briefly the day before, but without much interest. Now, however, he was interested. He picked up the four cookery books which seemed strange things to be owned by a man whose lover had said he was useless in the kitchen. He took them to the bleak room he was using as an office. The flowers he had bought two days before were wilting lifelessly: he threw them in the waste bin and made a mental note to replace them. He set the books down on his table and checked his watch. There was plenty of time before his lunch appointment with Frank Labbat from the District Attorney's Office.

There was a note on the table, asking him to call Captain Amstel. He got up and went to the general office, found Miller's desk and borrowed his phone. Amstel wanted to ask him to lunch on Sunday. Fathers accepted.

'Good,' said the captain. 'We have a cabin on Long Island. It'll make a nice break from the steam of the city. A family occasion. Lieutenant Grolsch and his wife are coming, too. Is there anybody you'd like to bring?'

Fathers said there was not.

'OK,' said Amstel, and told him which train to catch. 'We'll meet you at the station.'

'I look forward to it,' said Fathers.

'Sure. Have a nice day.'

Back in his temporary office, Fathers took off his jacket and began to look through the cookery books. Three were paperbacks. None seemed used. The fourth was a hardback, with its dust jacket still on. Not quite sure why he was doing it, Fathers began to leaf through it, page by page.

Occasionally he found his concentration slipping, and he read the recipes. Some were very interesting. It was a book of international cookery, and the Middle Eastern section was especially strong. Fathers kept having to repress his interest. He ended with page 344, closed the book and went through each of the others. Nothing out of the ordinary in any of them, neither in the culinary sense nor in any other. He put the last one down and checked his watch. A few minutes left before he should go downstairs to meet Labbat in the entrance to the building. He yawned, reflecting that he had had no coffee since leaving Rosemary's. He thought for a moment about her and about the night before.

Fathers yawned again and stretched. His mind flickered from Rosemary to his wife, Sarah, and to his two children. Before they made love, Rosemary had said it would mean nothing. He wondered if she thought that now. He wondered what his own feelings were.

As he stood up and put on his jacket, a thought struck him. He took the dust jacket off the hardback he had started with. Written in biro on the inside were some notes in a small, neat and legible hand. He looked at them for several minutes. They were jottings which meant nothing to him. If they had not been written on the inside of the dust jacket on a book that seemed to have no obvious right to be owned by Michael Sampson, he would not have paid them a second glance. He tore a sheet off his pad and laid it on the table. That way no impression would be left on the pad below the sheet he was writing on. He was not quite sure why he was taking that precaution, but doubts were starting to form into the beginnings of a hypothesis, and despite feeling a little foolish he decided to leave no trace for prying eyes – if there were any. He copied the jottings exactly:

FERRET−D ◄———► KAL7 ◄———► STS−8
                4½ BY C 141
                RC−135
                −10 MIN SAME FLT PATH
                DUMMY ?

3 PASSES   O 23: 28·5° N
CF 1964   024: ? +1−2° N ?
                                O 25:   DITTO
                                1400−2000 m
                                OR LESS ?
                                CF LAUNCH TIME

            CHECK CABLES

C OF C: STS−8 ——► CONTROL (NASA) ——► NS ADVISOR ——► ???? RR!
                                      FIRED (?) 6 WKS
                                      CONNECTION ?

When he'd finished, he folded the sheet up and put it in his
inside breast pocket together with the photocopy he had got from
the precinct. Feeling surreptitious, he put the dust jacket on the
book, took it and the other three back to the other room, and
took the lift down to the entrance hall where he found Frank
Labbat waiting for him.

Lunch was pleasant and uninformative. Both men did a little
fishing for information. Labbat was angling for a report on
Fathers' progress and conclusions, while Fathers was after any
little something about the FBI, but neither landed anything.
Fathers also mentioned the missing request for assistance from
the precinct; the other cocked his head at him and promised to
dig a copy out of his files. Fathers avoided alcohol, ate only half
his meal, turned down dessert, gulped his coffee and, without
being rude, managed to get lunch over in slightly less than an
hour.

When he had left his temporary office before lunch, an idea
had been forming in his mind. Now he thought about it some

more and it became a decision to do three things: first, to get some assistance to decipher Sampson's notes; second, since New York was not his city and there was too much rustling in the undergrowth of this case, to get it from London; and third, he had decided whom to ask. When he got into his room it was not yet two o'clock. He trusted to luck that today was not one of the rare days when the people he wanted would have left work before seven p.m., or one of the common days on which they were working outside the office on some emergency.

His luck was in. He spoke first to Detective Inspector Stevens, who listened to what Fathers said, and then transferred him without comment to Detective Constable Yarrow.

'Yarrow,' Fathers said, 'I need your help and your discretion.'

'Yes, sir,' said Yarrow. 'How can I help?'

'Have you got Finlay's telephone number?'

'Yes, sir.'

'Give it to me.'

'Home or work?'

'Both.' Yarrow read the numbers out.

'Now, then,' said Fathers, 'I'm going to phone him tomorrow morning, about eleven your time. But I want you to soften him up for me first.'

'Be honest, sir, I'm not sure I can.'

'I'm going to tell you how,' said Fathers, and explained.

'I think I get you, sir,' said Yarrow thoughtfully. 'I'll phone him this evening and set it up to go round tomorrow to spend a bit of time with him before you call. Can I just check that I've got it straight? As I see it, it's the seriousness of the case that counts, not his bit of naughtiness, but I chuck that in, gently though, for good measure.'

'That's right. Remember, the point is to get him to talk, which in his case means persuade him. You've got to convince him, not try to scare him. All right? And for the moment, remember what I said about discretion. Till I say different there's no need for anybody else to know.'

'I got you, sir. Is that it?'

'Yes. Transfer me back to DI Stevens, will you? Oh, and thanks.'

'Got what you wanted from the lad?' asked Stevens when he and Fathers were reconnected.

'Yup. How's it going?'

'Just fine. Those silly buggers went for Carteret's this morning and we've got them tucked up nice and snug.'

'Great. Is one of them going to cough about Terry the Talker?'

'I think we'll get Pelham to wear it whether or not one of these laddies spits it out.'

'Was he with them?'

'No, but the driver had an address in his pocket, and when we got there, who should we find but Pigface? We're working on him now, in shifts.'

'Stroke of luck, that.'

'The criminal mind is not always very large, guv, not always. When we spun them round, two of them turned and duffed up another.'

'He was probably the one who said it would be safe to go ahead.'

'Anyway, we're holding them all on a whole pile of charges, and if we need to we can threaten them with conspiracy to murder and accessories after the fact to flush out the goods on Pelham.'

'Sounds like some very good work, James. How're you getting on with Mr Bastin?' Stevens made a noise which sounded like a repressed snort. 'Getting up your nose, is he?'

'Right up there beyond where the finger nail can reach,' said Stevens. 'Have you ever wondered how he got where he's got to?'

'Fruitless speculation, James. He's a Knight Commander of the Crooked Pinky, if that's got anything to do with it.'

'By the way, two blokes from the Punter kidnap crew have been picked up.'

'Bastin do that?'

'No. Queen.'

'Did he indeed?'

'Yeah. The crafty sod went on working away on it, despite you. Didn't let anybody in on it, didn't even let us know he was

166

doing it. He put the word out and went over some previous cases. Got a whisper which meshed with some likely candidates from the form book. Went and put the frighteners on one and the bloke couldn't stop talking. So he turned up yesterday morning, pleased as Punch, with a villain under each arm. Decent bit of work, all things considered. Can't blame him for having a go really.'

'Not really, I suppose. Were there just the two of them?'

'Four in all. Queenie got the other two names from the ones he picked up, so we should get them pretty soon.'

'Anything else?'

'Zoe was found on Wednesday, dead I'm afraid.'

'Oh shit. Well, I suppose it was expected.'

'Yes. The pathologist reckons she was dead more than a week, since well before last Thursday night, that means.'

'So Queen was right about that. How's the evidence?'

'It wasn't clean, you know? So there were all kinds of traces to establish the link with the blokes Queen picked up – bits of skin and clothing, blood type with one of them.'

'Oh, it was like that was it?'

'Fraid so, poor little kid. Very, very nasty. I think that's what threw the one who talked, that it was so nasty – I mean, she was only a kid.'

'How's Punter taking it?'

'Badly, still swearing revenge for last week's cock-up. We'll be keeping our eyes on the Sunday papers for a few weeks. But he can't pin Zoe's death on us, so I suppose Queen has come out of it more or less all right. Can't really grumble with results, can you?'

Yes you can, thought Fathers, but he did not say it.

When Fathers put the phone down he considered his timetable for the rest of the day. He had John Franklin to see at three-thirty. He needed to get to the Consulate and type up a report to be telexed to London. And he wanted to see Rosemary again that evening. He phoned her first. Her 'Hallo' when he was put through was harassed and snappy, and though that changed to warmth when he said who he was, she still sounded busy and not in a mood to talk for long. They set a time and rang off.

Fathers sat and looked at the phone for a minute, then sighed and turned his mind to Sampson's cryptic notes. Why, he wondered, did he write them there? To hide them? From whom? He shook his head impatiently. Everything he knew about Sampson told against him acting melodramatically; hiding notes like that seemed wildly out of character. Or had he at some point needed to make notes and simply grabbed the nearest clean piece of paper? No, surely not: he would have as much stationery as he could use in a company like Franklin's. So Sampson hid them. Perhaps Finlay could help tell him why.

Fathers pulled from his pocket the photocopy he had taken at the precinct that morning.

When he had finished reading it, he knew its absence from the files at the Homicide HQ and Sergeant Coors' records at the precinct had not been accidental. Most of it told him nothing new. A lot of turgid prose was devoted to basic information on Sampson, what had happened at his office and his study and who had been interviewed and by whom. But the last paragraph explained why Fathers had not been able to see the document by asking Sergeant Miller, Lieutenant Grolsch or Captain Molson, and why Labbat, when asked, would pretend to have forgotten to get it from his own files. Fathers read it a second time:

A further item for your attention is the involvement of the Federal Bureau of Investigation, namely Agents Beck and Weiser. Their arrival at Dr Sampson's apartment on the evening of Monday, October 1, during the first visit there of precinct personnel, was cleared here only retrospectively, with no reason given or explanation of how the Bureau knew this precinct was investigating relevant to Dr Sampson. I point out that precinct officers arrived at the Sampson/Willis apartment nineteen minutes after receipt of the emergency call, and that Bureau personnel arrived some thirteen minutes after that. Their prior interview with Mr Franklin (Pres. Franklin Res.) was remarked by him, and later confirmed by the Agents. Likewise, their interview with Miss Willis was not cleared here, and confirmed by them only on my asking, after the Investigating Detective had received a telephone call from Miss Willis in the course of which she mentioned it. While not unduly concerned by Bureau presence and involvement, and while I understand that the nature of Dr Sampson's work involves wider issues, the level of cooperation is questionable. On raising this, I have been informed that Agents Beck and Weiser are not investigating Dr Sampson's apparent disappearance and have a prior interest in him. There is an entangling of issues, agencies and jurisdictions here to which you may wish attention be given.

So much for the comment by Agent Broderick Weiser of the FBI that he was only keeping a watching brief and that neither he nor any other FBI agent had been actively involved in the investigation.

The document did not actually state any reason for the request for assistance; it simply outlined the case and requested help. Fathers guessed the decision had already been made to take the case out of the precinct's hands, and Captain Molson had simply had to send through the formal request as a matter of routine bureaucracy. Thank heavens for the demands of bureaucracy, he thought, and for bureaucratically inefficient detectives like Zberg (and even for efficient and helpful bureaucrats like Coors).

Fathers put the two pages down on his table, got up and took a few steps around the room. He paused to light a cigarette, then stood looking out of his window. He began to speculate and reconstruct.

After a while he shrugged irritably. Time to go to his appointment with John Franklin. There was still no hint of what actually had happened to Sampson.

12

Fathers groaned into consciousness in his hotel room at the sound of his alarm, switched it off and got out of bed. He turned to tuck the sheet up around Rosemary's neck, pausing a second to look at her.

'What a way to start a weekend,' she muttered, nestling back into the pillows and sleep.

He looked at the clock: it was five-thirty a.m. He had had less than four hours sleep. He used the phone to order coffee from room service and then went to the bathroom for a shower. He was dry and mostly dressed by the time the coffee was delivered.

Sitting with his coffee, Fathers pulled from various jacket pockets several pieces of paper: Finlay's phone number, his copy of the writing he had found inside the dust jacket of Sampson's cookery book, the document from the precinct, the carbon copy of the report he had typed for telexing to London the previous afternoon, some notes he had made for himself the previous evening. He looked them all over, refreshing his memory and his emerging sense of the possible order of things. He pulled the telephone over and, with a pad of paper and two pens within reach, he dialled.

The phone rang twice before it was answered and Fathers heard Finlay's 'Hullo'.

'Hullo, Dr Finlay. Fathers here. Is Mr Yarrow with you?'

'Yes, he is.' Finlay's voice was flat and neutral; Fathers wondered if it was a bit subdued.

'And has he explained the situation to you?'

'Yes, he has. It really seems as if Mike's disappeared, does it?'

'Yes.'

'Is, er, that is, does it look as if he's been murdered?' Finlay's flat voice emptied the question of drama.

'Maybe. It's really not at all clear. Now, are you going to help me?'

'I'm not sure if I can. Your man tells me it's technical advice of some kind that you want.'

'That and your discretion, Dr Finlay. I'm going to take you into my confidence and I expect you to repay me by not breaking it.'

'If it will help find out what happened to Mike, I'm prepared to help. If I can, that is.'

'Oh, I think you can,' said Fathers. 'Do you have a pen and paper handy? Because I'm going to read you over some notes of Dr Sampson's that I came across. They mean nothing to me. I'm hoping you can make sense of them for me. All right?'

'I'm ready.'

Fathers picked up his copy of Sampson's notes and began to read them. He did it slowly and precisely, detailing the columns and the arrows.

FERRET −D ◄────► KAL7 ◄────────► STS−8
4½ BY C141
RC−135
−10 MIN SAME FLT PATH
DUMMY ?

3 PASSES
CF 1964

023: 28·5° N
024: ? + 1−2° N ?
025:   DITTO
1400 − 2000 m
OR LESS ?
CF LAUNCH TIME

CHECK CABLES

C OF C: STS−8 ──► CONTROL (NASA) ──► NS ADVISOR ──► ???? RR !
FIRED (?) 6 WKS
CONNECTION ?

When he had finished, Finlay read it back to him, more quickly but equally precisely. 'You seem to have got it down right,' Fathers said. 'So now, please, can you tell me what it means?'

'Well,' said Finlay, 'it's a puzzle.'

'Yes,' said Fathers. 'Does any of it mean anything to you? Because none of it means a thing to me.'

'It's not at all clear what it means,' said Finlay.

'Any help you can give me, Dr Finlay,' said Fathers, feeling a little desperate. 'Could we take it bit by bit? What does "Ferret-D" mean, for example?'

'Oh, that's straightforward enough. It's a type of reconnaissance satellite. What's interesting is the bit beneath it about nineteen sixty-four, because that was when the first one was launched.'

'And "cf" presumably means "refer to"?'

'Yes. And "3 passes" presumably means it made three passes. That is, three passes over the area in question, whatever it is.'

'Seems logical,' said Fathers. 'What about "KAL 7" in the middle column?'

'Er, can we come to that in a moment? It could mean something, but I've moved onto the right hand column.' Finlay's voice was less flat now. It had an interested but detached tone, that of an academic puzzling through an interesting conundrum.

'All right. "STS-8", then: what does that mean?'

'It probably means the eighth mission of the Space Shuttle. That's the way they're numbered.'

'As you know, Dr Finlay, that's what Dr Sampson was working on earlier this year.'

'As you say, as I know.'

'What about the figures beneath it?'

'Well, this is just a guess, mind, but I should think "O" means "Orbit". It probably refers to the latitude along which the twenty-third, twenty-fourth and twenty-fifth orbits were made. Number twenty-three was at twenty-eight point five degrees north and he's wondering whether the next one was one or two degrees further north.'

'And the next line in that column?'

'Yes, well, that's a real puzzle, isn't it? Because shifting the inclination by one or two degrees wouldn't change the footprint by that much. Or that little.'

'I beg your pardon?'

'Eh? Oh, yes, sorry, I'll try to say it in English. I think the fourteen hundred to two thousand bit refers to a measurement, but if you shift a couple of degrees north from a given point, you don't shift as much as fourteen hundred to two thousand miles, nor as little as a couple of kilometres – if the "m" meant metres rather than miles, I mean. Do you see?'

'Yes, I think so. What could it refer to?' There was a silence from the other end of the line. When Finlay showed no sign of breaking it, Fathers said, 'What about the launch time?'

'Ah, yes, well I was looking at the middle column, actually. I think I've worked it out. Not so difficult, in fact.'

'Go on then.'

'I should think "KAL 7" means KAL 007. Does that mean anything to you?'

'No.'

'It's the flight number of that Korean Boeing airliner that was shot down by the Soviets last year when it penetrated their airspace.'

'I remember.'

'The next line could be a map reference. It would be forty-one or forty-two degrees North, by a hundred and forty-one degrees East. It sounds about right, don't you think, for Sakhalin?'

'I beg your pardon?'

'That's roughly where the airliner was shot down. It's an island off the top end of Japan that the Soviets own, though the Japanese claim it.'

'And that's a map reference for it?'

'Well, could be. I don't know what it could mean otherwise, but I wouldn't be sure without checking.'

'Don't bother. What about the bit below it?'

'The RC-135 is an American electronic spy plane, and there was one in the vicinity when the Korean plane was shot down. Or, rather, there had been some while beforehand. Yes, it's coming back to me now. This is rather pedestrian stuff, I'm afraid. There's been a theory going around that the USA was using the airliner to test out Soviet air defences

173

and so on, and there was an RC-135 which followed the same flight path as the airliner for a few minutes. There's been an article about it.'

'I don't remember it.'

'No, well, it was in the specialist press, though I do seem to recall an article about it in one of the Sundays. There was more coverage of it in the States. Anyway, the dummy bit refers to the theory that the RC-135 was used to sell a dummy to the Russians as cover for the Boeing's mission. Now the distance makes sense, because according to that article the Shuttle's orbit at its closest point was fourteen hundred to two thousand miles from the incident, but Mike seems to be suggesting it might have been closer.'

'What's the connection?'

'The idea is that the Ferret and the Shuttle were used to monitor and control the mission, if that's what it was rather than an unholy, tragic balls-up. And the nineteen sixty-four thing refers to the fact that when the Ferret first went operational the Americans tried something on using military aircraft operating together with the Ferret. They did it twice. The pattern is rather similar – apparently accidental penetrations of Soviet bloc airspace, over East Germany I think. They both got shot down.'

'What's the launch time got to do with it?' asked Fathers.

'The launch time of that particular Shuttle mission was rather odd. And that has suggested to some that it was timed deliberately to coincide with the apparently accidental intrusion of a Korean airliner into Soviet airspace in one of the most strategically sensitive parts of the world. It's where the Soviets have a whole lot of major military bases, and it's also one of the two areas where they concentrate their SSBNs.'

'Their what?'

'Nuclear-powered submarines equipped with nuclear missiles.'

'I see. So does the view that the Korean flight deliberately intruded into Russian airspace seem likely to you?'

'Well, actually I regard the whole thing as a bit fanciful. I always tend to the cock-up theory of history, myself, and there have been reports suggesting that the whole thing was the

174

result of computer failures, which I find credible. But the most convincing parts of the conspiracy theory are, first, that the Americans have done it before, or something similar, and anyway they're always trying sneaky peeks into Soviet air defences, and, second, that the strange launch time is convincingly explained by this theory and not by anything else.'

'But it is all just theory?' asked Fathers.

'Until something more leaks out.'

'Well, let's go on. What does "check cables" mean?'

There was a long silence from the other end of the line.

'Are you still there, Dr Finlay?' asked Fathers.

'Yes, I am. Just pondering, that's all. There are some people, you see, who believe that the US has the ability to tamper with the USSR's undersea communications cables. It has apparently happened before, and I have heard a couple of rumours that it was done this time. Mike's notes seem to mean he was going to try and check up on it.'

'By tampering with the cables, do you mean cutting them?'

'Yes.'

'What would be the point of it?'

'It would force the Soviets to communicate everything by wireless, which makes it possible for the Americans to listen in. And the point of that is that it makes the whole of Soviet communications and activities in that area transparent to eavesdroppers, which of course gives them more data about how the air defence system works, what its weaknesses are, and so on. If it did in fact happen, it would strengthen the theory that the airliner's intrusion was deliberate – strengthen it up to the point of virtual proof, I'd say. But they are just rumours.'

'How about the bit at the very bottom?'

'Yes, I was wondering about that. Let's see. "STS-8" is the Shuttle. "NASA" is NASA – you know, the American space agency.'

'Yes. And what about "NS Adviser"?'

'Could mean the National Security Advisor who did, as it happens, leave his job some six weeks after the Korean incident, and it seems as if Mike, like that article I mentioned, is speculating about whether or not there was a connection.'

'How about this "RR" bit with all the question marks?'

Finlay chuckled. 'Good heavens, Mr Detective, there you are in America with the Presidential election going on all around you, and you can't think of somebody whose two names both begin with the letter "R"?'

Fathers whistled.

'In fact,' said Finlay, 'I rather think "C of C" means Chain of Command, and Mike is speculating about whether it went from the Shuttle right the way to the top. That part is not pedestrian.'

'No, it doesn't seem to be,' said Fathers, comparing his notes of the conversation with his copy of Sampson's jottings. 'You seem to have covered everything, Dr Finlay. Thank you very much.'

'Well, there's a few heroic guesses in there, but it makes a certain kind of sense. There is one thing, though.'

'What's that?'

'Well, actually there's two things. What I was going to say is, do you know when Mike wrote these notes?'

'No.'

'Oh dear.'

'Is it important?'

'Well,' said Finlay, 'it could be. I was just wondering whether Mike had been the source for that article I was telling you about, or whether the article was the source for these notes. Do you see what I mean?'

'Yes. Of course, the author of that article and Dr Sampson could have arrived at the same conclusions independently.'

'That's true.'

'Who wrote the article?'

'The author,' said Finlay, 'is anonymous.'

'Oh?' said Fathers. 'Oh.'

'Well, I see what you're thinking, but frankly I'd be a little doubtful that it was Mike. The editor of the journal it appeared in has sort of described the author, and unless he was telling a total fib, the description is not at all like Mike.'

'Well, I suppose we can find out from the editor.'

'I doubt it. He's resisted all blandishments to name the author so far.'

176

'What did it appear in?'

'A thing called *Defence Attaché*. I can look it up and give the exact reference to your man here if you like.'

'Certainly. You said there were two things. What was the other?'

'I said two, but like Monty Python's Spanish Inquisition, I now mean three. The second one was to say that Mike is not a fanciful person. Or wasn't. Er, I mean he wasn't when I knew him at the college. The very opposite, really. A bit stodgy and politically rather naive – not at all the kind of person who would assume the worst of our great ally. So if he subscribed to a theory that I have so far found fanciful, especially if it reflects badly on the USA, I think I'd probably change my opinion about the theory.'

'I understand, Dr Finlay, and thank you for telling me. You mean you think he was on to something real?'

'Well, removing for a moment all sorts of qualifications, which include saying that nobody really knows what happened with that airliner, the short answer is yes, especially if he went to any trouble to put it all together. Which is why I wondered when he'd written the notes. I mean, if he worked that lot out for himself, it probably took a lot of effort, and he wouldn't invest that much time in something unless he took it seriously. But if he was just making quick notes from somebody else's article, then it didn't take much time or trouble, so it wouldn't necessarily mean he believed it for a second. Do you follow?'

Fathers paused and thought about where he had found the notes and what Rosemary had said about Sampson having some kind of trouble over his work on the Space Shuttle during the spring and summer. 'Yes, absolutely,' he said. 'I follow. What was the third thing, or are there four now?'

'No, still stuck at three. I just wondered if you had found anything else about it in Mike's office. It's not in the paper he may or may not have sent, and which I may or may not have received.

'Oh, isn't it? Thanks. I haven't seen it. I'm told it's classified.'

'Yes,' said Finlay, 'I might have read that on it if I had, in fact, seen it.'

'Which you might or might not have?'

'As you say. Have you found any other references to the airliner incident?'

'No, there's nothing else, but then there wouldn't be.'

'Oh?'

'Everything else of his has been removed. Whoever did it missed this, which was rather well hidden.'

'Good heavens. Well, if he hid it, that probably means he thought it was for real.'

'Yes. That's my own conclusion. I have one last question for you. This article, which I expect I'll see at some point, does it include everything that we've been discussing?'

'Um,' said Finlay and paused. 'I think there are three differences. One, Mike's notes seem to imply he thought the Space Shuttle was, or might have been, closer to the incident – orbiting further north, that is – than the article says, though I think there is something about how the Shuttle might've been closer. If I remember. Two, the article speculates that the chain of command reached up as far as the National Security Adviser, but doesn't imply that Reagan himself was directly involved or in the know. Three, I don't remember it saying anything about the business with the cables.'

'I see,' said Fathers. 'Well, let me say that you have been a great help. I must ask you now to tear up the notes you have made about this conversation and forget all about it.'

'Don't be silly, Mr Fathers. I'm not going to tear them up, and even if I did I could write them out again as soon as your man's gone. I have a very good memory.'

'Now, look, Dr Finlay—' Fathers began.

'And if you think about it,' Finlay cut in, 'you'll see it as being a favour to you. If you think about it.'

Fathers paused and thought. 'All right, Dr Finlay, I suppose I can't do anything about your memory. Thank you very much in any case.'

'You're very welcome, Mr Fathers. Go carefully, now, and watch out for the Blue Meanies.'

Fathers chuckled as he hung up.

★

When Fathers took off his glasses and turned round, Rosemary was sitting up in bed, the covers pulled round her. He looked at her without focus or expression, a frown of concentration gathering on his face. He swivelled in his chair, put his glasses on and began to read through the notes he had made from Finlay's comments. He put his glasses down again, gave a little jerk of his head, as if shaking himself, and stood up, pressing his knuckles into the small of his back.

'We have a lot of ground to cover,' he said. 'I need to go through these notes again and make sense of them, and then we need to talk some more.'

'I'll take a shower,' she said, 'and then we could have breakfast.'

'Mm,' he said, and, ignoring her as she got out of bed, he sat back at his table and his notes.

Rosemary went into the bathroom. As she showered, she thought. Last evening Fathers had insisted on being more business-like than before. They ate a cheaper and quicker meal, then found a quiet bar but drank little. Throughout, Fathers asked her questions. She found it as easy to talk to him in his role as police officer, as she had the previous evening in the role she had designated to him of friend and then lover. His questions were brief, but he drew her into long replies. When she apologised for digressing, he brushed it aside. 'I don't know what the nub of the matter is,' he said, 'so there's no such thing as a digression. What you say in passing might turn out to be what I'm really interested in.'

Thus encouraged, she had rattled on. He was interested, it seemed in three things: in the FBI's interviews with her; in Mike's work and what he said about it; and in John Franklin, the head of the research company. He pressed her especially hard to recall the details of the FBI interviews. She did her best, describing how the two agents – Beck and Weiser – had seemed most interested in her relationship with Michael Sampson and in details of his personal life and habits. But the interviews had occurred when she was most shocked and numbed, and the account she gave to Fathers was, according to her, very incomplete.

He had picked her up from her apartment just after seven

o'clock. By eleven she was nearing mental exhaustion, and just when she was going to say she had had enough, he called an end to it.

'That'll do,' he said, 'for now. I'm sorry about this. What you have to understand is that I'm on an extended fishing expedition. And you're the only person I can go fishing with. I think I've got everything I'm going to from the police here, and Franklin made it pretty clear this afternoon that he doesn't want to give me anything. And since Mike worked pretty much alone, and nobody else at Franklin's place is going to talk either, not with Franklin's permission anyway, that leaves you. I'm sorry to put you through it, but I'm afraid I just have to turn your skull inside out, and hope that something drops out that will throw some light. Do you understand?'

'Sure I do,' she said. 'Has anything lightful dropped out?'

'I think so. I'll have a better idea tomorrow morning after I've made a phone call, assuming the bugger talks.'

'What bugger?'

'A man called Finlay.'

'Oh yes, Mike's old boss. Will he help?'

'Yes,' said Fathers confidently. 'If nothing else, I think it'll tickle his ego to be called from America and asked for his expert advice.'

'What's he going to advise you on?'

'Some notes I found that Mike wrote.'

'But I thought all his notes and everything had been—'

'Not quite all,' he interjected. 'These were hidden, rather cleverly.'

'He did what?' said Rosemary.

'He hid them.'

'Why?' Fathers did not answer. 'Yes,' said Rosemary, 'foolish question – he hid them to hide them. Who from?'

Fathers shrugged. 'It seems,' he said, 'that Mike may not have been quite as naive as you think.'

Thinking of that remark as she towelled herself dry, Rosemary felt the same stab of anger and puzzlement as when he had made it. What was this policeman doing, prying around and finding out more about Mike than she knew herself, changing her picture of

180

him, telling her he was not quite the boy she had taken him for? What was he doing, turning her skull inside out, as he put it, and examining its contents, arranging them in an order which told him something they did not tell her? What right had he to open her up, penetrate her recollections and her emotions, and give them their place in a version of events he was constructing for his own purposes? It was because she had talked more intimately with him than with anybody else recently, and especially because they had made love, that he was able so efficiently and dispassionately to obtain and dissect her memories of months of living and loving with another man. And she had decided then not to let the intimate side of their relationship go any further. They would not make love that night. He could question her all he liked because she wanted the truth of what had happened to Mike Sampson to be discovered – or at least to find out why the truth could not be discovered – but they would return to the roles of detective and witness, not confuse them with friendship and passion.

But as they left the bar and walked into a blessedly cool evening, he had gently taken her arm. He started asking questions again, but they were about her – her work for a public relations company, her background, the college she went to, her involvement with student politics in the era of Kent State and the dawning of the women's movement, her intermittent political activity since, her recurring disillusion with the Democratic Party. And she had felt herself warming to him anew, interspersing her answers with questions about his own politics, about which he said little, and life, about which he talked freely. Then she had asked him more about his work, picking up where they had left off in the restaurant the night before. She drew him into talking about the dilemmas of his profession.

'You begin by looking at everybody as a potential criminal,' he said, 'and anything's justified to get a conviction. But when you not only regard society as essentially lawless, but become lawless yourself, something's going badly wrong. I thought about what you said – that in the arms business, about anybody knowing what honest behaviour is any more.'

'That's long since happened in politics,' said Rosemary. 'And

181

in advertising, too, which is my line of work.'

'I know.'

'Maybe there are no honest corners left any more.'

'Maybe. But there ought to be, there sodding ought to be.'

His mood had been bleak, but also gentle. She changed the subject to keep him from such thoughts. When they reached the point where their ways would part if they were to continue alone to apartment and hotel, and he stopped and faced her and said, 'What do you want to do?' – she had replied, 'I want to be with you.'

'Come on then,' he said, 'we'll go to my place.'

'Mine's nicer.'

'Yes, but mine's where the notes are that I need to make my phone call in the morning.'

She had ignored the intrusion of his investigation into the moment of their closeness, linked her arm through his and walked with him to his hotel room where they undressed, and made love for a long time.

In the bathroom, as she finished drying herself, she pondered on the ambiguity of it. How far does he know, she wondered, that sex together makes me less able to hold things back from his prying policeman's qestions? Does he fuck to feel good or to keep me there as a witness?

She put on one of the bathrobes provided by the hotel and opened the bathroom door. She looked at him as he worked, jotting something down, pausing, writing something more, pausing again in thought. She decided he did know. She hoped there was more to it than that. The feeling of being manipulated was infuriating, yet it added to the excitement of it all and, she told herself, it let her maintain a sense of distance within whatever their relationship was so that when he shortly left for England, as he would, her equilibrium would not be disturbed.

At the table Fathers had written out Sampson's notes again in a single column on a large sheet of paper. Next to each item, he had entered Finlay's interpretation. Finally, he had written three separate words at the bottom of the sheet: 'Distance. Cables. Reagan.' He turned as he heard Rosemary leave the bathroom.

'That was a long shower,' he said.

'I was thinking.'

'Oh?'

'About you.'

'Oh.'

'Don't worry, it was all good, Well, mostly good.'

'You enjoy my interrogation methods, then?'

She smiled and leant over his shoulder to look at his work. He stood up and faced her, resting his hands on her shoulders, deftly placing himself between her and his notes.

'Don't you want me to see?' she asked.

He looked at her seriously for a moment. 'I think it might be better not to,' he said, 'better for you, I mean.'

'The less I know …' she said. He nodded. She put her arms round him and hugged him hard. 'Oh Christ,' she said, 'whatever are we into?'

'Whatever it is, there's no real need to be in it together. Do you understand if I say that there is a level at which it is important that you remain just a witness, whom I would naturally want to question long and comprehensively, and if I want to sleep with you, too, then that may be seen as unprofessional, but can also be seen as just my affair?'

'You don't confide in witnesses, do you?' she asked, standing back.

'Not usually,' he said, 'though it's a rule I'm increasingly breaking in this case.'

'Nor with casual lovers,' she added.

'Not necessarily,' he said.

There was a silence between them which she finally broke. 'I think I understand.'

'It's not between us, that level where you are just a witness,' he said, 'but when I've gone back to England you may find it useful to have a little reality to help the pretence along. If you don't know, you won't have to pretend you don't know, and then it'll be easier to pretend you were just a witness with a bit of sex on the side. If it should come up.'

'Do you think it will?' she asked, hugging him again.

He stroked her strong back gently. 'It's worth bearing in mind.'

'But that's not what it is between us?' she said in a small voice.

He took her head in his hands and lifted it so they looked into each other's eyes. 'No,' he said firmly.

'Places I've seen in the films,' said Fathers. 'Little Italy, Chinatown and Greenwich Village. No museums or art galleries. A walk in a park. A boat ride. And going up a tall building. And, of course, some tawdry souvenirs.'

'Sounds good,' said Rosemary drinking her coffee as they finished breakfast. They had agreed that Fathers would continue with his questions through the day while they wandered round New York being tourists, and she had asked him what he was interested in. 'Do you want the Empire State or the World Trade Center?'

'Which is higher?'

'The Trade Center. But the Empire State's older.'

'Yes, but we're in America,' said Fathers. 'Bigness matters.'

'You said it, buster,' said Rosemary and winked at him out-rageously. 'And they have the tawdriest souvenirs in the world at the top of the Trade Center. What first?'

'Whatever's most convenient,' said Fathers.

'Well, we could wander through the Village, down into Little Italy, on in to Chinatown, have lunch somewhere, take the Staten Island ferry, come straight back, switch across to the Trade Center and come on up back to Central Park. By which time we should both be looking and feeling pretty much like wet rags 'cause it looks like the day's going to be hot and sticky again. Or there's a boat trip right around Manhattan. We could do that, or would you prefer the Staten Island ferry?'

'Oh, definitely the Staten Island ferry,' said Fathers. 'That's where detectives always go for clandestine meetings with low-life characters.'

'Thanks a lot,' said Rosemary. 'If we're going to start with the Village, there's no point starting yet. Got to let it come to life. This is much too early.'

'Oh dear,' said Fathers, drumming his fingers ostentatiously on the table. 'What're we going to do to kill time?'

184

13

Rosemary Willis was a good guide. She had lived in Manhattan since she'd left high school. She and Fathers left the hotel at ten o'clock and caught a bus. 'This is the Village,' she announced as they got off.

The day was hot and humid again, and they walked slowly. At first, Fathers was unimpressed by Greenwich Village. It bustled only in exactly the same way as Camden. 'In the summer,' said Rosemary, 'we'd probably find some street festival on a Saturday, but not this late in the fall.'

'How hot is it in the summer?' sighed Fathers.

'Like this but worse,' she said.

Washington Square, however, Fathers admitted, was lively in a way that was foreign to London. People of all ages and colours were out to play. Children played as they do. Adolescents – and some a little younger or a little older – zipped round and round on roller skates. Three or four people in different corners were doing exercises that Fathers supposed were Oriental; passers-by gave them a respectful berth. Two men and a woman stood in a triangle throwing Indian clubs to each other, watched by a large circle of people who applauded and cheered any spectacular toss and groaned when one of the clubs was dropped. There were tables where several pairs played chess. Some people's play was to sit and watch the activity. Fathers stood and watched dreamily. He took Rosemary's hand sweatily in his and squeezed it. On a street off the Square, she took them to get a cold drink in a café that was strikingly beautiful and cool despite being almost full. 'Here and in San Francisco and nowhere else that I know,' she said, 'you can find places like this.'

They walked south out of the Village, through Little Italy.

'Should be pretty much home from home for you,' said Rosemary, 'all that crime.'

Fathers grunted and looked up and down the street lined with small shops and restaurants.

Rosemary wanted to know why known crime rackets were allowed to flourish. They talked a little about corruption and power. She wanted to know if it happened in London.

'Course it bloody does,' said Fathers glancing away from her.

'Well, why do *you* let it go on?' she asked pointedly. 'You're in the Serious Crimes Squad, aren't you?'

Fathers began to turn stiff and defensive. 'We don't *let* it go on,' he said as she pressed him more. She softened her manner slightly but carried on.

'The truth is,' said Fathers eventually with a sigh, 'that the police actually have to sanction a lot of crime.'

'You mean, like corruption?' asked Rosemary. 'Why do you have to?'

'No, I don't mean corruption at all. Not in the ordinary sense anyway. Not that it doesn't happen, of course, but I'm talking about coppers who by their own lights are honest. What do I mean, their own lights? By our lights. I do it too.'

'Do what?'

'Oh, we let a lot of crime go by without a whisper in exchange for information on a crime we're really interested in.'

'That is bad,' said Rosemary.

'The police couldn't function without it. Information received is the commonest way of getting leads and finally convictions. And to get information you usually have to trade – sometimes money, sometimes a blind eye.'

'And that's not corruption?' asked Rosemary indignantly.

'Yes, in a sense, I suppose it is. But what would you rather – convict the man who trades dodgy motors and let the protection racket keep going, or put the thugs inside and leave him to flog his wares?'

'Tough play to call,' she said. 'Why can't you put them both inside?'

'Because,' said Fathers patiently, 'we'd only get the dodgy motor man. It's a matter of priorities. It's not perfect, but it's not real corruption. I can tell you about that if you like.' But he walked quickly on and showed no sign of wanting to tell her. She let it go.

They left Little Italy and walked into Chinatown. As they went in and out of one fascinating small shop after another, Fathers asked, 'Why are Chinatowns so magical?'

'Is the London one like this?'

'On a smaller scale, but the same kind of thing. I was thinking of the films, too.'

'Well,' she said, 'this is really how it is.'

They had lunch standing at a street stall that sold Chinese delicacies. Fathers accepted Rosemary's advice about what to eat. It was all delicious. They strolled on.

'Courage, man,' she said, 'only a little further and you'll be in the heart of corporate America, and a little ways after that it's the ferry.'

Fathers nodded and looked over his shoulder.

The walk from Chinatown through the Wall Street area to the ferry was longer than Rosemary had made out. As they waited tiredly on a wooden bench in the terminal Fathers gently returned to the business they had agreed to intermingle with the pleasure.

'Ohh,' Rosemary said, and smiled at him a little sadly.

'I know,' he said, 'but ...'

'I know,' she said. 'But.'

He nodded agreement. 'But,' he said. 'But, but, sodding but.'

She smiled and rested her cheek on his shoulder. As he put his arm around her, she looked up and kissed the corner of his mouth. He smiled and kissed her perspiring forehead. She put up a hand to hold his head still and kissed him gently on the mouth.

'Go on,' she said. 'I told you last night that I understand.'

Fathers looked into her eyes for a moment and nodded. 'I realise,' he said, 'that Mike did his actual research alone. He doesn't even seem to have had a research assistant at Franklin's, only a secretary.'

'That's right.'

'Did that bother him?'

'No, I don't think so, not that he ever said. You see, Franklin's is set up so that he got a lot of the assistance he needed without having to have an assistant all of his own. I mean, they have people there who provide the kind of help that a librarian would, and if he needed any calculations done that were beyond his scope, they'd either be done by somebody on the staff or they might even contract it out if it were a big enough job. But it was always possible that Mike would work on a project where he would have one, two, or even three assistants. In a way, it's no big thing to have a research assistant or not to have one.'

'But who did he talk about his work with, who did he work out ideas and discuss problems with, or did he just keep it all to himself?'

'Oh no,' said Rosemary. 'Hey, ferry's in.'

On the deck of the ferry there was almost a hint of what might have been a breeze. Fathers leaned with his back against the rail, Rosemary standing beside him facing out over the water with both hands clasping the rail. 'He didn't keep it all to himself?' prompted Fathers looking up and down the boat at the other passengers.

'No,' said Rosemary. 'There's a system at Franklin's where they have weekly discussions about this or that person's research. Whoever's turn it is presents a paper and they all discuss it. I think the idea is to go round in fairly strict rotation among the staff researchers.'

'Does everybody go to every discussion?'

'Well, I think that's quite strictly controlled. Of course, Mike was a Vice-President of the company and that meant he could go to every one he wanted to, though I don't think that was all of them. But I remember him saying about somebody being mad because he'd been kept out of one of the sessions. I forget who. Look, that's Ellis Island.'

Fathers turned round. 'Where the immigrants went when they first landed?'

'Not all the immigrants, fella, not the ones who had means and money, just the poor ones. First sight of the land of the free was to be treated like prisoners. Literally.'

Fathers turned his back on Ellis Island. 'Why was he kept out? Or was it a she?'

'It was a he. They all are. I'm not sure, really. I guess it could've been for security reasons, you know? But maybe something else. And there's old Liberty, but you get a better view from the Trade Center.'

Fathers looked but could barely see the Statue of Liberty through the haze. It looked very green.

'They have some sort of – I don't know, code of conduct is too strong a word,' said Rosemary, 'but a kind of accepted practice that people who make presentations at these sessions keep off extremely sensitive areas. They've all got some sort of security clearance, of course, or they couldn't do the work at all, but they seem to pride themselves on taking security very seriously and being careful not to talk out of turn. I remember Mike talking about it once before he was going to do a presentation, sometime during the summer, saying how difficult it was to know what to leave out and still make it interesting.'

Rosemary stopped abruptly and concentrated on something far out across the water. Fathers stopped looking up and down the boat and turned towards her. He put his hand over one of hers and she picked it up and rested her cheek on it for a second.

'And then, of course,' she said, 'he'd talk with John Franklin.'

'And argue about it.'

'During the summer, yes. Not before, I don't think, not seriously anyway. Is there a reason why you're looking everybody up and down or are you just interested in people?'

He smiled at her vaguely. 'Is there anything to see on Staten Island?' he asked.

'If you go a fair ways there's woods and things,' she said, 'but right round the terminal, nothing at all.'

'So we might as well come straight back?'

'Sure.'

'Fine,' he said. 'Let's go up the front of the boat and watch ourselves coming in.'

'OK.'

They found an empty spot on the rail near the bows, but there were too many people around for Fathers to feel happy pressing on with the questions. He stood with his back to the rail again and watched the other passengers.

'Real corruption,' said Rosemary.

189

'What?'

'You were going to tell me about real corruption if I liked, which I do, so shoot.'

'You're fascinated by all this aren't you?'

'Better believe it. Come on, give.'

He told her about a detective he had known. 'He began like I told you,' he said, 'getting information and turning a blind eye in return. Standard stuff.'

'Sure. Standard.'

'Then he developed it a bit. In return for the old blind eye, he got information and money.'

'Blackmail.'

'True enough. He got a lot of convictions, got promoted and made a load of money on the side.'

'What happened to him?'

'Oh, the next stage was he started to rook the insurance companies on a few large thefts, pretending the information he'd got didn't come from the blackmail side of the game, but from some other citizen, with whom he'd then split the reward. He raked it in. Got caught in the end and did a stretch. Had a rotten time inside, of course. I think he lives somewhere in the Caribbean now, so he must have put a lot to one side. It was a real shame – he was a good policeman before he turned, nice bloke too.'

'How did he get caught?'

'Grass.' Rosemary looked at him blankly. 'Someone told on him,' he explained.

'Who did that?'

'Somebody who got fed up with it.'

'One of his blackmail victims?'

'Well, they weren't really victims. Bent as corkscrews, the lot of them. No, it was someone he was doing for a major theft who was so outraged that he took another detective to one side, and that was that. Of course, he was lucky. Some coppers he could've chosen wouldn't've taken it any further.'

'But this one did?'

'All the way.'

Rosemary contemplated for a moment. 'It must mean you can't trust anybody you work with, if you know that kind of thing could be going down.'

'No,' Fathers said, 'it's not like that. But there's an awful lot of temptation lying around, so it's always worth keeping an eye open.' He lapsed into silence, looking round the crowd.

'Did you ask John Franklin about Mike's rows with him?' asked Rosemary suddenly.

'No. I was going to but he pre-empted me by saying how well they got on, and how smoothly Mike's work had been going.'

'That's just not true,' she said.

'I know.'

'But I mean he's lying to you.'

'Yes,' said Fathers, 'lots of people do. It goes with the job.'

'What a job. Can you tell when people are lying to you?'

'Often. Not always, but often.'

When the ferry had docked, Rosemary wanted to stay on board. But Fathers insisted on leaving in the crowd, waiting in the terminal for a few minutes and then getting back on. 'It's the same ferry,' said Rosemary.

'Yes,' said Fathers, 'but I want to say I've been on Staten Island.'

'Sure. How do you like the place?'

'Oh, lovely, lots of atmosphere.'

They found an unoccupied patch of rail. As before, Rosemary looked out over the water, and Fathers faced the other way and let his gaze fall on the passengers.

'What did it mean to be a Vice-President?' he asked.

'Do you know, I never really asked about that. John Franklin told me at some cocktail party that he'd met Mike once and then seen his work, or some of it, and asked a couple of people in England about him, and then invited him to join the company. Mike never said so, but John thought he was rather reluctant to leave England, so he made the Vice-President offer to tempt him. There are three of them, and they have some administrative

191

responsibilities as well as doing research. Exactly what Mike's were, I don't really know. He never talked about them much, except sometimes to complain they were getting in the way of his research. That's what he was really interested in, what he talked about all the time.'

'Did any power come along with the title?'

Rosemary reflected for a moment. 'I don't think so. Responsibility, yes, and also a higher salary than the regular researchers, or than most of them anyway. But I think the company's small enough that all the real power of decision rests with John alone. I mean, there's only about twenty or thirty staff all told.'

Fathers nodded thoughtfully. 'That's what I assumed,' he said. 'I suppose that would be the power of hiring and firing and deciding company policy, what research contracts to go for and so on.'

'Yes, doing the negotiations with the Pentagon, or the foundations, or the companies who fund the research. Deciding what research proposals to put in and so on. Also, John is the one who keeps his eyes and ears open to see what the best field is to be in at any time. He has very good contacts, so everyone says.'

'Did Mike ever talk about why he came to New York?'

'Oh yes, a whole lot. He never seemed real miserable about not being in London, but I guess it was quite a wrench for him, though he did once say the States is where the action is, and London's where it isn't.'

'It's also where the money is.'

'Especially in this field, especially since Reagan was elected. But money wasn't so important to Mike. I mean, he liked to live reasonably well, of course, like anybody, but he wasn't extravagant. He'd go out to eat lots, and in nice places too, and we used to go to the shows and keep up with the movies, but he wasn't one to live in the fast lane, you know? He dressed appallingly left to his own devices, not like you. Or are your clothes the result of your wife's taste?'

Fathers smiled. 'No, all my own idea. So did you dictate Mike's wardrobe to him?'

'Not dictate,' said Rosemary, 'but I encouraged him along the right lines, like dragging him by the ear into good stores every now and again.'

'So perhaps John Franklin was wrong to think that the Vice-President thing tempted Mike to New York when he was reluctant?'

'Well, that could be. At least, I'm not sure the extra money would have had anything to do with it. But Mike was always very pleased with the idea that he was a Veep, you know? I mean, the image of being a Vice-President before he was thirty. Not that he was really vain about it, but like when he introduced himself to people he'd always say he was Vice-President of Franklin Research Associates. So he might have been a bit tempted by the status, although I do think the research it opened up for him was the main factor.'

'Did he miss London? The place, friends, whatever?'

'Not seriously. He always talked quite happily about his time there, but I didn't get the impression it broke his heart to leave. He could get pretty irritable about America, in a cultural sense, if you know what I mean, but when he calmed down he'd usually add some compensating remark about something in London that used to get him down. But those things weren't to do with work but with, you know, life in general, different ways of doing things.'

'Such as?'

'Oh, he hated American television and always said the only good shows were the British ones on the PBS – the non-commercial station. And he'd get mad at the news whenever he watched it and complain about how parochial it was and how bad the newspapers are at covering foreign news. And he used to say how much less helpful people are in New York if you're looking for somewhere, compared to London. And there'd be little things – like he'd get pissed when somebody in a shop or something didn't understand his English accent. But, you know, none of these things were important to him. It's not like he pined for home.'

'How about people? Anybody he particularly missed?'

'Not that I recall. It's interesting, because in a lot of ways he was a real social animal over here. He used to accept just about every cocktail or dinner invitation that came his way, for instance, but I sort of got the impression he hadn't had very many real friends in London. One thing he said several times was that one of the good things about moving to a new place is you leave everything behind you and start with a clean sheet.'

'That sounds as if he was rather unhappy in London,' Fathers said.

'Not really, not the way he put it. If you want to know, I think what he meant was more to do with what kind of person you're seen to be by the people around you. And there comes a time – I know because I felt like this when I came here to go to school – college, I mean, not high school – there comes a time when you feel you've outgrown what you used to be and you want to behave like a different person, but all the people round you think you're still how you were and it makes it hard for you to change. Do you know what I mean?'

'I think so.'

'The way you are sets up patterns of particular responses in other people, and they keep responding the same way even when you've changed internally. It's a bit like with parents who think you're still their little girl in braces when you're snorting cocaine every night and changing your lover every second Tuesday. Begging your pardon, Mr Policeman.'

'Snorting cocaine every night,' said Fathers, 'is very silly. Changing lovers every fortnight – well, that depends on circumstance.'

'But you know what I mean.'

'Yes, I know what you mean. Doesn't everybody? But he missed Finlay, didn't he? You said he looked on him as some kind of father figure.'

'Yes, he did, to some extent. But I don't think he missed him as such. They weren't really friends. Mike respected him a lot and thought he was really clever and so on, but I don't think they were close, and I know from what Mike said that they didn't agree about politics.'

'Finlay thinks he was politically naive.'

194

'He's right. And I have the idea that he used to let Mike know that at every conceivable opportunity. In fact, I think Mike found him a bit suffocating, you know? One part of him was quite glad to get out from under.'

'Did you and Mike talk politics much?' asked Fathers.

'Some, not a lot.'

'What were his attitudes? What did he think about the President, for instance?'

'I think he was mainly baffled by him and his appeal. But then, so many of us are. Mike would've voted Social Democrat in last year's election in Britain, he told me. He said the Labour Party was a scrap-heap and the Conservatives were wrecking the country. I guess he'd vote Democrat in America, though he was always confused by the party system over here.'

'It seems very different from in Britain.'

'Oh, totally, as far as I can understand.'

'And what did he think about Reagan's policies, as opposed to the man?'

'He didn't understand economics, so he said, but he used to comment on how badly poor people get treated in the US, so I guess he favoured expanding the welfare system. But on foreign policy and the military and so on – I don't know, he was odd. Maybe because it was what he worked on and everything, but it was very hard to pin him down, even when he'd had a few drinks, to saying it was good or bad. He could talk for ever about the problems in the policy, and he could list the good points and the bad, the contradictions and inconsistencies, but he'd never come right out and say it was a bunch of shit. For everything he found wrong with it, he'd find another thing right. And he never showed much sympathy for any foreign policy critic, whether it was something somebody had written, or an expert appearing on television. Whatever they said, you could be sure he'd find something wrong with it. And if it was someone supporting the policy, he'd find something wrong with them, too. It's not that he had no views – he had lots of them, but no conclusions, that's all.'

★

195

They took a cab from the ferry terminal. Fathers spent most of the short drive looking out of the back window commenting on buildings they had just passed. Not till the journey was almost completed did he grunt with satisfaction and turn round in his seat. At the World Trade Center the lift shot them to the top floor and they climbed the steps up onto the roof. Rosemary walked over to the parapet and leaned on it. 'Oh, it's not such a clear view as you can get sometimes, but even so,' she said. 'Hey, what are you doing standing back there?'

Fathers walked gingerly over to join her and stood stiffly. 'Look,' said Rosemary, 'right over there, that's the ocean. And if we go round this way you can have a look at the Statue of Liberty through one of the telescopes if you want. Hey, is anything wrong?'

'We can look at it from behind several inches of plate glass on the floor below,' said Fathers, 'and I think I'd prefer that.'

'But it's much cooler here, probably the coolest place in the city today.'

'But we don't have to stand by the parapet to feel the breeze.'

She looked at him and took his hand to lead him away from the parapet. 'Don't you like heights?'

He grinned bashfully. 'It makes my stomach turn over to stand there,' he said, 'or even just to see somebody else standing there.'

'Yeah, I get that feeling too, sometimes. Do you get it always?'

'Pretty much, yes. Ever since I saw somebody jump.'

'Oh Christ,' she said, 'if you're going to talk like that, let's go downstairs this minute.'

They looked down on Manhattan and its surrounding areas through the plate glass for half an hour, and then went to the café. They took cold drinks to a table and sat sipping in pleasant silence.

'I'm glad you don't like heights,' Rosemary said finally.

'Makes me seem more human, eh?'

'Oh, Inspector, I think I know you're human all right,' she smiled.

'So it gives you pleasure to think of me suffering,' he suggested.

'No, smartass, it's just that – well, you come over so strong and capable and unflawed that it's kind of nice to know you have a weakness.'

'Ah, if only you knew the whimpering me that hides inside this tough shell.'

'Yeah, well, let's not go overboard on this.' She leaned over the table to whisper, 'What say we go back to my apartment and fuck?'

He let out a roar of laughter. She pretended to be aggrieved. 'I'm sorry,' he said, 'it's just that I was thinking about starting in on some more questions.'

'Oh,' she said. 'I thought maybe you'd finished.'

'Fraid not.'

'OK, shoot.'

'Well,' said Fathers, 'I wanted to go back to something I asked before, about people Mike might have talked with about his work. I got the impression from Finlay that people working in this sort of field keep in contact with each other and maybe chat things over quite a lot. I was wondering if there was anybody Mike did that with, not necessarily people he actually worked with at Franklin's, other people.'

'Oh yeah, I see what you mean. Actually, Mike was sometimes quite pompous about it. He used to refer to what he called the research community as if it was some holy band of brothers. And he was always zipping down to Washington, especially since the spring, I guess.'

'Did you meet any of them?'

'Oh, there were various people who passed through, and I met one or two of them, though only briefly. I remember a really nice Australian, but I don't think Mike liked him much. There's also a guy called Bradley Waddup in Washington. He's a Congressional staffer. I've known him some time. I introduced them, in fact – at least, I gave Mike Bradley's name and number and suggested he call him up when he was down in DC. Now I think about it, it was soon after Mike met him I first realised that he was having trouble at work over this Shuttle thing. Oh, and Mike told me about a guy who he said really reminded him of Paul Finlay. Now what was his name? Mike met him at some seminar or other

I think, quite some time ago now. Ted something.'

'How did he remind him of Finlay?'

'Um, Mike just said he reminded him, that's all. I think it was his manner, or his attitude. Yes, it was something he said that when Mike told me, he said was typical of Finlay. I don't recall it, though. It's kind of there, but it's like a joke you can't remember the punchline to, and since I don't know Finlay it was lost on me. But Mike seemed quite struck by it. I know, Mike said something about that guy, Ted whatever, having a reputation as somebody who had lots of lines into the Pentagon. Apparently he used to be involved in a lot of whistle-blowing, though not so much recently, so Mike said.'

Fathers looked at her uncomprehendingly.

'You know,' she said, 'blowing the whistle, spilling the beans, letting the cat out of the bag.'

'I know now,' he said. 'But you can't remember his second name?'

'Mmm, it'll come to me, it'll come.'

'Anybody else?'

'Yes, a guy who worked in a company exactly like Franklin's but doing more technical work, rather than the policy stuff that Mike was involved in. He worked for what Mike used to call a Beltway Bandit.'

'I know what that means,' said Fathers.

'And his name,' said Rosemary slowly, 'is Simon Goldsack. Yes, that's right.'

'And Mike went to see these people a lot, did he?'

'Well, he went to Washington a lot this year, a couple of nights almost every week for several months, I guess, through the spring and summer. I don't know that he always went to see them, and there were others as well. I think he went to the Pentagon a fair amount, and there was a guy who he'd known for quite a long time who works at one of the very big research institutions – but I don't think he works in Mike's field, more sort of arms control from what he said. David Gay, I think. And you know, the thing is that at various places Mike would really meet quite a lot of people and he'd look them up from time to time.

There was another Congressional assistant he saw quite often, but I didn't know him.'

'And does the first one you mentioned, Bradley Wadham – is that his name? – does he work on the Space Shuttle?'

'Waddup. Yes, something like that, and this Simon Goldsack as well. Both in the holy band. But I don't know exactly what they do, except that the second one, Goldsack, is more technical. It's not much help, is it?'

'You never know. Can you think of any other names?' Rosemary shook her head. Fathers finished his drink. 'Let's take a look at the souvenirs, then,' he said. 'I think you recommended them as the most tawdry available.'

Rosemary had not misled him, and they had fun picking our T-shirts and pencil cases for his two children and a paperweight for his wife. Fathers was interested that he felt no twinge of guilt or even ambivalence making these purchases with Rosemary. She revealed nothing either, and he wondered if she were merely hiding it or if she really felt nothing. It was, in its way, a very sharp reminder of how short a time he would be in the USA. As he queued to pay, he wondered how he would think about this affair when he was back home, and wondered about the nature of what he felt about her. As they walked to the lift he put his arm round her shoulders, and she smiled with pleasure and rested her hand on his.

'Gullick,' she said suddenly. 'Ted Gullick.'

'The man with the whistle?'

'Ted Gullick,' she said again. 'I knew it would come to me.'

'Good girl,' said Fathers and patted her bottom. 'Er, were you serious back there?'

'About my apartment?'

'Mmm.'

'As serious as a good girl can be.'

14

Sunday, 28 October, was another hot and sticky day. The Fahrenheit temperature in Manhattan was in the seventies; the humidity was ninety-five per cent. It was the day of the New York marathon, thousands of runners pounding and padding and struggling across hot tarmac. Many collapsed from the heat and the effort: one died.

Harry Fathers, in clothes as light and as casual as he could manage from the limited range he had brought to New York, went out to Long Island to Captain Amstel's weekend and holiday house. He was surprised at how long the train journey was, how far out of the city it took him. He had not realised how long Long Island is.

What Captain Amstel had described as a 'cabin' was a pleasant, four-bedroomed, wooden house on two floors. A large garden at the back ran down to a road on the other side of which was a slope to the beach. The sea, but not the beach, was visible from the house. Fathers was met at the station by Captain Amstel in a car. As they drove, the captain explained that there were more guests than he had first said. As well as his own family, there would be Lieutenant Grolsch and his family, Labbat from the District Attorney's Office and his wife, and Sergeant Miller and his girlfriend. When they got to the house it was close to noon. All the others had arrived and were drinking together on the good-sized terrace. Fathers, like the other men, accepted a very cold beer.

Fathers soon realised he was in for a teeth-grittingly excruciating time. Although they were out of doors, with five children of various ages from seven to eighteen present and everybody dressed casually (with Amstel the most casual in shorts and T-shirt) the mixture of apparent bonhomie and strain was familiar to Fathers from more formal occasions with colleagues – juniors and superiors – from the Yard. Amstel ('Please, Harry, call me

Pete'), the most senior as well as the host, was also the most boisterous, serving drinks and making jokes at which everybody laughed to different degrees. His wife ('Hi, Harry, I'm Jerry') popped in and out of the house in her floral print dress, bringing out the food and plates. When she had brought it all out, the captain took over and started to barbecue steaks. Miller, in jeans, was restrained – quite unlike his manner in Grolsch's office the morning Fathers had first met him and the others. His girl-friend ('And this is, er, Wanda, is that right?'), who looked a few years younger than he, and who, wearing shorts and a halter top, was the most scantily dressed of the party except the children, sat primly quiet for the most part, occasionally sipping her cocktail at Amstel's urging and smiling wanly at the remarks he passed at or about her each time his wife went back into the house. Grolsch sat drinking in a chair, looking hot, occasionally returning Amstel's banter, while his wife opted entirely out of the adult party and went to play down in the garden with the youngest two children. Frank Labbat, in a striped shirt and white slacks, and his wife, Eileen, elegantly if casually dressed with a patrician look to her face and carriage, stood together on the edge of the terrace looking out at the sea, appearing sociable and friendly, chuckling occasionally, but taking no larger part in the gathering.

On behalf of all of them, as well as for himself, Fathers felt uncomfortable and embarrassed. He had no small talk to initiate since he knew nothing about any of them, except what little he knew of them professionally. Pete Amstel had begun by banning any discussion of work, and he was not eager, in any case, to discuss his own investigation, though he assumed that was the point of this get-together and would follow at some point. So he limited himself to replying in brief and general terms to the pleasantries Pete or Jerry Amstel tossed in his direction about how he was liking New York and wasn't it very different from London?

The problem of small talk seemed serious. Talking shop was out, and neither Pete nor Jerry Amstel had anything to say about films or the theatre. Pete filled in some time collecting, noting down and checking how each person wanted his or her steak cooked, but his supply of jokes was apparently not endless, and once his wife had brought all the food out and permanently joined them he refrained from making more remarks about Wanda. Politics provided no refuge. When Jerry responded to a comment from Grolsch by declaring her intention to vote for President Reagan and her belief that everybody there would do likewise, Eileen Labbat's mouth tightened and her eyebrows flickered in an unmistakable statement that she would be voting for Mondale, while her husband coughed and looked away at the tree tops as if he might have seen a rare bird coming to perch. Jerry's attempt to cover up the moment of tension consisted of passing the ball to Fathers by asking what the British thought about the President, but he managed to dispose of it by saying that he didn't follow American politics. It was Miller who provided a safe topic by denigrating the chances of the New York Knicks in the coming basketball season. He even managed to draw Labbat into the conversation, but the women and Fathers were excluded from it by disinterest and ignorance. Like many gatherings of people drawn together only because some of them worked together, it was an uncomfortably mismatched group and Fathers' respect for Miller rose at his ability to find common ground among any of them. When basketball was exhausted, Miller turned effortlessly to football. Fathers toyed with his beer, feeling very English and withdrawn, but enjoying the slight breeze as a welcome relief from the city's heat.

Amstel managed the barbecue efficiently, his wife fetched garlic bread and the children and Mrs Grolsch were recalled to eat. The steaks were expertly cooked according to each person's taste and the salad was crisp. To drink there was cold red wine or beer. Afterwards there was ice-cream and fresh fruit salad followed by coffee, and Amstel brought out cigars. The women and children took the plates, cutlery and glasses indoors to load the dishwasher, and the men were left to themselves on the terrace.

'Well, Harry,' said Amstel, 'this is really a social occasion, and it seems a shame to spoil it by talking about business, but I guess since we're all here we might as well take the opportunity to review things a bit, huh?'

The moment had come. Fathers waved his cigar in vague assent and got up to look for an ashtray.

'What do you say, Frank?' asked Amstel.

'Easier than fixing up a special meeting tomorrow or the next day,' replied Labbat.

'How's it going then, Harry?' asked Grolsch.

'Do you have an ashtray?'

'I'll get it,' said Miller and went inside. Fathers smiled and stood silently until Miller returned, with the ashtray, but also with Wanda, who was explaining that they were going to take the younger children down to the beach and asking if any of the men wanted to join them.

'Oh leave them to it, honey,' said Jerry Amstel emerging onto the terrace. 'When the men light up the cigars, it's time for the women to withdraw discreetly. Isn't that how you do it in England, Harry?'

'In the last century,' replied Fathers, unable to contain himself.

'Sure,' said Jerry unabashed, 'sure, in style. C'mon, honey, we'll get the kids together and we'll leave them to it, whatever it is.'

'I think,' said the captain when the two women had gone, 'that we might find it easier if we went indoors. This is kind of a major intersection when the beach party is getting its act together.'

The men filed indoors bearing coffee cups, cigars and, in Grolsch's case, a fresh glass of beer. Amstel showed them into a large dining room and they sat down around the table. Noises of children being harried into getting ready for the beach intruded through the closed doors of the room and the open windows.

'Well, Harry,' said Amstel, 'I guess we're waiting on you.'

'I'm not sure there's much to wait for,' said Fathers. 'I've gone over things a bit, but I don't have any better idea than you as to what happened to Dr Sampson, unless anything has broken your end?' He looked at Grolsch and Miller.

'No,' said Grolsch, 'but I guess we're pretty tied up with our serial killer. We're keeping our eyes open, of course, but nothing yet.'

'What does that mean?' asked Fathers. 'Keeping your eyes open?'

'Checking the John Does in the morgue, mostly, and looking out for names on the inter-state reports,' said Grolsch wearily.

'I think, Harry,' said Labbat, 'that you can take it you would have been informed immediately if Homicide had discovered anything.'

'Of course,' said Fathers.

'In fact,' Labbat continued, 'it's really you we're looking to hear something from.'

'Nothing to report really,' said Fathers.

'But you've been keeping busy,' Labbat pressed.

'Oh yes,' said Fathers. 'I've read all the reports, all the available reports, and I've been to see John Franklin, and I've spent quite a bit of time with Rosemary Willis trying to see if I can dredge up anything which would give a bit of a lead. And I've reported back to London, which is to say I've told them what I'm telling you: that I've looked around but haven't made any progress finding out what happened to Dr Sampson, except that we assume that, dead or alive, he has disappeared pretty much for good.'

'You went to the precinct, too,' said Labbat.

'As I said to you at lunch the other day.'

'Sure, but you said you had no luck there.'

'None.'

'You talked to Detective Zberg.'

'Yes. Chaotic fellow, isn't he?'

'I talked to him, too,' said Labbat.

'Oh really?'

'Yes, really. I talked to him after we had lunch together, after you had asked me to give you a copy of the precinct's request for assistance.'

'Yes,' said Fathers. 'You said you'd dig a copy out of your files. Did you?'

'And he told me that he gave you a copy and you took a xerox of it.'

Fathers paused and shook his head thoughtfully. 'He thought he did, and I thought he did, but when I looked at it after we'd photocopied it, it was the wrong one, something I'd already seen.'

Labbat looked at Fathers in silence. Fathers could feel the tension in the other three as they watched the exchange. 'You told Sergeant Coors you didn't get it, but you didn't go back and ask Zberg for the right one?' asked Labbat finally.

'No,' said Fathers.

'I'm surprised you didn't,' said Labbat.

'Why? I checked through his folder, thought I had what I wanted, but I was wrong, it wasn't there. Or do you mean it was there?'

'I'm not sure, Harry,' said Labbat, 'that you're entirely levelling on this.'

'What a shame,' said Fathers.

'It sure as hell is a fucking shame,' said Labbat raising his voice. Fathers wondered if Labbat would slam his fist on the table, but instead he stood up, continuing in his louder voice, 'It's a fucking great shame that you have such a bullshit story that it is fucking obvious you are not playing straight.'

Fathers leaned across the table and spoke so quietly that the others had to strain and lean forward themselves to hear him. 'Is this your court-room manner, Mr Labbat? It might impress some people, I suppose, but I think you're making a fool of yourself.'

'Now, Harry, Frank, please,' said Amstel placatingly.

'Hard man, soft man, is it?' asked Fathers sneeringly.

'Please, Harry,' objected Amstel, but Fathers interrupted him.

'You're making me think, Mr Labbat, that there's something special about this particular document, that it has been lost all over the place accidentally on purpose, that the promise we received of full cooperation is not being fulfilled. Is that right? Is there some reason why you're so upset to think I might have seen it?'

Labbat opened his mouth to reply but Amstel raised his hand and cut him off. 'I'm sure, Harry, that that is not what is getting

205

Frank a little heated. Because, as you say, full cooperation was promised, and full cooperation is what you got, as I hope you'll make a point of reporting to your superiors back home. But there is, let me put it like this, a seeming inconsistency between, on the one hand, the fact that you wanted to see that document and were asking all round about it and, on the other, the way you didn't go back and press Zberg for the right document when, as you say, you took the wrong one. Especially because, if you'll let me say this, we've all been mighty impressed by your attention to detail as you've gone through this material. Do you see the point?'

Fathers did indeed see the point. It was the kind of small but glaring inconsistency on the basis of which he had on many occasions so pressured suspects that they had ended up signing their confessions.

'Well, well,' he said, '*mea culpa*, I suppose. He seemed very busy, and I've been very aware that I'm trading on the goodwill of people who, especially at the precinct, as Captain Molson made all too clear to me, are not particularly interested in this case any more. For reasons which I can thoroughly understand, I assure you, and I wouldn't dream of bringing it up in my report. I do think you're making a little much of it, unless there is some reason why you wouldn't want me to see the document.'

'Zberg says he gave it you,' said Labbat forcefully.

'Frank!' snapped Amstel with a crackle of authority that so contrasted with his earlier goonish sociability that Fathers felt a shiver of alertness down his spine. He would have to be more on his guard with Amstel than Labbat.

At Amstel's voice Labbat turned away from the table and went to look out of the window, watching the women and children saunter down the garden on their way to the beach.

'Look,' said Amstel, 'let's just clear the air a bit by going over it again.'

'No,' said Fathers, 'let's not do that.'

Amstel looked at him in surprise. Fathers could feel Amstel testing and searching him out, looking for the right strategy to respond, like a chess opponent considering an unexpected gambit.

206

'After all,' said Amstel playing for time, 'there is Frank's point that Zberg told him he gave you the precinct's request for our assistance.'

'It's quite irrelevant,' said Fathers trading on the degree of social nicety that Amstel had reintroduced when he took over from Labbat, 'and you know it is. Frank has promised to dig out of his files a copy of the offending document, which I'm sure will prove to contain nothing that isn't repeated several times in the reports I've already seen. And then it won't matter whether you think I was slack not to keep on badgering poor Detective Zberg or whether you think that slackness was atypical of me, grateful as I am for your kind comment, Pete. Anyway, talking of slackness, I'd be surprised if you couldn't accept at least the possibility that Zberg was mistaken about what document he xeroxed for me, not that I want to put him down in any way.'

'He was pretty certain,' said Amstel, and Fathers knew he had spotted the weak point in their case just as accurately as they had identified the inconsistency in his.

'Actually,' said Fathers, 'he didn't see it. He was with some-body – a suspect, witness, informer, I don't know. Somebody. He was called out and shouted at by the formidable sergeant they have down there. He grabbed a folder out of a pile in his drawer. He thought he'd found the right thing. I thought so, too. He copied it, gave me the copy and got back to his whoever-she-was as fast as he could without looking at it. Go and look at Zberg's desk for thirty seconds, and then come back and tell me he couldn't have made an honest mistake.'

'Anyone can make an honest mistake,' said Grolsch. Amstel looked at the lieutenant speculatively.

'Especially Detective Zberg,' said Miller, thus encouraged.

'Anyway,' said Fathers, 'if Zberg thinks he gave it to me, that presumably means he's got it, or thinks he's got it, in which case, just to keep up my reputation for attention to detail, I can always go back and ask him for it again. How would that do? Then Frank wouldn't have to bother himself with it – unless Zberg hasn't got it, of course.'

207

There was a silence. Labbat still looked out of the window, although the beach party had gone. Grolsch and Miller exchanged a glance and a shrug. Fathers relit his cigar. It was Amstel who broke the silence before it became too strained.

'Well, Harry, maybe you have a point. I'm sure if you look at it from my point of view you'll be able to see the inconsistency there, but never mind. We seem to have reached some kind of impasse.'

'So we do,' said Fathers cheerfully. 'Of course, there are one or two questions still hanging, but I think I can survive without pressing them. One thing, though. Where's Agent Weiser these days? I've been wanting to talk to him, but I can't seem to get hold of him.'

Amstel, Grolsch and Miller looked at each other almost theatrically and exchanged more shrugs.

'No?' said Fathers, still cheerfully. 'Well, never mind. Do you mind if I get some air?'

He left the room and went and stood on the terrace where he was joined in a few minutes by Miller.

'What a horse's ass,' said Miller with a chuckle. 'You do have that document, don't you?'

Fathers looked at him, smiled and shook his head. 'It sounds like I ought to,' he said. 'What's in it – the truth about the sinking of the *Belgrano*?'

'Huh?'

'Never mind. Never mind.'

'Why do you want to see Weiser, anyway? Haven't you had enough of the back-end of horses?'

'Oh, I've never had enough of them,' said Fathers. 'I just wanted to know why he's having me followed, that's all.'

'Oh,' said Miller after a moment. 'What if I say he's not having you followed?'

'I wouldn't mind. I wouldn't believe you, but I wouldn't mind.'

'That's very generous of you, Harry. He's not having you followed. There, I've said it.'

Fathers nodded amiably. 'How's the serial killer case going?' Miller shrugged. 'Making progress,' he said, 'but not enough

to get him before he does it again. We're building a picture of him, but we don't have enough yet.'

Fathers shook his head sadly. 'Thank God we don't have that problem at home.'

'Really,' said Miller. 'You don't know how lucky you are. I bet you don't have the teenage suicides either, huh?'

'What?'

'We have a plague of teenage suicides. It's the second leading cause of death for youths between fifteen and twenty-four. They've just set up a special task force on it in New York State. I was reading a report. There were six thousand suicides across the country among people that age last year.'

'Christ,' breathed Fathers. 'What is it? Pressures of the economic crisis: no jobs, no hope, no future?'

'Can't tell,' said Miller. 'It happens a lot in the better areas around New York City – Westchester, Putnam and Rockland. Those are really affluent counties. There've been eleven this year on Long Island, which isn't poverty stricken. There's a town in Texas where they had about that many in the last school year. It's like an epidemic.'

'Christ,' said Fathers again.

'Pressures of poverty,' said Miller, 'pressures of wealth. Take your pick these days.'

They stood in silence for several minutes. Fathers could think of nothing to say. He wondered what to do.

'Do you play chess, Harry?' asked Miller finally. 'If you do, how about a game? I'm not much good and you'll probably beat my ass off, but how about it? One way of passing the time and taking our minds off the various bits of crap that surround us.'

Fathers agreed, and Miller went back inside and came out with a fine chess set. They played three close games – one to a draw with one win each. All the while they played, the other two detectives and Labbat stayed indoors. When the beach party returned, Labbat and his wife left almost immediately. The others had coffee, chocolate cake and some conversation on the terrace until the party broke up. Miller and Wanda drove Fathers back into town.

15

On Monday morning Fathers left Rosemary's apartment before seven, caught a cab to La Guardia airport, and took the eight a.m. Eastern Shuttle to the National Airport of Washington, DC. Sunday evening had been a warm and gentle time with Rosemary. Fathers had put aside his detective's role and asked her no questions connected with the case. They talked past midnight, exploring each other's thoughts and feelings, opinions and tastes, before they went to bed and made love.

Fathers slept for most of the short flight. There were four men he wanted to see. Three were the researchers Rosemary had said Michael Sampson saw particularly often on his frequent trips to Washington. The fourth was David Able, formerly a crime reporter in London who had since changed papers and subjects and was now the Washington correspondent for a London weekly. They had met through their work ten years before, when Fathers was first at the Yard. Friendship developed and their families became close. When Able moved to Washington they kept in touch with Christmas cards. On Saturday evening, Fathers had thought of his friend and phoned him to arrange a meeting as soon as he arrived. He had asked Able to come equipped with any information he had, or could find, about the three researchers.

'Can do,' Able had confidently replied. 'Is there a story in it?'

'No. This is a one-way favour.'

'Well, I suppose I still owe you.'

'Yes,' said Fathers. 'You'll be reducing your deficit to three hundred and eighty-four.'

'What do you mean?' asked Able. 'You got coverage, didn't you? – and look at you now.' He suggested meeting in a café near his office and told Fathers where to find it.

Fathers walked into the café and saw his friend sitting at a corner table. He got himself a coffee and doughnut and went over.

'Hello, sailor,' grinned Able.

'Seaman,' replied Fathers shaking his friend's hand.

'It's good to see you,' said Able. 'Are you in town long?'

'No, I'm going back tonight if I can.'

'That's a shame. Frances would love to see you again. We hoped you'd eat with us this evening. It's been a long time.'

'Well, if I have to stay over I'll take you up on it.'

'And stay with us?'

'That would be great, but if I can get back I really must.'

'And you would never invent a reason that absolutely prevents you from doing what you probably ought to.'

Fathers smiled. 'It's good to see you again, David.'

'The pity of it is, I can't give you much time right now. Election time, you know. So I guess it's no how's-the-wife-and-kids, but straight to work. How is Sarah, by the way?'

'Fine. Kids, too. Yours?'

'Blooming, one and all.'

'Good. Have you got anything for me?'

Able passed over a sheet of paper on which were written three names with addresses and telephone numbers.

'So tell me about them,' said Fathers.

'Bradley Waddup,' said Able, 'is a staff aide to Senator Huggett. I'm not sure how senior he is. He advises the Senator on strategic policy, which is one of Huggett's interests. He's on the Armed Services Committee – Huggett, I mean. He doesn't run his mouth a whole lot, but what he does say on the floor of the Senate and in committee is regarded as pretty competent, and that would be down to good staff back-up.'

'Which means this Bradley Waddup is pretty competent himself,' said Fathers.

'Most definitely. Simon Goldsack I don't know much about. He works for one of the Beltway Bandits. You know what they are?'

'I've been told.'

'Well his company, Systems South, is well thought of – it's not actually on the Beltway. Not the largest of them, but reasonably well established. It specialises in high-tech systems research, and

211

it was one of the first to move into space defence after the President made his Star Wars speech in March last year.'

'That was when he launched this Strategic Defense Initiative thing,' said Fathers.

'Like a bolt from the blue, shortly after his Darth Vader speech.'

'What are you talking about, David?'

'That was the one when he called the USSR the evil empire. Next month he did the Star Wars number. And just last month he offered to share Star Wars with the evil empire. Weird country this, isn't it? Of course, it is election time – but that only explains it, it doesn't excuse it.'

'So the company this Goldsack works for was in sharpish.'

'Indeed,' said Able. 'Which speaks well for their business acumen, but in the time you gave me I couldn't find out anything more either about Goldsack or his company.'

'And this last fellow?'

'Ted Gullick. I know him. He's very interesting. Not so old – about our age – but he's been around a lot. At different times, he's worked for the State Department, in Congress for one of the House committees and for a while on some congressman's staff. He's held an academic job or two on the West Coast, and right now he's got some kind of senior position with an outfit called the Futures Research Center. One thing I will say about him, as long as I can count on your discretion, is that in the past he's been one of Washington's information conduits.'

'I've heard that, but explain it to me,' said Fathers.

'Information is one of Washington's two most precious assets,' said Able, 'the other being a dinner invitation to the White House. As regards information there are three categories of valued people. There are those who have the information and will release it – people in government, for example, or on a Congressional Committee. There are those who want the infor- mation and can use it – mostly reporters. And there are the people in the middle who know people who got it and people who want it.'

'Middlemen,' suggested Fathers, 'cut-outs.'

'That's right. Someone like Ted gets given something juicy,

maybe by someone who's pissed off with what's going on and wants to stir up some trouble. Ted then farms it out to a reporter, say, who gets it printed in his rag. And there you are: another leak, another scandal.'

'But the middleman's name doesn't get mentioned,' said Fathers.

'Right again. The reporter protects his source, who protects his source, and so on. Cut-outs, like you said.'

'You said he used to do this. Has he stopped?'

'Well, he left town for a while, was away a couple of years – came back some time last year I think – and that's enough time to get a bit out of touch. Maybe he's started up again, but he hasn't told me if he has.'

'And what does he get out of it? Money?'

'Oh no,' said Able. 'That's much too cynical, and too naive at the same time. He gets a certain aura out of it. He becomes someone other people want to know. It's kind of an open secret when somebody's playing that role. And of course it's pretty exciting dealing in illicit information, but also reasonably safe since there's not much chance of getting caught if you're at all sensible, and no real punishment even if you are nabbed.'

'Do either of the other two deal in information like that?' said Fathers.

'Goldsack, I don't know. I could ask a pal or two and see. Waddup, yes, I think that if his Senator wants something leaked out, Waddup is the one to do it, but whether he would independently receive information from someone on the inside, I don't know. It all depends on who you know.'

Fathers sat for a moment in thought and finished his coffee. 'Anything else?'

'I don't think so,' said Able.

'Well, I'd better get to it. Find a phone box and make some calls.'

'Well,' said Able, 'if I were you I'd go to Union Station – or rather to the National Visitors' Center, which is right next door to it. There are loads of public phones there, which nobody ever seems to use. And it's pretty convenient for Capitol Hill, where you'll find Waddup, it's only a few blocks from Gullick's office, and you can take the Metro from there to Crystal City, where Goldsack hangs out. Assuming they're all in, of course.'

'It's probably better than the office I've got in New York,' said Fathers.

'You can get there by Metro. I'll show you. The station's just round the corner.'

As they walked there, Able had one more piece of advice.

'I don't know how you're going to handle this, Harry. I don't even know what it is you're handling. You'll find people in Washington like to talk, but they also like to listen. If you're looking for information that's at all – how shall I put it? – at all delicate, you may find the going easier if you're willing to trade. Even if it's information they can't use, swapping makes it easier. Use my name if you like to get an intro with Ted Gullick. And if you are going to stay overnight, call me any time during the day. I'll be through by about seven and we can go out together. For you, Frances won't mind the short notice.'

At the Metro station he showed Fathers how to use the ticket machine that accepted dollar bills. On the train Fathers noticed that, of the other passengers, the largest proportion by far was black. The predominance of black faces since he had arrived at the National Airport now struck him forcibly. He vaguely remembered reading somewhere that Washington's population was eighty per cent black. It was, in reality, an entirely different city from the one which appeared in the television news and in films. In that sense, it was like New York: nothing he had seen of it in the cinema or on television had prepared him for the amount of advertising in Spanish he had seen there. To an Englishman, the USA was a very strange place; he wondered how Americans felt about it.

Ted Gullick was the first person Fathers phoned.

'I'm afraid Ted's out of town right now,' said the woman who answered the phone, 'but he'll be back late this afternoon and said he'd look in here on his way home. Can I take a message?'

'Yes please. My name's Harry Fathers. I work in London. David Able is a mutual friend and suggested Mr Gullick could help me with something I'm working on. I'd be very grateful for some time with him, tomorrow morning first thing if at all possible. What time will he be back?'

'About five, he said, but he wasn't sure.'

'Well, I'll try to call again then, or at his home this evening. But please leave the message anyway.'

'Certainly, Mr Fathers. Let me see I've got it straight. Harry Fathers, London, friend of David Able, would like to meet, will call again. Do you have a contact phone number?'

Fathers gave her Able's phone number. 'I'll be there from about eight,' he said. 'Thanks very much.'

Next Fathers tried Waddup, with more success. 'Well,' said Bradley Waddup, 'my schedule's a little tight today, but I think we could manage lunch. How would that do?' Fathers said it would do fine. 'Good. So come along to the Old Senate Building, call up from the front desk, and we'll go eat in the Supreme Court cafeteria. Would twelve noon suit?'

Simon Goldsack was also busy, but equally willing to see Fathers if he cared to come out at five o'clock and provided detailed directions. Fathers went to buy a newspaper and have another coffee to kill the forty-five minutes before lunch. In London, he wondered, would somebody from out of town find it so easy to fix appointments with people who are extremely busy and total strangers?

Fathers and Bradley Waddup sat down together at a corner table in the large cafeteria in the basement under the Supreme Court. Waddup was a neat, medium-sized man in his mid-thirties, wearing a dark blue blazer, a bow tie, white shirt and grey trousers. He was having a quiche and salad, Fathers a lasagne and salad. The food looked good and the room was large and airy, slowly filling with lunchers from various offices of the judicial and legislative branches of government.

Fathers had not said he was a policeman. His explanation that he was working on some aspects of the Space Shuttle seemed enough introduction. Waddup appeared to assume it was research, which in a way was true, and did not bother asking what

215

kind of research it was. He did ask, though, if Fathers knew Paul Finlay. Fathers nodded.'Quite well,' he said. Waddup nodded, and commented with a grin that Finlay was quite a guy.

'And Mike Sampson who used to work with the good doctor?' asked Waddup.

'I don't know him so well, though I know Rosemary pretty well,' said Fathers through his lasagne.

'Mike's a real nice guy, very smart, too. I haven't seen or heard from him in awhile. He was doing some work on the Space Shuttle too, wasn't he, over the summer?'

'That's right. But you'd know all about that. Wasn't he coming down here almost every week to see you about it?'

Waddup paused and chuckled. 'That was his story, was it? Well, I guess if Rosemary ever confronts me I'll keep my end of the story up, but I wish he'd told me.'

'What do you mean?'

'Well, this is kind of out of court. I don't know how close you are to Rosemary, but better not tell her if Mike hasn't told her himself.'

'You mean ...?'

'Sure,' said Waddup. 'He's been two-timing her. Oh, you should see the pretty Miss Sanders. Any man with a half a chance would be a fool not to take it up with her.'

'Where can I find her?' asked Fathers.

Waddup chuckled again. 'Think you could pull her, huh? Well, no blame to any man for trying. She's a secretary in the State Department. Least, she was last time I saw her. She's twenty-five, sweet as anything, and what a figure.' He chuckled again and gestured roundly with his right hand in front of his chest. 'I don't know if she had anybody else on the go. But I do know that she's the real reason Mike kept bombing down here. Business was strictly second place. Now I come to think of it, maybe they've called it off, which would be why Mike hasn't blown through in awhile. Haven't seen her in a few weeks either.' He munched contentedly on his salad.

'But he used to see you each time he was down?'

'Yeah, well, most times, I guess. And other people. But you know, the telephone company's cheaper than the Eastern shuttle

216

if you just want to say "howdy", and I don't know that Mike and I ever said much more than that. Of course, there could've been other people he wanted to see more – you know, more substantively, more professionally.'

'You don't work on the Space Shuttle, then?'

'I keep abreast, you know? But the Senator's got other bones to chew. We're heavily into the whole over-pricing issue on Pentagon contracts. You know, six hundred dollars for a hammer and so on. We just found a beauty: over ten thousand dollars for – guess what? Go on, guess.'

'Cheque books,' Fathers hazarded.

Waddup laughed. 'I like it, I like it, good one. But no – better yet.'

'I give up. Tell me.'

'Hair cuts,' said Waddup. Fathers looked at him open-mouthed. 'Hair cuts for executives. Takes some believing, doesn't it? But I kid you not.'

'How do they get away with it?' asked Fathers when he got his mouth working again.

Waddup shrugged. 'Conspiracy, incompetence, mutual back-scratching. Take your pick. You're right: somebody should've checked and spotted it. In fact, I can't believe it wasn't spotted. Nobody bothered to do anything about it, is all. But now the heat's coming on about the whole thing, people on the inside who don't like it are beginning to find a market for their little nuggets. Hair cuts, can you credit it? Next thing we'll find they've been charging up their saunas. Not for long though, not for long. We're going to get a proper investigation, going to tie all these different bits and pieces together. It'll build up to be bigger than Northrop and Lockheed in the seventies, I'm telling you. There's gonna be a massacre of top executives, you wait and see.'

Fathers wanted to ask more questions, but remembered he was supposed to be a researcher and didn't want to display an ignorance incompatible with the role, so he contented himself with mild expressions of shock.

'You people,' said Waddup, 'should look into your own sink of corruption as well.'

'In Britain, you mean?'

'Sure. You have – what? – one fifty, two hundred defence officials a year getting jobs in the arms industry and you've gotta think, hey, there may have been a little hanky-panky here to sweeten their path into corporate life, you know? How come you don't look into it?'

'I, well – two hundred, you say,' said Fathers, 'I suppose I'm more on the, er, technical policy side of things.'

'Sure,' said Waddup. 'Still, I'm surprised somebody doesn't take it up. Anyway, how can I help you? The Shuttle, you said.'

'Well,' said Fathers carefully, 'maybe not at all. I rather had the impression you were working more on the Shuttle than it seems you are.'

'Sorry about that,' said Waddup. 'Looks like your trip's a victim of Mike's perfidy.' He chuckled again. 'Anyway, what're you working on?'

It was a polite, casual enquiry, one researcher to another; Fathers could not turn it down.

'I'm just scratching around a bit,' he said, 'to see if there's anything to this business of Flight 007.' He left it at that for the moment. He had few cards to play in this trick and did not want to commit himself all in one go. Waddup said nothing for a moment as he drank his coffee, looking at Fathers over the top of his cup.

'If I were you, Harry,' said Waddup, leaning forward and speaking quietly, almost conspiratorially, 'I wouldn't scratch around at that one, not in this burg anyway.'

'Oh?' said Fathers. 'Tell me more.'

'What I should be telling you,' said Waddup, 'is that since that anonymous article in that British magazine, it's been thoroughly looked into and there's no connection.'

'What are you going to tell me instead?'

'There's a lot of embarrassment over that article. Not that, even on the q.t., it's being admitted that it was right. But the clear sense is that there's something very heavy involved, and people who like to sleep peacefully in their beds at night should stay well clear. It is not – believe me – it is not at all on the level of over-priced contracts.'

'If you don't mind me saying, you sound a bit scared.'

218

'You bet your titty I am,' said Waddup raising his voice, then lowering it again as he went on. 'So much that I don't want to ask you any more about what you're doing. If there's something there to find out, and if you've found anything out, I don't wanna know. If that makes me sound a bit rabbit-like, OK, we rabbits are great survivors.' He picked up a leftover piece of lettuce and popped it in his mouth with a flourish as he sat back.

Fathers smiled. 'It all sounds a bit outlandish to me,' he said. 'But you needn't worry. I've got nothing yet. I've only just started.'

'Well,' said Waddup, 'if you're smart you'll stop there.'

'Has Mike ever talked to you about it?'

'No,' said Waddup a shade too quickly.

Fathers smiled. 'What did he tell you?'

Waddup looked affronted. 'I said no,' he said.

'And I heard you. But he did tell you, didn't he?'

'Well, OK, he mentioned a rumour or two.'

'And?'

'Yeah, I mentioned a rumour or two back to him. But I didn't want to talk about it then, and I don't now. It's a bit too hot in that particular kitchen for me, and I've got other fish to fry, real juicy ones too.'

Fathers drank his coffee. 'How do I find Miss Sanders?' he asked. 'And what's her first name?'

'Now that's more like it. That's what a wise man should spend his time doing. Her name's Gail. She works, last I heard, for a man called Tanley in State. He's on the European desk. Nice guy. I met him at a cocktail party last year. If you're in town long, why, maybe you can fix a date with Miss Sanders. I tell you – what a looker, what a dresser. On the other hand, what a mouth – never stops talking. Well, I don't know about never; I haven't had the opportunity to find out, nor will I, delectable though it would be. Good luck.'

Fathers phoned Able. 'I am staying tonight,' he said.

'Great,' said Able. 'I'll tell Frances. How's it going?'

'How do I find somebody who works in the State Department? A secretary.'

'Mm, that's not so easy. Do you know who she works for, assuming you don't mean the Secretary of State?'

'No, a typing secretary. She works for a man called Tanley in the European section.'

'Oh, that's easy. What we do is we reach out a hand for the State Department telephone directory, then we flip through to the European desk, then we look down till we find his name and his telephone number, and then we read it out to you.' He did so.

'Thanks.'

'You're welcome. Must run now. Phone me around six, OK? I'll tell you then what time I'll be free. You would have to come to town on a Monday. See you.'

Fathers phoned the number Able had given him. A woman answered.

'Miss Sanders?' he asked.

'No, this is not she. I am Miss Wright. Miss Sanders is no longer with us. Do you wish to speak to Mr Coyle?'

'I'm sorry, I thought this was Mr Tanley's office. I must have the wrong number.'

'No, you have the right number. This was Mr Tanley's office, but he's moved to a different section. Is it Mr Coyle or Mr Tanley that you wish to speak to?'

'Er, no, actually it was Miss Sanders herself that I wanted to talk to. Where can I find her now?'

'May I ask your name, sir?' persisted Miss Wright. 'Are you a friend?'

'Well, I'm sort of a friend of a friend. How do I get in touch with her?'

'And your friend asked you to call on Miss Sanders?'

'That's right. He hasn't seen her for a while, sends his best regards, suggested I look her up since I'm just visiting and so on. Is she working somewhere else in the Department?'

'I don't think I caught your name, sir.'

What Fathers said in reply was 'Shuttleworth', but he mumbled and turned half away from the mouthpiece as he said it.

220

Turning back, he said more clearly, 'Do you have a phone number for her?'

'I'm afraid I have to tell you, sir, that Miss Sanders is dead.'

'Oh good heavens,' said Fathers. He had no need to inject the tone of shock into his voice. 'That's awful. When? And how?'

'Just three weeks ago. It was a car accident. A hit-and-run late one night.'

'Oh, that's awful. She – she sounded such a lively person.'

'Yes,' said Miss Wright. Her tone had changed and was more gentle. 'She was. We were all very upset. I'm sorry to have to tell you this. But I'm also afraid that I must go now.'

'Yes,' said Fathers. 'Yes, of course. Goodbye. Thank you.'

When she had put the phone down, Miss Wright pressed the button on her desk intercom and, at the response, got up and walked into a larger office next to hers. 'That was another phone call for Miss Sanders, sir,' she said to the man sitting behind the desk.

'Thank you, Ella, What was the name?'

'I didn't catch it. I did ask him twice but he mumbled when he said it. He was English.'

'Ah. Thank you, Ella, What kind of call was it?'

'Personal, sir. He said he was a friend of a friend. He sounded very shocked when I passed on the news.'

'I'm sure he did. That's all, thank you.'

'Should I keep telling you when we get calls for Miss Sanders?'

'Until further notice, please, Ella.'

When Miss Wright had gone, the man picked up his phone and dialled. 'Coyle here,' he said when he was connected. 'The last call to Miss Wright's number was for Sanders. Check the tape and transcribe it, and pass it on as usual, OK?'

The weather in Washington was cooler than it had been in New York and sunnier. Fathers walked from Union Station down to the long Mall which leads away from Capitol Hill. The grass was green, the trees were changing colour, there were plenty of people out strolling, the Capitol looked imposing in the sun. He found a bench and sat down in the sunshine to think.

The case was beginning to close up on him again. When he added up what he knew and separated it from what he guessed might be possible, he was left little better off than when he had first arrived in the country.

Most of all, he felt frustrated that this was not an investigation he could pursue in London. Here he had little time and almost no resources. In London he would have been able to fill in the details. He would have had help he could trust, the authority to question people, and the contacts to find out more about them without them even knowing. He could have answered a dozen questions, bit by bit, till they satisfyingly built into the right answer. Where his items of information were connected, he could have established that connection; where they were unconnected, he could have shown it to be so. He sighed and decided to walk in the sun until it was time to take the Metro to his next meeting.

Simon Goldsack could spare Fathers only half an hour. He took him into his small office and they sat down on each side of the large desk that dominated the room. Everything was modern and neat. Goldsack himself was in his twenties, bespectacled, dark, lightly built, wearing a short-sleeved white shirt with a tie under a sleeveless sweater. Fathers again introduced himself in the role of a fellow researcher and, having thought about it for some time on the Metro train, again presented himself as beginning to study whether or not there was a connection between the Space Shuttle and the Korean airliner.

Goldsack's reaction was entirely different from Waddup's. 'There's a lot of meat there, I'll bet. Do you know Mike Sampson? He's English, too, lives in New York. He's shown some interest in that aspect of it. Of course, it's not the kind of thing we get into here, nor, properly speaking, should Mike be getting into it.' Goldsack spoke rapidly and with an air of

222

authority that belied his relative youth.

'I know of Mike,' said Fathers. 'Has he talked with you about it?'

'A little. But the work we do here is not only mostly classified, it's also very technical, and we tend to concentrate on fairly narrow areas. Frankly, we've largely moved on from the Shuttle, though the company did take part in some definitional studies in the early days. From our point of view, you could say it's yesterday's news. So I couldn't really help Mike out much.'

'What was he asking about?'

'He mostly wanted to know about the business with the cables. I take it you've heard about that? Yeah, most people have. It's kind of an open secret, though as far as I can make out it's mostly rumour.'

'Most of it seems to be mostly rumour,' said Fathers.

'I think that's right. What's your own view about it?'

'Well,' said Fathers carefully, 'I think there are some discrepancies in all the accounts that say it was just a tragic accident – the intrusion, I mean. But actually, those are the accounts I believe. I can't really credit that the USA would risk a civil airliner in that kind of way. Yet there are other bits and pieces, including some that haven't been published, which together with those discrepancies... Well, the answer to your question is that I don't know, so I'm looking around a bit to see if there's anything that will settle it one way or the other. There probably won't be, though.'

'I guess that's so,' said Goldsack. 'Let's face it, this administration is capable of almost anything, but that? It's pretty farfetched.'

'What did you tell Mike about the cables?'

'Nothing. I don't know anything about them. They're under the sea and our interest is focused right up outside the atmosphere. Like him, and like you, and like everybody's second cousin, I just know there are rumours circulating. But, hell, there are rumours circulating about most things in this town, and the more dramatic it is, the faster it gets round. You need to carry more than a couple of pinches of salt in your coat pocket. Come and ask me about the software problems for the SD and I'll burn

223

your ears off, but on undersea cables I've got zilch. Sorry.'

'You said he was mostly interested in the cables. Was there something else, then?'

'Oh, yeah, though that was part of his actual research for darper.' The way he said it gave Fathers the feeling he should know what 'darper' meant, so he forbore to ask. 'I'm not sure I should really tell you,' continued Goldsack tantalisingly, 'but, in outline terms, he wanted some calculations the company did years back about orbital inclinations.'

'Did you give them to him?'

'Yeah, no reason not to. Checked first, got the OK, and handed them over.'

'Why did you say Mike shouldn't get into the business of the cables?'

'Oh,' said Goldsack carelessly, 'if he wants to keep getting DoD dollars he's got to learn what he can pry into and what he can't. You know what I mean? Reporters and research institutes, academics and public pressure groups, and even staffers on the Hill can all buzz round the honey pot making as much noise as they want, you know? But we who dine on honey every day, we should just answer the questions set for us, turn in our reports and ignore the rest. Step outa line and there goes your classification. If I did something like that and my boss got wind of it, I'd pretty soon be packing my bag. One rotten pea spoils the whole can, and he can't afford to risk the company for the sake of my curiosity. He wouldn't be on my side on that one, and I wouldn't blame him, you know? But sometimes I envy them. It would be fun to just poke around for the hell of it. But I know where I am and what my job is. I get the impression sometimes Mike isn't too clear about that.'

'You mean he thinks he's still working in English acadaemia?'

'Pretty much,' said Goldsack.

16

The evening with David and Frances Able was deeply pleasant – a celebration of an old friendship overflowing with news and reminiscence. Fathers allowed it to wash his mind for a while of his racing thoughts about the Sampson case. Even with Rosemary, except when they were making love, the case and its unanswered questions were never entirely out of his mind. This evening was a respite – and neither of his friends asked what brought him to the USA and its capital city.

Just once he mentioned something connected with the case. 'What's darper?' he asked Able.

'That's the Defense Advance Research Projects Agency,' said Able. 'It's a small outfit in the Pentagon that runs exotic research of various kinds. Take any wacko notion, put dollars into it by the tens of millions, and see if it means anything.'

He had phoned Ted Gullick's office from a call box after meeting Goldsack. This time he was in luck. Gullick was there and showed the friendly willingness to meet and give Fathers some of his time that he was now regarding as normal. Fathers simply explained that he was working on the Shuttle and that Able had suggested he get in touch with Gullick, and a nine-thirty meeting was immediately arranged.

Gullick's office was in a four floor house a few streets east of Congress. His room was spacious, airy and in a state of total chaos. Books, journals and newspapers lay in loose piles on the floor, on shelves, on any available surface. Papers were piled high on his desk. Several folders sat precariously on the open drawer of a filing cabinet. A computer on a table to one side had several newspapers and a couple of envelopes on top of it.

Fathers immediately understood why Gullick himself had reminded Michael Sampson of Finlay. He was large, though not that large – a couple of inches taller than Fathers and a good twenty pounds heavier, which still left him four or five inches shorter than Finlay and seventy pounds lighter. He wore an open-necked shirt, jeans and sneakers, and had a confident manner that Fathers judged was not at all superficial. He offered Fathers coffee, and disappeared with five mugs collected from various corners of the room, returning once to ask how he took his coffee before finally coming back with two full mugs.

'So you're doing some work on the Space Shuttle?'

'Yes,' said Fathers. 'I'm looking into this business about the Korean airliner, the Ferret and the Shuttle.'

'Ah ha,' said Gullick. 'At a guess I'd say the only way to find out the full story on that one is to have an inside line. Do you?'

'Not really. Have you looked into it at all?'

'A little, not a lot. I read what's available, but the stuff I know about the Shuttle doesn't include that aspect of it, if, of course, that is an aspect of it.'

'I share your scepticism,' said Fathers, 'but I think there are some avenues worth exploring.'

'Yes? Could be. But how can I help you?'

'Do you know Mike Sampson?'

'Yes, pretty well, very nice guy. The Space Shuttle is one of his special interests, of course.'

'Have you seen him lately?'

'No, I guess I haven't, not since last month maybe. Why?'

'Nor has anybody else.'

Gullick paused, his coffee mug in mid-air. Fathers levelly returned his gaze.

'Where do you do your research, Harry?' asked Gullick.

'In London mostly.'

'Who with?'

'Scotland Yard.'

'I beg your pardon,' said Gullick putting his mug down too firmly and spilling some coffee.

Fathers pulled his warrant card from his breast pocket and handed it over. Gullick waved it away without inspecting it. 'No, don't bother,' he said. 'I wouldn't know a forged London police ID if I saw one.'

226

Fathers stayed silent and watched the other man regain some of his composure. Gullick and Finlay were definitely two of a kind, he thought.

'You say nobody's seen Mike recently?'

'That's right,' said Fathers placidly. 'He's disappeared.'

'He's disappeared? Where to? Sorry, foolish question. If you knew that you wouldn't be here. But I don't know either, so what do you want from me?'

'No, Mr Gullick, if I thought you knew I wouldn't be here either. Others would. I'm looking for some background information to fill in the picture and help explain what has happened to Dr Sampson, and whichever way I turn this business of the Korean airliner crops up. I know he saw you quite often, and I know you work in the same field, so I thought there might be a chance you could help fill in some of the background.'

Gullick scratched his head and fiddled with his mug. 'Is this an official enquiry?'

Fathers paused to consider. 'It's an official *British* enquiry,' he said. 'I'm here at the instruction of my Assistant Commissioner, who was asked to second me by the Foreign Office and Defence Ministry. The New York police are cooperating and, when I'm in New York, I work from one of their offices. But as far as the police in Washington are concerned, it's not official. I doubt they even know about it. Certainly, I couldn't say from your point of view, as a US citizen resident here, that there's anything official about my presence here right now, or my questions. You are absolutely free to talk to me or ask me to leave this minute, as you like.'

Gullick paused to drink some more coffee. 'Were you kidding me about knowing Able as well?'

'I haven't kidded you, Mr Gullick. I told you I'm looking at some aspects of the Space Shuttle, and so I am. I merely let you get the wrong end of the stick. And I wasn't kidding you about David Able either. I stayed with him last night.'

'Well, if you don't mind, and even if you do, I'm going to check.'

Gullick reached for the phone and a battered address book, then paused before dialling. 'Maybe I'll call his home,' he said. Then he added conversationally, 'What's his wife's name? I forget.'

'Frances,' said Fathers smiling. 'Their children are Peter and Graham, known as Cokey for some reason. Their dog is a setter called Bosun, and I can tell you their number if you haven't got it there.'

'Well, it seems a little foolish after that impressive catalogue, but here goes anyway.' He dialled. 'Hello, Frances? ... Hi, it's Ted Gullick. Listen, did someone called Harry Fathers stay with you last night? ... Yeah, he said he was going to. Look, I was to meet with him this morning but he hasn't showed – when did he leave? ... Really? Well, maybe the Metro's in trouble again. Er, hang on – what's he look like? There's a guy looking lost across the street and I wondered if ... Yeah, that's him. Tell me, what does he do for a living? ... No, not really, I just wondered.... Is he? Well I'll be honoured to welcome a London bobby to my humble office. What does he want, do you know? ... Oh, he didn't, OK, well thanks, 'bye now.'

Gullick put the phone down and looked at Fathers. Then he rose and looked out the window for several minutes. He spoke without turning round. 'Well, as far as I can tell, you check out. I don't think Frances would be part of something weird, like vouching for you if you're not on the level. But how do I know if I tell you something you find interesting, you won't go blabbing around?'

'You could always deny it.'

'Not if you've got some kind of little tape recorder on you.'

'What do you want me to do? Strip?'

'Would you do that, you a big detective and all?'

'If that's what it takes to get you to talk.'

Gullick turned to face Fathers and grinned. 'I've never had a detective strip in my office before. What a first. But it would be too embarrassing. I'll take the risk. More coffee?'

'Please.'

Gullick left the window and took the mugs out to refill them. He brought them back filled, gave Fathers his, and sat back down at his desk. 'What do you know about Mike's work on the Shuttle?' he asked.

'Do you know Paul Finlay?' Fathers replied.

'Yes.'

'Well?'

'Pretty well. We correspond, meet whenever we can. I like him. Why?'

'Yes, I thought you'd like him,' said Fathers. 'I only asked because he already knows what I'm going to tell you. Sampson's disappearance dates from the last weekend of September. Precisely when, we don't know. We don't know the means of it either – whether it was voluntary or not, I mean, and if it was, where he's gone.' He paused to sip some coffee. Gullick looked at him without expression. 'What we do know is that all his work materials, both at his apartment and his office, were removed at the same time. So I don't know much about his work on the Shuttle. I haven't seen the report he wrote, though Finlay has.'

'Has he now?'

'Sampson sent it to him on the quiet. Quite why, we don't know. Sampson did leave some notes, rather well-hidden, which escaped the attention of whoever emptied his office, and I've found them. They're very cryptic, but Finlay's interpreted them for me – that's how he knows about what I'm telling you. In Finlay's interpretation, they refer to a connection between the shooting down of that Korean airliner and the Space Shuttle mission which, to put it at its lowest level, coincided with the incident. Compared to an article which Finlay told me about, but which I haven't yet seen, about that connection—'

'I know the one you mean,' said Gullick.

'Compared to it, Sampson's notes are apparently different in three respects: he seems to be speculating that the Shuttle was closer to the incident than the article reported, that something may have been done to certain undersea cables in the area where the airliner came down—'

'I've heard that too,' Gullick said.

'... and that the chain of command in the incident may have reached up beyond the National Security Advisor to the President himself. There's nothing about any of this, by the way, in Sampson's report, so Finlay says anyway. Sampson was asking at least one other researcher in this sort of field about the question of the cables. That's what I know. What I now want to know is if he talked to you about any of it.'

'Yes,' said Gullick after a pause. 'He did. It was those three things you mentioned that weren't in that article.' He paused. 'Jesus, but it's hard to take in. Disappeared?'

'Yes.'

'No trace of where he's gone? I mean, does it look as if—?'

'Yes,' said Fathers, 'I think the supposition has to be something very dramatic. Either he's dead or, one way or another, he's defected.'

'I find that impossible to believe, knowing Mike, impossible.'

'That he defected, you mean?' asked Fathers. Gullick nodded. 'Well, without knowing him, but knowing a lot about him, I find it hard to believe too. But not necessarily impossible.'

'If you don't mind me saying so, I think that's just a policeman's suspiciousness. If you knew him, you'd just rule it out. But shit, that means he's probably dead, poor bastard. In which case, who did it?'

'That's what I'm trying to find out, Mr Gullick. But if it makes you feel better to think he might have defected, I'm discovering many things about him that nobody who knows him would find credible.'

'Yeah, like what?'

'Well, for example, the fact that he was studying this connection was not in character as far as Finlay was concerned, or the British Defence Ministry, I shouldn't think. Nor was the fact that he hid these notes that I found. Other things too.'

'Well, maybe,' said Gullick. 'But it's no comfort, I reckon, to think that he's defected. What the shit would be his motive?'

'I'm sure you don't want a policeman's suspiciousness turned on that question,' said Fathers.

'I guess not.'

'So, what did he say to you about those three items which aren't in that article? Do you have a copy of it, by the way?'

'Sure. I'll let you have a xerox to take with you. Anyway, I guess Mike first mentioned it sometime in the spring. He was down here on one of his little jaunts.'

'He used to come down quite often, didn't he?'

'Yes, quite a lot. I think he used to check in at the Pentagon, talk around with various people, and so on. The usual thing.'

'And?'

'Well,' said Gullick, 'first time he referred to it he mentioned this thing about the cables. It was the first I'd heard of it. But I've since heard it from several people. I don't know where Mike picked it up. He wanted to know if I knew anything which could confirm it. But, like I said, it was new to me and I couldn't help him. I did ask one or two people if they knew anything more, but all they had was rumour.'

'Where and how do these rumours circulate?'

'Oh, lots of places. At various meetings and seminars you get people chatting over coffee or drinks. Cocktail parties, if that's your scene, are real rumour factories. Just in general, meeting people – reporters, for instance – you get to talking about the issues of the day. You know. Everybody likes to be in the know, or to think they are – it's that kind of town. Anyway, he also asked me about this business of the chain of command. I think this was actually before that article came out. He wanted to know if I thought it was credible that the responsibility for it stopped with the National Security Advisor. Frankly, I told him I wasn't even sure that there was any responsibility for it, not in that sense.'

'There does seem to be a lot of scepticism about it,' said Fathers.

'Sure. I mean, if it's true that the whole thing was fixed by the US government as a spying exercise – or that other theory, which leaves the Shuttle entirely out of it, that it was done to reap the propaganda harvest and get the MX money through Congress and the cruise missiles and Pershings into Europe – either way –

that they're really so cold-blooded, it's pretty hard to credit, even of this bunch of crooks.'

'I haven't heard about that theory.'

'No? It was in one of the British newspapers. The *Guardian*, I think, quite some time back. It has a kind of *post hoc* plausibility to it, because the administration did make a whole lot of hay out of it, but I can't remember that it had any really hard evidence to go on. I can let you have a copy of that too, if you like.'

'Thank you, if it's not too much trouble. So was that the only time he referred to it?'

'Oh no. A few weeks after that he told me he was sure the Shuttle was a good deal closer to the incident than that article reported.'

'Did he say why?'

'Uh huh. I asked him, and he went into some whole rigmarole that I didn't understand, and I'm not really sure he did either, about angles of inclination and orbital shift, but I gathered he didn't have any hard evidence. It was pretty much supposition, but I kind of understood him to be pretty convinced by it, and, frankly, I thought, without understanding it at all, like I said, that if Mike was convinced by it there had to be something there.'

'Because you respected him as a researcher?'

'That's right. I mean he's – or he was – whatever – a real cautious researcher, you know? He didn't just jump to conclusions, not usually anyway.' Gullick paused.

'Go on,' said Fathers.

'Some time in the summer – June, maybe, or even July – he told me he had absolutely firm evidence that the chain of command didn't stop until it reached the President, that Reagan had known about the mission and approved it, and that that's why the response was so fast when the airliner was shot down. He said they knew the risks and had an entire PR operation geared up ready to go if it all went wrong.'

'Firm evidence?'

'That's what he told me. He didn't say what it was, and I don't know where he got it.'

I think I do, thought Fathers, but he said nothing.

'He wanted me to see if I could check it out. He reckoned that with two separate sources it would be possible to go to a journalist and blow the whole thing. He said he thought I was the right person to follow it up. I don't know if you know, but I've been involved in leaking a few things out in the past and I guess he thought I might have the contacts to do it.'

'I do know,' said Fathers. 'And did you check it out?'

'Well, I passed a couple of questions to one or two people in a vague kind of way, but I didn't get anything back. You know, you have to be careful not to show your hand too much when you do that kind of thing, and this was pretty big potatoes. So I didn't want to go blabbing about what I knew. Had to be tactical, you know?'

'I think I understand,' said Fathers. 'But you didn't get anything?'

'No. The people I know happen not to be in the right kind of position to help on this one. So I had to tell Mike, no dice.'

'Did he talk to you about it again?'

'Oh yeah, just about each time I saw him he'd ask if I'd got anything. I don't think he knew what to do with it if he was the only who had it. These things are pretty tricky, and he may have thought that if it did come out the source would be too obvious, you know what I mean? And whether he was wanting to protect himself or his source or both, he wouldn't want to let it out in a way that was obvious.'

'Tell me,' said Fathers, 'did he ask you to pass it on to a journalist, or to somebody else to pass on?'

'We did talk about that a couple of times. But the thing is that no reporter worth anything is going to touch that kind of story without something pretty solid to back it up, and Mike was really unwilling just to pass on whatever it was he had, I guess because he thought it could be traced back – to him or his source. And you know, there's a thing you may not realise: Reagan is going to win this election partly because the press is so fucking soft on him. It really does make anybody think hard about handing over any kind of shit about Reagan to the press unless you're totally sure that it's going to stick. What if you gave it to some reporter and he says OK, but his editor just says, no, Reagan isn't like that? In Mike's shoes, I think I'd've kept it to myself, too, if I couldn't find a second source to act as some kind of cover for the original, real source.'

'So you don't think he told anybody else about it either?'

'Not to my knowledge.'

Gullick had nothing more to tell him. Fathers thanked him and left with a copy of the two articles – the one Finlay had first mentioned to him and the one from the *Guardian* – both plucked by Gullick without hesitation from the middle of two large piles and photocopied on a machine in the basement.

17

From Gullick's office Fathers walked to Union Station, took the Metro to the airport and flew to New York on the first available shuttle. On the plane, thoughts about what Gullick had said jostled with thoughts about Rosemary. He could concentrate on neither one nor the other, and realised how much he was looking forward to seeing Rosemary again. It seemed a long time since he had been with her on Sunday night. He was beginning to realise that leaving her would not be so easy.

New York was still sultry and sticky. He took the bus to the East Side Terminal and a cab to his hotel. It was just after two p.m. when he collected his key from the lobby desk. The clerk smiled and saying, 'Ah, so you're Mr Fathers,' handed over a sheaf of message slips. Fathers took them up to his room, where he ordered a pot of tea and a ham salad sandwich from room service, changed into clean clothes and then checked his room.

Before leaving for Washington, the policeman's suspiciousness to which Gullick had sceptically referred had prompted Fathers into an unfamiliar course of action. He had never, in any real sense, had the authorities against him. He had never had to bother about the possibility of his possessions being searched, his telephone being tapped, or his room being bugged. But since he had read the supposedly unavailable precinct request for assistance from the Homicide Department on Friday, he had been forced to the conclusion that such things might now happen to him. The telephone call to Finlay had been a calculated and necessary risk. He had, however, taken precautions in his room. When he had realised on the Saturday that he and Rosemary were being followed, at least as far as Staten Island, though he thought they had lost the follower there, he had felt justified, the more so when Miller had as good as confirmed he was being followed.

235

His precautions in his room had been elementary. Certain things were placed just so. Under his underpants in a drawer a matchstick was placed in a corner at an angle of forty-five degrees with its head caught in the gap in the Y-front of the bottom pair – it would be impossible to search the drawer without disturbing it. Even the most careful searcher would not know exactly where it had been before, and would not necessarily realise that it had been placed there deliberately. In another drawer a pile of papers had been arranged with particular sheets sticking out a few precisely measured millimetres; Fathers had noted the measurements on a scrap of paper and put it in his wallet.

He shook his head ruefully when he had completed checking. The matchstick had been moved. The papers had been put back carefully, but not exactly. What had they hoped to achieve? His notes and the copy of the precinct document had all gone with him to Washington in his briefcase.

He read the messages as he sat at the table with his snack lunch. Three were from Mary Wardingley, the woman from the Consulate he had met on his arrival. The first, received on Monday morning, read, 'London reply received – please call'. The second, on Monday afternoon, said, 'Please call urgently', and the third, at noon that day, 'Call immediately'. Lieutenant Grolsch had called twice – once that morning and again just half an hour before. The first message said, 'Please call in at once', and the second, 'Imperative you call immediately'. And there were two from Superintendent Bastin in London, both received that morning, one saying, 'Phone at once', and the other, 'Your return required: call at once'.

Fathers cursed the last message and debated whose calls to return first. He also wanted to call John Franklin to arrange to see him again. The messages could wait. He decided to begin with Franklin, who was not at all pleased to receive Fathers' phone call. When Fathers said he wanted to see him quickly, that afternoon, Franklin demurred. He was booked solid with appointments all afternoon, he said. 'I'm sure it will only take a few minutes,' said Fathers, 'and I'm sorry to press it so hard but

I'll probably be leaving soon for London and just wanted to get a couple of details straight.' Franklin, sounding no less intransigent, then erred by saying it was impossible because his first appointment was in only twenty minutes. 'I'll be there in five,' said Fathers. 'Thank you very much.' He put down the phone without waiting for Franklin's objection, left his room, had the good luck to find a cab right at the hotel door, and was at Franklin Research in four minutes.

When Fathers had seen him the previous Friday afternoon, John Franklin had been courteous but entirely unforthcoming. This time Fathers had decided to dispense with the indirect approach. A comment Simon Goldsack had made during their conversation in Crystal City had suggested a way to open things out a little and he was going to follow it up.

He walked into the reception area of Franklin Research, told the secretary he had an appointment with John Franklin and walked straight in.

'Good afternoon, Mr Franklin,' he said, 'it's very good of you to see me at such short notice.'

'I do not recall agreeing to see you, Mr Fathers,' said Franklin tightly. 'I am not prepared to accept—'

'I do assure you, Mr Franklin,' said Fathers sitting down and smiling, 'that it will only take a moment, concerns one matter only and that it will be quicker if we get straight on with it.'

Franklin sat down behind his desk. He was several years older than Fathers, wearing a white shirt and brown tie with darker brown trousers. The jacket and waistcoat of his suit were on a hanger on a coat stand in the corner of the room.

'Well then?' he asked.

'That's the way,' said Fathers. 'It's just one question. How did you react when Dr Sampson told you he'd stumbled across some information on the possible connection between the Space Shuttle mission numbered STS-8 and the shooting down of the Korean airliner last year?'

Franklin took his time to reply, too much time. Fathers waited.

'He never told me any such thing,' Franklin said at last.

Fathers remained silent and waited.

'Of course,' said Franklin after another minute, 'like anybody working on this subject at that time, he was aware of the article that was published in a London weekly magazine on defence affairs, and he may have mentioned it to me, but that's all.'

Fathers remained silent and waited some more.

Eventually Franklin said, 'I am certainly not aware that Dr Sampson knew anything more than is in that article, or was in any position to confirm its speculations. He certainly had no business to. Naturally, he would have told me if he had done so.'

'Naturally,' said Fathers and waited again.

'It is certainly not the policy of this company,' said Franklin, 'to engage in either investigative journalism or speculative hypothesis.'

'You know,' said Fathers quietly, 'this would go a lot quicker and be much easier if you simply answered my question. I know he had information, and I know he told you. Simply, how did you react?'

'He certainly gave me no details that—'

'No, Mr Franklin: how did you react? That's my question.'

'And I'm afraid I can't answer it since it is based on a false premise.'

'Do you know who arranged for my presence here?' asked Fathers. 'The British Defence Ministry and Foreign Office, and your own Departments of State and Justice. Please, Mr Franklin, don't play around. How did you react?'

Franklin again took a long time to consider his reply. 'I told him to forget it,' he said quietly, not looking at Fathers.

'There,' said Fathers, 'that's progress. Now,' he said encouragingly, 'who did you tell?'

'You said one question,' said Franklin with an almost childish resentment at a broken deal.

'Consider this a subset of the same question,' said Fathers. 'Who did you tell?'

'Obviously,' said Franklin, 'when Sampson refused my advice, I told the contracting agency.'

'DARPA,' said Fathers.

'Yes.'

'Anybody else?'

'Of course not.'

'I'll accept that assurance,' said Fathers getting up. 'Thank you, you've been a great help.'

'I had to,' said Franklin. 'We did argue, of course. He kept on coming back to it. I repeatedly advised him to drop it, but finally, when he didn't, I had to report it.'

'Of course,' said Fathers with his hand on the doorknob.

'I didn't expect ...' said Franklin.

'No,' said Fathers as he opened the door, 'nobody did.'

From Franklin's office, Fathers took a cab to the British Consulate.

'Mr Fathers,' said Mary Wardingley when he was shown into her office, 'you have been much sought after.'

'So I understand,' said Fathers. 'I had to leave town.'

'You might have informed us,' she said with mild reproach. 'I believe that was the understanding.' Fathers shrugged, looking as unconcerned as he felt. 'But no matter, now that you're here,' she continued. 'Let me see. I have two things for you. Yes, here it is. This is the reply from your office to the telex you had us send off on Friday evening. Now, if you'll just wait a moment, I'll fetch the other.'

Fathers looked at Bastin's reply to his initial report. As he had expected, it was brief: 'Your report received with thanks. Continue enquiries until you are sure all avenues are exhausted or further notice, whichever comes first'. Fathers shrugged and folded it away in a jacket pocket. Mary Wardingley returned.

'And here,' she said, 'is your ticket home on the seven-thirty British Airways flight this evening.'

Fathers looked at her.

'I expect you'll need a little while to pack,' she said brightly, 'and there'll be a car ready at your hotel at five o'clock. That should be time enough to get you there by check-in time.'

Fathers continued to look at her.

239

'Superintendent Bastin did say,' she added, 'that he would tell you about this himself. Didn't he?'

'I, er, I haven't yet returned his calls,' said Fathers. 'I was going to after I'd seen you. It's a bit sudden. I'm not sure I'll be ready in time. Isn't there a flight tomorrow morning?'

'Mr Bastin was most insistent that you take the first available flight, even if it meant a foreign carrier, though, thankfully, that's not necessary. We actually made bookings for yesterday evening and this morning, but had to cancel since we couldn't get hold of you. It was yesterday afternoon that he first called.'

Fathers was preparing an excuse and a protest, but Mary Wardingley cut him off. 'Actually, he did say that, if necessary, I should accompany you to the airport myself, but I'm sure he didn't really mean that, did he?'

Fathers smiled and surrendered. 'I suppose he just knows I sometimes don't like doing what I'm told. Could I use your phone?'

'By all means,' she said, and discreetly left the room as Fathers dialled the number for the Homicide Department. He was put through to Lieutenant Grolsch.

'Well, Harry, ain't you the hard one to find?'

'I had to leave town,' said Fathers, 'and it took longer than I expected. Is anything up?'

'Lots of things. I understand you're going home?'

'Yes, so I just found out. I was planning to come down and check I haven't left anything I might want in the room you lent me.'

'OK. Do that. Talk to you then.'

Fathers put down the phone and left the room. 'I'm off,' he said to Mary Wardingley in the outer office. 'Sorry if I caused you any trouble. Thank you very much for looking after me.'

They shook hands. 'You're most welcome,' she said. 'I hope you enjoyed your stay.'

Fathers was shown into Lieutenant Grolsch's office. 'Hi, Harry,' he said. 'Agent Weiser is in with Captain Amstel right now. You wanted to see him.'

'Wanted,' said Fathers. 'I don't think it matters now. Were you trying to get in touch with me about anything in particular?'

'Yes,' said Grolsch. 'Rosemary Willis is dead.'

Fathers sat down suddenly and said nothing. He was silent for a long time. Grolsch looked at him. 'How?' asked Fathers finally.

'Car accident,' said Grolsch simply. 'Hit-and-run. It must have been late last night. She was brought into the morgue before dawn this morning.'

'Hit-and-run,' said Fathers.

'Yeah,' said Grolsch.

'Late at night.'

'Yeah. Are you OK?'

Father said nothing for a while. He sat very still, very pale, hoping the shaking inside would not be copied by his hands or his voice. Images of Sunday night with Rosemary beat in his brain.

Grolsch walked round his desk and stood by Fathers. 'They said you had a thing going,' he said gently.

'Did they?' asked Fathers without inflection

'It's all a bit shitty, isn't it?'

'What do you mean?' asked Fathers, looking up.

'When somebody you're close to dies, whatever that closeness is, that's all.'

'Yes,' said Fathers, 'it's all a bit shitty. Come with me. Somebody has to know.'

He stood up and walked out of Grolsch's office and along the corridor to the room where the evidence from the Sampson case was held. Grolsch followed as Fathers opened the door, went in, and picked the large cookery book off the shelf. He took the dust-jacket off and handed it to Grolsch. 'There,' he said, 'that's what it's all about.'

Grolsch read the neatly written cryptic notes. 'What's it mean?'

Fathers looked at him for a moment. 'Probably better you don't know,' he said. 'Excuse me a moment, I'm going to xerox this.'

'Haven't you done enough damage with photocopies?' asked Grolsch.

'No,' said Fathers, 'not yet. Where's the machine?'

Grolsch showed him and worked the machine himself. Fathers folded the copy into a square and put it in a pocket. They went back to the room, and he replaced the dust-jacket on the book and the book on the shelf. He went into what had been his own office. Some of his original notes from the first two days' of looking at files lay in a neat pile on the desk. He picked them up, found a pocket that was not yet bulging with paperwork, and shoved·them in. He took one last look around the room, left it and closed the door. Grolsch was waiting in the corridor.

'One thing,' Fathers said. 'Have you checked Rosemary's apartment?'

Grolsch shook his head.

'Do,' said Fathers. 'Look for signs of breaking and entering and signs of somebody searching it, even if it doesn't look like anything's been stolen. I'd appreciate a quiet word from you if you come up with anything.'

Grolsch nodded. Fathers shook hands with him. 'Give my regards to Captain Amstel and thank him from me for Sunday's hospitality,' he said. 'Don't say anything to Mr Weiser.'

'I know you didn't take to him' said Grolsch, 'and I know he had you followed, but he's just a policeman, same as you and me.'

'No,' said Fathers, 'that I can't believe.'

'Well,' said Grolsch, 'will you believe me if I say I wish we could all have been strictly on the level with you?'

'Yes,' said Fathers, 'I can believe that.'

'I never directly lied to you, Harry.'

'And I only occasionally lied to you,' said Fathers. 'Only when I had to.'

Grolsch nodded. 'Lots of tough shots,' he said.

Fathers turned on his heel and walked back to his hotel to pack.

18

Early morning at Heathrow Airport on Wednesday, 1 November, was cold and grey. Fathers phoned home once he had cleared Customs. He had forgotten to call Sarah from his hotel or from Kennedy, his mind alternatively too full and too blank to deal with anything apart from the basics of checking in and getting on the aircraft. During the flight, he had had several whiskies to make himself sleep and dull the bitter edge of alternating guilt and rage he felt about Rosemary. By the time he made the phone call he was tired and hungover. Sarah sounded surprised and pleased to hear him.

By the time he got home the children had gone to school, but Sarah had delayed going in to work and had prepared him a cooked breakfast of welcome. 'How was it?' she asked.

'Not good,' he said. She looked at his tired, white face and left it at that. When he had eaten in silence he went to bed and slept, and she went to work.

When he woke up it was early afternoon. He mooched around the house for a while, then left a note for Sarah and went into work. There he went through the motions of accepting welcome-backs from the detectives in his team. But even the most boisterous of them noticed his quiet, internalised air and quickly went back to their duties. He went into his own office, ignoring the large pile of files on his desk, and phoned Bastin.

Chief Superintendent Bastin looked almost as grim as Fathers felt when he walked into his superior's office, but he too made the motions of welcome.

'Good to see you back, Harry,' he said. 'Sorry it was such short notice but we've been feeling the need of you here, and since you appeared not to be making much progress I decided to get you back straightaway. But you do look rather tired. If I were you, I'd take the rest of the day off and settle back into work tomorrow. Got to watch out for jet-lag and disorientation, you know.'

'I think I made some progress in the end,' said Fathers. 'I'm just checking in now. I'll do up my report tomorrow.'

'Yes,' said Bastin, 'when you've time, when you've time.'

'And then you can arrange another meeting at the Home Office,' said Fathers, 'and I'll deliver my report.'

'I'm not sure that will be necessary.'

'I am.'

'Look, Harry, this is pretty much a dead case now. Do up the report, as you say, and I'll send copies along. There'll be a meeting if they want one for any comments, supplementary details, and so on.'

Fathers looked at him tiredly. 'Look,' he said, 'when I was instructed to go to New York, I was also instructed to report back in person to Messrs Foster, Hanson and Witherspoon. It's in the letter from the AC, in case you've forgotten.'

'Of course, Harry, of course. I'm just not sure they'll want to do it that way. It's simply not such a priority now.'

'Why don't you just fix the meeting?' asked Fathers. 'Any time after tomorrow.'

He left Bastin's office and went back to his own. 'A word with you, James,' he said as he passed Detective Inspector Stevens' desk. 'So tell me what's new,' he said, sitting down.

Stevens looked at him for a minute, then picked up the folders from Fathers' desk and tucked them under his arm. 'Go home,' he said and went back to his own desk. Fathers followed him out. 'Go home,' said Stevens again, 'I'll tell you tomorrow.'

They were gathered again in the same Home Office room: Hanson, the stocky balding Scot from the Home Office; Foster, thinner and rather aristocratic from the Foreign Office; Witherspoon, taller and slightly overweight, from the Ministry of Defence; Bastin, wearing a permanent frown; and Fathers, feeling relaxed, recovered and confident, wearing a grey winter suit.

They were not all gathered again, however. The pair sitting in the corner before – Mrs Redmond and the other note-taker, who had remained anonymous – were not present this time. The five men helped themselves to the usual tea and biscuits from the trolley.

It was Thursday morning – two days after Ronald Reagan was re-elected President of the United States – the week after Fathers returned from New York. The weekend with his family had restored him – as it always did. A renewed surge of warmth at home had overridden his guilt about Rosemary. He had shopped with Sarah on Saturday morning and pottered in the garden for the afternoon. In the evening they found a babysitter and went to a film. Sarah was delighted with having him around for a full weekend. She sparkled, and he responded. After the film they went home and made love for the first time since he had got back – for the first time since over two weeks before he had left, in fact. Fine weather on Sunday had allowed them to make a long winter outing to Epping Forest. A form of normality had returned.

The guilt he felt about Rosemary was not because he had had an affair with another woman. It was not something he or Sarah did much, though he knew for sure of three occasions when she had slept with other men during their marriage, and he had done so with two other women before New York – with one just once, and with another in a chaotic month-long affair which had sparked wildly, run quickly out of steam and petered out amicably. Although he often worried that Sarah would find a man who would satisfy her in every way more than he did, he did not worry that such brief flings would rock their marriage. And infidelity held no resonance of sin for him. But he believed agonisingly that he had put Rosemary in danger. He could justify their affair to himself on grounds of pragmatism – he had no doubt that she had been more open and spoken more freely and usefully because of their sexual relationship than she would otherwise. At the very least, it needed friendship to open her up. Sex and passion simply took it further. He could also justify it to himself on the grounds which need no justifying – they were attracted, she had needed something to restore her sense of herself, another if not him, it had been good, warm and gentle, they had given each other something. But he could not justify or

245

forgive himself for how exposed it had left her in that dangerous world. If, he thought – if, and he really didn't know, he could only guess, suspect, fear – if she died because of him, not all the guilt was his, because he could not lose, and did not want to lose, his rage at her death. But enough of it was.

Guilt was not a new companion to Fathers. I will live with it, he thought, diminished but still here.

He did not tell Sarah about Rosemary, and she had easily taken his pale quietness for fatigue, especially as he began to shake it off. When she asked about the case, he gave her a heavily censored version: neither Rosemary nor various other aspects figured in his account. He let her understand that his enquiries had been entirely frustrating and unproductive. On Sunday evening, before they made love again, she told him she felt he had returned to her in more senses than one. He accepted that, putting it alongside both the bright and the dark of his memory of Rosemary, which he held now under control, not allowing it to affect his new closeness with Sarah. Habits of secrecy and compartmentalising his life were deeply ingrained.

The day after his return he had received a phone call from Lieutenant Grolsch. Rosemary's apartment had been broken into, but the case was now closed. Working late, Fathers completed the report on his American trip. He had spent the next day, Friday, re-familiarising himself with two pending court cases delayed by his absence, catching up on the new crimes, taking up the reins again from DI Stevens. Since the weekend he had settled back into his routine, doling out the work, checking on his subordinates. He had taken Detective Constable Yarrow out for a drink, thanked him for his help, reminded him of the need for discretion and, in a general review of the young detective's work since joining the Serious Crimes Squad, congratulated him on his progress. Yarrow had seemed surprised, pleased and encouraged in equal measure. Each morning and afternoon he had chivvied Bastin about arranging the meeting with the civil servants. His boss surrendered to his persistence on Tuesday afternoon, when he ran out of excuses on the others' behalf.

The three civil servants and two detectives sat down at the table in the same arrangement as before: Hanson at its head, Witherspoon and Foster on his right, Bastin and Fathers on his left. Hanson cleared his throat and Fathers immediately chimed in with, 'No notes today?'

'No,' said Hanson. 'I was about to mention that. It was felt that, with your written report before us, we could dispense with the requirement for an *aide memoire*. The Foreign Office concurred on this point and Defence again saw no need. Should we feel the need of an unified account, I feel sure we can exchange an agreed memorandum.' He looked at Witherspoon, who ignored him, and at Foster, who gestured assent with his left hand. 'However,' he continued, 'it appears we do not yet have your written report.'

'No,' said Fathers. 'I thought it made more sense to give it to you now. Here.' He gave Bastin, on his right, four copies of his thick report. Bastin kept one and passed the others to Hanson, who did likewise, passing the other two on to Witherspoon, who handed the last one to Foster at the other end of the semicircle.

'Should we take a moment to read it now?' asked Foster.

'That's not really necessary,' said Fathers. 'I can probably summarise as quickly as you can read.' Foster nodded, but Witherspoon began to read it anyway.

'The report,' said Fathers, 'is in several parts. Part One is a bald summary of what we knew up to the point I arrived in New York, together with a record of my written and verbal instructions. As you recall, Mr Witherspoon, you told me that I was to report not only on what hard information I found and what events I could prove had occurred, but also on my assessment of the probabilities of what happened.'

Fathers paused long enough for Witherspoon to feel he had to say something. 'That is so,' he said gravely and returned to his reading.

'And it's also what my Assistant Commissioner told me in writing,' said Fathers. 'Part Two sets out a series of proven facts: things that I know happened. As you will see, they're organised

247

in three categories. You could think of them as inner, middle and outer circles. At the core are those things that beyond doubt or argument pertain directly to Dr Sampson's disappearance. In the middle circle are things that are almost certainly connected with either his disappearance or his work in the period shortly before it. In the outer circle are things that, while directly connected with Dr Sampson or his work, might not initially seem related to his disappearance. Do I make myself clear?'

'Admirably,' said Hanson.

'All ears,' muttered Witherspoon, still reading.

'Part Three is a hypothesis I have constructed in the form of a narrative which links and explains the various facts in Part Two. Part Four briefly outlines alternative, less satisfactory, hypotheses. And there is a conclusion and an appendix of copies of various documents. What I propose to do is tell you the main hypothesis.'

'Please proceed,' said Hanson.

'On the night of thirty-first August and first September, nineteen eighty-three,' Fathers began, 'a Korean airliner was shot down on its second intrusion into Soviet airspace.' Bastin looked up in surprise; the other three showed no reaction.

'There has been considerable speculation,' said Fathers, 'about how and why the tragedy happened, and especially why the airliner was so off course. One theory concentrates on human errors and mechanical failures. Another, less widely supported, suggests that the airliner was there deliberately, as part of an American ploy to test out Soviet air defence procedures in that area. In support of this theory, evidence has been advanced about the presence in the vicinity some time before the incident of an electronic reconnaissance aircraft, about the orbits of a Ferret-D reconnaissance satellite, and about the relative proximity of the US Space Shuttle. The fullest public statement of this theory is a magazine article published in this country; a copy is appended to my report.'

Fathers paused to take a sip of tea. Witherspoon was looking at him with interest now, Fathers' report open before him on the table. Foster was staring at a point in the middle of the table. Bastin and Hanson were both making notes.

'There is also another theory,' said Fathers, 'though it appears to have little credence and I don't mention it in the report. According to it, the intrusion was deliberate, in order to provoke the Russians to shoot the plane down so that the Americans could reap the propaganda advantages of that. I have appended a copy of the article containing that theory, but I have given it no attention.'

'Good,' muttered Foster.

Fathers continued. 'For most of this year, Dr Sampson's work on the staff of Franklin Research Associates was a study of certain aspects of the Space Shuttle programme. During it, he came across further information relating to the tragedy of the Korean airliner, but not contained in that article. One aspect of this concerned the possible cutting of Soviet undersea communications cables in the area where the tragedy occurred. This is a widespread rumour in Washington at the moment. Everybody working in this field seems to know about it, but nobody appears to know how or where it started, or to be able to confirm it.'

'Are you suggesting Sampson might have been the initial source for it?' asked Witherspoon.

Fathers shrugged. 'It doesn't affect the hypothesis one way or the other,' he said. Witherspoon nodded. Fathers continued. 'The second item concerned the distance of the Space Shuttle from the incident. Sampson firmly believed it was closer than the magazine article put it. His reasons derived from technical calculations he had made himself.'

'How much closer?' asked Witherspoon.

'I don't know,' said Fathers. 'The few notes he left didn't say. It doesn't affect the hypothesis, either.'

'And do you know where he got the data for his calculations?'

'From another research company, with approval, but again it's irrelevant to the hypothesis.'

'Please continue, Mr Fathers,' said Hanson, casting a look at Witherspoon.

'The third piece of information Sampson got from a woman he was having an affair with who worked as a secretary at the State Department in Washington. He believed it proved that President

Reagan knew in advance of the Shuttle-airliner mission.' Foster looked up suddenly with his mouth open. Witherspoon grinned and put a restraining hand on Foster's arm.

Fathers continued without pause. 'Sampson told his superior, John Franklin, about his information. He also encouraged a friend in Washington to confirm the information from a different source, but the friend was unable to oblige. Franklin attempted to persuade Sampson to drop the subject and continue with his main, contracted study. When Sampson refused to, Franklin felt it necessary to report to the Department of Defense what Sampson was up to.'

Fathers paused again for another sip of tea. Nobody else spoke.

'Sampson was then put under surveillance by the FBI, probably for some weeks. Whatever happened to Sampson, they know. If I can just digress into my reasoning at this point, there are two possibilities: either Sampson has defected, or he's been killed. The possibility that he has gone into hiding on his own account seems ruled out by his non-reappearance when the FBI must be looking for him very hard. Unless they were incompetent, it would take a very professional and experienced set of operators to spirit Sampson away with all his work materials. It's unbelievable that Sampson could do that himself, or that he would know people who could do it for him, or that he had the funds to pay them on his own account, fix a new identity, cover, all the rest. I assume such things would come as expensive in New York as in London, where they would cost several thousand pounds in initial outlay and a continuing supply of cash thereafter. My view that the FBI know what happened to him is strengthened by the fact that, without being notified by the local police, they turned up at Sampson's apartment at about the same time as the police, when his disappearance was first reported. If he defected, it's more than a month since it happened – wouldn't one expect him to have surfaced by now in Havana or Moscow to make embarrassing allegations about the American President?'

Nobody answered.

250

'So my money is on him having been murdered and his body efficiently disposed of. If that happened, again taking the FBI's surveillance into account, it was done by some official organ of the US government. I suppose they do have people available for such things *in extremis*?'

No response again.

'Since then, the two women with whom Sampson was intimately involved have both been killed, both in the same way: hit-and-run car accidents late at night. There were signs at Rosemary Willis' apartment that it was broken into. Since nothing was stolen – or rather, since items of value weren't removed – the conclusion must be that it was entered to be searched. It seems likely that she was the victim not of a car accident, but of a deliberate killing. The assumption is less strong but plausible for the woman in Washington.'

Fathers drained his cup.

'In sum,' he said, 'Dr Sampson came across information embarrassing to the US government and was removed from the scene because his discretion couldn't be trusted. The source of that information and the woman to whom he might have confided it – though in fact he didn't – were dealt with likewise. That's the hypothesis.'

A long silence followed. When Fathers broke it by standing up and going to refill his teacup, Hanson did the same. 'Yes,' he said gratefully, 'more tea I think, gentlemen, more tea.'

When they sat down, it was Witherspoon who started in on Fathers' account. 'Though your hypothesis fits all the facts, I wonder if it is right to assume that all the facts must be made to fit the hypothesis.'

Foster looked approvingly at his colleague from Defence. 'Yes,' said the Foreign Office man, 'for example, car accidents do happen and need not be related to your central story. Or again, the fact that valuable items were left in the woman Willis' apartment doesn't mean that others weren't removed. The conclusion may point to either discriminating or incompetent crooks, rather than to a search.'

251

'And the status of certain components of your hypothesis may be in doubt,' said Witherspoon.

'Indeed,' said Foster. 'For example, do you know for a fact that the FBI had Sampson under surveillance? It seems a key part of your hypothesis, but is it more than a guess?'

Fathers spoke carefully. 'It's a reasonable inference from the available facts. They were interested in him before his disappearance. It's mentioned in the local precinct's request for assistance, which is appended.'

'Even that,' said Foster, 'may rest on a misperception on the part of the precinct.'

'So why were they so reluctant to let me see that document?' asked Fathers. 'And how did the FBI turn up at the apartment so fast without being told by the police?'

'Ah,' said Foster, 'I cannot claim to know American police procedures well, but I am sure there may be an alternative explanation to your own.'

I bet you are, thought Fathers.

Witherspoon flipped through the appendix and found the copy of Sampson's notes. 'I see,' he said, 'that the reference to the President in Dr Sampson's notes, assuming they are his, which seems likely I agree, is cryptic – consisting only of the letters, "RR" – and is surrounded by question marks. That doesn't sound like Sampson being in possession of hard evidence and might even refer to somebody or something else.'

'No,' said Fathers, 'it was one of his friends – the one who Sampson asked to provide further confirmation – who told me that. If Sampson made any other notes, they were taken. That's all I saw.'

'The New York police and the FBI did let you see that,' commented Hanson.

'No,' said Fathers, 'they didn't know about it. I found it for myself inside the dust-jacket on a cookery book that hadn't been taken from his office along with all the other things. I only looked because I accidentally discovered he wasn't interested in cooking.'

'Still,' said Foster with a very reasonable smile, 'if Sampson thought he had hard evidence, why did he want further confirmation from this unnamed friend?'

'So that it could be convincingly leaked to the press without implicating Sampson or his source,' said Fathers pleasantly, watching Foster's smile fade.

'Be that as it may,' said Witherspoon quickly, 'we are notably lacking in any documentary evidence, even for some of what you state as certain facts, for which I think you are over-dependent on second and third-hand accounts.'

'Well,' said Fathers, 'since both the New York police and the FBI were holding various things back, and since Sampson himself wasn't around to help, second- and third-hand is all there was.'

'Perhaps,' conceded Witherspoon, 'but I would contend that, even if what you have is the most reliable evidence available, force of circumstance has left it something less than adequate.'

Hanson intervened. 'I believe you referred to other hypotheses, Mr Fathers?'

'Indeed,' said Foster, 'you did. Perhaps you could elaborate.'

'Well,' said Fathers, 'as Mr Witherspoon put it, the facts don't all have to fit the hypothesis. You can, for example, leave the deaths of the two women out, although the fact that Rosemary Willis' apartment was broken into is something that ought to be explained. If you do that, however, I think there are two main possibilities. Either he defected and whoever oversaw his going arranged to remove all his work material, or perhaps he did surprise intruders in his apartment, was killed, and then the FBI removed all the material for security reasons. Going back to the old theory of a burglary at both places, plus murder by burglars disturbed in the act, is stretching coincidence a good deal too far.'

'Agreed,' said Foster, 'yet you are left with two perfectly satisfactory alternative hypotheses.'

'No,' said Fathers. 'Neither is satisfactory. If Gail Sanders, the woman in Washington, was, as seems likely, the source for

253

Sampson's information about the President, her death needs to be explained. Coincidence is possible, but the double coincidence of a man and his two lovers all being killed within a month is going too far, especially since you have the break-in at Miss Willis' apartment. And there's still the original problem with the disturbed intruder theory: if a burglar, or two or more, were surprised and killed him, they'd just run. If they took anything with them it would not be his body and it would not be his work materials. It is all entirely unconvincing.'

'Defection, though,' said Witherspoon, 'might cover the lot.'

'Yes,' said Foster, 'I'm very inclined to that explanation myself.'

'Except that he seems a very unlikely figure for such an operation. Other people have far more access than he ever had to classified secrets and far more technical knowledge to offer. And you're still left with the coincidence of the two women.'

'Perhaps only one was coincidence,' said Foster. 'The Washington woman, perhaps, while Miss Willis may have killed herself in grief – either at Sampson's death or his perfidy.'

'No,' said Fathers.

'Or the other way round,' said Witherspoon.

'And the break-in?' asked Fathers.

Foster and Witherspoon remained silent.

'Don't you find it difficult to be scraping the bottom of the barrel so much?' said Fathers.

'On no,' said Witherspoon, 'we do it all the time. It's our job, you know.' The look Foster directed at him was almost murderous.

Hanson intervened again. 'I see your objections to these alternative hypotheses, Mr Fathers, and at first hearing they are convincing. But surely there are similar objections to your own preferred explanation, even leaving out the objection that the thought of the President's involvement in such an action as you suggest over the Korean airliner is simply too monstrous to contemplate, while the action you suggest the United States government took against Dr Sampson is preposterous. It's a democracy, for heaven's sake.'

'Our major ally,' said Foster, 'leader of the Free World.'

254

Fathers frowned, but said nothing.

'Let's look at the flaws in your preferred version,' said Witherspoon. 'For example, you provide no explanation for why Sampson was removed – if he was, which I don't necessarily concede – at the precise time he was, rather than sooner.'

'Nor,' said Foster, 'for why Rosemary Willis was removed – if she was, speculating without prejudice – some weeks after Sampson's disappearance, rather than sooner.'

'Well,' said Fathers, his calmness over his racing thoughts requiring a major effort, 'she proved to be a very cooperative witness. Perhaps that was the problem.'

Foster's mouth opened and closed a couple of times. 'Do you know what you are suggesting?' he asked finally.

'Yes,' said Fathers.

They were silent for a moment before Foster took it up again. 'Given the flaws and the unanswered questions in your main hypothesis,' he said, 'alternative explanations could be made to carry as much weight as the one you have chosen to concentrate your imagination on. The report would be better framed if you reworked the balance of your theories. Defection, I think, should receive rather more attention, as should the possibility of murder by disturbed intruders. The one you outlined at the beginning should be somewhat de-emphasised and its shortcomings highlighted, while the most judicious conclusion would be that we do not know, and I fear probably never will know, exactly what happened to Dr Sampson.'

'That seems the most solid conclusion,' said Hanson.

'So I hope,' said Foster, 'you will emphasise that conclusion when you redraft your report along the lines we have been suggesting.'

'Oh, I can't do that,' said Fathers.

'Why not?' enquired Foster. 'I think we are of an accord that it would be more satisfactory all round.'

'Because I've already deposited the necessary copies in the appropriate files and registers.'

Hanson cleared his throat, but Foster was the first to respond. 'I'm not sure as to the precise propriety of that, Chair,' he commented.

'Why not?' asked Fathers.

Hanson took it up. 'I imagine the Foreign Office view is that, since your instruction was to report to this group, and especially since you yourself were insistent on making your report in person, there would be a chance here for a preliminary discussion before any documentation was irrevocably committed to the archives.' Foster nodded.

'I must say,' Hanson continued, 'that was my own impression and one of the main reasons for consenting to this meeting, so as to have a chance of avoiding any misunderstandings or misleading nuances.'

'Routine procedure,' said Foster 'especially in cases of inter-departmental consultation.'

'It may be routine for you,' said Fathers, 'but I'm afraid it's not for us. I was instructed to report: here is my report. I was instructed to report to you in person: here we are, in person. You're here to receive and discuss my report, not to change it.' He paused and sipped his tea. 'Anyway, how could you change it? You weren't there.'

Hanson fiddled irritably with a pencil, looked at Bastin and coughed.

'I'm afraid,' said Bastin, speaking for the first time, 'that Harry is right – right about our procedure with reports, right about his instructions. Right is what he usually is, in fact,' he added gloomily, but offering a degree of support that Fathers had not expected.

'I can scarcely believe, Chair,' said Foster, 'that the police never amend a report after its first draft. That would suggest a quite extraordinary institutional facility in the drafting of reports.'

'A junior officer,' said Fathers, 'might ask for, or be told to accept, assistance. But tampering with reports after they've been written could be quite a serious internal offence.'

'Tampering is not the issue,' said Hanson.

'Nor are misunderstandings and nuances,' said Fathers. 'What you want to change are the conclusions and half the substance. I'm sorry to disappoint you, but if you wanted to co-author the report, you could have informed me beforehand, and I could have refused then.'

'This is hardly satisfactory,' said Foster.

'I ask you to bear in mind,' said Fathers mildly, 'that I made my unwillingness to undertake this enquiry in New York very clear – too clear, in fact, as you'll recall, Mr Foster. I went because I was instructed to go, and I went under protest. That is also on file. I was required to report not only on the facts but also on my assessment of the probable explanation for them. Not only Mr Witherspoon verbally, but also my Assistant Commissioner in writing, were quite explicit about that. I have done as I was told, and none of you has any ground for complaint. If you disagree with my hypothesis, so be it, but that is my report and it stands.'

'Anyway,' said Witherspoon, 'the report's been filed now.'

'Moreover,' said Fathers, 'you've received it and, just for the sake of completeness, I'd like you to sign for it. Here.' He passed Hanson a document his secretary had typed up. It was an acknowledgement, dated that day, that a report from Detective Chief Inspector Fathers, concerning his enquiries in New York into the disappearance of Dr Michael Sampson, had been received by Hanson, Foster and Witherspoon. There was space for each man's signature above his name.

As Fathers passed it over, Bastin gave a near shudder and seemed to duck his head into his shoulders. The Home Office man looked at Fathers.

'Is there any problem?' asked Fathers innocently. He could see Hanson thinking, You know what the problem is. 'Purely routine,' he said coaxingly.

Hanson scribbled and passed the document on. When Fathers received it back from Foster, he saw that the nimble Civil Servants had all added qualifications to their signatures: 'With strong reservations' by Hanson's name; 'Received but not accepted' by Witherspoon's, and 'Ditto' by Foster's.

'Thank you,' said Fathers.

'And now,' said Foster acidly, 'I suppose you have suggestions for further action?'

'No,' said Fathers. 'You pulled me out in time to stop further action. We can't do anything from here.'

'This isn't really evidence, is it, Harry?' asked Bastin. He had been looking increasingly miserable as the session went on, but this remark was brightly made.

'Not at all,' said Fathers cheerfully. 'It wouldn't stand up in a court of law for a moment.'

'Case closed then,' said Hanson. 'Thank you one and all.'

Bastin and Fathers got up, said goodbyes and left. When the Civil Servants were alone, Witherspoon stood up, stretched and swore.

'I think we shall be exchanging that memo, Fossie,' said Hanson. Foster nodded.

'Let that be a lesson,' said Witherspoon through a yawn. 'Next time we send an experienced investigator off on his own, let's be sure we want the product of his investigations.'

'Point taken,' said Foster.

'It would also be an idea,' said Hanson, 'if you wouldn't change your minds half-way through.'

'Out of our control, Jock, as you know,' said Foster.

'One thing, though,' said Witherspoon, 'you notice that every hypothesis includes the premise that the FBI know what happened.'

'I tried to shake him on that,' said Foster.

'You tried,' said the man from Defence condescendingly. 'You do know, don't you, that the defection theory is poppycock?'

'Who's to say what's poppycock and what's not in these times?' asked Foster. 'I do know it would be embarrassing for you people, though, after you gave him your bill of good health.'

'The view, I take it,' said Hanson, 'will be that though this is an experienced, competent man who did his best, his array of evidence is not adequate to support his hypothesis, and so we cannot know what happened to Sampson and no further action can be taken.

'That should do it,' said Witherspoon closing his copy of Fathers' report.

'And perhaps I'll just have a wee word about Mr Fathers,' said Hanson grimly.

19

Fathers returned to his office after a frosty drive from Whitehall with Bastin, and a quick, solo lunch time drink. Though Bastin's silence shouted his disapproval of his subordinate, he had said nothing since he knew of nothing for which to reprove him. This time there had been no loss of temper, no rudeness – merely a precise carrying out of his instructions. That, Fathers decided, was why Bastin was so disapproving: he had done wrong only by doing right. He was not about to change Bastin's perception by letting him know about his affair with Rosemary, his phone call to Finlay, or his occasional deceitfulness with the New York authorities.

As he entered the general office, Yarrow, emboldened since their session together two evenings ago, said, 'We've struck gold.'

Stevens loomed up behind the younger man's shoulder. 'May have struck gold,' he corrected him.

'What kind of gold?' asked Fathers.

'Bullion kind of gold,' said Stevens, 'from a Heathrow warehouse.'

'You remember the case,' said Yarrow.

'Of course,' said Fathers. 'Come and tell me all about it, James.' And he walked into his own office with Stevens, leaving the excited Yarrow standing bewildered. Fathers, it seemed, had not changed.

'Is this for real?' asked Fathers sitting down at his desk.

'Could well be. If it is, it's down to the lad.'

'Yarrow?' Stevens nodded. 'Bring him in then. Sorry, I thought he was just a bystander.'

Stevens went to the door. 'Yarrow!' he shouted. 'Bring three coffees, one the way you like it.'

'I don't like it,' Yarrow called back.

'At least his name isn't Gregory Schlitz,' said Fathers.

'Eh?'

'The coffee carrier where I was in New York was called that.'

'Poor bugger,' said Stevens.

Yarrow came in, carrying three coffees. 'Thanks,' said Stevens, 'siddown.' Yarrow sat. Fathers put his feet up on his desk. Stevens lit a French cigarette.

'Proceed,' said Fathers comfortably.

'I'll tell it,' said Stevens to Yarrow, 'then it won't sound like boasting when it comes out how clever you are.' Yarrow grinned and squirmed a little.

'Do you remember the name Peter Hughes?' Stevens began. 'No? Nor did I. This clever sod did, though.' He paused.

'How pleasing,' said Fathers. 'Do get on with it. I know you want me to acknowledge our lad's cleverness – you're making it painfully obvious – but please get to the point so I can be suitably stunned.'

'Peter Hughes,' said Stevens, 'works for Jason Security – a name you will remember.'

'Handled the security at the warehouse where eight million pounds of gold was lifted,' said Fathers, nodding.

'Said Hughes was picked up at the weekend, one of a group emptying a large house near Henley. One of those total removal jobs. Owners away on a little trip to the West Indies for a winter break – you know the kind of thing – and chanced to return a week early. The owner is something in the City, and apparently his something was facing a bit of a crisis and he had to interrupt his holiday.'

'How frustrating,' said Fathers. 'Isn't life a bitch?'

'Seeing a pantechnicon pulled up in their modest driveway, he acted quickly and drove straight to the nearest police station, which, with the same commendable dispatch, sent a bunch of flatfeet along who copped the lot.'

'Go on.'

'You don't need telling that we've been centralising reports on this kind of blag, so in the fullness of time a report came our way

260

and landed on the desk of our young hero who, quick as a flash, came to tell me that Peter Hughes had been picked up, and politely filled me in when I expressed my ignorance of the man.'

'I did check first, actually,' said Yarrow.

'Smart work indeed,' said Fathers.

'Anyway,' said Stevens, 'we bombed out there this morning. The Hemel lads have done a fine job of putting the frighteners on them all, and it seems they'll wear a few other jobs in this line as well.'

'So you went to see this Hughes,' said Fathers, 'and found him nicely softened up, whereupon, you pair of lying gits, you told him you had him bang to rights for the bullion job and he spilled the old beans.'

'Straight into our laps, guv,' said Stevens delightedly, 'straight into our laps. Cough, cough, cough. Coughed the lot.'

'And?'

'And,' said Stevens, 'and … No, you tell him.'

'And,' said Yarrow, 'we have an address which …'

'Don't tell me,' said Fathers, 'let me guess – an address which happens to feature among the two dozen or so thrown up by your computer work.'

'Got it in one,' said Stevens. 'But we don't only have an address.'

'There's more?' said Fathers. 'Oh, happy day.'

'What they've been a doing of,' said Stevens, 'is filtering the gold out of the country bit by bit and selling it to a bloke in Paris.'

'Good,' said Fathers, 'we need to do a favour for the frogs. Does this mean there's still some left?'

'According to Hughes,' said Yarrow, 'unless they've moved it since he was picked up.'

'If they know he's been picked up,' said Stevens.

'Right,' said Fathers getting up. 'Let's roll it over.'

'Ready to go,' said Stevens.

'Ha ha,' said Fathers walking round his desk, 'they are going to hate him. Let's get going, keeping our fingers crossed. Nice one, Cyril.' This last remark was to Yarrow, accompanied by a slap on

261

the shoulder. The three detectives left the office in high delight.

Late on Friday morning, Fathers sat in Bastin's office. He was enjoying himself quietly at the expense of his superior, who was visibly seething from a mixture of emotions. As the senior officer in the Serious Crimes Squad, he naturally benefited from any of his Squad's successes, just as Fathers benefited from Yarrow's quick thinking on seeing the name of Peter Hughes in the middle of a report. Bastin had, therefore, not only had to congratulate Fathers on the breakthrough in the bullion case as a matter of form, he also was genuinely pleased. A feather in Fathers' cap was a feather in his own. On the other hand, when Fathers annoyed senior Civil Servants and started ripples in New York which spread to Washington and thence to London, it was Bastin who bore the brunt of criticism, blame and pressure. What made it worse was, first, that Fathers seemed not to care and simply stood by his assertion that everything he had done had been according to reluctantly accepted instructions, and, second, that he was obviously right. Bastin's comments about displeasure in high quarters could not shake Fathers from his stated view that he was prepared to argue his case with anybody, and that if Bastin cared to set up another meeting with any or all of the interested parties then he, Fathers, would be happy to attend.

The raid on the address in the Berkshire countryside given by Hughes had been a total success. The house had been surrounded, then entered. Two men were there, along with what a hastily summoned expert estimated to be about half the stolen bullion. The press, already alerted, had been sent for. Too late for the Friday morning newspapers, the arrests were nonetheless reported on the morning radio and television news and wholly favourable coverage was expected to continue for a day or two. Separately, Detective Sergeant Pardoner had been sent to arrest the house's owner. All three men had reacted to their arrests exactly as Hughes had when Stevens and Yarrow spun him the story that they knew everything there was to know about the bullion theft. None of them saw good reason why they should be the only ones to be charged with it and, with little pressure, had supplied a fine list of names. Arrests had continued through

Thursday night and into Friday morning. Meanwhile, the telephone wires were burning up with the Paris police's gratitude; they had raided three likely addresses on advice from Fathers, and at one of them had found four gold bars, immediately identified as part of the haul from the warehouse near Heathrow.

As a result, what Bastin had originally intended as a session in which he would convey disapproval to Fathers, had begun with him offering congratulations on a major success. Fathers was, in any case, not at all prepared to be contrite about the way he had handled the previous day's meeting. But the successful conclusion to an investigation he had long since given up on had provided a welcome strengthening to his position. A case cleared up always provided all the defence that was needed against recriminations for past boobs, blunders and bloody-mindedness. He found a way of implicitly communicating this to Bastin, and left him to twist in the conflicting winds.

Fathers had no sympathy for Bastin's predicament. In his own view, his boss could deflect all the pressure by standing on the ground of correct police procedure, and asking whose idea it was in the first place to send him to New York would start enough recriminations going to leave Bastin well-covered until the whole fuss blew over. What he did not know was that Bastin had already started to mobilise his defence on exactly those lines, adding to them – during a telephone conversation with Hanson earlier that morning – by commenting that since the front page of every newspaper the next day would be headlining Fathers' bullion coup, this was really no time to be issuing any sort of reprimand to him.

With a loyalty and a toughness which would have surprised Fathers as much as pleased him, Bastin had also given Hanson a warning. 'I know you've been under pressure all round on this,' he said, 'and I know Harry was causing problems. I certainly agreed with pulling him out when we did. But if you want to scapegoat him, think again. He's well-respected and it will cause a lot of difficulty between the Home Office and the Yard if you go out gunning for him. You may also find him quicker than you on the draw. Close the case and let it lie is my advice. In the end, you can't fault him for doing what he was told.'

Bastin's last, weak comment on the Sampson case was a question: 'Harry, do you really believe in this theory of yours, or what?'

Fathers paused. New York already seemed a long time ago. 'It leaves a lot of questions unanswered,' he said, 'but I think it makes more sense than the others.'

Bastin never mentioned the case to him again. In the weeks leading up to Christmas, Fathers supposed his superior had found a way to divert the pressure.

'If you just look at the facts,' said Fathers, 'I can see their point – in the abstract, I mean, leaving any other considerations to one side.'

'And there's plenty of them,' said Finlay. 'Other considerations.'

They were sitting in a pub. In an envelope on the table between them lay a copy of Sampson's research report that he had sent to Finlay earlier that year. Finlay had made an extra copy and brought it for Fathers.

'True. But on its own merits, it's not a case I'd go to court on. If you look at it, there's a dozen other explanations. Car accidents are car accidents. We don't know how Sampson disappeared, but New York is a violent city. There's no reason why those three deaths should in any way be connected. He could be a victim of a random killing. His research involved classified material, and you could suppose that the FBI acted quickly to remove all his work material just to be on the safe side. If they did have him under surveillance – which is only my supposition – they might even have seen him killed but have been unable to arrest the killer. That would explain their silence, on grounds of embarrassment at their own incompetence, as well as how they got in on the act so fast. Then again, Sampson had a few thoughts about the Shuttle and the airliner and, being young, melodramatically committed some of them to a ludicrous hiding place. So what? He talked to a few people in Washington about his thoughts. The place is a rumour mill. Can I be sure his secretary woman really had the goods? Can I even be sure that any of my witnesses were telling the unvarnished truth? Can I shit.'

'So why are you telling me?' asked Finlay.

'Somebody has to know,' said Fathers. 'For Rosemary.' He sipped his beer. 'If they'd let her live I really don't think I'd be talking to you now.'

'You're pretty sure about it then?'

'Sure?' said Fathers. 'What am I sure about? I don't know – while I was there, America seemed the kind of place where that kind of thing could happen. But maybe that's just what you pick up talking to policemen – a policeman's suspiciousness.'

'There's plenty of people who'd say this year that Britain isn't so very different.'

Fathers did not respond. He drank some beer and was silent for a while. 'Hypothesis is a fancy word,' he said eventually, 'but it just means guesswork, no more. No proof, no nothing. The facts are that Sampson has disappeared, that Rosemary is dead, that his other lover is dead. Those are the facts, but what do they amount to?' He drained his beer.

'Facts,' said Finlay scornfully. 'Don't give me facts. What about the fucking truth?'

'Facts and truth,' said Fathers. 'Different as chalk and cheese.'

'East and West,' said Finlay, 'and ne'er the twain shall meet. Have another?'

'Thanks,' said Fathers.

When Finlay returned with the second round of drinks he said, 'So it's a mystery without a solution. We don't know who done it.'

'We don't even know what they done,' said Fathers.

'Do you want me to do anything with it? Is that why you're telling me?'

'I don't know. I've been behaving so unprofessionally about this case that it seemed a shame to stop now. Anyway, you helped a lot, I owe you, and I knew you'd be interested. What could you do with it?'

'Don't know, really. Give it to a journalist, I suppose, but there's a lot of holes in the story, aren't there? Entertaining

265

suspicions is one thing, but for a story as big as this there'd have to be a lot more.'

'Yes. The thing is the whole background has disappeared now – all the people, all the documents, all the first-hand evidence.'

'Anyway,' said Finlay, 'even if somebody did write it up, it would leave you in deep trouble. It'd be so obvious where the story came from. And probably wouldn't do any good. Reagan's safely back in the White House now. Do you want to end your career over this?'

'No.'

'There we are then,' said Finlay with an air of finality. 'Doesn't seem a lot that can be done. Our little secret.' He drank his beer.

'You could always write a novel about it,' said Fathers.